8   £1.25

D0619064

THE PEACOCK RING

Robert took a step forward and at last looked down at Laura and saw the sum of all his life, everything he had ever done, all his dreams and desires gathered and centred round that sleeping face, the gentle curves of that relaxed figure. Laura, his first and only love. For a single moment he knew the future with complete certainty. This was his future, this the only woman, in youth and in age, here lay the dear companion of all his years.

The certainty lasted for a breath. Then everything was swept away in the passion of feeling that overwhelmed Robert when he saw the tear stains on Laura's cheeks. He bent and gathered her into his arms.

The Peacock Ring

Katharine Gordon

CORONET BOOKS
Hodder and Stoughton

Copyright © 1981 by Katharine Gordon

First published in Great Britain 1981 by
Hodder and Stoughton Ltd.

Coronet edition 1982
Second impression 1984

British Library C.I.P.

Gordon, Katharine
   The peacock ring.—(Coronet Books)
   I. Title
   823'.914[F]   PR6057.069

ISBN 0 340 27913 3

Printed and bound in Great Britain for
Hodder and Stoughton Paperbacks, a
division of Hodder and Stoughton Ltd.,
Mill Road, Dunton Green, Sevenoaks,
Kent (Editorial Office. 47 Bedford
Square, London, WC1 3DP) by
Cox & Wyman Ltd., Reading

To Mary with love

Chapter 1

Gulls were calling above the grey roofs of Dover, and there was the constant urgent whisper of rain along the quays as Robert Reid boarded the *Sedalia*, the ship that was to take him to India.

He stood at the rail, looking down at the group of people who had come to see him leave. His grandfather, Sir Robert Reid, for whom he was named, was taller than anyone there. His father, Colonel Alan Reid, lately wounded in action in South Africa, was leaning on a stick, his leg obviously troubling him. Holding his grandfather's arm, Jane Reid, his beloved grandmother, had her face turned away because she could not bear to see him go. The woman beside her, small and elegant, waving a handkerchief, was his godmother, Lady Caroline Addison. He knew that of all the four people saying goodbye to him, although she loved him dearly, she was the only one who was glad to see him go.

As he watched, Caroline Addison put her arm round his grandmother and led her away. The two men gave him a last wave, and followed. So they were doing as he had asked, which was good of them. It hurt him so much to see his grandmother's grief that, as they all vanished into the shadows of the customs shed, he felt a selfish relief.

The ship was moving. She rolled out of harbour, and, looking back, Robert saw the white cliffs rear up briefly through the rain-soaked mist and then vanish as the ship gathered speed and bent to the rough seas.

England's uncertain spring was left behind. The ship heaved and wallowed in a grey winter seascape, drenched with driving rain and pounding salt water that swept up and fell back on the decks in cascading, thundering waves. Robert thanked all the gods for two mercies, that he had no more fare-wells to face, and that it appeared that he was a good sailor.

He left the soaking decks because there was nothing more to see, and went below, where even the smells of cooking, and other smells of worse origin did not affect him. He went into his cabin and lay down on his narrow bunk and then, with nothing to distract his mind, memory attacked him like a beast that had been hiding in ambush waiting for the right moment.

He thought of the fifth person who should have been down on that melancholy quay to see him go, and of the reason why she was not there, and his eyes blurred with shaming tears.

Laura, his dear love. Laura Addison, sent away a whole week before he was due to leave. He felt the ring that he wore on his finger, it shone emerald bright, the Peacock ring. Given to his mother by the Ruler of Lambagh, Muna had passed it to him so that it might, one day, be a betrothal gift to his bride, the ring that he intended to give Laura. He thought of all he had wanted to say to her, and all that he wanted to hear her say. The ring blurred and sparkled through his tears, glowing green fire, and he remembered then that, even if he had had time to give it to his love, and to say what he had longed to say, it would have all been of no use.

Memory was sharp, like a physical pain. He heard again the words that Laura's aunt, Caroline Addison, had said to him, the words that had torn his world apart.

"There is no question of marriage between you and Laura, Robert. Her parents would never hear of it."

"Because we are too young?"

"No. It has nothing to do with your age. Dearest Robert, you know that this is not my wish. I dislike having to tell you this, but it is my duty. I cannot allow you and Laura to continue to live in a fool's paradise."

"But you must give me a reason!" Even in his shocked pain, Robert knew that he had all the attributes that should have made him a most eligible match; he had great wealth, good looks, perfect health, and one day would inherit his

8

grandfather's title. Yet he was not to be considered as a husband for Laura Addison?

"You must tell me why," he repeated stubbornly, and had looked up into the compassion of Caroline's eyes, and had known the answer to his question and cursed himself for asking it. Behind Caroline, in the shadows of her drawing room, he had seemed to see another figure standing, looking towards him with loving eyes as she had so often done in life.

His beloved dead mother, beautiful and adored, and the reason why his love for Laura was despised.

Muna the Dancer, the Rose of Madore.

His father had met her in India and married her and brought her home to life in England. In spite of her matchless beauty and charm, and the fact that she had been accepted everywhere, it seemed that she who loved him so much brought him to grief after all. He was regarded by Laura's parents as a half-caste, a person of no standing, someone to be despised.

Robert had worshipped his mother, and had broken his heart when she was killed in a riding accident. He had been proud of his mixed blood, and the thought that because of it he was despised by people like Laura's parents tormented him. Nothing that Caroline Addison had said to try and comfort him had had any effect. He had flung out of her house in a rage that had blunted the edge of his grief at not seeing Laura again. In the grip of that rage he had thought, "To the devil with all these anaemic die-away English girls. I shall find me a girl like my mother, a warm, loving girl, instead of an English Miss." He had visualised the girl he would find when he went out to take up his post with the Ruler's Forces in Lambagh. Such a girl! She would be dark, and richly curved, round of breast and hip, with long, tilted eyes, sparkling like moonlight on a deep lake, and she would love him with all her heart and give him many sons, and they would live together in that warm and distant country, the land of his mother's heart, where it was always summer.

So he had dreamed in anger. Now, lying on the hard, narrow berth, he could no longer think of the Indian beauty he was going to find. All he could do was remember Laura.

He saw her eyes and her mouth, her slender, long-legged grace, and remembered the scent of her hair, and the feeling of her body in his arms the only time he had kissed her, and for a time he suffered very much. His blood rose and thundered in his body, drowning the noises of the ship, until at last he fell asleep, to dream of Laura and her tumbled, curling hair spilling over her shoulders. He woke to empty arms, and instead of Laura's soft imagined whisper, heard the high shrilling of the wind. It took him a long time to fall asleep again.

In the morning he awoke to the smell of incense strong in his cabin, and smiled at his own foolishness. One day out of England, and he was already smelling the perfumes of the fabled East! Idiot! said Robert to himself. But the smell was very strong. The cabin steward, coming in with Robert's shaving water, brought a gust of the smell in with him.

"Good heavens – the ship smells like a church," said Robert.

"Well it may, sir. There is a monk, or someone of that sort, in the next cabin." The steward wagged his head, and added darkly, "Very bad luck it is, sir, to carry the clergy. Specially odd clergy. Him in there, he's burning this stuff, and going on in front of some picture – likely set the whole ship on fire."

Later Robert saw the priest in question, a broad, stocky man in black robes. The most noticeable feature about him was his eyes, which were a very pale cold blue. He stared fixedly at Robert as they met in the corridor, and Robert did not care for the man's look, and thereafter ignored him.

The steward's prophecies of bad luck on the voyage did not come true. The days went easily, moving past as smoothly as the ship on the painted stillness of the sea as they entered eastern waters. Robert walked the decks, and played cards with three other young men who were on their first voyage too, and with them paid laughing court to the four girls on board, giving each of them equal attention, so that none of them could take him seriously. He was in great demand because of his looks, and the girls and their mothers pursued him assiduously. He flirted with them all outrageously, all through the long warm days, but at night he vanished. Up in the bows of the ship, lying behind a coil of rope, he watched the night skies alone, seeing the great unfamiliar constellations swing into view, and always among the strange stars he saw Laura's eyes, and her tender, smiling mouth.

One night, lying in his hiding place, he felt that the breeze was very warm, and there was a smell of spices and sandalwood on this warm breeze, and the smell of coconut, and then a very strong, a sweet, rotten smell, the smell of putrefaction. Robert went to the rail and strained his eyes at the horizon, but the night was velvet dark, and kept its secrets. Robert lay down again and fell asleep behind the coil of rope, with the alien scents still blowing about him, and when he woke the voyage was over. The *Sedalia* was dropping anchor in Bombay Harbour, and there was the slap of running feet as the lascars moved to the shouts of the ship's officers, and the rope ladders began to snake down the sides of the ship to where a fleet of small boats clustered. A precarious gangway was also lowered, and various officials began to come on board.

Robert looked down at the chaos of small boats and felt disappointment and dismay. His companions of the voyage had no time for him now except to call their farewells. They all seemed to have friends or family meeting them, they were organised – and he, who was arriving in a country he had always thought of as home, was alone, and had very little idea of how he should set about the rest of his journey.

Someone came to stand beside him, throwing a shadow on the rail. Robert turned and found the priest beside him. Having avoided him throughout the voyage, it seemed hard to suffer him now in this uncertain time of arrival. Like a bird of ill omen in his black robes, the priest stood there smiling at him, his blue eyes cold and expressionless above his smile.

"So your family have not met you, young man?" His voice was thick and guttural and it was a surprise to find he was not English.

"My family? My family are in England."

"I speak of your people in Lambagh."

"I have no family in Lambagh. I am not expecting anyone to meet me." Robert felt very angry, and at the same time, uneasy. The priest was looking at him as if he did not believe a word he said.

"You mean that your – your *friend* the Ruler of Lambagh is not sending anyone to meet you, on this your first trip to India, although you have come out specially to join his army? Very strange surely!"

"You appear to know more about my business than I do myself, Father. If you will excuse me –" Robert turned to walk away, but the priest stopped him.

"Wait, young man. If indeed you have no-one to meet you, then allow me to offer you a seat in the boat that is coming to collect me – there will be room, I am sure."

"Thank you but no, Father – I have already made all my arrangements." This time, Robert walked away and did not look back to see the priest staring after him, his smile gone, his black robes like shadows round him in the brilliant sun.

Robert went to a spot near the rickety gangway that hung down the side of the ship. He could not understand how the priest knew so much about him, and felt an acute sense of uneasiness, as if the priest had given him some bad news.

There was a disturbance on the gangway. A man coming up had slipped and almost fallen into the water. He was an Indian monk, his orange robes kirtled high about his skinny legs. He made a strange figure among the disembarking passengers, and Robert watched him, wondering what business a Hindu holy man could have on the ship. Perhaps he had come to meet the priest.

It was a few minutes later that he saw the monk finish his climb and stand safely on the deck. The passenger who went forward to meet him was indeed the priest. An odd combination, Christian and idolator, thought Robert idly, and stared at the two men standing apart and talking urgently together.

As if they felt him staring, both men turned to look at him. The monk then walked quickly to the side of the ship and began to climb laboriously down the ladder again and into a small boat which moved off as soon as the monk had seated himself. The priest was not with him and, when Robert looked for him, he had vanished. Robert was left with a greater sense of uneasiness than he already had. There had been something secret and urgent about the two men talking so privately together on the crowded deck.

"Sahib? Reid Sahib?"

Robert turned sharply as he heard his name spoken, and looking at the man who had spoken to him, he could neither look away, nor could he speak for a few seconds.

Here was a legend from his childhood, a dream made flesh. His mother had spoken to him so often of this man. She had known Ayub Khan most of her life. He was part of the Lambagh family, and had married Muna's Scottish maid Bella, the woman who had been present at Robert's birth, his mother's loved friend as well as her faithful servant.

"Ayub Khan," said Robert at last, "Ayub Khan Bahudar."

"Sahib, it is I. I am sent by the Ruler to meet you and bring you up to Lambagh."

The big man was staring at Robert, astonishment on his face, as if he too could not believe what he saw. They stood together, searching each other's faces, each lost in a different amazement.

Finally Robert said, "Now I know that I have arrived at last."

"We have waited long for you. Eh Boy, this is no place for us to talk. Let us get your baggage and leave this vessel. Even tied up it makes me queasy."

He had brought a small army of men with him it seemed. In no time they were off the ship and down into a small boat, bouncing over the waters of the harbour, with Ayub holding his mouth grimly closed until they were safely on dry land. The baggage was loaded onto two tongas and despatched to the station. Robert and Ayub sat in comfort in a magnificent landau, drawn by two splendid horses, outstanding among the pathetic bony creatures that were pulling the other carriages.

To Robert's enquiry, Ayub said, "We have some hours to spend before the train leaves. We go to the house of a friend. These are his horses and his carriage. You speak Urdu well, Sahib."

"Do not call me Sahib, Ayub Khan, it puts me at a distance. Yes, I spoke Urdu before I spoke English. How not?"

"How not indeed. Muna's son learned from her. Did she teach you Lambaghi also?"

"The language of her heart? Yes, and I was fortunate. A retired colonel had brought his servant back to England from India. He was a Lambaghi and I spoke with him when my mother was away so that I never forgot the tongue that she loved," Robert replied in the Lambaghi tongue, and Ayub Khan was delighted. He forsook Urdu immediately, and they spoke in his own hill language, and Robert found it came easily to him, and thanked his mother in his heart. He imagined how she would have enjoyed returning to India with him, and felt the familiar sense of loss that thought of her always brought.

"She died too soon," he said, and Ayub Khan answered, knowing without being told that he was thinking of Muna.

"We die when it is our time, Boy. Do not think of your mother with sorrow. She brought joy with her always, she would not wish her son to be unhappy."

Robert remembered his mother's laughter, her lovely smile, and her delight in anything beautiful. His heart lifted. No, Muna would never wish to see her son unhappy. He turned to the understanding giant beside him.

"Tell me about our host for today, Ayub Khan. Is he an old friend of the family?"

"His State borders on Jindbagh. He owes fealty to the Ruler, and is a very old friend of mine. Once we were poor together – now he has inherited much wealth. His name is Ali of Pakodi."

He looked at Robert to see if the name meant anything to him, but Robert was looking at the crowds in the streets, and did not appear to have heard the name Pakodi before.

"He knew your mother." The pause that followed his

14

words was long. The dirty streets, with their piles of terrible rubbish in which bone-thin dogs, crows, and skeletal children all scavenged impartially, had been left behind. They were climbing, and the air was cooler and scented with the flowers that bloomed unseen behind high walls. For a moment Ayub thought that Robert had not heard what he said. Then Robert turned to him.

"Was he also a friend of my father?"

Ayub shifted uneasily. How much did this boy know about his beautiful mother? Things that were taken for granted among Ayub's people might be a shock to a boy brought up on English ideas. He slanted a look at Robert.

"Nay, I do not think that he met your father."

"So. The Nawab of Pakodi knew my mother in the days when she was Muna the Dancer. Was he one of her lovers?"

Ayub let out his breath on a long sigh.

"Wah! She told you everything, your mother."

"How not? She made me a present of her life, painting a picture of it with her words, leaving out nothing. Do you think that she would have let me come to India knowing nothing about her? That would have been a coward's action, and she was not a coward. Nor was she ashamed. Should I then be? Nay, Ayub, my mother only had a short time with me after she came back from India, but in that time, before she was killed, she knew that I would come to her country and made sure that I would have no surprises. She did not mention Pakodi by name, but I am sure he was one who loved her."

"He loved her greatly. He wished to be her only love, but she laughed at him. She laughed at all her lovers except one."

"My father. She must have loved him very much to give up her life here, and live with him in England. He must have taken her heart completely."

Robert stopped speaking and looked frowning back over the years, and Ayub said nothing, watching the crows and kites wheeling and swooping above a tall tower on the hillside. So there were one or two things that Muna had not told her son. Ayub decided to keep silent, too, until it was necessary to speak. He had much to tell this young man.

The carriage lumbered on, the horses pulling strongly as the hill grew steeper. They passed a temple and Robert saw orange-robed men, and smelled incense and saw through the high carved door of the temple a fire flickering in front of a seated god. He was sharply reminded of his strange conversation on the ship that morning, and of the meeting between the orange-robed monk and the priest. He would have been very surprised if he could have seen into an inner room in the temple. Here his travelling companion, the priest, sat talking to a circle of men, not all of whom were of the religious order. The priest's black robes had gone, his head was shaved bare and he was indistinguishable from any one of the orange-robed monks who moved about the temple on bare silent feet.

The men who spoke with the transformed priest called him Tovarish, and listened to all he had to say with deference and interest. One, darker skinned and more richly dressed than any of the others, asked a question.

"You are sure the boy is the heir, Tovarish?"

"I am sure. I have seen Kassim Khan, the Ruler of Lambagh, many times. This boy is his mirror image. Also he was met by Ayub Khan, who is the Ruler's close relative by blood. They leave for the north tonight, but today they stay in the Palace of the Nawab of Pakodi. I have a man there, as you know."

"So you have. Then you think –"

"I do not think. I know what I will do. Listen." He outlined plans in a few quick sentences emphasising his words with gestures of his strong, long-fingered hands. When he had finished speaking the older man nodded approval.

"This sounds well. What do you wish from me?"

"That you send word to your Lord. There must be men ready to take the boy down. I do not wish to travel the southern roads this year. I have much to do in the northern States."

"Very well. I send word at once. Now I go to Sagpur by road. I have your permission to go?"

"You have leave, Khaji." Tovarish was dressed in the

coarse cotton robes of a monk, and the other man was richly attired in silks, but it was obvious who was the master.

Alone, Tovarish sat cross-legged on a strip of coarse matting, a rosary of large, carved wooden beads running through his fingers, his eyes half-closed in contemplation. It was easy to him to slip from one role into another; like a chameleon, he took his colour from his surroundings. He had indeed some small right to his present image. He had once trained for a short time in a monastery, before leaving it for other training. A paid agent of the Tsar, he travelled in many places and in many different guises, but he felt at home in this temple atmosphere, it was one of his favourite roles. He sat quietly, looking calm and gentle, his hand at last relaxed and still.

So looks a leopard lying soft and drowsy on a green branch, waiting for his prey.

Robert turned to speak to Ayub Khan about the priest, but they were now on the crown of the hill with all the town laid out like a picture below them and the sea stretching beyond, and he forgot what he was going to say in the beauty of what he saw. There were trees round them, and a high white wall in front of them with scarlet-flowered creepers tumbling over it. There was an open gate and a curving drive that led to a second gate in an inner wall.

The carriage stopped at the second gate. Ayub climbed out and Robert followed him. The Durwan at the gate salaamed deeply and swung the gate open.

Here was the India of his mother's stories. Green lawns, brilliant flowers, splashing fountains. Birds as brightly coloured as the flowers screamed from trees that threw a thick refreshing shade over the glare of white marble paving. Robert took a deep breath. Here it was, part of the magic land that he had longed to see.

Everything was suddenly full of excitement and movement. Ayub was held in the arms of a man who could have been his twin brother, who was shouting a boisterous welcome. The two men were of a height – they stood, laughing into each other's eyes. Then the Nawab turned to welcome Robert, and for a moment his eyes widened, and into all the noise and laughter a silence came, and a strangeness. Only for a moment. Ayub moved forward, and said quietly, "Ali, I bring you Muna's son."

"At such a time, with no warning! Boy, if you were not already welcome because of your mother, you would be welcome for your own sake. Tell me of your mother. I have had no news of her for many years, not since a day long ago when she left us all with no music and no laughter, taking it all with her when she went so far away. I trust that she is well. Has she returned to live among her own people and her beloved mountains at last?"

Robert could think of nothing to say, no way to break this smiling man's happiness.

Ayub Khan took the Nawab's arm, and his voice was gentle for such a big man.

"Ali, you do not read your letters properly – or perhaps you did not receive my letter. The Rose is dead. She sent her son back to Lambagh instead of coming herself."

There was nothing then but the gentle sound of the fountains, the sound of water falling on the broad leaves of the waterlilies that grew in the pool. The water fell softly, to lie on the dark leaves like pearls, or like tears.

The Nawab looked down at the lilies among their pearled leaves, and shook his head. He took Robert's arm, so that he and Ayub Khan and Robert stood like old friends, holding together against grief.

"How many dreams died with the Rose, how many golden dreams? Your mother brought nothing but pleasure wherever she went, and I am very sure that she would not wish mourning to attend her son's arrival in my house. Come, Boy, let us not grieve. Come in and be welcome."

He led his guests to an inner court, where water ran splashing and gentle from one level to another, and the air was cooled by manufactured streams in their marble courses. Servants brought wine, and the three sat talking, and after a few minutes the Nawab began to speak of Robert's mother, making no secret of his adoration for her.

"When I was young, I was mad for her. I remember a day when I filled a goblet with rubies and gave it to her after she had danced for me, and I can hear her laughter now as she poured the rubies away on the grass and asked for wine. There has never been another woman like Muna."

Robert, listening, felt that he could see his mother dancing, hear her laughter.

He could hear laughter, and the voices of women, but this was present laughter, not the memory of mirth. Somewhere behind one of these flower-draped walls there were women, the women of Pakodi's household, hidden away, kept from the eyes of strangers for his pleasure alone. The wine ran in Robert's veins, and he thought of the hidden laughing women, and envied the Nawab. This was the way to keep women, safe among cool fountains and singing birds, safe from all harm.

Like a bird flying over his mind's eye he had a sudden flashing picture of Laura leaning over her horse's neck, urging it on, leaping a high thorn fence. That slender free figure – would she be content behind flower-wreathed walls, among the whispering fountains?

In the long hot afternoon he slept, and women's laughter sounded in his dreams, while the slow-moving punkah creaked and fluttered to and fro above his head.

When the day was cool with the coming of evening, he woke, and found clothes ready for him; not his own clothes. Two servants, northerners by their dress and their light skins, were moving about the room. When he turned, one brought him a glass of steaming, scented tea, tea that was pale as straw, and very refreshing. Then he went into a marble-walled bathroom and bathed luxuriously under a cascade of water that fell continuously from a pipe high up on the wall. He was assisted in his dressing, each garment being held out for him to put on. The clothes fitted as if they had been made for him. Perhaps, thought Robert, living by this time in a dream, perhaps they had been made for him, by magic. Now he was dressed exactly as Ayub Khan was, except for his *puggaree*, his turban. But that

19

was there too. First the embroidered cap that rose to a point, the *kullah*, was put on his head, and then the emerald green muslin was wrapped and folded round it, one end left sticking up like an open fan.

There was a mirror on the wall, and Robert walked over and looked at his image.

Robert Reid had gone, leaving a stranger. Who was this fierce-looking man with eyes that were full of questions? Would his mother, had she seen him thus, have given him an English name? 'Robert' certainly did not fit the man who looked back at him from the glass. He moved his shoulders inside the silk shirt, enjoying the feeling of freedom. He tilted his turban to a more rakish angle, and was pulling on leather boots as soft and supple as kid gloves when he heard the clatter of horses below his window. He went over and looked down and saw the Nawab talking to a *syce* who was holding a horse.

"Have you a mount for me?"

The Nawab looked up at him, delighted.

"You wish to ride? Good. Come down at once, and there will be time before we meet Ayub Khan and drink our farewell drinks. We will go to the beach at Worli."

It was wonderful to be riding on the beach, the sunset streaking the sky and the sea with scarlet, and the heat of the day blowing away on a fresh sea wind. Robert exulted in the air and the movement after the long inactivity of the voyage. His mother had been killed by a fall from a horse, and at one time Robert had thought that he would never enjoy riding again. Life had moved on, the pain of loss was still there, but not so fierce. Now, galloping on the sands, hearing the steady thud of his horse's hooves above the sound of the sea, Robert remembered his mother without sorrow. Her body lay in a grave beside the rose garden in Morton Park, the rose garden where she had so often walked. Her spirit? The sea rolled and tumbled on the beach, the waves breaking in a thunder of white foam, and Robert, the sea wind blowing about him, knew with certainty that his mother's spirit was as free as the white bird that rose and dipped above the breaking waves, and in its freedom had set him free from grief.

The courts of Pakodighar were shadowed and silent when they returned. Servants were lighting lamps that bloomed like bright flowers among the creepers. The fountain was whispering to itself, the pool ringed with little oil lamps. It was the blue hour, the hour for lovers to meet. Robert thought of Laura with a sharp twist of pain in his mind. How long would it be before he saw her again? He had no doubts in his mind about whether she would be happy in India, among such people as he had met today, and in such a setting. He placed her graceful figure leaning over the fountain, and could almost see her turn and smile at him as he walked towards the pool.

But it was Ayub Khan who was waiting in the shadows, impatient and thirsty.

"Ali, if we are not to ride all the way to Madore, which would take upwards of three weeks, we will be leaving shortly –"

"Eh, Ayub! I know, you are thirsty, and have been working while we rode. Now we drink, and there is plenty of time before we leave for the train." They followed him into the cool, water-loud inner court, and servants had set out a low table, and there were plates of various things to eat while they drank their wine.

"Ayub Khan, remember I told you I had something for the boy? Let me show you now."

A servant who had been standing beyond the lamplight, stepped forward, holding on his outstretched hands the most magnificent sword that Robert had ever seen. The scabbard was jewelled, the sword hissed gently as Robert drew it. It was certainly not intended to be an ornament; in spite of the gilded hilt and the chasing on the blade, the steel shivered with blue light down its length under the lamps.

Robert could not believe it was for him. He had just enough sense left to raise the sword and hold it out, hilt first, to the Nawab, saying, "In your service, Nawab Sahib!"

The Nawab did not touch the hilt as was customary. He embraced Robert, kissing him on each cheek, and giving him a rib-cracking hug.

"Boy, you honour me by accepting my gift. Offer your fealty

21

to Kassim Khan Bahadur. It is to him that you owe your loyalty, and it is his army you join. I would have been happy to have such an heir to give my sword to! Here is the dagger as well. Wear the weapons in health, and with good fortune." He leaned forward to fill Robert's goblet again, and clapped his hands.

Outside the wall music began, the throbbing beat of a drum, the clear notes of a flute. The drum and the flute were joined by the sound of little bells, and there was a harsh broken cry, high and shrill as the cry of an eagle, and three girls ran into the court and began to dance.

There were naked except for a narrow binding around their slender hips. They wore face veils, veils as light as mist that covered their faces, hiding nothing. The dance was fast and acrobatic, a whirl of slender arms and legs, little pointed breasts jouncing in time to the fast stamp and shift of small hennaed feet.

Robert, enchanted and dazzled, felt his breath shorten as the dance ended with a series of wild leaps, so that the girls seemed to be flying straight towards him. The same harsh, broken cry sounded, the music stopped, and the girls were gone into the shadows beyond the lamplight.

The Nawab laughed at Robert's bemused face.

"They are good, no? They make the blood run faster, those little ones. They come from beyond the black sea of Turkestan, and they were very expensive. Which one pleased you most, Boy?"

Robert answered out of the hot tumult of roused blood, words that seemed to speak themselves without any intention on his part.

"The one in the centre, the smallest one."

"Yes. You chose well. Sweet and fresh like wild fruit. She is still a virgin. It is a great pity that Ayub Khan is in such a hurry to return to Lambagh. You might have found many pleasures here."

"You know why we must return."

"I can guess why. Ayub Khan, truthfully, I could not read that spider-scrawled letter of yours."

22

"Would I put such things on paper? Maybe someone who can read more easily than you can would have taken the letter."

"True, oh wiser than wise. Very well then, Ayub, let us now be serious. You do not have to remind me that I owe fealty to the Ruler. I am his man now and always. Only tell me what he wants from me, it is his."

"He wishes to know how your borders are guarded. Do you know, oh one who is always absent from his hills?"

"I know. My borders are safe enough. There is trouble?"

"Wah! You know that your borders are safe, but you ask if there is trouble? Such a neighbour to have on our eastern side!"

"Ayub, do not anger me. You know that my borders are well guarded. They are held by the Ruler's own men. You prod me with words like a man trying to wake the bees in a hive with a stick. Take care that you do not get stung."

"Still quick to take offence, Ali. Good. It shows your heart is still young."

"We were speaking, I thought, of trouble that is causing anxiety?"

"The trouble has not begun, but as a wind rises before a storm to give warning, so the wind has risen. It is blowing strongly, and has blown many strange tales into the valleys."

"The wind blows from what quarter?"

"You need to ask that? You have been too long among your flesh-pots, Ali."

"Not so long. It is the Russians as usual?"

"As usual. Now there is talk that they take the game into Tibet, to make their plans there, and the British are taking this talk very seriously."

"Russia has only to turn in sleep and the British take it seriously. Is this not just another move in the game that Russia and Britain play all the time?"

"It seems more serious than usual. More important, the Ruler is not happy about the situation. There are a number of things that worry him –"

"He has things that worry him now, when his heir has only

23

just returned? I should have thought the State would be full of rejoicing. The heir was gone for a long time –"

"Well, the heir is back, true, and that is good, but . . ."

There was a gesture from the Nawab, a hand movement so slight and so swift that it barely caught Robert's eye. Ayub stopped speaking and began to laugh, and the Nawab laughed too, and said, through his laughter, "Ah, Ayub, you give yourself away. I know why you long to return to your valley. But please do not tell me long stories or give me wild reasons why you should return quickly. The reason is that you ache to return to your leopardess . . ."

The man who had come, feet noiseless on the grass, put a tray of ice and small things to eat – meat on sticks, and saucers of different relishes, and chutneys – before the Nawab, and he filled the Nawab's glass and stood back. The Nawab waved him away with a careless hand.

"Well thought, Salih. Do not wait. We will serve ourselves. Now tell me, Ayub, tell me of the green-eyed one. She is well?"

"The woman of my house is well. Very well, Pakodi. She is unwilling to leave the valley even for a day. She has become as one of our women. She is content in my house."

"Ah, alas for the hunting leopardess! You have tamed her. I would have kept her wild, and chained her with gold, and collared her with emeralds."

"And I would have killed you."

The Nawab nodded, while Robert stared from one to the other, completely confused.

"Eh, son of Muna, you wonder at us, as well you may, for we speak of things long past. Yes, Ayub, I verily believe that you would have killed me. I have never forgotten what you said that night. Do you too remember? 'There is always the one woman –' You are fortunate. I also found the one woman, but she would not have me. So, since then, I have found many women. Well – to each his fortune. I found another, and married her."

As the Nawab was speaking, Ayub Khan had risen to his feet without sound. Like a ghost he moved over the grass to a

24

door that was hidden under creepers on the wall. He flung the door open, and seized the man who leaned close against it. Robert leapt to help him, and together they dragged him over, as he struggled and fought, and threw him down before the Nawab. He made no effort to escape, but lay at the Nawab's feet, his turban gone, his clothes torn. Now he lay still, looking at nothing, it seemed, for he did not even move his eyes when the Nawab spoke to him.

"Salih? There is something you needed to know?"

"No, lord. Nothing."

"Then perhaps someone else needed some information, and asked you to get it for them?"

"Perhaps."

Ayub Khan had gone out of the court. Now he returned with some men hurrying and jostling behind him.

"Wait!" The Nawab looked back at the man lying so quietly at his feet.

"Now I ask for information, Salih. Who is this man who needs news so badly that he pays you to listen outside my door?"

Salih's shoulders rose in an almost imperceptible shrug.

"Who knows?" he said, and his voice was almost a sigh, "Who can tell?"

The men behind Ayub Khan moved a little forward, and one of them spoke. He was a tall, broad man, and he must have been roused from sleep, for he was only half dressed. His great shoulders and muscular body were pale, and his head was completely bald. When he spoke it was like an animal growling.

"You know, Oh Salihbhai. You know. And so we will know soon. I take him now, lord?"

The Nawab turned away. "Take him," he said, and the men moved up like a tide on the shore and lifted Salih to his feet. Then he looked round him once, and once he looked at the Nawab, and then, held by a man on each side, he walked from the garden.

"Salih!" said the Nawab disbelievingly, as the men left the court, "Salih Mohammed! I would have staked my life on him.

He is of the hills! Well, all men have a price, I suppose."

They were all silent then, there was only the sound of falling water and the smell of jasmine.

It was a still night, with half a moon just showing above the trees, and somewhere a bird called suddenly. Robert remembered his mother telling him about the bird they called the hot weather bird, whose cry was supposed to drive men mad in the heat of summer. The cry rose higher and higher until the sound lost itself in a scream so high that the note cracked, and broke into silence.

A bird? The Nawab and Ayub were both on their feet and turning for the door in the wall, with Robert close at their heels.

Then Ayub put his hand on Robert's arm, and speaking very low, said, "You stay here, Boy. That is torture, and the Nawab did not order it. He will not wish you to see – for his sake, you stay, or he will lose much face."

So Robert perforce stayed, ashamed of feeling relief that he would not have to witness whatever had caused that terrible crying.

The shock wave of the capture of a possible assassin within the Nawab's Palace spread through the flower gardens and over the high walls of the women's quarters. The women sat in clusters, murmuring of nothing else, their faces pale and frightened, their security threatened by the attack on their lord. In an inner room an old woman with fierce, determined eyes stood over the bed where a girl lay looking up at her with horror.

"If I am caught, Mother, it is death!"

"You will not be caught if you come now. They run about the Palace like headless chickens, seeing nothing. I have found the old secret way to the Nawab's court. Come girl, *now* – or do you wish to end your days sitting with the other women caring for their growing children while your beauty ages and your empty womb shrivels? Come, I say."

Under the lash of the pitiless voice, the girl got up, wrapped herself in a dark cotton sari and followed her mother from the room, down a curving staircase and out into a shadowed court where the fountain basins were empty and there were no flowers. The girl shivered and pulled her sari closely about her. This place of shadows had a name – the Court of the Forgotten Women. In the Nawab's father's day, his unwanted, ageing concubines had lived here with little comfort. She pressed on towards the wall, but her mother held her back.

"We wait here. If there is a chance it will be soon. Do not look as though you go to a monster, daughter. Toori says the young man is very personable. Think yourself fortunate that you do not have to bribe a low-caste servant to make you with child. The blood of this one is as good as that of the Nawab. The boy is of the Lambagh line. Wait now – see the light there? That is Ooriya. He makes sure that the prince is alone." The girl did not speak. She stood quiescent, and when the man in the shadows waved his lantern she made no demur. Her mother snatched the sari from her and pushed her forward. She moved over to where the man stooped beside a low door.

"This is the door. Here you will come out also, so mark it well, lady." An old servant of her house, he put a silver jug into her hands, opened the door and she walked through it. She heard the door close softly and she found she was in a scented garden with the sound of falling water gentle in her ears and a young man standing with his back to her. She stepped forward, took a deep breath, and spoke.

"Lord?"

Robert turned, his hand automatically feeling for the dagger that hung at his hip. But it seemed that no danger confronted him. One of the dancers stood behind him, the shadows of the trees dappling her naked body. She was holding a silver wine jug.

"They sent me with fresh wine, lord –" She spoke with a lilt in her voice as one who speaks a language not her own. She moved out of the shadows into the lamplight, and her eyes were wide and dark above her smiling mouth.

Robert could not look away from her. She came, step by step, holding out the wine jug until she was only a handspan away from him. Her skin shone like silk, and he could see a

27

little pulse beating in her throat. Robert wondered, while he could still think, why she had been sent. Was she supposed to keep him from following the others, keep him entertained, so that the Nawab could investigate the torture that had been inflicted without his orders? Then his body shut his mind away. The wine he had taken, the warm night, the smell of her flesh and her hair all conspired against him. It seemed to him that he was still watching her dance. He saw the tumble and swirl of her legs and arms, the movement of her breasts in the dance, her wild, flying leaps.

He put out his hand blindly and touched, not the silver jug, but the warm cup of her breast.

The silver jug fell to the ground and was forgotten. The cry that was not from the throat of a bird came again and again, and then died away. There was only the warm night, full of stars pressing close, and beneath the sound of the falling, lulling music of the water was the girl's soft breathing, and her muffled voice. Robert, lost in the scarlet thundering of his blood, moving in the heat of an ecstasy he had never known, heard nothing, until the night seemed to engulf him, and all his mind and body were filled with a burst of shooting stars. He lay, tangled in long scented hair, in soft arms that held him close. Long scented hair – but the little dancer's hair had swung shoulder length! The girl in his arms had hair that must have hung below her waist. Robert raised his head and looked down at her.

This was not the face of the little dancer. He had deceived himself. This girl had enormous shadowed dark eyes, and a mouth full-lipped and made for kissing.

"Who are you?"

"Lord, thou knowest, I danced for thee this evening –"

"You did not. Who are you?"

He was unprepared for the swift twist that took her out of his arms. He heard her breathless gasp and then he was alone. Her slender, naked figure had slipped through the trees into darkness as silently as a shadow, and he did not know where to look for her.

Chapter 2

The moon was well above the trees when the Nawab and Ayub Khan returned. Ayub Khan looked sickened and angry, and the Nawab had a fine sheen of sweat on his face.

"What can one do? That man is an animal. I swear to you, Ayub, that is not my way of gaining information. Flogging, yes. But torture – ach, I am sick."

"Why do you keep that brute? Where did you get him? He is not a man of our country, neither of the north nor of the south."

"Nay, he is from another place. He saved my life in the harbour here, when the boat I was in overturned and I was thrown unconscious into the sea, having had a blow on my head. This one was on a ship nearby, and dived in and brought me to safety, and begged for work, being but poorly paid by his employer. I took him from gratitude, and indeed he has served me well. He is as tender as a woman with horses, and I swear he thinks as they do. I did not know the animal that slept within him." The Nawab shuddered, and wiped his face.

"Stepan his name is. A savage. But what to do? I cannot punish him. He saw treachery and tried to obtain information in the only way he knew. He was guarding me, his master. One does not kill a good watchdog."

"Nor does one keep a man-eater as a watchdog. Have a care that he never turns on you, Ali. Well, it is over, one cannot call back the dead. We will get no information from Salih now, we will never know who paid him."

They spoke as if Robert did not exist, they seemed to have forgotten him completely, and he sat listening to them, glad to be forgotten, for something was worrying at the back of his mind and he could not think what it was.

Then, as the Nawab picked up his goblet, Robert remembered what he had seen, and jumped up to knock the drink from his hand. Both men stared at him as if he were a ghost. The Nawab recovered his senses first.

"You think of poison, my friend?"

"Yes. That man – Salih. He gave us no wine, he only filled your goblet. He was clumsy as he did it, he spilled some – see, here is the stain."

Clear on the cloth was a long streak of brown, yet the wine in the Nawab's goblet was white, and when Robert put his finger to the stained cloth, it crumbled into a tear beneath his finger. With staring eyes, the Nawab placed his goblet back on the table, and shouted.

Armed men came running. It was obvious that the Pakodighar was now as alert as a disturbed hornet's nest. The Nawab sent his wine away and a servant brought a fresh cloth and fresh wine, pouring himself a full goblet and drinking it under the Nawab's watching eye before the man was allowed to fill all their goblets. Ayub refused his, but Robert drank with the Nawab.

The Nawab finished his goblet at a draught and held out his goblet for more. He then noticed the wine jug lying beside the low table, where it had fallen from Robert's visitor's hand.

"What happened there? Was that also poisoned?"

Robert had forgotten all about the wine jug. He did not care for the thought that it might have been poisoned too.

"I do not know. I did not drink from it."

It was sent away, and Robert sat wondering uneasily if the girl who had lain in his arms, and who had lied about being a dancer, had been sent to poison him.

While they waited for news about the wine, Ayub paced restlessly, speaking disjointedly as he put his thoughts into words. Finally, the Nawab begged him to sit.

"I cannot think while you growl and prowl, Ayub. I cannot think why anyone should wish to kill me. I have no enemies."

Ayub Khan continued his prowling as if the Nawab had not spoken. Finally he came to stand beside the Nawab.

"Ali, you asked me a question just as that assassin came in, and you moved your hand, and stopped me answering. Can you remember the question?"

"Wait. Ah, I have it. I asked why the Ruler should be worried, when he had no reason, his heir having returned safely . . . by the Door of the House of the Dead, Ayub, there we have it!" The Nawab had risen and was now pacing beside Ayub Khan.

"Let us think back," said Ayub. "Yes. There are many reasons for error, it is not necessary to think that all plans have been uncovered. First I come down from Lambagh, with a half troop of the Ruler's men. Then I bring the boy here, in some state, in your carriage. Then –"

"Then we speak of the return of the heir. Ay, Ayub Khan, it was my death cry he waited for, so that he could raise the Palace. In the tumult that would have followed, it is not hard to see what would have happened." The two men were looking at each other when a quiet knock on the door in the wall brought their heads round, and Robert stood up, his sword in his hand. The knock had been so quiet. But the Nawab shook his head at Robert.

"All is well, Boy. I know that knock."

An old man came into the court, walking slowly through the shadows of the trees on the lawn below the terrace where they were sitting, and after ceremoniously asking permission to approach, he came up to them, to salaam low to the Nawab, and to his companions. He was dressed in tight white trousers that wrinkled to the ankle. Over them he wore a fitted tunic, buttoning from a high collar at his thin neck. He stood in silence, until the Nawab gave him permission to speak.

"The wine in the goblet was poisoned, your honour. That in the jug was clean. The poison was very strong. Only a very little would have been necessary, a mere wetting of the lips."

"A sip, and then to sleep, eh Hakim?"

"As the Nawab says. The sweet wine of sleep."

"The sweet wine – yes. Sometimes the wine of sleep is sweet. Thank you, Hakim Sahib."

"May the Gods guard you against such sleep, Huzur." The old man salaamed again and walked slowly away, and they

31

heard the door creak open and then shut, heard it clearly, as if, after his words, even the water ran more softly. Death had been very close to the Nawab that evening while he sat among friends in his moonlit, safe garden, a place made for peace and pleasure.

When the Nawab spoke, his voice was muted from its usual cheerful roar.

"So, as a pretext, I was intended to die, in order that the heir should be taken. My death was of no importance, the reason for the killing is. But why? How could they make such an error? The heir is safe in Lambagh. Has no-one heard that he is there, that they should think that he arrived today? Someone is a fool, I think."

"I wish I thought so." Ayub Khan was frowning heavily, and looked years older than he had when Robert had seen him in the sunshine of the deck that morning.

"Ali, have you declared your heir?"

"My nephew is waiting for me to declare him. I have many children born out of wedlock, but I have married lately a girl from the hills. My nephew will have to wait, for this is now my Begum, and her child will inherit, be it girl or boy. I have never married before."

"Is she with child?"

"Not yet. But as I say, I have fathered many children, so I know my seed is potent. If she is barren, I must put her away, but I do not so wish. She is sweeter than honey, and as gentle as a dove. I will keep her for at least another year, for she is very young."

"Well, while you wait, who have you named as heir until you have one from her? One of your sons by one of your other women?"

"What, and have her strangled in case she gives me a child? Nay, I am not a fool. She lives with the others in the court of the women, and how long do you think she would last if they knew she was to bear my heir? They are all happy and peaceful, living together like sisters *because* I have no heir. Each son has his portion, no-one is neglected. I have named the Ruler as Regent, you know that, and so all are content."

Ayub expelled his breath on a long noisy sigh.

"You wonder why you might have an enemy? With Allah knows how many sons, and how many jealous women, and that nephew of yours roosting like a vulture up in Mehli, waiting for news of some calamity overtaking you? I feel pity for your young wife, Ali. If you do not get yourself out of this net of music and fountains and women and hidden conspiracy, she will be a widow before she is ever a mother – if she is not killed first!"

The night breeze was rising, sighing among the creepers and the flowering trees, and splashing long shadows over the streams of water and the smooth grass. The Nawab looked uneasily over his shoulder at the high wall behind him.

"Do you ill wish me, Ayub Khan? Be silent, say no more. I will come up as soon as I have made certain arrangements. I will come, and bring my Begum. She will be glad to see her hills again, no doubt, and she will be safe up there."

"Well, let not the desire for music and beauty delay you. If your Begum is a hill woman, she will be glad to leave here and will not need many arrangements – leave those to your servants, and come with us tonight. Come, Ali, I ask you from my heart."

"I would if I could. But I must arrange the doings of my household. A week, a little week is all I need."

"Very well. We look to see you in a week. Now –"

"Yes, Ayub. We must leave. That iron beast that carries you will not wait. I shall come the old way, in my own time, by road."

They went to the station in greater style than they had arrived, travelling with the Nawab, with outriders before and behind, and a man with a drawn sword sitting beside the driver.

The flower-scented courts, the fountains and the lamplit trees were left behind. Robert looked back once at the white walls as they drove away, remembering the smell of sandalwood and the close clasp of soft arms, and the long, tangled hair of the girl who had not been a dancer.

From a window, high up in the wall, eyes watched him go. The older woman drew the girl away.

"Lie down, *pyari*. The purpose was accomplished. You did

well. Now put him from your mind and sleep. Ooriya is here, and Krishna, outside the door, and I will watch also. Do not fear."

The girl turned with a last backward look, and walked over to the low bed on the other side of the room.

"What if my lord should come?"

"So he comes. What is strange in that? Does he not come to you almost every night to take his pleasure? All is as it was. If he comes, he will be late because he has gone to the station to see the Railgharry go, but you will welcome him as usual, with pleasure. Sleep while you can."

Obediently the girl lay down, lifting her long heavy hair so that it hung over the pillow, almost to the floor. As her eyes were closing, she smiled.

"It was sweet, Mother. Love can be sweet –"

"Love can be sweet. But a son is a crown of gold, and a strong wall against the winds of life. Let us hope you have made a son tonight, since your lord does not seem to be able to plant one in you, in spite of his successes with all those she-wolves in the court of the women. *If* those are indeed his sons."

"Mother! Have a care! You speak of your own death if you are heard."

"There is no-one to hear. Sleep now."

The girl sighed, and turning her head away from the window where the moonlight slanted in, she fell asleep, and in her sleep she smiled.

Outside the white walls the road went steeply, winding down towards the city. The landau passed the temple, which was blazing with lights, and noisy with worshippers. Robert saw many orange robes, monks going about their duties, and a group of shaven-headed men gathered about a tonga outside the temple gates. He could hear chanting, and he smelled incense, as if the air round the temple was impregnated with the smell because incense had been burned there for so many years. He knew that scent so well! It was part of his childhood, the faint smell that always clung about his mother's room. Remembering her, he forgot the German priest and the monk who had come, so improbably, to the boat to meet the foreign

34

priest, and had then left again without him. He had no thought of the ship, the voyage seemed to be years ago.

The road turned again, and the temple, like the white walls of the Pakodighar, was gone.

The air grew warm and foetid. They had left the fresh smell of the hill behind and were entering the city again. Although it was late, the streets were still crowded and noisy. People were sitting outside the tenement houses, and the grass-roofed *bhusties* that stood side by side in strange alliances of ancient and modern. Many were sleeping on the ground, or, the more fortunate ones, shrouded from head to foot and lying on string beds pulled out on to the pavements for coolness. Goats and cattle wandered along the streets, and a great brahmani bull nosed unchecked at a vegetable stall, helping himself, safe because he was sacred, though no-one had thought to do anything about the suppurating sore that disfigured his back. The smell of the streets was terrible, as if the odours of the day had been saved and distilled for the evening.

At last the journey was over. The horses drew up outside the station, and with Ayub Khan's men all round them, they walked into chaos.

There was little time to spare before the train left, and they stood outside their compartment, the Nawab and Ayub Khan speaking urgently together in Lambaghi, and Robert listening and watching everything. Ayub Khan's men, the same that Robert had seen on the ship that morning, stood round them, and Robert saw that they were as alert and ready for trouble as hungry panthers. The crowds surged round the group of men, leaving them in an island of comparative peace. The station was like a madhouse, ringing with noise and packed with people. Bundles that lay unattended in the middle of the platform would suddenly stir into life, and turn out to be people sleeping, waiting out interminable delays, with their household goods all round them. There were stalls set up near the entrance to the station, and from them the food-sellers came, carrying pots piled one upon the other, balancing their way through the crowds to the packed carriages. Women veiled like ghosts, with nothing showing from their covered heads to their slippered feet, chattered and clung behind their menfolk, dragging innumerable children at their heels.

Robert had never seen, or smelt, or heard anything like that station. His head began to feel as if it were bursting, and he had to raise his voice to a bellow when he spoke to make himself heard at all. He found to his astonishment that Ayub Khan and the Nawab had chosen this moment to discuss fortifications and armies and the troubles in the north, and then realised that they could not have chosen a safer place to speak their fears and their plans. No-one beyond the circle of Ayub's men could have heard anything they said. He himself could only hear snatches, and he was tormented with curiosity, longing for the time when he could question Ayub Khan, for the evening was becoming a puzzle to which there did not seem to be any solutions.

Far down the train two orange-robed monks climbed into a third-class compartment, but Robert, engrossed in what he could hear of the conversation beside him, did not see them. He heard the Nawab say, "Has he been told?" and saw Ayub frown and shake his head, and then there was a great deal of shouting and running about among the crowds on the platform, all of whom surged towards the train. A bell began to clang noisily, a cloud of smoke rose up from the front of the train where the engine was snorting and then all the other noises were lost in the loud blast from the engine. The Nawab embraced Ayub, shouting something, and took Robert into his arms. Ayub climbed into their compartment and Robert, escaping from the Nawab's bear hug, followed him, and the train jolted into movement.

The Nawab, the crowded platform, the noise and the smells, the beautiful ride along the beach at Worli, all the events of the evening receded into the past. Ayub locked the compartment and the carriage became their home. The train rattled over a small bridge, there was a fugitive gleam of dark water, some lighted houses, and then nothing but the night and the pattern thrown by the lights from the train windows on to the dark ground, and the sound of the train hurling itself into the darkness.

In the compartment Ayub Khan removed his turban and passed his hands through his thick thatch of greying hair.

"Allah be praised who has brought us safely from that cess-pit. Boy, there is wine there, and ice, and I do not need to send for a wine-taster. Our men be men from Lambagh, not sweepings from the cities of the plains. Let us wash the taste of this evening's doings from our mouths. I have much to say to you that I could not say in that place of walls and whispering water. I spoke more fully with Ali of Pakodi on the station than I could within his courts. You heard what I said?"

"A little of it. There is trouble on the Lambagh borders?"

"Ach, not yet. The harvest is not in. Once the harvest is gathered and stored there is always trouble, because the harvest being safe there is nothing for men to do except finish old feuds, until winter comes to close the passes. Listen, Boy, do you feel yourself entirely an English Sahib, or are you of our people in your heart?'

The question was so unexpected that Robert stared at Ayub Khan, wondering if he was joking. Ayub Khan was watching him with narrowed considering eyes. So the question was neither a joke nor a casual enquiry. It required an answer.

An English Sahib? Certainly England had seemed to be his country, and he loved it dearly. He thought of his childhood in the wide lands attached to his grandfather's home, and remembered with a frown his grandmother's tears when he left. She had wept when he first went to school, but her tears had dried quickly because she knew he was coming back. When he had sailed her tears had been more bitter, for he was going so far away, and there was no date for his return. Robert knew that a corner of his heart would always hold to English ways because of her.

Set against that tender memory was the memory of his days at school, days of utter misery at first, when nearly every day had found him fighting desperately, fights that had left his knuckles permanently scarred, because he was 'different', and the other boys had sensed the difference. Slowly, as he grew into adolescence, his strength and prowess at all sports had made him acceptable to the rest of

37

the school, acceptable and admired. The admiration had been sweet balm, but had not healed the original hurts. He had hated school.

He remembered his constant longing to come to India, his frequent disagreements with his father all caused by his determination to join, somehow, the Forces of Lambagh State, instead of taking his place in his father's old regiment. Those bitter arguments had all ceased when his mother was killed. After her death, everything she had ever wanted was a sacred charge to his father, and it had been well known that she had wanted Robert to visit her valleys.

Leaving England had not been hard, he had felt no home-sickness, no desire to return. He was at ease with Ayub Khan and the two languages that his mother had taught him came as easily to his lips as English did. His clothes were comfortable, he did not feel strange dressed as a man of the northern States, was not at all self-conscious. He had certainly not felt English on this, his first evening, accepting treason, poison and torture as a matter of course; he flushed, remembering something else he had accepted, but he did not regret his encounter with the girl. How could he? He had taken her as easily and with as much pleasure as he would have accepted food if he had been hungry, but he doubted if he would have behaved so naturally in England, even if the opportunity had offered.

So – Indian? Entirely turned towards the eastern world, with no backward looks?

Without warning, in the dusky shadows of the shuddering carriage, Laura seemed to stand, delicate and quiet, a white rose of a girl. What would she think of the man he saw when he looked over at the clouded mirror that was fixed to the door opposite?

Robert found that after all he could give no answer to Ayub Khan. He looked up and met the watching eyes.

"I know not what I am, Ayub. You tell me, when you know me better. But I came here of my own will, because I had long wished to come. Of my very own will, against all opposition I came."

"Enough. That is a good answer indeed. As to my speech with Pakodi – as I said to you, the trouble on the borders is nothing. I spoke to him of matters of greater importance. Did you hear anything I said?"

"I could hear very little. That station rang like a bell."

"Then listen. I tell you now. The matter of Panchghar is the news I gave to Ali. That State lies beyond the northern borders of Pakodi State, and is therefore, with Pakodi State, a buffer between Thinpahari and Tibet. You know that Thinpahari is the name the old Ruler gave to the three states of Jindbagh, Lambagh and Diwanbagh when he brought them under his rule. Panchghar is a small State, but suddenly that petty Raja is preening himself like a cock with two hens. He has received much gold from some quarter, and it has not come from the British because they are also watching him as we are. News has come down to us by devious ways that strangers have been in Panchghar, men who were said to have come to look for plants and flowers, and who asked many questions not pertaining to these matters, and became very friendly with the Raja, who is a man of no *jat*, his mother being a low-caste whore from the street of cages in Bombay. The Raja of Panchghar allowed those foreigners free access through the State, and they came across the borders into Mehli, which is the capital of Pakodi State. There the British have a foothold, they have put an adviser there, called an Agent, a man of little brain, but he was a good assistant. He returned the foreigners back where they came from, and sent a message to his masters in Delhi, and now the British are putting a small detachment of their soldiers into Pakodi State, and this is bad, and has angered the Ruler, who is, after all, the Regent of the State, and whose permission should have been requested had things been done in order. Kassim Khan wants no foreign presence in his State, friend or foe. So – I was told to warn Pakodi that he must return and take up his duties in his State, and I was also told to discover how deeply your English training has bitten into you. *That* is why I asked you the question which you say truly you are unable to answer."

"I do not understand why my English blood should worry

39

the Ruler. I come to enter his Forces, and take an oath of service. Does he think that my father's blood will make me break faith, and that I will be a coward, or betray him in some way? The English do not have *that* reputation!"

The young voice was rough, and held a man's anger in its tone.

"Boy, do not fly at me with your eyes like sword points. The Ruler has his reasons, which, if you will sit in peace with me, I will tell you. Give me time, and I will tell you all. I have a message for you also, and you have the right to give your own answer to the message, which also contains a question. Will you hear me?"

Robert sat back, not able to understand his own sudden rage, but still almost trembling it had been so hot. Ayub Khan waited until he saw the flash of temper die out of the grey eyes, and then smiled.

"Boy, I do not think that the hand of England lies on you very firmly. You rose like a man of the hills, in a rage like theirs. The English have great tempers also, but theirs is not sudden, and when it comes it is cold and bitter and lasts a very long time. Now, listen you to me, in calm, for this matter touches you very closely."

His hookah had been left ready for him in the compartment, the charcoal glowing on the strong native tobacco. Ayub Khan took up the silver mouth-piece and drew in a great lungful of smoke. As if it had given him strength for a task that he dreaded, he then leaned forward and began to speak.

"May God, the one true God, keep us from all harm. May the matters of which I now speak be far from us, and may the Guardian of us all, who sees the future into which we grope, be with us." The sonorous prayer rolled out, as if Ayub was a priest speaking to an acolyte. Robert waited, feeling his heart begin to beat fast as it did when he was waiting in the boxing ring, or on a duck shoot as the first birds came over.

"Should aught of evil happen to the Ruler, and then, in disaster compounded, to his heir, Jiwan Khan – if this should come to pass, you, son of Muna, you have been named the next heir to the Guddee of Thinpahari. Two precious lives

40

stand between you and the Guddee. If Jiwan Khan marries and has a son before calamity strikes, then you will still rule, but the Guddee will revert to Jiwan Khan's son when you are ready to relinquish your Rule. Our Rulers seldom die as Rulers, unless in battle, or by murder. They hand the rule to their heir when they feel the time has come for them to go. You have heard me so far, Boy?"

"I have heard. But I understand nothing."

The train thundered and swayed along the ringing rails. The night roared by, the plains of India, dust and thorn bush, rock and dark banyan tree, the everlasting land that nothing could change lay outside the windows, the ancient land that accepted the roaring monster that ran across it on gleaming rails, just as it had accepted the marching feet of Alexander the Great and his hordes. Beneath the shelter of a great rock, a jackal, eyes green in the light of the lamp on the front of the engine, howled defiance, unheard. Robert sat, seeing nothing, dazed and unbelieving while Ayub Khan talked.

Ayub's quiet, unemotional voice made sense at last. The statement that he was heir, third in line, to a man he had never seen, and a hill state of richness and strategic importance, began to seem possible, instead of the ramblings of a tale that might have been told to a rapt audience by a professional story-teller. Ayub saw that Robert was no longer looking as if he had been struck by a thunderbolt.

'It is good, Boy. You understand now why it is necessary that you came of your own will, because you loved the valley already, and because the hills called you. You are our protection against great danger. A state with no heir is like a chicken run with a leopard prowling about. Many have their eyes on Lambagh State, and not only in the north. There is a worse danger from the south, the family of the Sagpur Kings, who have a spurious claim to the Guddee, which has been suddenly revived."

"Sagpur? I thought that Sagpurna, the Raja, saved my mother's life, and had become a friend of Lambagh?"

"Had your mother lived in Sagpur, possibly Sagpurna, the new Raja, might have become a different man. But after the

41

news of her death he changed, and then his Rani, who was a Pahareen, died giving birth to his son, and slowly the Court became what it had been before. He is very rich, that young Raja, and he uses his money in strange ways and in strange places. We have news up from Sagpur which has added greatly to the Ruler's troubles. But that tale will do for another time. Now this matter we speak of is of more importance. Give me an answer to my question, Boy."

"I have heard no question, Ayub Khan."

"I ask you if you accept the Rulership of the Three States, should the Ruler and his son perish."

"My mother told me that she took a vow as a child. She swore the oath, and it bound her for life, and through her it bound me. My life for the Ruler's life, now and always. Does that answer your question?"

"Wah! I said that the hand of England lay on you lightly. That was a Prince of the House speaking." Ayub Khan got to his feet clumsily, the train swaying beneath him, and held out his sword hilt, his words ringing out loudly above the noise of the train.

"My life for yours, Lord – now and always!"

"Ayub! That oath is not for me, nor ever will be, I trust!"

"It is fitting, Boy, indeed as heir, it is fitting. Take my fealty, I am the Ruler's man, and therefore I am your man. We are bound, each to the other – but as the heir, I owe a special loyalty to you."

Robert put out his hand and touched the hilt of Ayub's sword, and felt as if a legion of men of his blood said the words "It is well" as he said them.

The moment passed. With a gusty sigh Ayub settled back in his seat and took up his hookah again.

"So. It is very well. We speak now of other things. Boy, you have never seen Kassim Khan Bahadur. But you have looked in a mirror."

As Ayub spoke, a great many things that had been tangled and confused in Robert's mind all at once became clear. The noisy train vanished and he was back in England, on his last night, talking to his father in the library of Moxton Park.

They had been sitting together, his father with one foot raised on a stool because his wound pained him. He had spoken to Robert of his time in India when he had first gone out there as a young man, and had met the young Kassim Khan who was now Ruler of Lambagh.

"He is a splendid fellow, a loyal friend, and a very brave man. You may not always understand him – there were times when I found him strange to say the least – but none the less it is impossible not to like him, and you will certainly enjoy serving under him. He was my friend, although I sometimes thought he hated me." Alan Reid had stared into the fire as if he could see pictures of his youth in the embers. Then he said a strange thing.

"One thing is quite certain. You will recognise him at sight, just as he will recognise you. It will not matter when or where you meet, you will know each other immediately."

His father's words still sounding clearly in his ears, Robert returned from the past to the present, and Ayub's eyes watching him.

"I resemble the Ruler?"

"You are more like to him than is his own son. You even sound like him, the timbre of your voice is just as his when he was young. You took my breath with surprise when I first saw you on that boat."

"How can this be? You, of all men, Ayub Khan, you, married to the woman who was present at my birth, you know that I am the son of Alan Reid, and no-one else."

"Yes, Boy, I know. So does my wife, though not having seen you for many years I think she too will be astonished. It is impossible to believe that you are not the son of Kassim Khan, *although* I know. Therefore, in this land there will be none who know you both, and who knew your mother, who will not be sure that you are indeed the Ruler's child. Maybe, long ago, in your mother's blood line, there was a man who resembled the Ruler. Be not distressed. It does no-one any dishonour! You are doubly the heir, should an evil day come. Your mother has once more reached out her hand to aid the family she loved more than her life – and the man."

"Kassim Khan was the man she loved! Of course! I have been very blind. She spoke of him to me so often, telling me nothing in words, but now I can hear the sound her voice had when she said his name. She loved greatly."

"Muna did all things with her whole heart. Be at peace, Boy. Acceptance is all. This was intended, it is plain that the hand of God has led us all. May He be praised, the Compassionate, the one God."

Ayub Khan relinquished the mouth-piece of his hookah, and stood up and opened the window to look out as the train began to slow down.

The fresh night wind came blowing in, cool and sweet, and with it came a voice, a whisper.

"Love is strong," said the whisper, soft as a dying echo, "Love is very strong."

Ayub drew in his head, and reached for his turban.

"We be at Wardhar," he said. "They will come in here and make up our beds for the night, and we will sleep. Will you walk, and stretch your legs? We have spoken of many great matters on this your first day in your mother's land, and much has happened to you already. Come, eat the air, and be at peace with yourself. All things are in the hands of the Compassionate, He who knows the ending before we have seen the beginning. Come, Boy."

The train had juddered to a halt at a wayside station. The night was full of noise, sellers of fruit, and tea, and hot food, and the passengers who were buying through the windows of their compartments all shouted together. Above the chaos stretched the great night sky, studded with larger stars than Robert had ever seen. Beyond the station with its dimly burning lamps lay the wide empty plains of India, and this time, above the noise of the crowded platform, Robert heard the crying of the jackals, the voice of the wilderness.

He walked beside Ayub Khan and slowly the silence of the plains overcame the noise around him, and he found peace of mind.

Robert was entering more and more deeply into his new life. As Ayub Khan had said, acceptance was all.

Chapter 3

When they re-entered the carriage, it seemed as if they had always lived in it. The bunks were made up into comfortable beds and there was a savoury smell coming from some covered dishes. Robert remembered suddenly that he had eaten nothing solid since midday. The dishes were empty when the servant came to see if they needed anything more before the train left. Ayub sat contentedly puffing at his hookah, deep in thought. Robert stretched out on his bunk, prepared for sleep. One window was still open. The chaos outside made the carriage seem a haven of peace. The platform was full of noise and disorder, and reminded Robert of the larger chaos of Bombay station, and from that memory his mind strayed back to the quiet and cool of the Nawab's garden, and to the various events that had taken place there. All desire to sleep left him. He sat up, and began to question Ayub Khan. The answers he got were confusing.

"But I do not understand why the death of the Nawab was necessary to cause a disturbance. I would have thought that was killing an elephant to take a fly from its ear. A little shouting of 'Thief' or 'Fire' would have sufficed, surely, to make the Palace guards run about?"

"Nay. Those men guard only the Nawab and his women. There are others to watch against thieves. Also, you have forgotten the nephew, sitting up in Pakodi State, waiting for the Guddee, and the power."

"So you think he ordered the Nawab's killing?"

"He has not the courage to order his death. Someone has strengthened his arm. His killing would have brought gain to the nephew – and to someone else."

"Someone wanted to make a great disturbance as cover for something else. What?"

"You are not a fool, Boy. After all you have heard and seen today, you know the answer to that question."

"I think I do. Someone – this strange, powerful someone – took me for the real heir, newly returned from England. While the Nawab lay in his death throes, and the Palace guards were occupied and the whole place in disorder and distress, I, as the heir to the Lambagh States, was to be taken. It is seen that this person wishes to put pressure on the Ruler. Am I right?"

"You are right."

"I was alone for about five minutes in that court, when you and the Nawab ran out. Then one came. I thought she had been sent to keep me entertained."

"She?"

"A girl came to me in the garden, with fresh wine. I, not seeing her properly, thought she was one of the dancers."

"Now I see the matter of the fallen wine flask. So?"

"So, she was naked. I was sure because of the nakedness that she was one of the dancers. She was very beautiful, and did not struggle. But then, afterwards, I remembered that the dancers had hair that was cut short to the shoulders. This girl had hair that hung below her waist. She was certainly not one of the dancers."

"I suppose she tried to knife you?"

"Ayub Khan, she did me no harm, but gave me great pleasure. But she was not one of the dancers. Was she sent to keep me quiet?"

"I do not know who could have sent her. Certainly it was not Ali; he was too occupied in trying to drag that brute servant of his away from the already dead body of Salih. Aiee, Boy, I have seen many things in my life that make me wake shivering in the night, but I shall remember what I saw *this* night, all my life. Let us speak no more of that. So. You took the girl. How not? I do not understand why she was there. No knife, no drugs, no companions to seize you, no cries for help –"

"No clothes. Also I do not think she was a virgin."

"You do not *think*? You must know – Boy, was she your

first?" Ayub's eyes had opened wide in astonishment.

Robert felt diminished and stupid. No doubt this large and charming man had deflowered his first girl when he was twelve.

"Not altogether the first," said Robert, attempting to turn various unsavoury episodes with one or two of the village girls into full-scale seductions in his mind. "Not *altogether* the first. But the first in that way –"

"How many ways can you take a girl for the first time in the name of God?" enquired Ayub, astounded. He saw Robert's high flush, and said, "Boy, in your country I understand that the customs are different. Feel no shame. So the girl was your first, and you do not think she was a virgin. She was young and beautiful and had a splendid length of hair. Did she speak to you?"

"She – she said one or two words –"

"In what language? Could you understand?"

"I was not listening, but I think she spoke in Urdu. Yes, I remember, she spoke in Urdu. She told me, when I asked who she was, that she was a dancer."

"I am beginning to understand. I do not think she was an enemy." For some reason, Ayub was smiling broadly.

"Ali of Pakodi has fathered many children, and he has been a great lover of women all his life. Perhaps now it takes a little time for his seed to take root, and his Begum, with much at stake, grows worried. Boy, you may very well have fathered the next heir to the Pakodi State. Come, there is no need to look ashamed! This is not a crime. Woman all over India have done this if they were afraid that their husbands were not potent and it was necessary for them to produce an heir. Let us hope you gave her a són! Now, Boy, what is it? Have you seen a ghost?"

"Not a ghost! A priest!"

"A priest?" Ayub stared in amazement at Robert who was standing up, pointing at the window. Ayub pulled him back, snibbed the lock on the door home, and pulled the window up.

"Now, Boy. What is it?"

"Something I should have told you before." Robert told his story, forgotten all day, about the priest on the ship, and the Hindu monk who had come out to the ship to speak to him, and had then gone away.

"Just now, two monks in orange robes passed that window, and they were looking in, staring, as if they were searching for someone."

"Did they go? Very well, we will see what they wanted, if they wanted anything. They may have been curious. But I will send Yar Khan down the train, to see what sort of monks they are. I like not the orange robes. They have caused much trouble up and down the country, and the robes are not always worn by monks." Ayub had his hand on the door when there was a rending crash, the carriage ran backwards and then jerked violently forward, there was a wild shriek from the front of the train, and the glasses and dishes on the side table began to tap and ring together as the train jerked into movement. Robert rescued the glasses and dishes and Ayub sat back on his berth.

"Too late. The next stop will be at first cock crow. I will go out then. I wish that you had told me before."

"Yes," said Robert, and remembered his grandfather's maxim – never make excuses. Ayub, used to the voluble explanations and excuses of the East, noted this and admired Robert's dignity.

Robert then described the European priest minutely.

"Why do you call him German?"

"He spoke very thickly, and also he had pale blue eyes and his head was a strange shape. His head was flat at the back."

"You use your eyes well. None the less, I am not sure your priest is German. There are others that look and sound as you say he does. Well, we will see into the matter of these monks when the train stops at the next station, which will be just before dawn. Sleep now."

Ayub looked across at Robert and saw that there was no need for him to tell Robert to sleep. Nature had already taken over, and he was stretched out, flat on his back, and very sound asleep. Ayub remembered his father very well, and a strange and tragic night journey unlike this journey in the comfortable carriage drawn by the iron monster. He wondered how much of Alan Reid was in his son, and wondering, fell asleep himself.

As soon as the train stopped, Ayub was awake, and ready to get out and start looking for the two monks. He opened the door on darkness, and saw that this was not the scheduled stop. There was no station, and he realised that the stop had been sudden and even more jerky than usual. The brakes must have been applied with violence.

The cessation of movement woke Robert too. For a moment he lay confused by sleep and darkness and wondered where he was, thinking himself back on the ship and surprised by the heat and the lack of air. Then Ayub cursed fluently and opened a window on the other side of the compartment, and Robert knew where he was.

He opened the window beside him and leaned out into the desolate darkness. There was no sound, no light. It was the hour before dawn, the hour when true darkness ruled.

The silence was broken as the passengers awoke. Voices called question and answer up and down the train. As the glow-worm of the guard's lamp approached, Ayub shouted to him and did not understand the answer he received.

"Stupid down-country fool! He mumbles like an owl in a sack. Wait you here, Boy, I go to try and find out what has happened. We would have done better to come by road. Allah alone knows how long this stop will be. I have heard of trains standing, broken, for days at a time –" Muttering, he lit a hurricane lantern, and climbed down and hurried after the guard. Robert watched him until the darkness hid his figure, and all that could be seen was the dim flicker of his lamp.

The dark plain seemed unbroken by any hill, rock or tree. Black and formless, it stretched to an unseen horizon. Dark earth and dark sky seemed to be one, a bowl of darkness that swallowed the querulous questioning voices of the passengers, and made the few lights glimmering along the train seem as small as the flare of a match. Robert looked out of the open window on the other side of the compartment. Here the

49

plain ended. He looked down and by the light that came from the lamp behind him, saw that the railway ran along the edge of a deep ravine. The light from the window reached the beginning of the drop. After that the earth itself seemed to end. Robert turned away, and went to lean out again to see if Ayub was returning.

He heard something, or perhaps it was some other instinct than hearing that gave him warning.

He was starting to turn when the smothering folds of a quilt fell over his head and shoulders. He tried to fight his way out, but the hands that held him were too many. He tried to shout, but the quilt was pressed too firmly over his face and his throat, there was no air to draw into his lungs, he could make no sound. Wrapped closely, gripped firmly, he was dragged to the other side of the compartment and thrown like a sack, down to the ground. His last conscious thought was of the ravine that dropped away, down and down into darkness, close to the rails. Then something thudded against the side of his head, and he joined the darkness that he had been thinking about, and fell into a hole that held no light and no sound.

He came up from the darkness like a swimmer from a deep dive. He felt no pain, but knew that he was tied, trussed like a pig for market, with ropes round his wrists and ankles and knees. However, he could breathe, the smothering cloth had been taken from his head. He lay with his eyes shut and did not move, because he knew that pain, though unfelt now, was waiting to pounce on him. His head felt strange, light and large, like an air balloon. Perhaps if he moved, his head would float away, taking his body with it, out of this place where voices sounded all round him.

As he became more conscious of his surroundings, he began to listen to the voices. There were several, all speaking Urdu, and he began to make sense of what they were saying. They were certainly speaking of him, and one voice was urging some course on the others, and another voice, which cut in suddenly, silenced all the others.

"Fools and sons of fools! Were you not told to be careful,

and bring him safely to Safed? So you bring him, with a broken head, and then begin to speak of murder, because through your own efforts you have rendered him unfit to ride, and you can think of nothing but your own skins, and getting away quickly. Oh that I should have to work with such as you! Give me *one* of my own countrymen instead of ten of you – useless sons of goats!" The voice was like a lash, and was familiar. Robert lay puzzling over the familiarity, his brain still hovering on the edge of blackness. The next voice that spoke brought all his senses back with a rush. It was like the growl of an animal.

"Am I not of your country, Tovarish?" Robert now listened with all his might. This man he certainly knew.

"Do I not come from your land? Be careful what you say. *I* will not have my father's name insulted by such as you. Furthermore, I tell you –"

"You tell me nothing! Back to kennel, dog! Now, listen to me, listen and obey – for I lose nothing by killing all of you! I will not have my plans destroyed by a parcel of mudheads. Get water and get brandy. We must revive him. He is young and strong. A knock on the head will not prevent him from riding, I swear. Move."

Robert allowed himself to be brought back to consciousness, groaning with genuine agony when they moved his head, but none the less determined to ride. Once on a horse – they would have to free his legs for that – he would have much more chance of getting away from these men. He groaned again, swallowed a little of the fiery brandy they were dribbling over his chin, and opening his eyes, tried to sit up. This he could not do, because of his bonds.

"Untie him," ordered the voice that must belong to a man in authority over this band. Robert's ropes were loosened, and he sat up and looked about him.

It could not be dawn. The sun was in the wrong place. Therefore he must have been unconscious for about twelve hours. God alone knew how far he had travelled in that time. The scene around him was desolate enough for it to be part of the moon. Bare, sandy and featureless, the plain that had seemed endless still stretched round him. There had been a fire and they had been cooking. He saw cooking utensils scattered about, and some saddles lay on a horse blanket close by. Of the horses he saw no sign. As his sight cleared, he saw that the plain was not altogether flat. There were rocks and thorn trees, and a gully cutting across the flatness. Perhaps the horses were there, the gully possibly held water. Robert looked at it all with an eye that searched for possible ways of escape. His mind was clear now, but his body felt as if it belonged to someone else, and he knew that there was no hope of him indulging in any hard physical effort. Looking at the men ranged round him, his chances of escape seemed remote. His eyes went from face to face. Stupid, brutish and thoroughly unprepossessing, they stood about him, scowling. All but one. He was different.

He wore a loose belted tunic, over trousers that were caught into high red boots, fitted with spurs. He was taller than the others, and had a broad, strong body under his loose tunic. Raising his eyes, Robert looked at his face and gasped. The pale blue eyes looked back at him, as cold and expressionless as they had been on the ship. The mouth smiled, the eyes did not.

"Good evening, Nawab Sahib," said the priest, who, it seemed, was no longer a priest. "Good evening. We meet again."

Robert was silent, staring at the man, and marvelling at the change in him. Gone with his black robes was the subservient priest. This man was a leader, and he was in a towering rage. He gestured to one of the other men, who came forward with a cup, and Robert this time drank deeply of the brandy and water that was in it. Another man brought a wet cloth and held it to the side of Robert's head. Robert forced back the cry that he could hardly avoid giving. The pain in his head was so intense he was afraid that he might faint. The watching leader muttered something, and coming over, snatched the cloth away and dealt with Robert's wound himself. His touch was skilful, and he did not hurt Robert any more than he could help. He bathed the wound, examined it and called to

52

one of his men who brought a small black case ornamented with silver. The leader rummaged in it and then applied a salve to Robert's head before binding it with a clean length of stuff, obviously part of a turban.

"That is easier?"

"It is. Are you a doctor as well as a priest?"

"I am many things. Do you think you can ride, Nawab Sahib?"

"Why do you call me by that title? You know my name."

"Why are you dressed as you are – and travelling to Lambagh with a retinue? You have not answered my question. Do you think you can ride?"

"I can ride. Where do we go?"

"You will see, in due course."

During this conversation Robert had heard the sound of horses. Now two men came from behind the rocks leading two horses, and as they came up, Robert lowered his eyes and hoped his face had shown nothing. The man in front was the big man that he had last seen in the court of the fountains in the Pakodighar. He was the torturer, the man who had so mistreated Salih while he was questioning him that he had died. Robert felt that he must be dreaming, that he would waken suddenly and find himself lying on his bunk in the train. He looked up and found the man's little slit eyes fixed on him. The eyes were like small almonds set in that strange, high-cheek-boned face, which seemed enormous because there was no hairline, only the high bald dome of his head. He was staring at Robert, and there was an air of such malevolence coming from him that Robert felt a chill of horror. This was a man who enjoyed killing and suffering, and would not kill in hot blood, for he would never be enraged. He was without normal reactions. He would kill for necessity, because without other people's pain and fear he could not live. He stared now at Robert, a look of pleasure coming into his little eyes, and Robert knew that the brute had already sensed Robert's fear of him. He forced himself to meet that beastly stare, to meet it, and to allow recognition to come into his eyes.

"You have changed masters, Bald Head. You were the Nawab of Pakodi's faithful servant last night, I thought." The man took a step forward and Robert used every inch of strength he had, both mental and physical, to avoid flinching. He cursed himself. He knew he had made a bad mistake.

"Stepan! Get back, and bring the rest of the horses." The leader spoke as one speaks quickly to a dangerous dog, a dog who is about to attack. The big man stood for a second longer, eyeing Robert, one hand fingering the hilt of a long knife. Then he set his mouth into a tight line, and turning, went back the way he had come.

The ride over the plain was one that Robert never forgot. Mile upon mile of sand and rock, nothing to break the monotony, nothing on which to fix the eye.

There was no sign of any human habitation. No animal ran across their path. The horses moved in an empty landscape, and the night came down with no break between the flaming sky of sunset and the darkness that made the plain a place out of another world, and to Robert, in great pain, it seemed that he was also riding in another time, perhaps with the ghosts of some old invading army, led by the devil, or by death. For the big bald-headed man, Stepan, had been sent to ride ahead, leading the way. Perhaps the man they called Tovarish had seen the look of hatred he had given Robert, and wanted to keep him as far away as he could from his prisoner.

The half moon of the night before rose straight out of the line of the horizon, a yellow moon, with a yellow light that made every rut on the ground seem like a deep hole, and every small thorn bush or rock became a crouching animal. They had stopped several times and Robert, almost fainting, had been revived with a drink and a rest. There was no question of him escaping. That had been a mad dream. Even if he had been strong enough, he would not have been able to do anything. His hands were bound and his body was tied into the saddle, and his horse was led between the man they called Tovarish and another. Robert rode in a daze and thought of nothing, least of all escape. He rode with closed eyes most of the time, and when they finally stopped, and he opened his eyes as he was lifted down from his horse, he was astonished to see the first streaks of a magnificent sunrise lighting the sky. They had ridden all through the night.

Tovarish came over and changed the dressing on Robert's head.

"We rest here until nightfall. Sleep now. You will feel better tonight. When you wake, I will give you food – but I think you need sleep more than that just now." Before he had finished speaking Robert had dropped back into the dark hole he had first found the night before. Tovarish set guards, then, with a saddle for a pillow, he stretched out beside Robert. The horses were tethered some little distance away. Beside them sat Stepan. As the dawn brightened into day he sat, unmoving, and his eyes never left Robert's sleeping body. Unmoving, silent, as if he was a rock or a tree himself, he sat and stared, his face without expression, his eyes burning, hidden in the deep hollows about his cheek bones, the long knife in his hand.

When Robert woke he felt very much better. They brought him food and he ate with appetite. Looking at the sun he judged that it was midday. Cautiously he moved his body, trying his arms and legs, freed from the ropes that had bound him. Only his head hurt. He felt that strength had returned to him.

He had been careful. His appearance of weakness and his total submission during the night had lulled his guards. He was left unbound and, it appeared, unwatched, while they refreshed themselves and the horses and began to collect up the cooking pots and the food containers and pack them away in bags on the back of the two pack ponies.

Robert lay, resting up on one elbow, and took stock of his position, weighing his chances of escape. A horse, the animal he had ridden the night before, was near him. Looking about him, Robert formed the opinion that they were resting not far from a road, for every now and then he thought he heard voices, and the horses were restive, looking in one direction, towards a line of trees which Robert reckoned were about a mile from where they were. If he could get to that horse and head for the road – was there a chance? He looked at the men without moving his head. They were all occupied, and the leader was relieving himself beside a rock. Of course! Robert stood up, and fumbling at the front of his pantaloons, moved a little way from where he had been lying. One of the men looked round and Robert staggered on, his pantaloons still occupying his entire attention. The guard turned back to his duties, and Robert was almost within grasping distance of the horse.

Two, three, four more staggering steps. He stopped and made water as the guard turned and looked at him again. Then he lowered his pantaloons and squatted, and the man lost interest. Robert stood and pulled up his pantaloons, tying them securely, taking his time. No-one was paying him the smallest attention. He could not believe his luck.

He put out his hand, grasped the reins and scrambled into the saddle. The effort made his head swim, but he was up – and freedom was surely within his reach. He set his heels to the horse and braced his body for flight.

The knife, arching like a splash of blinding light through the sunshine, reached its target. Robert fell, one foot caught in the stirrup. He did not feel the way his body was dragged for a few yards by the frightened horse before it was brought to a halt. He lay, his eyes open, looking up into a high blue sky, and remembered Laura's eyes. They were just such a blue. He smiled, and looked up again, but the blue was gone; there was nothing but darkness, and cold, and silence.

Chapter 4

It was bitterly cold in Jersey, although it was late spring. Laura Addison, now entering the second week of what she considered to be her banishment, looked out of her window at the rain-lashed camellias in Lady Redmayne's garden and saw a seagull perched on top of the folly, looking as disconsolate as she felt.

Laura felt that she had done nothing since she arrived, reluctant, to stay with Dorothea Redmayne, but drink tea. She had either been taken out to tea, or had attended one of Lady Redmayne's tea parties in the great cold drawing room downstairs. Every afternoon, it seemed, she had sat, balancing a plate with a tiny sandwich on it, and a cup of china tea, and listened to two or three old ladies discussing whichever other old ladies were not present. She had certainly had plenty of time to think. When she was not having tea she sat in her bedroom and thought, and the subject of her thoughts was always the same.

Robert Reid. When would she ever see Robert again? Or worse, *would* she ever see him again? It seemed a century since they had talked and laughed together, a long cold century since he had kissed her and whispered his love.

Of course, whatever her parents did or said she would never marry anyone else. It was becoming obvious to her that she would never be allowed to leave Jersey until her parents returned from India, and that was not for two years. Robert must have already left for India, so there seemed little chance of them ever meeting again.

Laura, not quite sixteen, decided that she would go into a decline. She was not sure how one did it, but she had heard of girls going into a decline and dying. She pictured herself lying gracefully on a sofa, uncomplaining, with everyone murmuring pityingly about her youth and beauty. She saw herself asking someone to cut off a lock of her hair and send it to Robert after she had died. She saw Robert, bareheaded, standing beside a grave on which was a stone bearing the simple inscription 'Here lies Laura Addison, who died, aged seventeen, of a broken heart.' She was not sure how long it took to die of a decline, nor, indeed, how one got into one, but the picture of Robert, her darling Robert, standing lonely beside her grave, was so affecting that she burst into tears.

Maria, Lady Redmayne's elderly maid, knocked and came into the room.

"Oh for goodness sakes, Miss Laura, not crying again, are you? Whatever shall we do with you? You'll lose all your lovely eyelashes if you go on like this. Come now, let me wash your face and tidy your hair; her ladyship would like to see you in the morning room at once."

"Not *more* tea?" groaned Laura, submitting to Maria's ministrations with a large wet sponge.

"Tea? I don't know I'm sure, miss. But she wanted you quickly. Let me just run a comb through your hair – there we are. Off you go, and no more tears, there's a good girl."

She watched Laura go slowly and draggingly down the stairs and clicked her tongue. "Proper little fountain that one's been ever since she came. Wet enough outside, without Miss crying all over the house," thought Maria, and began to put Laura's room to rights.

As Laura went into the morning room, Lady Redmayne greeted her with more animation than usual.

"My dear child, how nice you look. That is a very becoming dress. Now come and sit here beside me. I have a lovely surprise for you."

Dorothea Redmayne managed to disguise the fact that it was also a lovely surprise for her. Laura had been so obviously bored and unhappy that Lady Redmayne had been distressed.

"That child could easily go into a decline," she had

58

confided to her best friend, the Archdeacon's wife.

"She was so thin when she arrived that I was shocked. Now she is just a shadow, and barely eats a thing. The only thing she wants to do is ride, and I cannot send her out alone, and it is not always convenient to send Mead with her. In any case, Mead gets *tired*."

Mead was Lady Redmayne's elderly groom. Dorothea continued, "When she is not riding, she just mopes. It is terrible to see." She sighed deeply, and her friend had been suitably sympathetic and wondered aloud if perhaps a little helping in the parish – visiting, you know – but Dorothea Redmayne as well as being kind was sensible.

"I do not think that she is of an age to go parish visiting. That would be enough to throw *me* into a decline. No, I shall just have to think of something. I shall find some young people; I wish I knew more people with daughters of her age, but of course they mostly go abroad to finish. I shall think of something, no doubt."

Now it appeared that she would not have to cudgel her brains to think of suitable entertainment for an unhappy young girl too young to put up her hair and go about, and too old for nursery entertainment. Now all was well since the letter had come.

"Dearest Laura," said Lady Redmayne, taking Laura's hand, "I have had a letter from your Mamma. You are to join your parents in India."

Laura heard no more, just the magic word 'India'. She repeated it softly, looking up at her kind companion.

"India?"

"Yes, my dear, India. You will leave at the end of the month. Your mother has arranged for you to travel out with a Mrs. Soames, who is taking her own two daughters to join their father. They are a little older than you are, but no doubt will be pleasant companions for the voyage. We must start getting your wardrobe together at once. Will that not be exciting!"

Clothes! Laura did not care if she went out in rags. She was in a daze of joy, wondering how this miracle had happened.

Each morning she woke, she hugged the thought to her that she was one day nearer to starting her journey. She slept dreamlessly, willing the night away as soon as she put her head on the pillow.

Time passed and the day came.

Lady Redmayne said goodbye to Laura with tears. She had become fond of this girl who had arrived in such misery and had now become so happy. Mrs. Soames, who knew nothing about Laura but who had been asked to chaperone her on the voyage as a favour to her sister, a friend of Laura's mother, looked at the girl with alarm. She was very young to be going out to India. Had she misbehaved in some way that she must be bundled off to join her parents before she was properly 'out'? Such a slim girl, with her hair still down her back. Mrs. Soames hoped that she was not going to be a trial on the voyage.

But Laura gave no trouble. From the time she boarded the ship on a boisterous, rainy day, Laura was like a person living inside a bubble of glass. Her manners were beautiful, she sat decorously on deck beside Mrs. Soames, holding a book which she did not appear to be reading, for she never turned a page. She walked round the deck with Mrs. Soames and her daughters once the ship entered calm waters and the two girls were able to emerge from their cabins. Laura had not been troubled by the rough weather. Laura was quiet, did exactly as she was told, and was as animated as a wax doll.

Mrs. Soames was greatly relieved, but felt sorry for Laura's mother. Laura showed signs of becoming a beauty, that was true, but if she continued to be so withdrawn, she would be hard to get 'off'. Mrs Soames looked at her own bouncing, giggling girls, and reflected complacently that they would, no doubt about it, both be married by the following season. They already had a crowd of admirers on the ship. Of course, it was right that Laura should not attend the dances or the musical evenings on board, she *was* too young, but one would imagine that she would have shown at least an inclination to flirt. Mrs. Soames would have nipped anything in the bud at once, of course; but it was odd that there appeared to be nothing to nip.

Laura, her eyes dreaming, knew nothing about Mrs. Soames' thoughts about her. She looked past any young man for no reason other than the fact that she did not even see him. All she saw was a mirage floating ahead of the ship – a fabled country where there were elephants and maharajas glittering with jewels, and palm trees sighing above seas that ran blue into green in the shallows where silver fish swam above silver sand. There were beautiful women dressed in floating silks, who walked like Muna, Robert's mother, had walked. There were jungles where the trees grew thick and the shadows were black and the flame-striped tigers stalked deer with polished black horns. The evenings in the country were scented with flowers, and the stars were as bright as the moon, and the people were all beautiful and kind, and, above all, Robert was there.

Robert! At the thought of him all other thought stopped, and Mrs. Soames thought that Laura looked positively vacant. The young Third Officer who was of a poetic turn of mind thought that Laura looked like an enchanted princess, waiting to be wakened by a kiss.

Laura looked over the rail at the blue sea, and saw her fabled country, and thought of Robert, and saw nothing else.

Chapter 5

Far away on a wide plain in India the men stood round in appalled silence while Tovarish knelt over Robert's body. He opened Robert's torn shirt and put his head down to lay his ear against the dusty, ripped and scraped chest. Then he stood up and walked over to where the man Stepan stood. He stood in front of the hulking figure, and stared into the little shifting, animal eyes.

"Stepan!"

"Tovarish, he would have escaped. Also he knew me. He knew why Salih died. He could have led our enemies to you through me."

"He could. He may still, for although your aim was good, he is not yet dead. Pray, Stepan, if you have a god. Pray that he lives. For if he does not –"

Like a threatened cur, Stepan cringed. The others, watching, marvelled and were afraid, because they had never seen Stepan show fear before. These men were brigands, men of no account, paid assassins and trouble-makers. This assignment was becoming less and less to their liking. These two men talking in front of them were outside their knowledge, they did not understand the fear they felt, and with one accord wished to leave, and would have crept away, but fear of the man Tovarish held them. He issued fast orders and enforced them with a look. Afraid to disobey, afraid to leave, the men did as they were told. One rode away in the direction of the line of trees. Robert's body was covered with a horse blanket. Stepan, lashed by Tovarish's tongue, took the horses into the shade of an outcrop of rocks and sat down like a beaten dog, his eyes following the figure of Tovarish as he moved to Robert's side again.

Presently a creaking, grinding sound broke the silence of the plain, and a cart came into sight, a long plume of dust blowing behind it, and the man who had gone to find a cart on Tovarish's order came galloping back.

The cart was piled high with chopped green stuff, *bhusa*, food for cattle and horses. The cart-driver, sitting dumb with fright at first, began to protest as soon as he saw Tovarish, a European.

"Sahib! This man of yours has behaved with great dishonesty. He had taken me from my right route and forced me at gun-point to come here. I cannot allow you to take this *bhusa*, it is for the market at Sardara. Who is to pay me for my time that I am losing, and also the sun will wither the green stuff – what doest thou?" The cart-driver's voice rose in a cry as the men, at an order from Tovarish, began to pull the green stuff from the cart.

"Sahib! In the name of the gods – what are these men doing – my *bhusa* – who will pay me?"

"You will be paid. Now be silent."

With staring eyes the cart-driver saw the body of Robert, bleeding and apparently dead, laid in the middle of his *bhusa*, and then covered with the green stuff that had already been unloaded. When the men had finished the cart looked as it had, a cart loaded with cattle food.

"Which of you can drive?" asked Tovarish, looking round.

His men looked from one to the other.

"Drive a bullock cart?" asked the senior amongst them. "Drive a *cart*? Nay, Sahib, we be horsemen. We have no knowledge of these lumbering carts."

"You will then take it in turns, until I see which of you does it best. He will be well paid. You – you start. Take the driver from his seat."

Dumb now with fear, the driver was tumbled on to the dust of the ground and made no protest, while the man Tovarish had pointed to climbed up to take the driver's place.

"Show him how to guide the beasts, you," said Tovarish, and trembling, the driver obeyed, hoping for nothing now except his life, and the chance to return to his village, and his family. He showed the man once or twice how to manage the iron-tipped stick and direct the bullocks from one side to another.

Finally Tovarish was satisfied.

"Very well. Now head for the road." He gave an order to the men who stood by the driver. The driver did not hear what he said. The cart, creaking and groaning on an erratic course towards the trees, was his whole life and he stared after it, deaf to everything else, watching his life going away from him into a distance that became eternity. He did not see the knife that killed him, knew nothing of the shallow trench hurriedly dug to receive his body. The earth was flung over him and stamped flat and his killers mounted and rode away.

Ayub Khan, returning to the compartment where he had left Robert, stood looking about him for not longer than a few seconds. Robert had managed to struggle a little, and in the struggle had left signs that his departure from the train had not been voluntary. The wine flask lay smashed on the floor, and some of the plates of food had toppled from the shelf that served as a table and were lying on the bunk and on the floor beneath the window. There was no wind to have caused any of this. The door swinging open on the wrong side of the train, with the ravine lying below, did not make Ayub think that Robert had fallen from the carriage. He wasted no time, the train was due to move. He rushed to the next compartment of the same carriage where his men were already seated. His orders were crisp and sharp. Three of his men tumbled out beside him. The others were to go on to the next station, hire horses, and return. Messages were to be sent to the Old Ruler in Madore. By the time the train pulled out, Ayub and his three men were fully armed, and the others of his troop knew exactly what they had to do.

Robert's captors had left very few traces, but there were some. However, the kidnappers had been mounted. It took Ayub Khan and his men two days to find their way to the place where Robert had been revived and had been mounted on a horse. There they waited, and in due course were joined by the rest of Ayub's men and the horses. Ayub made no effort to follow any trails. Indeed, on that rocky ground it would not have been possible. Instead he sent his men out on wide, sweeping searches.

They were rewarded. A herdsboy, lying amongst his sleepy, lumbering buffaloes, remembered seeing, on the skyline of the flat plain, a party of horsemen. He pointed out the direction they had taken.

A village woman, out at dusk gathering firewood, had seen nothing but had heard voices. She showed them the direction from which the voices had come. Another villager, out hunting *chikor*, had found horse droppings. One of Ayub's men found traces of a fire.

So at last they came together at the edge of the great road, the Grand Trunk Road of India, and there the trail ended. The road teemed with humanity. It would not be discreet to ask too many questions. There was no way of telling friend from foe, among this many-coloured, many-tongued crowd. Ayub and his men joined the travellers. The signs had all pointed towards the north, so they went north, and after a long and frustrating day came to a camping place, and drawing off the road, made camp for the night. It would not be a wise thing to become exhausted. Robert must be found, but when found, they must be strong enough to get him back.

They chose a site and made a fire and sat round it, talking in low voices, while they waited for their food to cook. There was nothing noticeable about them. Twenty or thirty other parties, very like them, were doing exactly as they did, talking together quietly, resting after a long day's travel.

The girl sitting behind the curtains of the domed, red-curtained palanquin noticed them however. She had opened her curtains a chink, so that she could watch the activities of the camp, and she saw Ayub Khan at once and recognised him. She knew nothing about him – or only one thing. The night before, when she had been getting off the train at Wardhar Station, she had seen the most beautiful young man she had ever seen in her life. This big man had been with

65

him, and they had walked up and down the train talking. She had left the train and the platform with reluctance, looking over her shoulder and peering at Robert through her veil. Her new master, Ram Chandra, had been too busy ordering the coolies about to notice her wandering eye, but the woman he had engaged to look after his new possession had seen, and had jostled the girl hurriedly out of the station, scolding her under her breath.

Meeta, the girl, was only thirteen, and had just been given to Ram Chandra the money-lender to pay off her father's debts. She had accepted her fate philosophically. She had two brothers, and her father was not a rich man. There would have been no dowry for her. At best she would have been married, without a dowry, to some old man, who would have despised her, unless she immediately had a son. At worst she might have found herself sold to one of the low-class brothels in the nearest big town. Ram Chandra seemed preferable to both these alternatives. He had given her two saris, a red one, and a white one for every day, and two gold bangles, and a small ruby to put in the hole that had been pierced for the purpose in her right nostril. On the whole he had been kind. He had contented himself in the train by stripping her and examining her every part, like a child examining a new toy. His fat fingers had strayed about her young body like slugs on a ripe peach, but she had expected worse, and was relieved when, the train stopping at a station, the carriage had filled with people and he had been forced to leave her alone.

But seeing the young man at Wardhar Station had unsettled her. She had never seen anyone like him, and could recall his every feature, his voice and his laugh, for he had laughed at something this big man who was now sitting beside the fire close by had said.

She peered about hopefully, but there was no sign of the young man. She even remembered what the big man had called him – 'Boy' – as if it had been a title of honour. Where could he be? While she was trying to see, she was careless. The old woman who was looking after her, Khera, saw her curtains moving and came to draw them close, and scold her.

"If our master sees you, he will beat you. Behave yourself, girl."

"He will not beat *me*," said Meeta firmly, "he will beat you."

This being perfectly true, Khera became cross and sat firmly down beside the palanquin, so that there was no way that Meeta could look out. She was forced to sit in a scarlet dusk, with nothing to distract her mind but her gold bracelets, slipping up and down on her thin arm, and thoughts of the journey they had made that day.

It had been exciting, the last three days since she had said goodbye to her village and set off with Ram Chandra. First the train – it was something she had never imagined that she would do, travel in the Railgharry. Then seeing the young prince – for of course he must be a prince. No ordinary man could look so like a god. He looked like the dancing gods in the temple that her father had once taken her to, the Krishna who danced with milkmaids. Her mind dwelt pleasurably on the idea of herself as one of the milkmaids, and then, as another party arrived, shouting and throwing down their goods as they settled for the night, she wondered who the new arrivals could be.

"Khera," she said beseechingly, "Khera, may I not open the curtain even a needle's width? You have travelled much, all this is an old tale to you. But I, alas," said clever Meeta, "I have never been anywhere before, and would like to look – only a very little open, Khera, please? Also, it is hot in here, I feel I cannot breathe."

Khera's bad temper had passed. She graciously agreed to opening the curtains a small crack, and went off to get Meeta a glass of sour milk with which to refresh herself while the supper was cooking. Meeta looked out and saw that the newcomers were a family she had noticed early that morning when she had started her journey in the palanquin. Meeta being light, and Ram Chandra being well mounted on a good pony, they had made good time, with Khera swaying and shaking on top of the mule that carried the baggage. They had passed most of the travellers on the road. For lack of anything else to do, Meeta began to count them over to herself. There had been the elderly farmer and his wife and two daughters in a bullock cart. They were on the other side of the clearing, the wife and daughters working over their cooking pots, while the father sat comfortably smoking his hookah. Then there had been three young soldiers, going on leave. They must have been in a hurry to get to the next town, for they had passed Meeta and her master early on, and she had not seen them again. Soon after midday they had come upon a bullock cart and a band of men, and had almost had an accident, the bullock cart-driver must have been drunk or asleep, for the animals were straying all over the road, the green stuff that formed their load toppling dangerously, and the other men had been cursing him with terrible curses and had turned on Ram Chandra and told him to go on. Something in their way of speaking had made Ram Chandra hit his pony smartly and gallop off, leaving Meeta and her palanquin coolies to follow as well as they could, and poor Khera had shrilled and scolded as the baggage mule balked and jerked, excited by all the noise. Once they had stopped to re-adjust the baggage on the mule, and also to allow Meeta and Khera to go discreetly to the side of the road and relieve themselves. The bullock cart and its attendant men had passed them again, and Ram Chandra had decided to wait and give those people time to get well ahead.

"They be *goondas*, bad men and better left alone," he had said, and had sat in the shade of a tree and smoked, and Meeta had dozed. And then it was evening and the sun was low on the horizon, and they started off again, going slowly, looking for a good camping place. There had been few people on the road then, and no-one had reprimanded Meeta when she had pulled her curtains back to watch the sun creep down the sky, and the birds flying home.

The road had been creamy with thick dust that spurted up between the toes of the carriers and blew back at Meeta, so that she wrapped the end of her sari over her face. She thought the dust was like the goat's milk that had spurted between her fingers when she milked the goat in the little courtyard of her father's house. Thinking of this she felt a spasm of homesickness, and tears filled her eyes, and she put a careful finger up to catch them before they fell on her beautiful red sari. She loved the red sari, it was the brightest and most beautiful thing she had ever owned. Such a brilliant red. Like the ruby in her nostril, it gave her great pleasure. She squinted down her nose to admire the ruby, letting the sari fall from before her face, and as she looked down, she saw on the dust ahead a bright red drop, like a red bead. Only for a moment, then the leading coolie's feet had trodden it down into the dust and it was gone. But there was another, and then another. At regular intervals, there were these red drops. Meeta, bored, began to count them, watching how evenly they were spaced. What were they? Had some woman broken a precious red necklace, and they were spilling out of her cart? Should she call out to the coolies and ask them to stop and pick them up? She leaned forward to see more clearly.

They were not beads. They were drops of blood.

They meant nothing. A traveller had cut his foot, or a bullock had a wound, or one of the thin, rangey dogs that ran beside the camel trains had a torn ear. They meant nothing, but those evenly spaced red drops had suddenly made Meeta shudder. They had seemed so very fresh and red against the white dust of the road.

Chapter 6

The bustle of arriving at the camping place, the choosing of somewhere suitable and private to set down Meeta's palanquin for the night, had driven everything else from her mind. This too was something new, this camping under the trees, with cooking fires blossoming and voices making the quiet grove ring like a village at night when the men come home from the fields. Here, as in the villages, people sat round the fires, talking, and someone was singing a long quavering song about a broken heart and a lover who never came, and a dog yelped aside from a dish of food, and a baby cried monotonously. She would have liked to get out of her palanquin and wander among the various groups, to hear what they said and see what they ate, and talk to the women. It was not long ago that she had run free, a child among the other children, because she had been late in starting her womanhood. Now she was a woman, and though not married, she was a man's property, and must stay hidden away, like a muslim beauty in a harem. It was not the custom in her village or in her family but Ram Chandra, being a man of consequence, insisted that she should stay private, and she had no thought of not doing exactly as she was told. Her mother had always obeyed her father, and as the only girl child she had, after her mother's death, had three men to obey and cook for and do everything else for. Sitting at ease like this, her little work-worn hands empty, was so unusual that she felt all her muscles jumping with the desire to get up and do something, anything, to relieve the boredom of being shut away. Khera had not come back with the sour milk. Meeta moved her curtain a little wider.

As the darkness gathered under the trees, the fires seemed

to grow brighter. Meeta looked again at the party that held her interest more than any of the others. The young Prince was not there, but perhaps he would come later. She settled to watch the big man who was his friend, and as the voices slowly died down in the grove as the rest of the camp settled to eating or sleeping, she found she could hear clearly the speech of the men at the next fire. She learned the name of the big man. Ayub Khan, a man of the north.

Her mother had been a Pahareen, a hill woman from the foothills round Chalka, and she could understand the hill tongue that the men were speaking. Their voices were low, but she heard enough to make her realise that they were worried and distressed. Something was lost, or had been stolen, a valuable horse perhaps. Meeta wondered if that was where the Prince was, searching for his favourite horse. She went off into a splendid daydream in which she rode away on a magnificent horse, and found the Prince in some terrible danger, from which she rescued him with invincible courage. He had just said to her, "Lady of pearl and silver, I shall take you for my queen," when Khera came back with the sour milk, and Meeta was brought suddenly out of her dream. Ram Chandra came to look at her, a man making sure that his newest possession was safe, and then rolled off to sit talking with some other money-lenders on the far side of the camp. Khera settled under a tree nearby and took out her little twist of paper which held a very small quantity of *bhang*, which she was used to smoking either put in with the leaves of a *bidi*, a native cigarette of great power and rank smell, or else, as now, poured on to the ball of glowing charcoal in her small hookah. Meeta knew that, after pulling at the hookah for a little while, Khera would fall into a sound sleep for several hours. No-one would watch Meeta now, unless she actually climbed out of the palanquin, so she opened her curtains wide, and sat enjoying the evening air, and was able to watch the whole camp at once.

The fires were built up. The singer started on another love song, and the men from the north were still talking, and planning about how to get back what they had lost. There

71

was no sign of the Prince. Meeta's eyes began to grow heavy, but something Ayub Khan said brought her back to wakefulness.

"If only the Boy had spoken of the priest on the ship. It is plain to me that priest was there to watch him, and that the two monks who were on the train are the men who took him. But how? He was no weakling. Yar Khan, when you questioned the men in that carriage, what did they say?"

"They said that the only people who had left the train at Wardhar were a money-lender and his women – two women. No-one else."

"Two women – could the monks have disguised themselves as women?"

"Allah knows – but I think I saw the man, and the women with him were not big enough to be men disguised."

Meeta had been beaten frequently for understanding and seeing more than a girl child should. She was far from being a fool. Now, listening to these men who spoke as her mother had spoken, she did not stop to think.

"The man lied," she said, her young voice carrying clearly to Ayub Khan and his companions although it was not loud.

"The man lied to you. After we got down from the Railgharry, I saw four men get down and go round to another carriage, they came from another place on the train to take seats with us because they were cramped they said. Being holy men, we made space for them, and then –"

"And then?" Ayub Khan, and another of his men had turned and were imperceptibly nearer. Meeta, after a quick look at Khera, sleeping over her hookah, went on with her story, pleased that her audience had the sense not to get up. If they had risen, and come close to the palanquin, Ram Chandra would have been over at once. As it was she felt perfectly secure.

"And then two more men came in, and they had friends further down the train, because they spoke of the baggage they wanted being in another compartment, and one said to the other, 'We must take it an hour after we leave Wardhar. The train will halt there. It is arranged.' I heard all this," said

Meeta importantly, "I heard what they said because I was with Ram Chandra, who is a Bunnia from Nucklao. But as to where the train halted I know nothing, for *we* got down at Wardhar, as this one saw."

"Sister, your eyes are bright as well as beautiful. Did you hear or see anything else?"

Meeta, delighted, thought for a second.

"Yes. I saw that one of the orange robes had strange eyes. His eyes were the colour of snow-water, green and blue together. Also one of the other men was very big, he took two seats to himself alone, and he had a voice like a beast, he did not speak, he growled. Where," asked Meeta, greatly daring, "Where is the Prince?"

"The Prince?"

"The Prince with whom you walked and talked on Wardhar Station."

Ayub Khan took in a deep lungful of air.

"Listen well, sister. Where is your master? Will he come soon?"

"He speaks with friends over there. I do not think he will come until he has eaten with them. As for my woman, she sleeps deep. *Bhang.* She smokes it very often, and afterwards nothing wakes her."

"So. It is seen that you are a woman of great sense, as well as having youth and beauty." Yar Khan, in spite of the terrible anxiety that held them all, could not prevent a quick roll of the eyes at the other men. This little thin child, with her cheap sari and her protruding teeth – Ayub Khan had certainly dipped his tongue in honey. Ayub Khan continued talking to a delighted Meeta, who had never been called either sensible or beautiful in her life before.

"Listen well, sister. The Prince is in danger. Will you help us?"

Meeta, saucer-eyed, nodded.

"I thank you. Now we are searching for the Prince. Tomorrow, as you journey, will you keep those bright eyes open, and remember everything you see. We will continue our search, and then at nightfall we will come along the road

73

until we see your palanquin, and we will camp nearby, and one of us will find a way to speak to you, and then you can tell us everything you see – everything. Do not forget, it does not matter how small the matter is, tell us. Sister, can you do this?" Mute with excitement, Meeta nodded. Ayub Khan glanced round, and then turned back to his fire.

"Pull your curtains, little sister. Your master comes."

By the time Ram Chandra had returned to the palanquin, and had kicked Khera into wakefulness because he wanted her to bring him his glass of *lhassi*, sour milk, Meeta's curtains were firmly closed, and her eyes too. She did not stir when he opened the curtains and peered in at her, and grunting, he went away. There would be plenty of time to pleasure himself with his new toy when he got to Nucklao. He looked suspiciously at the men round the next fire, but they were deep in conversation and did not even look at him. Satisfied, he rolled himself in a blanket and went to sleep.

Meeta slept herself in the end, and when she woke the whole camp was astir with departure. The Prince's retinue, as she thought of them in her mind, had already gone. She had planned her actions carefully, and when Ram Chandra came to part her curtains she greeted him with a smile, and wriggled with pleasure at his questing hand. Almost, Ram Chandra decided to spend the day under the trees. This little creature showed promise – perhaps the *hakim* had been correct, and his manhood would return, renewed by her youth. However, there was the time factor to consider. His fellow Bunnias would be going on, and he did not wish to arrive last when there were debts to collect or land to be taken in lieu. He dallied a little longer with Meeta, and when she asked him, her eyes cast modestly down, if she could ride today with her curtains drawn open, he was disposed to agree. "I will keep my face covered of course, lord, but it is very hot within the curtains, and I cannot see you ride, like a prince of horsemen, also I feel sickened by the swaying of the palanquin when I cannot see out."

A prince of horsemen! It was enough. With a last wandering of the hand, Ram Chandra graciously agreed to the curtains being open, on condition that she kept her face covered, and Meeta smiled her gratitude and suppressed a shudder at his crawling hand, and was at last alone.

All that day she watched, straining her eyes, and gradually learned what to watch for. She looked keenly at any band of men riding together on good horses. Covered, curtained bullock carts were remembered, also palanquins, and she stared at the bands of wild-eyed, naked fakirs that padded along in the dust, their begging bowls and the tongs that they clicked together as they walked, their sign that they were mendicants. If only the big man could have told her what danger the Prince was in! Her eyes ached with staring. She forgot to look down at the road, where the dust had almost obliterated the brown stains that had been bright red the day before.

By sunset her eyes were aching, and she felt her mind had nothing in it but the dust of the road. When she shut her eyes she saw an endless procession of people, and muttered over to herself everything she wanted to pass on to Ayub Khan.

She waited with impatience, enduring the attentions of Ram Chandra, who had drawn off the road early in order to have a little time alone with her. He was growing more ardent, and for some reason Meeta found it very hard not to bite the hand that took such long investigations of her body. At last he left her, to eat, and Khera brought her food which Meeta could not eat, because she felt sick, and wanted to do nothing but lie back, her curtains open a chink, and wait for the man she was sure would come.

It was full dark and the camp fires were beginning to be built up for the night before she heard the sounds of another arrival. Khera was settled with her hookah, Ram Chandra, his account book on his knees, his brow furrowed with concentration and a lantern throwing its wavering beam on his columns of figures, was some distance away, and in any case was not for the moment interested in anything but tomorrow's money collection. Meeta heard a whisper and put her mouth to the line of light that showed the opening of her curtains.

75

When she had finished, Ayub Khan thanked her gravely, and asked if she would do the same for him the following day.

"Of course. But is it possible for you to tell me what is the danger that threatens the Prince? Then I would know how to look."

Ayub Khan made up his mind.

"Listen well, little sister. The danger is very great. The Prince, as you call him, has been taken."

"Taken?"

"He has been taken by enemies, and truth to tell, we fear for his life. He is indeed a prince, but in our country you understand, we call him a nawab. He is of great importance to his – to the Ruler of Lambagh. We can find no trace of him, and tomorrow we turn off the road and go to Faridkote, because we will have to send word to the Ruler – we can keep it from him no longer."

"But if you leave the road, how can I get news to you?"

"One of us will find you, do not fear. But I will wait at the turning to Faridkote, so that you know it, and then, if you can so arrange it that your master camps close to that turning, it will make it easier for me to come – or I will send a man. He will say to you these words, so that you will know him. He will say 'I come from the son of the Rose.' Can you remember that?"

"Of course I can remember that. But there are many palanquins like mine. Should I not say something?"

"Well thought, little sister. You will reply with a question. You will say, 'From the Rose of Gold?' So. Is that pleasing to you? You have done very well, little sister. We will hear your news tomorrow. Do not distress yourself if we come late. Faridkote is a long way. Be assured though that we will come."

She did not hear him go, but when she opened her curtains a little wider there was no-one there. Tired though she was, she lay awake a long time thinking, and was heavy-eyed in the morning, though she pleased Ram Chandra by her reception of his attentions and won open curtains again. Ram

Chandra rode his horse just in front of her palanquin with the reins held high and one hand resting on his fat thigh, as he had seen the young nobles ride their spirited horses. His pony was quiet, and plodded gently along, but Ram Chandra saw himself as a young man on a prancing horse, and was very content.

The sun was still high when they came to a bend in the road, and there a smaller road broke away and began to climb up into the foothills beyond the fields of maize.

Ayub Khan and another man were at the side of the road where it branched off, bent over the hoof of a horse, talking to each other. They did not turn their heads to watch the tinselled, red-curtained palanquin carried by at a smart trot, but Meeta saw them, and marked the road in her mind by the spreading shade of the big neem tree that grew just after the turn.

The bend in the road hid Ayub from her sight. She was carried along, the road now heavily shaded by a thick grove of old mango trees. She risked much, and choosing her moment when there were not too many people to hear her shameful behaviour, she called softly to Ram Chandra.

"Lord!"

Astonished, he turned back, and rode beside her, half proud, half angry at this bold behaviour.

"What is it, woman?"

"I have a boon, lord. I am weary of this jogging. Could we not stop somewhere here, and spend the night? See, here is a place that has been used for camping. Also there is good shade . . ."

Meeta, child and woman, let her voice tail away suggestively. Not for nothing had she watched the girls in the fields round her village when their mothers' eyes were turned elsewhere. Ram Chandra was pleased, but the coolies were muttering together, and at last one of them said, looking at his brother carriers for help, "Heavenborn, this is a place of ill luck. This grove has a bad name in these parts. There is a shrine to Kali –"

It was enough. The name of that goddess is not said lightly.

77

"We go on," said Ram Chandra firmly. Then, as Meeta lifted beseeching eyes, he nodded to her with a wet smile, saying, "We go on. But not very far. There is a place just about three kos from here, and we will spend the night there. It is full early yet to stop in any case. But do not fret, woman, we will stop in good time."

His eyes were full of unspeakable promises. Meeta smiled back, and resigned herself both to a camping place that was further from the turn off for Faridkote than she had hoped, and also to the look in Ram Chandra's eyes.

When they finally drew off the road the camping place appeared to be empty. Ram Chandra barely gave her time to refresh herself before he came to her palanquin.

"Come, *piyari*," he said hoarsely. "Come with me. There is a place –"

Ignoring the smirks of the coolies, he led the veiled girl through the trees to a small half-ruined hut. Perhaps it had been a pilgrimage shelter once, or a priest's house, for there was a small shrine near it. Now it was a ruin, and the roof was gone. Here Ram Chandra took all Meeta's clothes from her, and after much effort, mounted her, and attempted what had been impossible for him for some years.

It proved to be beyond his powers even now, but his attempts were so nearly successful that he was pleased, and at last he allowed Meeta to pull her sari round her. He then fell asleep, his head on her knees, and Meeta sat, disarrayed and disgusted, wondering at what she had been told were the pleasures of love.

Dappled by the lowering sun through the green shade of the trees, Ram Chandra's head heavy on her knees, she sat, so still that the birds came close to her, rustling among the fallen leaves like whispers in the night.

Meeta fell to dreaming of how love might be, which naturally led her to thought of the young Nawab, as she now called him. She had seen little to pass on to Ayub Khan. She began to think, with despair, that the men who had captured the Nawab had taken him on some other road and that he would not be found. This brought her to misery and she wept, catching the tears with her fingers before they fell on Ram Chandra's face. He was snoring, and the birds had flown. Presently Meeta had cramp, and moved her leg. Ram Chandra woke, and after a little dalliance, pulled his clothes to rights and strutted back to the camp site, Meeta, her sari across her face, at his heels. Khera was waiting and had water ready.

Khera had grown steadily more respectful to Meeta as Ram Chandra's signs of interest in her charge increased. Now she assisted Meeta to bathe herself, holding up a curtain for privacy; then she took the rumpled red sari and Meeta dressed herself in the more ordinary white cotton with the red and blue border. She was glad to settle back among the cushions of her palanquin, her body felt bruised and mauled, as indeed it had been. It was still daylight but she left her curtains open, and the camping site being deserted except for their party, Ram Chandra said nothing.

It was sunset when she heard a bullock cart creaking and groaning towards the camp. Ram Chandra lifted his head from his account books and she twitched her curtains into place, leaving a crack open.

The long rays of the setting sun diffused through the dust made a scarlet-shot mist under the trees. Through this mist she watched the bullock cart rock into the clearing. It was laden with cattle food, piled high and roped into position to stop the load slipping. The men with the cart were hill men, in woollen robes girdled with rope. They wore the eared caps of the men who come from the high passes beyond Ladakh. If it had not been for that, she would have thought it was the same bullock cart that she had seen days before, for the green stuff did not look fresh.

The men did not unyoke the bullocks but fed them at once, so they were not spending the night. They spoke little. One of them sat apart, telling his beads – a priest, perhaps, or a holy man. A man of great stature leaned against the cart and did not eat with the others.

The sun sank, and the blue smoke from the fires added to the darkness under the trees. The newcomers had eaten and were repacking their utensils; they had good horses with them and that was strange, for hill men ride the small-bodied, short-legged *tat*, the pony that can climb like a panther. These horses were of a very different kind. That flea-bitten grey, with the silver crescents ornamenting its saddle – she had seen that before! The stallion, squealing and snapping, and quick to use its hind legs, that black stallion – she turned her eyes to the man sitting alone under a tree and mentally put on him a belted tunic instead of his duffle robes, a belted tunic and splendid red boots with silver spurs.

Meeta leaned back and tried to think, while her heart thundered. These were the same men who had cursed and laboured round that same bullock cart loaded with *bhusa*, while the bullocks, badly driven, had panted and snorted and pulled in different directions.

What reason could these men have for a complete change of clothing They were not hill men. She strained her ears to listen, but they were too far away and she could not hear what they were saying, except that it was plain that they were all arguing and all bad-tempered. Somehow she must get close to them.

It was agony, that time of waiting. She prayed that a voice would speak soon outside her curtains, saying the magic words "I come from the Rose", so that she could tell Ayub Khan or his man of her suspicions.

They were more than suspicions. Meeta was convinced that these men with the cart loaded with withering *bhusa* had something to do with the disappearance of her Nawab. She lay, rigid and sweating behind her drawn curtains. Ram Chandra did not come. She risked a look through a chink in the curtains. Ram Chandra had put his account books away, and rolled in a *rezai* was asleep. Khera, however, was close by and was still smoking her hookah. Soon, prayed Meeta, soon let the whispered words sound, or she would have to get herself across to that laden bullock cart to hear what those men were saying.

She was very afraid that the men would be leaving soon, because they had neither unsaddled their horses, nor had they unyoked the patient, cud-chewing bullocks. However, they were still sitting close around their fire and their voices were rising. She saw the man who was sitting apart raise his head, and then get up and join the others.

Khera was asleep. It was dark now. No other people had come to this *parao* beneath the trees. The carriers of her palanquin were already asleep, blanket-covered mounds lying close to the fire, as if the dark shadows of the trees, blacker even than the night, frightened them.

It was time. She could wait no longer.

Silent as an eel in water she slid out of the palanquin and lay flat, glad of the shadows that had made the coolies look over their shoulders with rolling eyes as they had first entered the grove. From one pool of darkness to the next she fled, a shadow herself, until she was kneeling behind the thick trunk of a tree and could hear everything that was said by the men near the cart.

She had had a terrible fear that they would speak some language that she would not understand, if they had come from the south or from the very far north. But they were speaking Urdu, and what they said so terrified her that she had to clap her hand over her mouth to stifle a scream.

The big man was speaking, he who had been leaning against the cart most of the evening, as if he were on guard. Now he had come to join the others and was arguing in a voice like the growl of an angry beast.

"Leave the horses? What is this madness? I have stood beside that cart for over an hour, and have heard not a sound. He is dead, I tell you, there were flies gathering this afternoon – now that it is dark, let us take him out and bury him under those trees, and then take the cart and leave *that* on the road, and use the horses to get away. That is what *I* say."

"And who are you, that you speak so loud in my presence? You dunghill beetle, be silent! If he is dead, you are dead, whatever you do. Look at me, swine-dog. Look in my eyes, and tell me what you see!"

The man who had been sitting alone was speaking. At the sound of his voice the others were silent, even the big man.

This must be the chief of this collection of terrifying men.

The big man finally seemed to summon up courage.

"Tovarish –"

"Do you dare to speak? *Look in my eyes, I said!*" There was silence, and when the man they called Tovarish spoke again, his voice was a whisper.

"What did you see in my eyes, Stepan? I will tell you. You saw death. Death for you will come very quickly if what you say about that boy is true. So hope, Stepan, hope for his life, as you hope for your own. Now. Listen you to me, all of you. We go on with the cart, and we take the horses further into the grove and tether them, with food and water for a day and a night. You, big mouth, will return here from the next *parao* and bring the horses, and then you will take the cart on to Safed, to the House of the Pundits. Do you understand? Then obey – and quickly. We leave here in an hour." As he finished speaking, Meeta had begun to move. The flurry of activity as the men began to round up their horses woke Ram Chandra, but after sitting up and looking round him he lay down again, and was soon asleep and snoring. Meeta gained the palanquin, and lay back, shaking with fear and horror.

The blood trail on the road! The Nawab lay somewhere under that load of green stuff, and was so badly wounded that he could now be dead. She had not looked for blood stains. She pushed a finger between the curtains to widen the gap and put her eye to it. The horses were being led into the grove and the bullock cart was being turned towards the road, the man called Tovarish beside it. Once he looked over in the direction of her palanquin and she leaned back, in deadly fear that the firelight might have caught her eye, glistening through the crack. But no-one came near. She heard the bullock cart creak and groan into movement. It was too ordinary a sound to wake the sleepers. Then she heard the heavy footsteps of the men returning from the grove, and held her breath. The cart's complaining axle sounded less and less as it went further away. The *parao* was silent at last, except for the bubbling snores of Ram Chandra, now in a deep, sound sleep.

Meeta waited and waited until she could be sure that there was no-one standing over the palanquin. With infinite caution she pushed the curtains aside and saw the camp site, firelight and black shadow, empty except for her own party.

She could not wait for Ayub Khan any longer. Every minute might make a difference between life and death for her Nawab. Meeta unwound her white sari, and fumbling among the bedding in the palanquin found a pair of wide cotton pantaloons which she had been accustomed to wearing about her work in the house in the village. She pulled them on, and then took a piece of cloth and bound her head, tying her long hair up inside it.

She stood beside the palanquin for a minute. The grove was blacker than night, and the palanquin seemed a very safe haven, even Ram Chandra's snoring seemed companionable. She took a deep, steadying breath, and walked into the grove.

The moon, in its last quarter, threw a dim and yellow light. Once she had put enough distance between herself and the camp fire, Meeta began to walk as quickly as she could. As she walked she prayed to every deity she had ever heard of, and among the great ones on whom she called was the goddess whom everybody loved and feared, Kali the destroyer, Kali the dark dancer, the mother and the lover, she who was both day and night, life and death.

Meeta passed, as she prayed, a thick grove of trees. The shadows in the setting moon's strange light were very black, and the chill of winter seemed to lie in them. Meeta hurried through those shadows, feeling as if she were swimming in dark water.

A voice spoke in her ear; closer than that, it spoke somewhere within her, a voice that took her breath with fear, and halted her step like a hand on her arm.

"Go in safety, my daughter," said the voice. "Fear nothing. You are in my hand . . ."

Meeta stopped, in a terror greater than any she had ever known, but there was nothing moving, no-one beside her in the dark shadows. Chilled to the heart she began to run, and did not stop until she was away from that grove of trees.

Deep in the shadows of that grove stood a crumbling plinth where another woman had given up her life long ago, and behind that stood a small shrine beside a tank of clear water, where a Ruler's wife had bathed, and had heard that same voice that Meeta now fled from. But that had all been very long ago, and Meeta knew nothing of it. Only she knew the fear of the cold darkness from which the voice had spoken.

A faceless ghost in the strange yellow light of that terrifying place, Meeta hurried on, her feet making firm prints in the shadow-barred dust, her breath coming short.

From behind a great mango tree came a flurry of sound, and Meeta, all courage lost, stopped and buried her face in her hands, afraid to look death in the eyes.

The noise continued, a trampling of great feet and a deep sigh, and then a soft wind blowing over her shoulder. Meeta, country born, turned with a sob, and took the great wise head into her arms.

"Oh deliverer of widows and orphans! Oh guardian of the poor, and comforter of the fearful! I thank thee. Oh thou whose name I dare not speak, take my life in thanks," said Meeta, weeping, and gentled the big, flea-bitten grey, who had not been tethered very well, for a piece of rope hung from his neck and he was trembling, his skin moving under Meeta's fingers like the skin of a beast tormented by flies.

He answered to her voice and her kind hands comforted him, he was glad of her company in that dark place. She took the rope in her hands and then took a firm grip of his mane, and managed somehow to scramble on to his back, she who had never ridden anything before but a scrawny bullock.

Once safely seated, wide-legged, on his back, ignorant and clumsy, and not at all the sort of rider he was used to, she guided the frightened animal by voice and hand, along the way that she wanted him to go, and when he went from a walk into a trot, and from that back-breaking movement into a canter as smooth as clouds sailing over the sky, Meeta clung on like a baby monkey on its mother's back, and was carried at a speed she had never imagined.

They reached the turning Ayub Khan had shown her well before dawn. Meeta turned off the Great Road and the pace slowed, for they began to climb almost at once. Once she fell off, but to her amazed gratitude the horse did not run away; his training held good and he stood beside her, his nostrils wide, his ears back, but standing there. Bruised and frightened, she managed with the aid of a big rock to clamber up on his back again and force him on, thumping his side with her heels and begging him to go on in a frightened whisper. Then suddenly he seemed to become more confident of the road. His speed increased, even though the road sloped upwards. The air was cold and Meeta, in nothing but her cotton clothing, shuddered as she rode.

The horse seemed tireless. It was hard to make him stop, even for a short rest. They passed a great chenar tree soon after dawn, and then crossed and recrossed a river. Meeta made no further effort to guide the horse for he seemed to know the way, as if he were going home.

The day began, and ended, and still there was no sign of any village or town. Meeta saw mountains ahead of her, their peaks scarlet with sunset, and then black and jagged with dusk. After that there was nothing but starlight, and the horse slowed to a walk as the road grew steeper and rougher. The hill wind blew like ice on Meeta's body but at last, as they came to the crest of a hill, below her, miles away still, it seemed, she saw the lights of a town. Faridkote? She did not know. She pulled on the rope, and by some magic the horse stopped, as reluctant as always, and they rested. But he would not stand for long and soon they were off again. Slipping and sliding, his haunches low on the ground, his forefeet often in a straight skid, the animal took his own way, and Meeta, thrown far forward on his powerful shoulders, clung on with all her strength.

The lights grew brighter, paling the stars. A great bulk reared up in front of her, and the horse stopped of his own accord, blowing and stamping. They had come to the walls of the town.

Faridkote was boiling with life, even at this late hour, but

Meeta and the horse were on the wrong side of the wall, and the gates were closed.

Meeta did not dismount, she fell from the horse's back, and just in time gripped his nose as he drew breath for a neigh that would, no doubt about it, have brought out the guards on the great gates. Meeta had no way of telling if this was a friendly town or if it might not harbour more enemies of her Nawab. Somehow she had to find Ayub Khan, but how? Why had no messenger come, as he had promised? She held the horse's head firmly against her body and wept in exhausted frustration, and the horse stamped and tossed its head, almost breaking her grip. A voice hissed from the wall, a clear and penetrating whisper.

"You – whoever you are! You, with the horse. Come closer to me."

It was a woman's whisper.

Meeta looked up and saw, balanced beneath the stars themselves it seemed, a gleam of mortal light that blew this way and that in the night wind.

Again the voice spoke, the whisper as clear as if the speaker's mouth was against Meeta's ear.

"Come! Who are you, weeping there in the darkness, outside the walls at this time. Come, I say, and tell me. Do you come from the Rose?"

Meeta's head whirled and her legs buckled. Clinging to the horse she managed a husky croak, like a frog speaking from the edge of a well.

"From the Rose of Gold?"

"Ah, that is good. Keep that animal quiet. I come."

Something snaked down the wall, there was a soft rustling, and then two firm hands pulled Meeta closer into the shadows of the wall.

"In the name of the goddess! It is but a child. Girl, I must get you in. Say nothing, I will do the talking. Come."

The horse, freed of Meeta's grip, threw back his head and neighed loudly.

A man shouted, "Who comes?"

"It is I, Janki, and I have my sister's daughter with me. She missed her way, and was late, and I went out to find her. Open, Osman. We be tired, and would get home."

"At such an hour you come? Eh, Janki, when did you go out? I did not see you go?"

"Are you become my keeper, that I have to tell you of my comings and goings? Open, Osman. Are we to stand here throwing words about in the cold until the gates open at dawn, or will you let us in?"

"Ohe, Janki, wait. I come. Indeed, you are a woman of no patience coming so late, and expecting the gate to be opened for you in the shutting of an eye! The town is humming like a hive of bees and half my men have been taken to patrol the streets at Ayub Khan's command, and I am here alone, with three men who sleep because they have been on duty all day. *This* is your sister's child? I did not know you had a sister –"

"Osman Ali, you are as full of talk as an old market woman. My sister and her child are no business of yours. Come, little one, you will soon be warm and fed, once this windbag decides to stop talking."

Osman's eyes were resting on the horse with astonishment.

"Your sister must be wealthy beyond most – that is a very splendid beast. If I did not know it was your sister's horse, I would say it came from some illustrious stable."

The woman Janki pushed him in the stomach, laughing.

"Eh, Osman bhai! You have an eye for horseflesh, like you have an eye for women. Let us go now, and come and discuss matters with me another day."

Osman fell back, the gate creaked shut behind them, and Janki gave the horse a sharp slap so that it clattered on ahead before Osman could say anything more. With an enveloping arm around Meeta the woman hurried past the large figure of the guard, calling her farewell before the last bar of the gate had thudded into place.

Pushed by that firm, kindly arm, Meeta walked down a street and turned off into a narrow lane, and there was an open door from which light streamed. As they came up to it the light went out, and Meeta was pushed into darkness. She heard the horse's hooves clopping on stone ahead of her. The woman spoke softly, a door opened on a lamplit room and they entered warmth and light. There were two boys in the room, boys almost in their first manhood. No-one spoke. The door was barred behind her and she was taken up some stairs and into a big room where a fire burned blue and yellow in an open charcoal stove. Janki gave various orders and Meeta was soon sitting before the stove, warmly wrapped, with a hot drink burning her cold hands and the woman and the two boys sitting beside her.

"Now, child. Speak. We be all people of the Rose."

Warmth that was almost agony was spreading through Meeta's body. Her head had a life of its own and kept falling forward, struggle as she would to keep it upright. The thought of the young Nawab was all that made it possible for her to speak.

She told her story in a voice that was broken and husky, but she told it meticulously, trying to remember every detail. The woman and the two boys listened to her without interruption, and towards the end of the tale, one of the boys got up and opened a big chest against the wall, taking from it a strange assortment of clothes. She watched him dress, and as she said the last words he stood there, completely changed. His last action was to tousle his hair, and then he was a perfect example of a very dirty beggar, dressed in rags so old that they had no colour and no shape. He dragged his fingers through the ashes under the stove and pulled them through his hair again. His long-fingered hands now ended in black rimmed nails. He stood before Janki, and she looked at him and nodded.

"It is well. Have a care, and if Ayub Khan thinks it fit to come here, let him be brought along the roofs. He can take his men out this way; it is better than being seen going through the gate when he has only just returned."

The boy was gone from the room as she finished speaking, and all Meeta heard was a noise a little louder than the rustle of the ashes falling from the glowing stove. The other boy got up and put more charcoal on the stove and fanned it. Meeta's head fell forward and the drink dropped from her hand. Janki straightened her body and pulled the quilt a little higher up the thin shoulders. Then with the other boy she went out onto the balcony to wait.

Ayub Khan was sitting fuming in a house known to all as the House of Paradise. His message had gone to Lambagh, and he waited for a reply. He had sent Aziz to track down Meeta and get her news, and he had not yet returned. Ayub Khan sat in a vacuum, unable to do anything, and felt that every minute that passed put Robert further from any hope of rescue, if indeed he were still alive.

He heard the high, nasal whine of a beggar outside the wall. It was like the hum of a mosquito, penetrating and aggravating. He heard the gateman curse, and then silence for a few seconds, and then the whine started up again, closer now, just outside the gate again he judged. It was a determined beggar who would risk Usbeg Khan's wrath twice. The whine had words, and he was suddenly alert.

"Oh Protector of the Poor, give alms for the sake of the peace of thy soul. Remember the poor in thy prosperity, oh Rose of generosity. Remember the sweetness of giving." The word 'Sweetness' was the name of the girl – Meeta, 'Sweet', had been her name. Ayub Khan got up hastily and went out. He gave a sharp order and the beggar was dragged in and brought to him.

"Did any see you bring him in?"

"I think not, lord. A man passing saw me clout him the first time. Why, fool, didst thou not say something to me?"

"I had no time. Thou art swift with thy great ape's hands – I was knocked down before I could speak."

"Well, no matter now, provided you got him in unseen. Speak, Rabindra."

As the boy repeated Meeta's story Ayub gave orders, and by the time the tale was told he and ten men stood armed and ready to leave. The boy was stripped, and finished the last of his news washing his ash-smeared body. Then he was attired in the same clothes as the men, and, armed as they were, followed them out, through a central courtyard sweet with the scent of roses, and up a ladder on to the first roof. After that, he led and they followed, and their progress was swift from one flat roof to another, then down and along hidden lanes so narrow that the balconies above their heads made a roof that hid the sky. When they could, they ran, soft leather boots making no sound. The last part of the way was above the streets, leaping from rooftop to rooftop, balancing on wooden balustrades and creeping along the high ridges of rich men's houses, which were tiled and not flat. Within half an hour they were all standing on the balcony of Janki's house, and the high bulk of the city wall was close above them. Ayub Khan took a few moments to go in and look down at Meeta where she slept, her little pinched face still grey with fatigue.

"Guard her well, Janki. God knows when we will return, or what news we will bring, but do not let her out of your sight. You say she came on a horse?"

"Yes, a flea-bitten grey, I think it carries the brand of Pakodi – a crescent and a star."

"Ay. Very well, Janki, that horse must be hidden. Can you do it? Otherwise, should any be searching, the search will end here, at your house."

"Do not fear, Ayub Khan. The horse will be safe, and no trail will end here. Go with the gods, and may you find your friend – and in good health."

Ayub Khan had gone, and his men with him, scaling the wall and down to a gully where horses waited for them. Rabindra the boy came back later, and after talking a little with Janki, went down to the horse, carrying a bowl and a rag, and whistling quietly between his teeth.

Dawn found a splendid black horse shifting and stamping in Janki's stable, ointment covering a wound on his left haunch. "Only a very small wound, Oh Magnificent One," muttered Rabindra who had not enjoyed the pain he had been forced to inflict on the horse. "Only a *very* small wound. Now you carry our brand, and it will heal with Janki's care. Come, eat, my splendid king among horses, eat, and forget."

*

Meeta woke, and lay, warm and relaxed, and thought that she still slept, held in a wonderful dream of comfort. Then a movement caught her eye, she turned her head and saw Janki smiling at her. In a great rush everything returned to her, and she started up, questions pouring from her, unable to wait for the answers. Janki leaned forward from her stool beside the low bed, and put a gentle hand on Meeta's mouth.

"Peace, peace, little sister. Wait. Ayub Khan has gone to find your Nawab. You are to stay here, quietly, until they return."

"Until they return, you say. Do you think the Nawab is alive? I saw so much blood!" Without warning Meeta found that she was weeping helplessly, weeping as a child weeps, with open, wry mouth and loud sobs, and streaming tears.

"Aiee, what a to-do! Shush! After so much bravery, you weep? Think with hope of your Nawab's return, do not ill-wish him with tears! Come, now, that is better. Now we bathe you, and find warm clothes, and we talk."

The mere mention of ill-wishing her Nawab was enough to dry Meeta's tears. Presently she was bathed, and dressed in soft woollen robes such as her hostess was wearing. Untutored and simple, Meeta still knew, somehow, that these soft cream folds of stuff were more becoming than the red and tinsel sari she had worn with Ram Chandra. Janki combed and oiled her hair, remarking on its length and thickness.

"No need to plait black thread into this hair, child. You have the hair of a beauty, hair like thick silk."

"Well, I have hair like my mother, and she was beautiful. She was a woman of Chalka and my father took her without a dowry because she had great beauty. I am like to my father's sister, and *she* did not marry, and now she sits in the house of my father's elder brother and looks after his children and works like a bullock at the plough."

As Meeta talked, Janki worked. Meeta's hair was plaited into a thick rope that swung below her waist. She was given a glass of warm milk, and a stack of thin chapatties with honey to drip on them. Replete, she leaned back, and Janki nodded approval.

"Good. Now we will talk. You have been a brave girl, and it will not be forgotten. The Lambagh family never forget those who serve them."

"But if the Nawab –" Meeta could not finish her sentence.

"Hush, girl! I said to you, do not ill-wish him. Ayub Khan will find him and all will be well. Think on that, and on nothing else. Tell me what you were doing on the Great Road, and why you left your village."

Chapter 7

The voyage ended. Laura woke in the night to feel the ship still at last. There was a strange smell in the air, not all pleasant. There was the scent of spices and of flowers, but stranger than that was a terrible smell of something rotten. The cabin was full of it, and now that they were at anchor there was no breeze, so that her skin ran with sweat, and the sheet that covered her was too much so she threw it off, and would have thrown off her nightdress as well if it had not been for Mrs. Soames sleeping peacefully on the other bunk.

The morning was very hot. They scrambled down a precarious gangway to a little boat that bumped and jolted them over the choppy waters of the harbour to the quay. This was a howling, jostling mob, and then, after a struggle, they were in the Customs shed, where Colonel Soames was waiting for them. He clasped his family to him with warm affection and greeted Laura kindly.

Laura, from living in a dream, had moved to living in a nightmare. The smells that assaulted her nostrils made her feel sick. Going out of the shed to the carriage that was to take them to their hotel, she saw a naked, crawling *thing* that moaned, and held up handless arms. It had no nose, and its eyes were deep in their sockets.

"Oh these awful beggars," said Mrs. Soames, whisking her skirts out of the way. Laura climbed after her into the carriage with legs that threatened to give way. There were dogs, so thin that they appeared to be skin stretched over a spine, nosing in unspeakable piles of rubbish, and beside them were children just as thin, except that their bellies were enormous, too heavy it seemed to be supported by such skinny little frames, and these children were scavenging for food in the same fearful rubbish.

The hotel was cool and dark, and the bathroom off her bedroom had a large earthenware jar in it and a wooden commode. To bathe one poured the water all over one's body from the jar, straight onto the floor, and the water ran out of a small hole in the wall. After one had used the commode one opened the door, and sitting outside was a little thin man, in a ragged red shirt and a loin cloth, who had a conical basket beside him and a rush broom. He was there to take away the contents of the commode, and put in a clean pan.

Laura sat in the bedroom on the bed, which had a hard coir mattress, and felt a stale breeze fanning her cheeks as the strip of cloth suspended from the the ceiling moved to and fro with a noise like a long sigh ending in a creak.

Was this India? She stretched out on the bed and closed her eyes, and at once was looking into the tormented eyes of the maimed beggar. She lay, keeping her eyes open, and watched the punkah sigh backwards and forwards, wondering how she had got into this nightmare world and where the real India was.

The journey up to Delhi took three long hot days and three long hot nights, on the rattling, shaking train that trailed itself over the brown plains of a country Laura could not recognise. Thorn, scrub, bare earth, scorching heat. The stations were bedlam, crowded with pushing, gesticulating people. None of them were in the least as she had imagined Indians to be.

In Delhi she was to be met by friends of her father's who would take her up to Mehli. Perhaps Delhi would be more like India?

They arrived early in the morning, before the heat had taken hold of the day. They drove to the Soames' bungalow, which was in the cantonment area, in an open Victoria, pulled by two horses that were so thin and poor-looking that Laura turned her eyes from them. The driver cracked a whip above their boney backs, and stamped on a bell that rang almost continuously, and shouted at the people who streamed over the road in front of the carriage. When they turned off the main road they saw a company of Indian troops, marching smartly, an officer riding alongside. Robert would now be in uniform. Laura looked eagerly at the officer. Perhaps – did not the State Forces come down to Delhi? But this was certainly not Robert. This officer was almost as old as Colonel Soames. They passed the soldiers, turned a corner, and drove through a gateway into a small dusty garden, where orange-coloured flowers clashed furiously with some bright pink things that looked like cocks' combs. A small collection of servants in white uniforms came forward salaaming. The Soames, at least, were home.

Laura spent two days with the Soames and grew more despairing each day. The Soames appeared to see nothing odd in the dust and discomfort of life. This was not 'home', this was India, and therefore bound to be uncomfortable. Laura was very quiet, and so pale that Mrs. Soames grew worried.

"If only the child does not get ill before these friends of her father's arrive. *Who* did you say there were, Bertie?"

"Oh, heaven-borns of course. Indian Civil, and very big nobs. I think their name is Lees. Why should she get ill, my dear?"

"Well, she has hardly eaten a thing since she arrived here, and I do not like her looks."

"What looks? She has none, poor girl. Now, our two – really, Luncinda, you have produced a charming pair of girls. I am looking forward to showing all three of you round the station."

Sir Richard and Lady Lees arrived the next day in a carriage with their own horses, and bore Laura off, rather as if they were rescuing her from a desert island. They offended both Laura's kind host and hostess, and embarrassed Laura, but nonetheless she was glad to leave the hot, dusty little bungalow where nothing was really comfortable.

The Lees lived in a large cool house, with a garden that would eventually be beautiful, but was suffering, like everything else, from the beginning of the hot weather. But at least the dust was kept down, and the grass kept green by clean, efficient servants. There seemed to be about twenty servants, not counting the grooms, or *syces* as Laura learned to call them. The horses were a delight.

Laura went out for her first ride the following day, getting up before dawn, before the sky was even streaked with the first signs of the sun, dressing in a dressing room that was almost as large as the bedroom. She had her own woman servant called Moti. Moti was slim and quiet and dressed in a full white skirt and a white bodice, and a white muslin head cloth which went over her head and was thrown over one shoulder to hang in graceful folds that did not impede her quick, skilled hands. She helped Laura into her habit, and combed and brushed her hair and tied it back securely with a wide black ribbon, and Laura went out to ride with Sir Richard feeling more cheerful than she had for some time.

They rode over dry fields, where the horses kicked up little spurts of dust with every step, and up a hill which was crowned by a ruined tomb which Sir Richard told her had once been part of Delhi, another Delhi, built hundreds of years before, and now crumbled away completely except for a few battlements of stone and this domed ruin. Delhi had been built and had fallen to invaders, or to time, and then been re-built many times over – seven times some said – but there were signs that beneath these ruins there were others, even older. Laura was fascinated and enjoyed talking to Richard Lees, feeling at ease with him. She asked about Mehli, where her father was now stationed, and was told that she was fortunate to be going there.

"It is a beautiful place and in the high hills. You will miss all the hot weather, which is going to be pretty bad this year, it appears, because the rains were late last year. Honor will go with you and stay up there for a while. I do not think that any woman should stay on the plains for the hot weather."

But Laura had only heard the magic words, 'the high hills'.

"Is Mehli near the Lambagh Valley?"

Sir Richard gave her a sharp look.

"Lambagh Valley? Well, fairly near, as the crow flies. About a week's journey if you are not a crow. The road winds about a great deal and there are some very high mountain passes between Pakodi State, of which Mehli is the capital, and Lambagh State."

Laura's eyes were glowing and she had a delicate flush on her pale face. He thought that the ride was doing her good, she was looking so much better already. He had been distressed by the little pale-faced waif they had picked up from the Soames; no wonder, poor child, what a place to have to live in! Well, she would enjoy Mehli at any rate, though come to think of it there were no young people up there. Perhaps her mother would invite some suitable girl to come and stay with Laura.

They rode home, taking a different route, following a rutted country road that meandered through the fields between great dark-leafed mango trees. Men were at work in the fields now, and Laura heard the strange creaking and squealing of bullock cart wheels and saw the cattle being driven out of the villages, the herd boy riding on the leading cow, drumming his heels against her side as he stared round-eyed at the English Sahib and the girl. The mango trees echoed with the screams of green parrots, and crows followed the bullock carts, carrying out exhaustive investigations into the cattle droppings. Across the fields a well wheel was working, the blindfolded bullock walking patiently round and round a beaten track, while the wheel droned and the water gushed out into prepared channels. Laura felt she had not enough eyes to see everything. They had to pull their horses to one side to let a bullock cart, piled high with freshly cut cattle food, go creaking by.

"There will not be much more of that this year," said Sir Richard, looking at it, "They will be scraping about for food soon."

Soon after they left the road and cut across the fields again, and they let the horses go, and Sir Richard was delighted with Laura all over again.

"That child can *ride*," he said to his wife later. "She can really ride! And how she enjoys everything! I cannot imagine why her parents are taking her to Mehli. There are no young people there, except the various sons and daughters of the hill Rajas. Not all of them are as civilised as the Lambagh family though."

"She will certainly not be allowed to have very much to do with any Indians. You know what her mother is like! They have great hopes for Laura. However, she is too young for them to force her into marriage yet, and I have every intention of persuading Clarissa to let me bring Laura back here next cold weather. It will not be hard to persuade her. There are all the young men of suitable age and standing that any mamma could desire here during the season."

"Yes, there are." Richard Lees spoke slowly, thinking deeply, and his wife looked a question.

"What is it, Richard?"

"Well – strictly between us, her parents may very well be down here themselves by next cold weather. Two reasons. The first is that there is a certain amount of unrest on the borders of Pakodi State, which may increase, and English women will be a responsibility no-one in the State will wish to take, and the second and more valid reason is that the Ruler of Lambagh, a very important gentleman indeed, is most displeased that the Addisons are there at all. Nothing against them personally, but it is Edward's official position to which the Ruler objects. The Ruler is Regent for the State of Pakodi, and no-one in the Secretariat thought to inform him that the nephew of the Nawab of Pakodi had requested a British Agent. They just sent Edward up. The nephew is angling for the Guddee, and in fact holds no position in the State at all. It is unfortunate, because we were very anxious to keep in good odour with Lambagh and this has really infuriated the Ruler. Another thing is that Edward and his lady wife, with their attitude towards our Indian friends, are the last people who should have been sent up there."

"Oh *dear*," said Honor, in such dismay that it was her husband's turn to question.

In answer to his raised eyebrows, she said "Oh dear – you

do not remember why poor Laura was first sent to Jersey and then suddenly brought out here?''

"No, my dear, I do not think I do."

"Well, it was all because of Robert Reid – you remember the Reids, Caroline Addison's greatest friends?''

"Of course I do. Who could ever forget that unlikely marriage. That beautiful woman, Muna, married to Alan Reid, who may be a good soldier but was a perfect stick of a man. Yes, I remember Robert Reid very well – Good God!''

"Dearest! What is it?"

"I have just remembered something more. Robert Reid is of course connected to the Lambagh family, and the other day was made the heir if anything should happen to the Ruler or to his young son, who is still unmarried. Robert Reid is out here now – he arrived, I believe, about a month ago. Now you are going to tell me that Clarissa and Edward disapprove of Robert as a suitor for Laura. I do remember hearing Caroline Addison talking about it. How very unfortunate that Edward is in Mehli. I can see that between them the Lambagh family are going to be extremely offended."

Richard and Honor sat in depressed thought, both depressed by different things. He stood up finally and kissed his wife.

"Well, I must be getting my breakfast, dearest. I have a good deal to sort out before we leave. But I must tell you I think that it is ridiculous to send Laura to Mehli. For any number of reasons. Let me arrange for you to go up to Simla, or to Dalhousie –''

"Oh no, Richard, all our plans are made! I do not want to go to Simla or Dalhousie, really I do not. I am looking forward to a quiet summer of walks, and painting, and collecting wild flowers for my pressed-flower book. Never mind Edward and Clarissa, she will most certainly not be offensive to any Ruler or Raja! *Any* title is better than none, as far as she is concerned! Really, I do not know why I bother with her, it was Caroline I was fond of – but there you are, we were girls together –''

"Honor, it is not only Clarissa's behaviour I am worried

about. I do not care for the rumours about the border disputes. If only our Government would stop behaving like a lot of old spinsters convinced that there is a man under the bed. Oh well, we'll leave things as they are for the moment. I want to get up there and see things for myself. You can collect your wild flowers. I am afraid poor Laura is going to be very bored.''

Laura was, at that moment, being bathed by her ayah, standing in a small round earthenware bowl and having water ladled over her, and then submitting to a thorough soaping and more pouring of water. It was the strangest way to take a bath, and no-one had ever actually bathed her since she was six. But it was pleasant, and she liked the ayah. She stood and was dried, and then sat down and had her hair brushed and brushed again until it shone like dark silk. Then, dressed in fresh muslins, she went to join Uncle Richard and Aunt Honor, as she had been instructed to call them, sitting at breakfast on the verandah overlooking the green of the lawns. She ate sliced mangoes and drank delicious coffee, while Richard tackled devilled kidneys and chops, and drank his coffee in a hurry, and left them sitting peaceably over theirs.

Chapter 8

They spent three weeks getting ready for their departure to Mehli. Laura discovered that this was called 'Going to the Hills'. In the meantime the house was put into its hot weather dress. All the chairs and sofas were covered with loose covers of white linen. The heavy curtains were taken down and folded away, and white linen took their place. *Chicks* were put up between each pillar of the colonnaded verandah. These *chicks* were cane screens lined with indigo-dyed cotton. They were lowered every morning as the sun came up, and rolled up again every evening, and they helped, with the thick walls and high ceilings, to keep the house cool.

Laura rode with Sir Richard every morning. They quartered the outskirts of Delhi, and Laura was fascinated by the many ruins and the temples and mosques and blue-tiled, domed tombs of emperors long dead, though never forgotten in this country of enduring memories.

During the long hot days she stayed indoors with Honor, and read or sewed, and talked. Honor found her an intelligent and amusing companion, with a quick wit and an easy sense of humour, and was more than ever determined to bring her back for the following cold weather.

When the heat grew less with evening they would drive out in the carriage, and either listen to the band concerts in the Cantonment Gardens or go to some party in a friend's house. These parties were always held in the garden, with white-uniformed servants to bring drinks, drinks kept cold by ice that had been wrapped in straw and buried deeply in pits, but which would not last through the hot weather. The hot weather was something that everyone wanted to run away from.

Laura wondered where the teeming hundreds of Indians went when the hot weather came.

"Oh the natives are used to it. It is their country after all."

"And my ayah?" Laura had grown very fond of Moti.

"Oh she comes with us of course, and my old Nila comes, and the two older bearers, Hassan and Ghulam, and several of the *syces*. We shall be quite a cavalcade, my dear, I think you will enjoy it."

Laura was taken about as if she were a grown-up young lady. She met many young men, and learned that to laugh a little and lower her eyes and then look up again suddenly had a most satisfying effect on any man. She enjoyed the company of these young men, but when they began to try to take her hand, or asked her to walk in the shadows round the big gardens, she would laugh, and shake her head, and stay close to Honor. None of these charming young men could lay a finger on her heart, which was entirely Robert's. "My true love hath my heart, and I have his," Laura thought to herself, and gained unjustly the reputation of being a bit of a flirt, and cold-hearted.

The day of their departure for the hills arrived. It was indeed a cavalcade. Baggage mules, horses, extra horses, tents, bedding, bedsteads, the inevitable necessary commodes – and an army of servants. All this left three days before the Lees, except for four *syces*, the two bearers, and Moti. Nila, Honor's old ayah, had gone ahead with the baggage, and Moti looked after Honor as well as Laura for the remaining three days of their stay in Delhi.

They started off very early in the morning, and Laura watched Moti swing herself up into the saddle and sit astride, riding as easily as the men. She recalled how Muna had ridden astride, and how angry her aunt had been when Laura had done the same, wearing an old pair of the stable boy's breeches. All the same, thought Laura, it was the easiest way to ride, and she envied Moti.

The first three nights were spent in Dak bungalows along the way, arriving just before noon when the heat became unbearable, and then leaving again before dawn.

The Dak bungalows were clean and orderly, because they were expected. There was water in the bathrooms, and a meal was cooked for them at night. They usually ate outside in the Dak bungalows' garden. All these gardens seemed to be the same, with dusty marigolds and cannas, and the string beds all smelled of paraffin because the legs of the beds were standing in little bowls of paraffin to keep away the ants. They slept under nets so opaque that neither mosquitoes, sandflies nor air could get in. Laura lay and sweltered for those three nights.

On the fourth day they left very early indeed; the morning star was just rising as they rode out of the dusty little garden, the custodian of the Dak bungalows salaaming on the verandah in farewell.

They rode all that day over an empty plain that seemed to go on for ever, a rocky plain, with the road losing itself among ant-hills and thorn trees, so that they could make no speed, but rode at a walk, and the heat overtook them and the sun was like a fire in the brassy sky. Honor lowered a green veil before her face, but Laura had only a topi, and felt the sun burning her skin, until Moti came up and gave her a piece of muslin, gossamer fine, and showed her how to hang it before her face like a little curtain. It was part of Moti's head cloth that she had ripped off, seeing Laura's discomfort, but she turned Laura's thanks aside and rode back down the line again to her place behind the two bearers.

The dust was thick; Laura felt it crawling with her sweat all over her body. How much worse it must be for Moti, riding at the rear of this snake of people and horses. Honor rode easily, just ahead of Laura, apparently feeling no discomfort. Sir Richard, too, although he mopped at his face and tilted his topi further over his forehead, did not appear to notice anything. Only Laura was unhappy, hot and dirty and exhausted.

"*Another* India," she thought, and wondered why no-one had told her of journeys like this. Her horse stumbled as her thoughts wandered, and she almost pitched over his head. Sir Richard turned back to speak to her.

"All right, Laura? It won't be long now. Look, you can see the walls of Madore. Once we get there, you will have a rest for three days. You will like Madore. Lovely old place." He chatted on, suiting his horse's pace to hers, talking to keep her from thinking of her discomfort, and Laura was grateful. Madore! The name rang like a bell in Laura's mind. Muna's stories of the beautiful city, the red walls, the Palace –

"This is Muna's city," she said aloud, and Sir Richard stopped speaking and turned to stare at her.

"What did you say, Laura?"

"This is Muna's city. She told me about it."

"*Muna* told you – child, what are you talking about?"

"Muna, who came from here. She lived near us, with her husband. She was really Mrs. Reid, but she told me to call her Muna. She was very beautiful."

"Beautiful! By God –" Sir Richard did not seem to know that he had spoken. He was staring at nothing, his eyes full of pictures that Laura could not see.

"Beautiful Muna," he said again, and then a kite, wheeling above them, screamed harshly, and he came back to the present and looked at Laura as if he could not altogether remember where he was.

"Did you know Muna too, Uncle Richard?"

"I did indeed. I was very young when I first saw her, and so was she. Muna the Rose they called her. But I did not realise that you had met her. She died so soon after she returned from that long time in India that I did not think you would have had time to meet her."

"I knew her very well. She used to ride with me – and – did you know her son? Robert Reid?" Laura's face behind the muslin veil was blushing, not only with the heat.

Sir Richard said slowly, "I never met him. I knew his father, of course."

"He is out here now. He came out to join the State Forces in Lambagh. I knew him quite well, Uncle Richard. He was – I like him," said Laura inadequately, and Sir Richard knew that she was longing to talk about Robert, but could not let her. Poor child! How unkind to bring her out here where the

104

young man would be so near her, before she had had a chance to get over what must be a very bad attack of first love! He felt he hated her parents. He swiftly changed the subject, saying, "Look, Laura, we are almost up to the walls."

Time had passed while they talked. Honor turned in her saddle and called, "What are you two gossiping about? Richard, there are camels. Should we pull off the road and let them go?"

Laura's horse, Roland, was already beginning to dance. Sir Richard shouted something and raised his arm, and then they pulled off into the scrub, the whole long snake of their entourage curling off after them. Laura heard the steady clanging of bells, but no other sound. Holding her horse still with difficulty, she watched the camel train go by, soundless in the dust except for the bells that rang at their necks. Men walked with them, and a woman, dressed in dusty black, her head and face swathed, only her eyes showing above the cloth. They were tall people, the woman striding and as tall as the men. Their eyes turned to stare at the Europeans who had drawn off the road for them, but they gave no greeting. They went by like dream figures, half veiled in dust, so that Laura felt that she was not looking at anything that was happening in the present. She was watching a bit of the past that had fallen out of context.

Then they were gone, the bells sounding fainter and fainter with distance. The journey started again, the red walls of Madore showing clearly ahead through the mists and drifts of the white dust that hung in the still, burning air.

The Circuit House in Madore had been prepared for the Lees and Laura, but before they had entered the cool darkness that awaited them, a man on a horse spurred up, and saluting, handed Richard a letter. Reading it, Richard called to his wife.

"We are bidden to stay with Sher Khan, my dear, and there is no question of refusing. Can you bear another half-hour ride?"

"Nothing, but *nothing* would make me refuse their invitation," said Honor firmly, and turned to mount her horse again. There was no need, however. A carriage was there, almost as they spoke, with uniformed driver and four riders, and Honor and Laura and Sir Richard were whirled off in a cloud of dust, leaving their servants to follow as well as they could. Laura was too excited to even think of poor Moti with another long ride ahead of her. Laura was going to stay in the house of the man who was Muna's adopted father, and therefore, was Robert's grandfather. Her face was so bright with anticipation that Honor said enviously, "Oh what it is to be young! Here am I, half dead, and Laura looks as fresh as if she had spent the whole day resting!"

Richard cocked an eye at Laura. The girl had certainly not looked fresh on that last stage of the ride to Madore, she had looked, in fact, as if she might faint. Now she was leaning so far forward to see where they were going that she almost fell off her seat when the carriage rocked over the rutted road through the walled city, and turning left, headed out into the plain. Then she looked at Richard in astonishment.

"But we are leaving the city! Is the Madoremahal outside the walls of Madore?"

"In fact it is, Laura. But we are not going to the Madore-mahal now. We are going to the house of Sher Khan. He does not live in the Madoremahal any more. He lives out beside the Rama Tank, a beautiful place."

The carriage rocked on over the plain like a boat on a rough sea. They came to a thick grove of trees, and green grass that followed the line of a wide, slow-moving river.

"The Kanti river," said Richard. The river widened into a lake that seemed to be as wide as an inland sea. It was impossible to believe that it was man-made. There was an island in the lake with a small white temple on it. The carriage was moving smoothly now, on a well-made road. It pulled up with a great jangling of harness and the horses stamped and blew before a high gate.

The gate opened on a garden that was all that Laura had imagined an Indian garden might be. Here were the bricked paths laid in herringbone pattern, the rose beds, the great trees where parakeets as green as emerald chips flew in animated garlands between the branches. The house was large and white and surrounded on all sides by colonnaded verandahs, and the lake lay, like a shining carpet of blue, reflecting the house, trees and flowers in faithful copy. Laura stood, lost, her dream picture of India at last beginning to come true.

The woman who came down to greet them was small and delicately boned, and dressed in robes that floated and trailed about her, robes the colour of cream. Her hair was coiled and piled on her head, and her eyes were deep blue, ringed with black lashes that needed no kohl to beautify them. She kissed Honor, and Sir Richard took her hands and kissed her, and then she turned to Laura, and before she could speak, Laura said, in the voice of one talking in her sleep, softly, "The Begum! The Begum Bianca."

The beautiful woman stared at her, and Laura said, "Muna told me," and the Begum took her into her arms.

"My dear child," she said quietly, "You are known to me. Muna wrote of you in her last long letter."

Then for a second everyone was still, Sir Richard and Honor staring amazed, and Bianca and Laura, a transfigured Laura, smiling with love into each other's eyes.

Sher Khan came down the steps, a big man shouting his welcome, bowing over Honor's hand, taking Richard into a warm embrace, turning to Laura to say, "Welcome, child! We heard of you from Muna, she loved you dearly. Come in, come in all of you, before the sun strikes us. Such a journey you have had, and then to insult me by taking your family to that Circuit House! Why?"

By this time they were in a big cool room, and were drinking champagne from silver goblets, goblets so cold that they almost burned the hand. Laura drank it too, Honor nodding permission, and the dream that Laura had moved into grew deeper as she sat listening to the talk around her and under the talk hearing the bubbles breaking in her goblet, each bubble whispering, "See, it was true! India is like *this*." Laura felt her whole body begin to relax, so that she became as limp as a rag doll and was afraid that she would drop her goblet.

With no idea of how she got there she was in a large room, and Moti was there to undress her, and then she was lying beneath a punkah that wafted cool air over her, and then, dreamless, because she was inside the dream, she slept.

Chapter 9

It was night when Laura woke, and there were lamps turned low set about the room, each one making a little island of light so that the shadows in the rest of the room seemed very dark.

Moti was there, sitting on her heels beside the wall, and she came forward as she saw Laura move. She turned up the lamps and the room glowed. It was a beautiful room, with one enormous window opening on to the darkness, a room that was cool and smelled of flowers.

Laura sat up and Moti took her into a marble-floored bathroom, telling her that there was no hurry, she could take a long time to bathe and dress, for the others were also resting. Everything had been unpacked, and Laura was dressed in due course in a light, white dress that covered her arms and her shoulders, as was fitting for her age. But the dress was cool, for it was made of muslin that moved and floated about her. She remembered that she had last worn the dress when she had been with Robert, and he had said she reminded him of a white bird. The dress seemed to bring him close, and she smiled as Moti did up the last little pearl button that closed the high neck. Moti brushed her hair and let it fall round her shoulders, and it was like a shawl, so warm, so hot, a thick silk shawl.

"Moti, my hair makes me very hot. I wish I could put it up."

"Why not, Missy? I put for you, make it very good, see, like this – only two pins. Then if the Lady Sahib say no, you take out the pins *so* and all fall down."

Laura was delighted with her hair, drawn up on top of her head, like a little crown. Moti went to the window and came back with a rose, a red rose so dark that it was almost black.

She tucked it into the coil of Laura's hair, and stood back admiring, and Laura heard Honor's voice. Honor came in and stopped in the door, staring at Laura.

"My *dear* —"

"Oh Aunt Honor, please may I keep it up? Just until we get to the hills? It is like wearing a blanket."

"Laura, of course you may. I was only dumbstruck because you look so beautiful. I am very proud of my adopted niece. Come and let me show you off."

The others were all gathered on a large open dais that was built out from the verandah and overlooked the lake. It was called, Laura was told, a *chibutra*. There were long chairs, and divans and carpets, and the most beautiful chased and ornamented silver lamps. Laura, a goblet of champagne in her hand, accepted the compliments that showered on her with grace, blushing but keeping her eyes steady and her head up. She remembered her Aunt Caroline's teaching.

"A compliment is something that you accept with pleasure and thanks. It is not graceful to wriggle and cast down your eyes, and say stupidities like 'Oh no, this is only an old dress', or 'But my hair never looks right'. Only fools accept a compliment like that." Dearest Aunt Caroline! Laura sat, composing the letter she would send her aunt, describing this wonderful evening.

Presently Honor came and sat beside her, and then Bianca drifted over, her silks seeming to move in a gentle air of their own.

"I insist on knowing how you and Laura became so well acquainted!" said Honor curiously.

"We never met, Lady Lees. Laura knew my beloved adopted daughter, Muna, and Muna wrote to me about her just before she died."

Sher Khan had turned and looked towards his wife, and she turned her head and met his look, and for a moment the atmosphere was not easy. Laura was too happy to notice. She was here, among Robert's people, and they were exactly as she had imagined they would be. Here she would get news of Robert. She decided to ask the Begum Bianca about Robert the following day, when she was alone. Laura had heard arrangements being made for a ride to the training stables, and decided to sacrifice the pleasure of that ride in order to get news of Robert. She did not wish to ask about him in front of Honor because she felt certain that her mother had spoken to the Lees about Robert; she was sure that they had been told that she was to have no meeting with Robert Reid. She sat dreaming, looking over the parapet of the *chibutra* into the darkness where the lake lay, and both Bianca and Sher Khan watched her and then looked at each other again.

Alone together that night, in Bianca's bedroom, Sher Khan sat watching his wife combing her hair and said, "That girl, Laura, is of great charm. She is very much in love with Muna's son. Poor child. If she knew what anxiety we are in about him! Will you tell her anything?"

"I will not. If it is the terrible news we fear, she will know soon enough. But I am full of hope, Sher Khan."

"You are right. Inshalla, it will be good news, but even so things look black for her. What fools her parents are! If they do not wish her to marry with my grandson, why take her so close to the valley?"

"I do not think that they realise that he is your grandson – it could very well change their attitude. What very common people they seem to be!"

"Yes. A bad *jat*, and yet they have produced that snow blossom of a girl. She is very beautiful, and very gentle."

"Yes."

"I know that tone of voice, my beloved. What do you think about so deeply behind that beautiful brow of yours?"

"I do not think that Laura will wish to live for ever in India."

"Pray God that there is no need. He only takes the Guddee if something that you and I could not bear to even dream about should happen."

"Do not forget his blood. He may feel the pull of Lambagh very strongly, and wish to stay in the Army there."

"And you think the girl will not? If she loves Robert as

111

Muna said she loved, she will stay anywhere to be with him. You stayed."

"Ah, but that was different. I may be Irish, but this is my country. I was born here, and I have never known any other."

"Do you tell me, oh my queen, that if I had left India you would not have come with me?"

Bianca turned her lambent eyes to the eyes that watched her from across the room.

"Whither thou goest, I will go – thy people shall be my people, thy God my God – I would follow you to hell and back, my lord!"

Sher Khan crossed the room and pulled her up into his arms.

"You did, my love, you did."

Much later, as they lay quietly, watching the night sky and the great stars, Sher Khan asked, "What was that verse you said to me?"

"'Whither thou goest'? It is from the Bible. It was said by a daughter-in-law to her mother-in-law."

"Such words of love! Most unsuitable from a daughter-in-law to her husband's mother! But from you to me – ah love, how your voice still touches my heart!"

The long night was their pleasure, the stars no brighter than her eyes looking at him.

The following day the opportunity to speak to the Begum did not come to Laura as she had hoped. It seemed that they were all making the expedition to the stables and taking a picnic with them. Laura was disappointed, but not for long. It was impossible not to enjoy riding along the lakeside in cool green shade, and seeing the magnificent horses that Sher Khan was so proud of. The picnic, sitting on piles of cushions and shaded by the green Sal trees, eating and drinking and laughing – there could never have been more laughter. Sher Khan and Richard Lees were old friends and had shared many experiences together. Old tales were told and new gossip passed on, and the day flew.

They rode back in the cool of the evening, with the sun throwing broad golden bars through the branches of the trees and filling the dust clouds that their horses raised with little golden motes. There were long shadows across the lake also, and all the birds were coming back to roost among the trees and in the reeds that grew at the edge of the lake. Sher Khan dared Laura to a race, and she almost won it, going down the road like a thunderbolt and being beaten, as Sher Khan said, "By the hair on my animal's nose! Who taught you to ride like that?"

"Muna," said Laura, and there was a little pause, and Sher Khan looked at his Begum, who smiled and said,

"Muna rode as you do, my lord – do you remember teaching her and Sara to ride on the shores of the lake in Lambagh?"

"I remember many things," said Sher Khan, and said no more.

Then there was only one day left, and Laura had not asked about Robert. She *must* have news.

She made up her mind, and that evening as they sat on the *chibutra*, she asked her question.

"Muna's son – Robert Reid. You know him?"

It was Sher Khan who answered her question, his words falling into a strange silence.

"Muna's son? Of course we know him! He is our grandson, you know that! We have not seen him yet, but he will come here one of these days. He has entered the Ruler's Forces, and is being sent to many places while he learns what he must do. I hear he is a very fine young man, a grandson to be proud of, and we are impatient to see him."

So there would be no real news about Robert, no word about how he was, what he said when he saw his mother's city, no extra link for her to hold to. Laura's eyes were full of disappointment. Bianca remembered how she had dreamed of Sher Khan when she had been Laura's age. She leaned close to Laura to whisper softly, "Laura – you will see him again soon. I am sure of that."

Laura flashed her a grateful glance, and was conscious that Honor was watching them both, and was more than ever certain that her mother had told Honor that she was to be kept away from Robert.

At dinner that night Laura was very quiet, watching Sher Khan. He was a most magnificent-looking man, sitting at ease at the head of his table, his long-fingered sinewy hand gripping the stem of his goblet, his grey eyes flashing with laughter as he told Richard some story. He looked what he was, a splendid highly-bred Indian Prince, and he was Robert's grandfather. If she married – no, *when* she married Robert, and had children, that splendid man would be their great-grandfather. Then she remembered that Muna had only been adopted, so none of this man's blood ran in Robert's veins, and yet there was a strong likeness. She was puzzling over this when looking up she saw Bianca watching her, and also caught Honor's interested eyes. Laura looked away quickly. She should not have mentioned Robert in front of Honor; she would be watched all the time now.

It was hard for Laura to leave Madore.

She felt closer to Robert there than she had for a long time.

On their last night Sir Richard and Sher Khan sat up late, talking. There was a great deal that they had to say to each other that could not be said in front of anyone else.

The unfortunate appointment of Laura's father, Sir Edward Addison, to the post of Agent in Pakodi State was among the matters they discussed.

"It was an action taken in a hurry, and performed with neither sense nor courtesy. Kassim Khan is very displeased."

"This is understood, in circles where there is more knowledge. My chief is very distressed. I am charged to inform you that steps are being taken to have Sir Edward withdrawn. This action will be greatly assisted if the Nawab of Pakodi comes back to his State and takes over the governing of it. There will then be no need for an Agent, and no face will be lost on either side. Sir Edward will be kicked upstairs, you understand."

114

"I understand, but Illaha! How strange are the workings of your Government! That man with the manners of a baboon will be given a post more senior, where he can do more damage by his truly disgraceful attitude to us – 'the Natives'." Sher Khan's voice was shaking with rage.

"No. He will be placed in a position where he is so important that other men do all his work, and they will be men of sense and experience. They will do his work very well, and he will get the credit, but he will be unable to do any harm. It *is* a strange policy, I agree, but at least it works. The men who are coming out now are good men who come because they love this country and its people. There will not be many more of Edward Addison's type, thank God."

"So, I would speak more of the Addisons. You know that this girl, who is already beloved by both myself and the Begum, knows Robert Reid, Muna's son?"

Richard shifted uncomfortably in his chair. He could see which turn the conversation was going to take.

"Can you explain to me why she is not allowed to marry the son of my adopted daughter?"

Richard looked at the handsome, angry man beside him. He could think of no valid answer that was not going to give offence, and as he paused, Sher Khan spoke again.

"I will tell you why. *Because* Robert is the son of my adopted daughter. He would be considered suitable if his mother had been a low-class white woman, provided he had plenty of money and inherited a title. But because his mother, Muna the beautiful, was an Indian, he is not to be considered. The fact that he is also the declared heir to the three States does not appear to matter. He is – how do they say it in your circles? – he is eight annas in the rupee. A half-caste. They forget – so is my nephew, Kassim Khan, the Ruler of Lambagh. I think, Richard, that the best thing for Laura is that she should stay here with us until the cold weather in Delhi, when I understand that your wife wishes to have her to stay. Should she go to Mehli she is bound to meet the Lambagh family, and also my grandson, and if Kassim Khan heard anything derogatory said about Muna, then I think it would be very difficult to get Edward Addison out of the States alive, let alone with dignity!"

He waited for a few minutes, and then spoke more quietly.

"Let us keep her here, Richard. She will be happy, and I know that my grandson will not come here for at least four months. By that time your lady will be starting to go back to Delhi. Come, my friend, is this not a good idea?"

"An excellent idea, Sher Khan Bahadur. But not possible."

"Why not?"

"If she were our daughter, my wife and I would be delighted to think that she was going to marry Robert. We have not met him, but we know his family in England and his family here. However, she is not our daughter, and we have no authority. We are merely her guardians for this journey. Please understand this, and do not make me say any more."

The splendid autocrat on the other side of the table glared at him with eyes that held, for a few moments, nothing but murder. Richard wondered if a very long friendship, which he valued, had now been broken for ever.

Sher Khan got up and came round the table to him.

"Richard, you are the brother of my heart. I cannot quarrel with you. I ask you two favours. Get that man out of Mehli, and the token force of troops with him, and if it is possible, be a friend to my grandson, Muna's boy. Let others put obstacles in his way. Not you."

"You have my word that I will have Edward Addison removed as soon as possible. As for the other request – Sher Khan, how could I be anything but a friend to the son of Muna?"

Laura had slept deeply and peacefully all night. She left with the Lees the next morning.

She rode away, looking over her shoulder at the white palace that Sher Khan had built for his wife, and the blue waters of the Rama Tank, until the whole beautiful picture vanished in the distance and the dust clouds of their cavalcade. Laura was young enough to believe that if you loved a place enough, you would return to it. In that sure and certain hope, she rode over the empty plain towards the hills.

116

Chapter 10

Ayub Khan went by short cuts and reached the Great Road before the sun set. Once on the road they went at speed, meeting Aziz posting back towards them, a dust cloud signalling his coming. Without drawing rein Ayub Khan gestured to him and he turned his horse, almost bringing it down in his haste, and rode alongside Ayub, leaning from his saddle to talk.

"I missed the girl. But I found something else. Some horses, tethered in the grove of Kali. Good horses."

"Yes. I know about them. The girl tired of waiting, and came for me."

"Wah! She left a wasp's nest behind her! That fat Bunnia was like an ape robbed of a mango. He was alternately searching the grove and beating his serving woman. But one thing was strange. When he saw the tethered horses he became quiet, and gathered up his belongings and left the place with speed. I think he had seen the owners of the horses and was in fear of them."

"Very likely. Listen. You are already tired, and your horse also. Go back to Faridkote, and wait for the message that will come from Lambagh. Take a fresh horse, then, and come after us, with the men that will come from the Ruler. I asked him for aid. Come back along this road, and if you do not find us in any of the *serais* or *paraos*, come to the city of Safed. Ask those who we can trust for the House of the Pundits and come there. We deal with serpents, so have a care."

Once again Aziz turned his tired horse and rode back.

Ayub went on, stopping at each camping site to rest, to

drink and feed and water the horses, and to get information. He wandered from one group of people to another, a big friendly northerner looking for a friend he had expected to meet. No-one seemed to have seen his friend, which was not surprising, for Ayub Khan gave a completely fictitious description of a man on a bay horse. While he asked his eyes were busy, but he saw nothing, and began to be very worried indeed.

It was close on sunset when they rode past a bullock cart drawn to one side of the road and saw the gleam of a fire further back among the trees. They were riding at speed and did not draw rein until they reached a busy *parao* some four miles further on. There they made a small fire, and sat close round it.

"You saw? That was the cart. Empty, so either they have sent him further on, in some other way, or –"

Ayub Khan could not finish his sentence. The alternative was obvious. Robert was dead and they were burying the body. He waited for a moment, and then said, looking round at the other groups already preparing their food, "It is necessary to know who, or what, is in any one of those covered carts, and the two palanquins. Yar Khan?"

That young man nodded briefly, and turned to speak to his brother who sat next to him.

What he said was not audible, but Dost Khan got slowly to his feet, looking down at his younger brother with starting eyes.

"Say you so! Son of my mother you may well be – but who was your father?"

"Allah! You with a dog's tongue, you insult your own mother? Bear me witness, Ayub Khan, I have had enough. I have eaten dirt from Kabul to Multan, and all because I saw the horse first, and not squandering my money on whores, was able to buy it."

"Buy it, forsooth! Horse thief! Go to Jehannum, son of shame!"

Yar Khan's sword was out, and his brother was trying to draw his, hampered by his friends, who were saying all the things that men say when a fight is imminent. To no avail. Dost Khan fell on his brother and the sparks flew like fireflies in the dark as they kicked and stamped around the fire, their friends dodging out of the way.

At other fires men were standing to see the fun, then as the fight moved and their own fires were in danger, they began to shout, and soon chaos raged through the various camps, as Yar Khan and his brother, swords clashing dangerously, turbans fallen, raged about the fires.

Ayub Khan stayed where he was, and presently two of his men returned.

"Nothing. Usbeg had his face scratched by a hell cat in that palanquin, and the other carts are full of women and children. You can hear them. Anyone would have thought we were demons from hell."

The noise under the trees was augmented by the yelling of disturbed children, and the shrieks of women more angry than afraid. Ayub Khan stood up and bellowed, and his voice, that had carried through many bloody battles, reached the ears of his two men.

"Enough," panted Yar Khan, leaning close against his brother's chest, his teeth bared in a grimace of rage, "Fall now, and I drag you back."

"*You* fall, brother – and *I* drag," said Dost Khan, and skilfully hooked a foot round Yar Khan's ankle, bringing him down with a thump. Then, sword in hand, he dragged his brother back to their own fire, followed by the vituperations of at least twenty disturbed and angry men.

"Sons of shame, both of you. See how you have disturbed this peaceful evening. Up, up! We cannot rest here now. We ride, and you ride without rest all night in return for this trouble."

Ayub Khan did not apologise, but he left a feeling of goodwill behind him. To be in charge of such hot-headed young fools could not be easy, and he had certainly done his best to stop the fight.

They rode out of the *parao* followed by derisive shouts, and no-one noticed that they had turned on their tracks and were

119

riding back the way they had come, towards the empty cart. They stopped a mile down the road.

"We will divide. Yar Khan, you go ahead, we will wait for ten minutes. Go behind the trees, and see what they are doing, and how many there are. We will come on slowly, riding on the side of the road to muffle the noise of the horses. We will leave our horses under that grove of mango to the left of the road, ten minutes' walk from where they are camped."

Yar Khan was off, swinging right-handed into the trees on the side of the Great Road. Ayub Khan and his men waited, as impatient and nervous as their horses. Before they could move they heard a horseman returning, and while they were loosening their swords, saw that it was Yar Khan, riding fast. He rode straight up to Ayub Khan and said breathlessly,

"He is there, and I think alive – they have him lying wrapped in a blanket, and it looked to me as if one of them was trying to give him water. Wah, Ayub Khan, such news! You know that animal that tortured Salih to death – that foreigner that worked for Pakodi? He is there. The others are all known to us, all *goondas* who work for pay, and run at the first sign of trouble. There is also another man, the leader, and he is a man from another country – one that we all know well. You remember the fight at the Bukree Well, where we fought on the side of the English whose speech is almost the same as ours? The English who wore skirts? Well, it is that man, the man who was shouting to the Raiders. Tovarish they call him. This will be an easy action. Those others will run, and all we have to do is take the big one and Tovarish."

"We take all. No-one lives except Tovarish. Him we want. Understood?"

"Understood."

"Very well. We go."

They tethered their horses under the dark trees and went swiftly and silently through the grove towards the fire they could see. They came up behind the men and stood for a second, taking stock. Then Yar Khan worked his way round to where Robert lay with a man sitting by him. The man went from life without a sound, and remained sitting propped against the tree, apparently looking at the others round the fire.

"One," said Yar Khan to himself, and began to worm his way round to the next man. The big man was left to Dost Mohammed. Now that Yar Khan had accounted for the man near Robert they were evenly matched – ten against ten.

One by one the men round the fire were taken – but now they were fighting, for, however unexpected an attack is, if the man sitting close beside you suddenly coughs and falls forward into the fire, it is not possible that you will not be alerted. But the grinning, determined faces of Ayub's men were enough to strike terror into the uncertain hearts of the paid assassins. They cried for mercy, and received none.

After a moment Ayub Khan left the ruckus of the fighting and went over to Robert, bending low over him to see if he was indeed the corpse he seemed. He heard Yar Khan scream a warning, and turned just in time to half avoid a blow from a sword wielded by Tovarish that would have certainly killed him. As it was he fought one-handed, unable to use his dagger. He stood astride Robert's unconscious body, for it was plain to him that his death was not the only thing Tovarish wanted – he was intent on getting rid of Ayub Khan as swiftly as possible and then killing Robert. During the fight he made several attempts to thrust his sword into the recumbent body between Ayub Khan's feet. Ayub Khan, hampered by his wound and by the fact that he had to stand still, was hard pressed, and heard Yar Khan's triumphant yell beside him with relief. Then, suddenly, there was no more fighting. He was staring at the empty air.

"Did you get him?"

"By Allah, that is not a man! He is a devil. Under my sword, while I had him almost at the point of death – I swear my sword was at his throat – he escaped. Listen –"

Like a heart beating they heard the distant sound of a horse going fast. Ayub Khan groaned with disappointment, and at that moment received another blow. Dost Mohammed came up, his handsome face not improved by a sword cut across his nose, to say that Stepan had gone.

"I cannot say he has gone. He was never here, Ayub Khan. Ho Bhai, when you looked and counted heads, was that brute here?"

"I told you he was, but you are right! I did not see him when we came into the grove the second time. I was not looking for him. I wanted the man near the young Nawab – Oh ten thousand, thousand devils! Shall I go after them, Ayub Khan?"

Ayub Khan, his shoulder bandaged by Usbeg, was bending over Robert again.

"Nay, it is more needful that we get this one to safety. He is alive, but he needs a *hakim*, and help. How many of us are wounded?"

"Only yourself and Dost Mohammed. They were very craven, it was like fighting women. Well, Peshawar and Kabul and Bombay will be cleaner places after this evening! One thing is certain, Tovarish does not know what kind of men to engage for his enterprises! He picks the kind of coward that he does not need. If we had known who his men were, two rupees and we would have had all the information we wanted from them."

They doused the fire, and made a rough stretcher from poles taken from the bullock cart. Robert did not appear to be breathing, and Ayub Khan was much exercised in his mind as to where to take him. In the end it was decided that they would make for Faridkote.

"If those two had died with the others we could have taken him to Madore, to the old Ruler, but that city has places to hide whole nests of serpents and it is very close to Safed. Better that we travel as fast as we can to Faridkote, where at least we are sure of safety."

It was a slow and weary journey. Robert did not move, he lay with his breath stirring the blanket they wrapped him in. He was cold to the touch, and as they started to climb and the hill winds began to blow around them, each man contributed some part of his clothing to put over the unconscious man. But

122

each time they looked at him he was colder, and a blue shade had begun to form round his mouth and eyes, which Ayub had seen before on other men wounded to death. Young Yar Khan handed his sword and his rifle to Dost Mohammed.

"Now for a space I act the part of the bride, and at the same time ride in comfort. Put the litter down, friends, and let me on. I regret the weight, but I will at least warm him."

He lay down on the stretcher beside Robert and pulled him into his arms, wrapping him close and opening his shirt so that the cold body was enfolded close to his warm one. "Eh, Yar Khan! Hast lost they heart to the white skin of the young lord?" asked an unwary friend as they prepared to lift the augmented burden of the stretcher. Yar Khan showed his perfect teeth in a snarl that was not pleasant.

"I shall remember that, Usbeg –"

"And I also Usbeg – we be two here," said Dost Mohammed.

Ayub Khan intervened angrily. "So, now, over a dying man, we seal a blood feud among the men of the Rose? Eh, that is excellent. Have you not all sworn the brotherhood of the blood? Enough, or I shall enter the fight and there will not be any of you left to have a blood feud here – you can all return to your own villages and kill each other one by one at your own expense. Take your turn at the carrying poles, Usbeg, and be quiet." Ayub Khan's voice was not weakened by his wound. Usbeg picked up the carrying pole with alacrity, and after a short time there was no more speaking, for all were exhausted, and the short cuts that they went by were more fit for goats than men and horses.

The lights of Faridkote grew closer and the sky lighter – it was dawn when they came up to the wall, and the lamps were being extinguished one by one as the new guard came on duty and the old ones prepared, yawning, to leave. The sight of the cavalcade waiting outside alerted them all, and there were many willing hands to lift the stretcher in and to take the tired horses and help tired men. The first questions were cut off by Ayub Khan who said briefly, "Words come later. Yar Khan, how think you? Does he still breathe?"

123

"Aiee – he is like ice. But he breathes. I would say that the House on the Wall would be best – Janki knows many things."

"The House on the Wall, then –"

Janki heard the trampling of many feet and the stamping and blowing of horses in the narrow lane outside her house. The door was already open when they arrived, and after one glance at what lay on the stretcher, she waved the carriers in. Ayub Khan and Dost Mohammed came in too, and the others were sent off to the quarters in the fort at the Pahari Gate.

Janki called and two girls came quickly down the carved wooden staircase. Their faces were still painted from the night before, and their arms jangled with gold and silver, but at her commands Ayub Khan's wound was skilfully dressed and Dost Mohammed, trying a little badinage as his face wound was cleaned, received a mouthful of soapy water, and was thereafter convinced that the ladies were off duty and had much to do. Yar Khan had nothing wrong with him, and sat awaiting orders, which were not long in coming.

"Thou are not injured, Yar Khan? Good. Carry him up into the big room and lay him on the couch there. The little one is on the balcony. Call her, and she will help you. I send for the *hakim* for that one. Rabindra!"

Rabindra went running and Yar Khan took his unconscious burden upstairs. Meeta, coming in from staring at mountain ranges that seemed to go on forever, saw the blue-shadowed face, the still, limp body, and stifled a scream with her hands.

"He is alive. Make up the fire, sister, for he is colder than death. The *hakim* comes."

Meeta, blowing on the coal in the stove until it glowed crimson with blue flames dancing above it, showed herself to be sensible in spite of her fright. She had bowls of hot water and rags ready before the *hakim*, an old man, climbed slowly up the stairs to stand looking down at what appeared to be a dead body. Meeta looked at him in apprehension. She had never seen such a man. He was very tall and very old – eighty years at least – and had a thatch of hair that was as white as the snows of the peaks that she had been watching

124

at sunrise. His eyes were a clear bright blue, and he talked to himself in a language that neither she nor anyone else there could understand.

Reiss was famous throughout the Lambagh States. He had walked up into Lambagh long ago, in the time before the bad year, when there had been great killing on the plains. He had stayed in the hills ever since, and it was known that he had saved many lives, including the life of the old Ruler's wife, the Begum Bianca. He was both loved and revered. He now lived in Faridkote because he suffered from a shortness of breath in the upper valleys. Here on these lower levels he was as healthy as a young man, and walked miles every day. Janki brought up everything he asked for, which was not much. He wanted a pot to put on the fire. Into it he put water, and then he put in some instruments, and when the water had boiled he asked for more water, and washed his hands and his arms. The rags were then boiled, and once all this was done Meeta, staring, was sent from the room, and Janki settled down beside the low couch while Yar Khan began to take Robert's clothes from him, one by one. The young man did not move, and did not appear to breathe. Ayub Khan came in, and shut the door firmly on Meeta, who then crouched, like a little animal, on the stairs outside.

Reiss stood above Robert and looked at the bloodless white face. Then he turned to Ayub Khan.

"This is he for whom the Ruler waits? Muna's son? If your wife had not been present at his birth we would know his father also, Ayub!"

"It is true. But he is the son of Muna and her Englishman."

"Well, now, let us see what is wrong with him – it was a knife wound? Good. In that case it is likely to be clean."

The wound, uncovered at last, proved to be a hand's breadth from Robert's shoulder blade, but appeared to be clean. Reiss bent over it and sniffed, and shook his head, smiling with relief. Then he turned to Janki.

"Oh woman of great knowledge, here is nothing for me. It is a clean wound. Your green ointment that you showed to me should do all that is necessary for it. He has lost much blood. It will take a little time, but when you have looked after him for a while no doubt you will be glad to get him out of your nest of chickens, for he will cause much trouble amongst them, I have no doubt." He looked again at Robert, who was beginning to move his head as Janki cleaned his wound with the boiled rags.

"Softly, softly lord," said Yar Kahn, holding him steady with firm hands. Robert opened his eyes and stared up at Yar Khan. Yar Khan smiled at him encouragingly, and Robert immediately smiled in return.

"Darling, where have you been?" he asked, his voice a bare whisper, but obviously the voice of a lover. "Where have you been? Bend closer, my dearest, I cannot see you properly –"

Yar Khan with raised eyebrows looked towards Ayub Khan and Reiss.

"Eh, who does he think I am? I do not know the words, but the tone would woo a houri down from paradise!"

"He has a love in England, I should judge, and speaks to her," said Reiss.

At that moment Janki's hands hurt Robert abominably – he swore with skill and violence in Lambaghi, and fell into unconsciousness again.

"That is better," said Janki, working with swift, skilful hands.

"Now I can do all without pain. Get me clean clothes from that chest – where is that girl?"

"I locked her out," said Ayub Khan rising to open the door. So Meeta had her wish, and ran like a partridge to fetch anything that Janki wanted, and was allowed to stand holding the clothes while Janki bathed the magnificent young body and then dressed Robert, and still he lay, unmoving, and finally Janki grew frightened.

"*Hakim* – did I do aught that was wrong?"

"Nay, he has lost much blood. Keep him warm, build up that stove, but keep the air in the room fresh, and feed him as soon as he wakes. Have you brandy? Then put some of this cordial in the spirit and give it to him a drop at a time." He smiled at Janki and took his leave and Janki went hurrying away to prepare a chicken for broth. Meeta was left to drip a little of the brandy and the cloudy liquid from the bottle that the *hakim* had left with her, between Robert's teeth. Drop by drop she gave it to him, and presently he moved his head away and groaned. Ayub Khan came forward.

"It is enough. Leave it now. He will wake. Go you, little sister, and tell Janki." He looked over at Yar Khan when the girl had left the room. That young man was staring at Robert, his eyes full of admiration.

"Wah! Such a man! He is stabbed, he lies for days beneath a load of cattle food, and can still wake up dreaming of love, and swear like his father. What a man – a man to trust and to follow." Ayub Khan contented himself with a nod of agreement. He did not know what the Ruler would wish to have said about Robert. Nor did he know what Robert was going to do when he fully recovered his senses. He was, after all, Alan Reid's son, and had been born and raised as an Englishman. His experiences so far in his mother's country had not been likely to appeal to the son of Colonel Reid.

Chapter 11

Robert recovered remarkably quickly. He was very young, and very strong, and had never had a day's illness in his life.

For two days he lay, obedient to Janki's orders, relaxed and content to be on the wide, low bed and to spend his waking hours, which were not many, watching birds fly over the patch of blue that he could see through the window, and eating and drinking anything that he was given. Meeta was the fetcher and carrier of anything that Janki needed. She did not walk when sent to fetch anything, she ran, and then stood waiting for the next order, and while she waited, she looked at Robert with devoted, loving eyes. Lost in the lassitude of weakness Robert barely noticed her – she was a little girl who did not speak but who moved without noise, and appeared and disappeared at regular intervals. He noticed Janki much more, for she was his mentor and his nurse, massaging strength back into his arms and legs, feeding him and scolding him, and he obeyed her without question. At night, if he woke, she was always there, sitting on cushions in a corner of the room, her face golden in the light of a little lamp. She would bring him a drink and look at his wound and tell him to sleep – and under her wide dark eyes he would feel sleep coming over him, loosening all his limbs, until her eyes were part of the darkness of sleep, and he knew nothing more of the night.

On the third morning he woke to find himself alone. The room was full of light and air, and he heard clearly the noise his mother had often described to him – the cry of the fish eagle. Was this room in Lambagh?

Filled with burning curiosity he sat up, and put his legs over the side of the bed and stood up, and the room turned in a slow circle, so that he thought he must fall, but he set his teeth and shut his eyes and stayed standing, while the room steadied at last, and he turned toward the big, low window. His progress towards it was slow, but he got there, and it was open, and there was a balcony outside, which he was determined to get to. It was not easy for he had to step over a deep sill, but he managed, and stood victorious out in the air that was so fresh that it seemed to burn his lungs – and there, over the rooftops, towered his mother's mountains, the lords of the snows. He looked as if he were not looking with his own eyes, he stared at them as a person long away looks at a beloved place when they have at last come safely home. He could not look enough, and his eyes followed each rise and slope, each rampart of rock, until, led up and upwards again, they rested at last on the high peaks and nothing else. There was no sound from the street below; he no longer heard the voices of the birds. It was as if that blinding, lonely whiteness had brought perfect silence, a peace that nothing could break.

Janki's voice from the room behind him was an intrusion that made his heart thump, and his legs suddenly lost their strength.

"Aiee – for this I stayed awake for two nights and made my eyes into plums! Oh ungrateful! Come you back at once. Meeta! Meeta, bring the broth – and some of the chicken curry as well, and the rice cooked with cloves. The lordling will eat today before he tries to climb over the balcony!"

The return to normal life was hard. Robert felt better, so to stay lying in the room was impossible. He demanded to be allowed to get up and get dressed. Janki stuffed his mouth with food and paid no attention. He then demanded to be shaved, feeling his chin with horror; it appeared to him that he had a beard like an old man.

"Shaved you will be, in due course. Eat now. Think of the toil I put into this food for you! Eat, and put back the flesh you lost, and gain strength. Then in two days, or three maybe, you can come down and walk in the courtyard to find your feet."

She was not a woman to disobey. Robert ate until he felt

stuffed like a Christmas goose. She came later and shaved him herself, and while he was feeling his smooth chin he tumbled into a sleep so deep that it lasted well into the night. Janki nodded at Meeta.

"Your Nawab is cured, my child. He will wake from his sleep a new man, and nothing we can say or do will keep him in bed any longer. His wound is almost healed also."

"Then he will go," said Meeta, and the eyes that were with her hair her only beauty overflowed.

"Child, did you think he would stay here with us? Nay, Meeta. We all have our dreams, child, but we know them to be dreams – otherwise our hearts break."

"I did not even dream," said Meeta quietly, "I saw him, and I loved him. That is all."

Janki put a kind arm round her and led her from the room.

"Come, Meetabhen, we talk together. It is time. We can leave him tonight. He will perhaps wake, but he will sleep again. Our work is done. Now, sit here, and drink this, and let us speak of you."

Comfortably seated on cushions Meeta sipped at a goblet of sweet wine and looked across the fire at Janki. She had already told Janki her story, and she wondered what more there was to say. She had given no thought to her future, there had been no time to think of anything but her Nawab.

"Meeta, what are you going to do?"

There did not appear to be an answer to this question, for Meeta did not know. Her life seemed to have come to a complete stop and there was nothing ahead of her but emptiness. She looked at Janki, and with eyes full of tears, shook her head mutely.

"Nay, do not weep, Meeta. There is no reason for tears!"

"There *is*," said Meeta, choking on a swallow of her wine. "There is. I have nowhere to go."

"Then do not go." Janki poured herself another generous measure of wine, and hands cupped round the goblet, looked at the big-eyed child opposite.

"You mean that I can stay here? With you?"

"What else? Or do you wish to go back to your village?"

"I cannot go back to my village. It would bring shame to my father – he has paid his debt to Ram Chandra by giving me to him. Ram Chandra might go and beat my father and take me again." Meeta shuddered at the very thought.

"Child, I do not think that Ram Chandra will go back to your village. I think he would lose too much face. Also if, as I suspect, he thinks you went with those *goondas*, he will do nothing to find you. He would be too afraid. If you so wish, I can send you back to your village."

Meeta shook her head firmly.

"No. I do *not* wish. My father would sell me to a brothel. He was going to do that in any case, if Ram Chandra had not come, and if no man offered for me."

"To be sold to a brothel would be very bad?"

Meeta shuddered again.

"It would be terrible – I have seen those women."

"Then you will not wish to stay here." Janki's voice was final.

"But I do wish – I would rather stay here with you than anything! I do not understand," said Meeta, staring across the fire at Janki.

"Where do you think you are now, child? This is the House on the Wall. This is one of the most famous houses in the north."

"*This* is a brothel?"

Janki nodded her head. "This is a brothel. I know the kind of places you have seen. We of the sisterhood are not like that. This is a place where men come for pleasure and comfort. What think you, little one? Do you stay?"

"Where you are lady, I stay."

"Eh, child, do not call me lady. I am Janki, and I need no other title. So, you stay. That is good."

Meeta though that it was very good. She had never been so clean or so comfortable in her life. She already adored Janki. Also there was another thought, far back in her mind. If she stayed here, might she not see the young Nawab sometimes? Janki was watching her and read her secret thought. She looked at the thin, peaked little face with the ruby incongruously perched on the curve of one nostril and the upper lip open a little over the beautiful strong teeth.

"Meeta. Are you still a virgin?"

At a loss, Meeta stared at her. "I think so. Ram Chandra attempted me once, but I do not think he succeeded."

"You would know if he had. Well, Meeta, I will train you until you are ready for work. You will not find it hard, child. There will, of course, be men you will not care for, but you can close your mind. In time you will find that they are all alike, men; the young and the handsome, the old and infirm. They come to us to ease their flesh, and to talk to us, and take comfort from us as if they were children again, with their mothers. All men come to us. We are the mother and the wife, the daughter, the lover and the friend, and as well, we are the solace of the flesh. So – in time it becomes very easy, for it is a service, and we are paid to serve. I promise you it will not be difficult."

"It will be easy to work for you, but could I not be your maid servant? For taking a man will be very hard for me."

"Why?"

"Because my heart and my mind are full of a man I cannot have."

"Eh, well, it is good that you have the wisdom to see that you cannot have him. But here you will forget your hopeless love. Oh child! Do not shake your head! He is the first to stir your flesh, that is why you think of him. I will drive him from your mind with the first man who takes you and sleeps in your arms satisfied. Meeta, listen to me, you who sit there with your eyes dazzled with dreams. I offer you a home and a comfortable old age, perhaps even a husband! One of my girls who was a virgin so pleased her first lover that he took her to his house. She bore him a son, and he kept her, and now she has a husband and a home."

"But I am ugly," said Meeta, and turned away her face.

"Wait till I have finished with you, and then tell me that, my child. But this must be of your own will. Do you stay?"

"You are my father and my mother." Meeta made the ritual gesture of touching Janki's henna-decorated feet as she spoke. Her eyes were sad and her mind rebellious. Janki looked at her with wise eyes, and taking her hand, led her to a room that she had not seen before. It was a small room with a window, and a string bed covered with a quilt and many hard pillows, and there was a charcoal stove that glowed redly in one corner.

"This is your room for a while," said Janki. "Later you will have a larger room and a balcony, but this is for now."

"Will he come *tonight*?" asked Meeta, eyes large with apprehension.

"Who, child? Will who come?"

"The man who is to make me forget everything. Do I have him tonight?"

"Aiee, *pyaree*! No indeed, for the young man I have in mind would be mightily displeased with me if I presented him fruit quite so green! First you have many things to learn, and you will rest and eat and think of nothing, and then, when your face is almond-shaped with food and rest, and I have taught you how to please a man, he will come, and I promise you that you will enjoy him, and *my* promises are not things of wind and water. Wait, child. Do not look like a caged bird! I will give you wings and teach you how to use them, until you are a woman who does not need to dream because your real life pleases you."

Janki went out then, and Meeta sat on the strong bed and leaned back against the hard pillows and fell asleep, dreaming of her young Nawab, of riding with him through the mountains to a future that was veiled in a mist of gold.

Upstairs Robert lay awake, looking up at the square of the night sky and thinking of Laura, wondering where she was and what she was doing and when he would see her again. He too fell asleep and dreamed, and in all his dreams he was searching through darkness to find the light that was Laura's face, the warmth that was in her arms.

It was only when Meeta woke him to bathe his face and hands with scented water that he realised, for the first time, that the ring that was to be Laura's, the Peacock ring, had gone.

133

Later he asked Janki. "You did not have it when you were brought here," she replied.

Robert looked away. "Then that man has taken it," he said with bitterness.

Janki put out her hand to Robert. "The theft may prove his undoing. Who can tell?"

Chapter 12

The Ruler's answer to Ayub Khan's message arrived two days after Robert had been allowed to get up and dress, and as a result had declared himself fit and well and ready to do anything.

He was sitting playing chess with chessmen of ivory and jade, furious because Janki was a better player than he was, when Ayub Khan came in to the House on the Wall.

"How goes it with you, Robert?"

"I am very well –"

"– and very restless," intervened Janki. "It is like living with a caged wild tiger. Dil Bahadur is not a peaceful companion at present."

"What did you call him?"

"A most suitable name. Exactly what he is, Lord of the Heart. Dil Bahadur."

"Well it has a more suitable ring than Robert, for the man I see before me now!"

Robert laughed. He ran a finger over a newly grown moustache, and tilted the embroidered cap he wore a little more steeply over his eyebrow.

"Eh, a peacock! Very well so. Dil Bahadur you will be from now on. You can come and be restless elsewhere. I take you out of here tonight. Is he ready, Janki?"

"As ready as I can make him. He needs more time; though the wound is healed, it will open if he exerts himself. It was very deep."

"I take him to Lambagh. Tonight to the House of Paradise, then tomorrow we start on a four-day ride. Can he do it?"

"Do I not have a tongue, that you talk over my body like two old market women over a plucked chicken?"

Ayub turned and looked into the angry eyes.

"A plucked chicken would have more manners, because it would be dumb, and could not speak so to a lady who has gone sleepless, night after night, tending you and bringing you back to health. You are discourteous, Dil Bahadur."

That young man flushed to his hairline.

"Janki, I am indeed. Forgive me, and know that you have, among all the other hearts you wear at your belt, a new one, to whom you gave a name he will wear with pride."

"Aiee – indeed, it is as well that you go, for I fear for my own heart with such a tongue of honey in the house!" She got up, stretching magnificently. "Alas, I grow old. There was a time – well, never mind. Come back and see me in a year, Heartbreaker." She went out laughing with Ayub to make arrangements for Dil Bahadur's departure, and he was left, feeling young and foolish, and certain that she thought him an oaf.

The voice at the door was barely above a whisper.

"Dil Bahadur!"

"Who is it? Meeta, come in, I have not seen you for upwards of a week. You come in good time, for I go tonight, and I wished to say my thanks to you. I live because of you –"

"And I, because of you."

"What?" Robert looked at the girl, not understanding what she had said.

Janki's training had begun to take effect. The parched thin look of her face had gone. Her eyes were carefully outlined with antimony, and were enormous. Her hair hung, shining like silk, about her shoulders. Meeta was still thin, but there were slight curves under the loose robes she wore. Her soft child's mouth, the upper lip caught open a little on her beautiful teeth, was endearing. She walked towards him and her walk had already a trained, cat-like grace.

Meeta would never be beautiful, but now she had something that took a man's eye, and pulled at his thoughts.

When she was close to him he saw that the big dark eyes were smudged with tears.

"What is it, Meeta?"

"You are leaving."

"I go tonight."

"So I weep. I shall never see you again."

Robert did not know what to say to this budding child-woman. He had thought of her as a brave little girl when he thought of her at all; there had been many other things on his mind. Now he was jolted suddenly into realising that even brave little girls have reasons for what they do. She had saved his life.

He looked at her, seeing the carefully painted eyes, the oiled sweep of her eyebrows, the little gold stud that had replaced the red stone in the delicate curve of her nostril, and as he looked, he searched for words. She was staring at him, as if she were trying to read something in his face.

"Meeta, what nonsense is this? Of course you will see me again. I will be living not too far away, in the Lambagh valleys, and I shall never forget you. If it had not been for your bravery I should certainly be dead. You will always have my gratitude –"

"Gratitude? I would have your love, Dil Bahadur."

"Meeta, what can I say?"

Wiser than many women much older than she, Meeta shook her head.

"Dil Bahadur, if you do not know what to say, then there *is* nothing for you to say to me. I do not need words. I love you."

Robert took her hand, still a child's hand in spite of all the oiling and the massage, and the pattern painted on it in henna. Seeing that little painted hand, and remembering the patterns on Janki's long-fingered hands hovering over the chess men, Robert suddenly realised what Meeta's life would be in this House of Women. She was certainly not going to be a servant. Her robes and the cared-for body told him that.

"Meeta, do you like living here? Will you like your life?"

Her answer was comforting if one only listened to the words.

"Janki is like my mother, the others are my sisters. This is now my home." She stopped, and looked away from him.

137

"There is only one thing."

"What?"

"I miss the plains! The mountains, of course, are beautiful," said Meeta, with pathetic courtesy. "But the plains – they were my home all my life, and they have beauty too. The villages are small and brown, but everyone is a friend. In the winter, when the fires are lit in the evenings, the smoke lies like a blanket, low on the ground, and the old men sit and smoke the hookah, passing it from hand to hand, and tell long stories, while the women sit a little behind and listen too. In the dawn the cattle are taken out, wading haunch-high in low-lying mist, and by midday the sun is hot and the fields have lost the white frost of the night and are green with spring grain –"

Robert held her hand and it rested quietly in his. What could he say to a homesick child, who could not go home because she had risked her life for him?

Her hand turned in his, so that her palm pressed against his palm.

"Dil Bahadur. They, Janki and the others, they are teaching me many things. When I am ready, they will give me to a young man for a night, and Janki says that when I have made love with him I will forget you. I will not. I wish that I could be taken first by you, I wish, even though I have not learned all that I should, that you could take me first."

Speaking, she slowly bent her head until her face rested against his hand.

"Dil Bahadur, if you took me first, none of the others would matter."

She was quiet after that, and Robert lifted his other hand and ran it down the length of her hair, feeling a response even in that, as the tendrils curled up againt his hand. He thought as he stroked the silk strands that if he had known, he could have pleased her, and not only because of gratitude. Meeta, offering herself so gently, was like a spark introduced into dry tinder.

But it was too late, and Robert did not know whether to be glad or sorry. He said nothing, because there was nothing to say. Presently they heard voices. Meeta lifted her head, pressed her mouth to his palm, and was gone, out of the door on to the balcony.

When Janki and Ayub Khan came into the room Robert was pulling on his soft leather boots, and there was nothing to show that he had had a visitor but a faint, lingering scent of the sandalwood oil that had smoothed Meeta's body.

"You are ready, Boy? Then make your farewells. We go now, while the streets are quiet, and most are within their houses eating. We walk."

Robert, held in the circle of Janki's arms, looked into her wise, knowledgeable eyes.

"The child – Meeta. Will she be happy?" Janki made no flowery answer. Looking into the handsome, worried face, she smiled.

"Believe me, Dil Bahadur. She has suffered nothing but good through her meeting with you. I swear on my life, she will be content."

If Robert noticed the change of words he ignored them. He was held close to Janki's heart, told to look after his wound, and kissed until he was breathless.

He followed Ayub Khan down the stairs, through the big room, which was empty, though it looked ready for visitors, with the cushions heaped high on the divans and the silver coffee pot glittering in the firelight. The courtyard was also empty, and Janki opened the outer door and called her farewells to them, thanking them for their company and asking them to return on their next visit to Faridkote. Her voice was purposely loud for all to hear that they were ordinary clients. Then they were walking swiftly down a dark narrow street and into another, and a door opened to let them in before they knocked. They walked through that courtyard and out with no-one speaking to them at all, and Robert saw that they were now four. He was finding it hard to keep up the swift pace, his breath was short and his wound throbbed. It seemed that they walked for hours, twisting and turning through lanes so narrow that they could have touched the walls of the houses on each side.

They passed a high white wall and stopped at a gate, and Ayub called out, banging on the wood with his fist. Had Robert not known him he would have thought he was drunk, he made so much noise. The Durwan came running and let them in – but only Robert and Ayub went in, the other two vanished. Still shouting at the Durwan Ayub went into the house, and once in and up the stairs into a room of painted splendour, he led Robert to the big, low bed and Robert subsided on to it, as completely exhausted as if he had walked ten miles.

"I am sorry, Boy, we came fast. It was necessary. The Ruler does not want your presence known, he wants me to get you up to Lambagh unseen. If they have traced you at all, they will have traced you to Janki's house. Let them continue to believe that you are there. They would not expect to find you among four men coming back from a drinking party." He gave Robert something to drink and helped him to undress. Robert was asleep before Ayub had finished looking at his wound, and did not stir all that night, sleeping without knowing that Ayub spent an uncomfortable night lying across his door, and that men were out quartering the city to make sure that his presence was not suspected. The Ruler's commands were never neglected.

The following morning, an hour after dawn, Rabindra, dressed soberly in the kilted robes of a hill labourer, his shining hair transformed into a tangled mess of dust and ashes, strolled out of the back gate of the House of Paradise carrying a basket strapped to his back. He went first to a charcoal seller, loading his basket with charcoal and getting himself remarkably dirty while he did it. He argued fiercely with the charcoal seller, ending his argument by leaning close to yell an obscenity into the man's ear. What the seller said in reply could not be heard, but it appeared to silence his customer, who fumbled in his kilted robe, brought out a handful of coins, and choosing three or four, flung them down and went off glowering, his back bowed beneath the load he carried.

He took a circuitous route to the House on the Wall,

stopping to buy other things, including a *seer* of great golden-skinned Kulu apples. He argued over their price too, but not so rudely this time. The seller was a girl, a hill girl with her ears weighted with turquoises and silver, her cheekbones so high that when she smiled her tilted eyes almost closed. She took his money, and his compliments, which were broad, and answered him with some of her own, and he walked on, well pleased. He went off the main street and followed little twisting lanes, where the houses and balconies were packed so closely together that it was like walking along a tunnel and a horseman could have easily picked a rose from the plants growing above his head.

So at last Rabindra came to his destination, and knocked, and the door was opened and he was inside the courtyard of the House on the Wall before his knock had finished sounding on the wooden door. Janki took his clothes from him as he undressed in the courtyard, and sluiced him with water, until his skin gleamed copper again, and his hair was once more ordered and clean.

In a small inner room, Janki had put out clothes for him, and while he dressed swiftly, he told her his news. She listened with her brow creasing with worry.

"There is a watch on this house?"

"The best. At the Ruler's orders. No-one will enter that is not clean. Provided Meeta stays out of sight of the streets, she will be in no danger. The city swarms with the Ruler's men now. Shanker will tell you all the news, he is within the temple, and takes food to that – that monk we know of. But he will come to you each day at dusk. Send word if the monk leaves, but if he leaves by the north gate, then he must be taken. Yar Khan is the guard commander. He will also come here each evening, being greatly enamoured of one of your girls – whichever one you choose." Janki nodded, her eyes thoughtful, her hands playing with a small, sharp knife with a turquoise-studded handle.

"Eh, Janki! He is to be taken alive!"

Janki looked down at her knife and laughed, and put it away somewhere within her dress. Her robes whispering

141

about her like the voices of the pigeons, came Meeta, fresh from a lesson on the sitar. Rabindra, fully dressed now, looked at her with raised eyebrows.

"Wah! What a treasure was locked into a small box! How long have you been teaching this one? Less than a month? The others had better learn something new. Here is a princess of pleasure already."

Meeta made him a low, dancer's salutation, smiled over her shoulder and walked away, while Rabindra made several appreciative comments. Janki nodded with satisfaction.

"The little one learns well and carries herself bravely, and a hidden love never does any woman any harm, provided she accepts the truth that love is one-sided, and for us does not exist except in dreams. She will be famous in due time, that one. Come, Rabindra, stop lusting after goods that are not for you. The horse is ready. You should go."

A short time later a young Punjabi, his turban cocked insolently over his eyes, a rose behind one ear, rode his horse through the narrow streets. He sang a love song as he rode, his voice harsh and breaking on the high notes. A sword, well-polished but old, hung at his belt, his waistcoat had been embroidered by loving hands and he was a very handsome young man indeed. The girls sitting at the side of the street on doorsteps, or pressed back against the sides of the houses with baskets of fruit or of walnuts, or freshly-made garlands of marigolds and pink roses, called out to him as he passed. The little flower seller, the hill girl in duffle robes with a bright embroidered cap on her head and long plaits snaking down over her shoulders, held up a bunch of roses, and he bent down to take it, still singing, and she offered him more than the roses, for he laughed and shook his head, and rode on to his rendezvous, clipping his horse to a faster pace and leaving her looking after him with wistful eyes.

Ayub Khan and Dil Bahadur were ready to leave when the young Punjabi tied his horse to the ring outside the gates of the House of Paradise and entered, shouting loudly for his old friend Yar Khan.

In the inner room, with the shutters closed, Ayub Khan looked in consternation at Rabindra.

"They have been seen?"

Rabindra removed the rose from behind his ear and twirled it, the light-hearted gesture in complete contrast to his worried face.

"Only one has been seen, the monk, but as they both escaped together, and the other is like a dog with his master, it is thought that he must be close by, though none of the watchers have seen him enter any of the city gates."

"Where is the monk?"

"In the temple. Where else? He came in as a hill priest, and most certainly he knows the ways of the priests of his people, who worship the Lord Buddha. The temple priests accord him respect, although he is not of their religion, and they have given him hospitality. We cannot take him while he is in there. There is a watch on him night and day, and if – no, *when* he comes out, he is to be taken if he turns for the north. The Ruler's orders. If he goes south, he is to be followed."

"Followed to the House of the Pundits in Safed, in the hopes that there we will find the leader." Ayub Khan wondered what message had been sent in warning to those who were known as the Pundits, and who risked their lives to bring information out of the far, closed regions of the north. He wondered too if the leader that was being sought was that strange man Dorjieff, about whom the British were so alarmed. Not only the British. The Ruler of Lambagh was constantly enquiring from his agents for any news of this man, who was known in his own country as The Abbot, and was a Buddhist priest. He was known to have travelled widely and to have been a welcome visitor at the Court of the Tsar. No-one in India had ever seen Dorjieff, no description of him had come over the passes from Tibet. Who was this monk who was now living in the great Hindu temple in Faridkote? Ayub turned to Robert.

"Boy, how looked that priest? Tell me again."

Robert dredged his memory for every detail that he could

143

remember of the priest on the boat, and the man who had been the leaders of his captors.

"You are certain he was the same man?"

"Yes. There is no doubt. His head was the same shape, round, with the cheekbones very high and padded with fat, and his eyes were set on a slant and pale blue. He smiled all the time, thus – and his eyes were like the eyes of a snake, cold, and with no expression at all."

"Ugh!" said Rabindra, and his shiver was not affected.

"You draw a picture of a monster. It was thus that the little one described him also."

"She saw him! Of course, I had forgotten, she saw him too. Is that child in any danger, Rabindra?"

"We have done all we were told. The guard is set, Ayub Khan."

"So. Then we had better leave with speed." Ayub Khan looked at Rabindra, seeing him as he was for the first time.

"Eh! You make a most handsome Punjabi, Rabindra. If you were a girl, would you not lose your heart, Dil Bahadur?"

"Doubtless," said Robert sourly, and the other two laughed as they went out to the courtyard, where a splendid curtained palanquin stood waiting.

A band of well-armed, splendidly-dressed men of Lambagh State left the House of Paradise.

They were led by Ayub Khan and a young Punjabi, obviously a friend of the family who had been seen about the city that morning by many. He was still humming his love song as he rode. A girl accompanied them, who seemed to be the Punjabi's property. She travelled in a well-curtained palanquin and he paid her much attention, riding close to the palanquin and singing his song to her bright eyes, and thereby throwing the carrying coolies out of step so that the palanquin swayed and rolled, and Ayub shouted at him. Thereafter he rode in the lead, shouting his songs, and yelling at the laden coolies that they met coming up the last steep incline to the city's north gate, bent double under their loads.

The cavalcade dropped down the steep path until it reached

144

the foaming, roaring river, where black stones marked the ford. The horses were led across, sidling and slipping up to their haunches in the rough water. The men had pulled their trousers off and stopped to dry themselves on the further bank. The Punjabi spoke with Ayub, and then dropped back to where the palanquin waited after a wet and rocking crossing.

"Come out, oh Queen of Hearts," said Rabindra, his voice dripping with tenderness. "Come out, and let the light of thy lovely face brighten our journey. Ayub Khan says you may come out."

The red curtains parted and a very rumpled Dil Bahadur emerged to stand cursing and stretching his long legs.

"That palanquin was made for a dwarf," he said, and turned gladly to take the reins of the horse they led up for him.

Whereafter the palanquin coolies went faster, and there was another rider in the van with Ayub Khan and Rabindra. Dil Bahadur, a young man of Lambagh, in full white pantaloons and embroidered waistcoat, an emerald turban set at an angle on his handsome head, a sword in a jewelled scabbard hanging at his hip.

They halted at the top of a steep climb.

"They should be here, or hereabouts," said Ayub, and as he spoke a man came slithering down the side of the hill towards them. He finished the last slope with a leap that sent Dil Bahadur's heart into his mouth, but the man landed safely at the very lip of the precipice.

"One day, Usbeg, you will do that and miss your footing, and finish your life with the fishes." Usbeg saluted smartly, waited while Ayub gave him concise orders, then saluted again and went back up the hill, moving as if he were walking on flat ground. Ayub raised his arm and the cavalcade continued on its way.

Four days later they took the last steep climb to the high pass, the Lungri Pass that was one of the ways into Lambagh.

In single file, strung out to give them plenty of room, the horses picked their way, sure-footed, unperturbed by the staggering drop to the river, foaming between narrow rocky banks far below.

The man lying along a ridge just below the skyline looked down on them as they passed. His gaze marked the emerald turban, and he drew his knife.

Clouds boiled up over the pass ahead, and he could see nothing. Bitterly he stared into the glittering mist, and settled back into his uncomfortable nest to wait for the mist to clear and darkness to come so that he could move.

Now the men he had been watching took the hardest climb. No-one could speak, they walked, leading their horses. They moved through the gold-streaked mist like home-going ghosts. There were a last few hard breathing moments, then the high, wind-beaten pass, and the mist shredding away like a torn curtain.

Ayub Khan took Robert's arm and led him up and forward.

"Look, Dil Bahadur. Look there –"

From where he stood at the highest point of the pass, Robert could see the whole valley laid out before him. Everything was small, scaled down by distance to thumbnail size. Everything but the mountains. Even the miles could not lessen their immensity, or take away the impact of those soaring white-capped peaks, the endless wall of the Himalayas, the Lords of the Snows.

Robert saw the river, a blue thread widening into a blue pool. He saw great dark bushes that were walnut trees, and tiny houses climbing up the green slopes towards the lake where the Kanti river was born.

Once again, as on the balcony in Faridkote, he felt that another spirit shared his eyes, that he must look long so that this spirit could see all that she wished. His sight blurred and he turned away. Muna did not need his eyes to see this beloved place. Her spirit was free, and could range those far peaks, this peaceful valley that she loved, as she wished. Robert drew the back of his hand across his eyes and went over to where Rabindra waited, holding his tired horse.

Chapter 13

The Lees and Laura had left Madore, crossed the plain and joined the great road, the Grand Trunk Road that ran from one end of India to the other, carrying with it an entire cross-section of the population of the country. Laura wished for time to look at everything and everyone that was on the road, but she had to give a good deal of attention to her horse, who was fresh and very restive. The creaking, groaning wheels of the bullock carts that took their own way along the road because their drivers were asleep drove her horse frantic. Sir Richard, watching her struggle, suggested that she pull over to the soft side and let him go for a bit. Laura did as he suggested and had a glorious gallop, which she enjoyed until a band of horse traders, taking their animals to a fair in a town nearby, pulled across her path without warning, and set her horse to shying and skipping sideways, almost unseating her. She got him under control, and found herself brought up short by a band of beggars – ash-smeared, with tangled hair hanging over their eyes. They were a fearsome sight, and Laura was as nervous as her horse. She turned to go back to her party and nearly ran one of the men down. He moved aside, glaring up at her with eyes that glinted pale as the eyes of a fish through his hanging locks. He raised a hand in blessing, or a curse, and she saw the glitter and flame of a jewel as she got her animal under control and cantered back to the others, thinking that this was indeed a country of fantasia, where even the beggars wore jewellery. She spoke of the band to Richard, who laughed.

"Not beggars, my dear! Fakirs, holy men. You should have dropped a coin into their begging bowl, and gained yourself much merit."

"They smelled terrible," said Laura, and thereafter, her horse being quieter, stayed close to Honor.

They left the Grand Trunk Road on the second day, after a night spent in a Dak bungalow, noisy because of its proximity to a *parao* or public camping ground. They turned off onto a small, winding road that began to climb almost at once. It was deserted compared with the great road, they saw very few travellers, and most of them were going the other way.

They reached their camp site two hours before sunset.

This was the first night that they would not spend in a Dak bungalow. Laura was delighted with their camp. The white tents, each of them as large as a small room, were pitched under pine trees. Laura had a tent to herself. A third of the tent was divided by a canvas curtain split down the centre, and behind this curtain was her bathroom, with a zinc tub, a basin on a tripod, and the inevitable commode.

Now she understood the reason for some of the servants and all the baggage mules and ponies being sent on ahead. The camp was absolutely ready for them when they arrived. Fires were already lit, the cook was at work outside the cook tent, and there was steaming hot water ready for their baths.

When she had bathed, Laura saw Moti her ayah shaking out the folds of a long woollen robe, the colour of the smoke that was curling up into the evening air from the wood fires.

"Moti, how beautiful! Am I to dress in that?"

"Yes, Miss Sahiba. Lady Sahib telling. Very good, very warm. This is dress of hill ladies. You like? Good. Now I do your hair like hill ladies also."

Richard and Honor were sitting beside the fire on canvas chairs. When Laura joined them in her beautiful robe her hair was coiled very high on her head, and they both exclaimed.

"Laura, my dear child, you look like a princess in a fairy tale!"

"Thank you, Aunt Honor. Then you look like the queen. These are lovely robes, where did you find them?"

Honor smoothed the folds of her own robe, which was russet colour, like autumn berries.

"Are they not beautiful? Do not thank me. The Begum

Bianca gave us these. We have three robes each, and the over-dress that matches, to wear when we get to the cold of the higher passes. I have *poshteens* of course, but no-one can describe them as being beautiful. I am always very conscious when I wear a *poshteen* that I smell exactly like a goat. But these dresses! Really, Bianca is a most thoughtful person."

Laura sat beside them, watching the short twilight fade into darkness, happy to think that she was warm and comfortable because of Robert's family. It was almost as if his arms were round her. She looked up at the night sky and the bright stars and was content.

Four days later they drew rein on the crest of a high windy pass and looked down into a green valley, and across that to a collection of houses clinging to the side of a mountain, looking in the vastness of distance like swallows' nests.

"There you are," said Richard, pointing with his whip. "There is Mehli." Laura looked at the clustering houses and the green trees that looked like bushes and the chequered fields. She drew a deep breath of the fresh, stinging air, and said quietly, "And Lambagh?"

Honor was not near enough to hear her. Richard moved his pointing whip.

"Do you see that river? Well, that is the Kanti river that you saw in Madore. Follow the curves of that river until they lose themselves at the foot of those mountains – see, there – over those mountains lies Lambagh."

The rampart of mountains, slope and rock escarpment and high jagged peaks, looked like an impassable wall. The wind was cold, and Laura pulled up the collar of her fur-lined *poshteen*, ignoring the slight smell of goat that enveloped her.

Those mountains could be climbed. One day she would climb them, and go down into the hidden valley of Lambagh.

Her eyes raised to those far peaks, she let her horse pick its own way, following Richard and Honor towards the hill village of Mehli, and whatever awaited her there.

The Agent's house was a large, double-storied house some distance from the village.

Sir Richard and his party rode through the white gate, held open for them by a uniformed Durwan, two sentries saluting as they passed. The manicured lawns, the ordered flower-beds, and the bushes cut into a firm dark green hedge came from a different world from the one in which Laura had been living so happily for the past weeks. Only the white roses, climbing riotously round the house, dripping over the verandah pillars and softening the outline of the building, had escaped regimentation. The roses are untouched, thought Laura, the roses, and high above, the mountains rising in majesty – they were unchangeable, remote from all control.

Men ran up to hold their horses, the baggage mules were directed round to the back of the house to be unloaded, and the party dismounted and were welcomed by Laura's mother, standing in dignified pleasure on the verandah.

"How like Mother," thought Laura as she waited for Honor and Richard to be greeted, "how like Mother, to make us come to her." Then she herself was taken into her mother's arms briefly, kissed, and given a keen critical look.

"Dear Laura! You have arrived safely. You look well, if a trifle disarranged. Agnes will show you your room. Honor, my dear, and Richard, come with me. I have put you in the room that overlooks the garden, such as it is!"

The two ladies walked off, and Richard, mopping the red rim that his solar topi had made round his head, followed them. Laura found a sallow-skinned woman in a black dress and a white apron standing beside her.

"If you please, Miss, come with me."

Laura followed her, but when she came to the door of her room she said firmly, "Thank you. What is your name? Agnes? Very well, Agnes, please will you find my ayah and send her up to me?"

"There is no need for that, Miss. My lady said I was to look after you." The woman had a strong accent, which Laura could not place.

"Thank you, Agnes. My mother did not know that I had my own woman. I will not trouble you. Just send my ayah up."

The woman looked askance, but she went away to find Moti, and Laura opened her bedroom door.

The room was small, but as there was nothing in it but a bed and a chaise-longue, this did not matter. A large dressing room opened off it, and there was a large bathroom. Laura examined the room and then stepped out on to a small balcony. She was delighted to find that her room did not overlook the garden. It looked straight across to the mountains, a view unimpeded by anything, and more beautiful and impressive than Laura had imagined. She decided that the balcony was where she would drink her morning tea, the chaise-longue could be put out there, and there would still be room for a little table.

Laura went back into her bedroom as Moti came in, followed by two youths with the luggage, which was put into the dressing room. Moti, who had been riding all that day, looked clean and fresh and cheerful in spite of it. She smiled at Laura and began to unpack. Laura turned back on to the balcony again and leant on the wooden railing where the white roses were climbing, and looked at the mountains, and lost herself in dreams.

She was there when her mother came in.

"Well, Laura, let me see you!" Laura turned to face her mother, who looked her up and down and clicked her tongue.

"My dear child, what on earth have you been doing? You are not changed yet, and they will be bringing tea soon! Your father will be back with Colonel Windrush and they will not want to be kept waiting. *Where* is Agnes? I told her exactly what to do –"

"I have sent her away, Mamma. I have my own woman. She is unpacking for me now."

Lady Addison compressed her lips into a line that Laura knew well, but as she waited for the words that would follow, she was surprised to hear her mother say with moderate civility, "Your own woman, indeed! I suppose it is a native servant, engaged for you by Honor? Well, they are quite clever, some of them. But, my dear girl, you cannot possibly wear any of the clothes that you have brought with

151

you! They will be impossibly creased. I have had some clothes made for you; they are in the *almirah*, in your dressing room. Where is your woman?"

"Moti," called Laura, and the ayah, immaculate in her white clothes, came in and salaamed. Lady Addison avoided looking at her.

"There are clothes for the Miss Sahib in that big *almirah* in the dressing room. The underclothes are in the painted chest-of-drawers. Laura, I suggest that you wear the cream wool, it will help to tone down your complexion a little; you appear to have caught the sun. Can you kindly have your bath at once, and be dressed and in the drawing room in half an hour? I shall send Agnes to do your hair. I see you have put it up."

"Yes, Mamma. But there is no need to send Agnes. My ayah does my hair very well and I shall be ready in time."

Lady Addison seemed to have decided that she was not going to argue. To Laura's surprise she nodded, and after giving her daughter another long, considering look, she told her to hurry and went away.

While Moti was bathing Laura, the girl reflected that she had not seen her mother for over two years. She had long given up looking for affection, but the coldness of her greeting struck her to the heart nonetheless. There were tears mixed with the water on her face. Mother! The word meant nothing to her at all, except authority. Honor and Richard, strangers to her until a few short weeks ago, had given her more kindness than she had ever had from her parents. The tears came faster, and Moti, patting Laura dry with a big soft towel, saw that she was weeping.

"Nay, child," she said in her own language, "do not weep –" then, changing to English, her voice holding a world of gentle comfort, "Not to cry, Miss Sahib. Making eyes all red, and doing no good. Better to laugh. Nothing here to cry for, this very good place. You wait. You like, I telling you. Now, coming here, and I am doing good the hair and the dress, and you going out in beauty."

"Oh Moti! What would I do without you? Yes, better to

152

laugh! I think I shall have to learn your language. You teach me? Yes?"

"Yes. Is much more better that you speak my language. I teach."

Laura was smiling when she went downstairs and into the big room where Lady Addison was entertaining Honor. There was no sign of Sir Richard, nor of her father, for which Laura was very grateful.

"Dearest Laura, how nice you look! That is a very becoming dress." Honor held her cheek up to be kissed, and Laura kissed her, and was astonished when her mother nodded.

"Yes, that is most becoming, Laura, and your woman has done your hair very well. Come and sit down and have some tea. You must be very thirsty."

Laura drank her tea, and listened to her elders talking without hearing a word they said. She had just received the first compliment she had ever had from her mother, and it took time for her to recover.

Horses thudded up the drive, and she heard men speaking – Sir Richard's laugh and another, unknown voice. Her father stamped into the room and her mother said quickly,

"Edward, my dear! You see we have our child with us at last –" and her father, who was bowing over Honor's hand, turned and came towards her like someone obeying an order. As she stood up he took her hands and said, "Well, well," very heartily, and bending forward, kissed her.

Laura said nothing because she could not. Her father had practically ignored her all her life. To be suddenly noticed by him was like being struck by lightning, or addressed by the Almighty. He too looked nonplussed, like a man who has forgotten half a speech that he was supposed to make, and her mother said, sweeter than honey, "Colonel Windrush, may I introduce our little girl?"

Laura looked up into a sunburned face, so brown that the deep-cut wrinkles round his eyes were white. His eyes were very blue, and until he smiled, very hard. But when he smiled his whole face was transformed, his eyes danced as if

153

they had some secret that she alone shared, and his teeth were very strong and white. He seemed enormously tall and broad, and was a man of her father's age. He took her hand and bowed, and said, "Miss Laura," and gave her hand a little squeeze before he let it go. Then he left her and went to stand talking to her father and Richard before the newly-lit fire, but every now and then she felt those hard blue eyes turned on her, and kept her gaze firmly away from the group by the fire.

The night was coming down fast; it was blue dusk in the garden, and with the dusk had come cold, a sharp chill, and Laura understood the reason for the fire. A bearer came in and drew the curtains across the closed windows, and Laura could no longer see the blue dusk creeping over the lawn and the flowerbeds. She looked at her mother, longing to ask if she could go to her room so that she could stand out on the balcony and see the last of the sunset, but her mother was deep in conversation with Honor, and she did not dare to interrupt. Colonel Windrush was suddenly beside her.

"Have you seen the sunset on the mountains, Miss Laura? No? Then, with your mother's permission –"

Permission was given with a broad smile, a fur-lined coat was brought – not a *poshteen*, Laura noticed as she was helped into it – and then she was outside in the garden standing beside Colonel Windrush, watching as the snows burned and faded and were gone into darkness and there was nothing more to see.

He did not speak until the last peak had vanished, then he sighed, "Extraordinary. I have watched that so many times and yet it is still something I could not bear to miss. I hope you did not mind me seizing on you as an excuse to come out."

"No. I was longing to see it. I am most grateful to you. I thought I would see it from my balcony, but this is a different view."

"Yes. Mehli is ringed by mountains, there is nowhere that you can look without seeing this incredible splendour. Are you warm enough? Then let us stay out here a little longer. We could possibly hear a bulbul, which might remind you of a nightingale. I do not think your mother will mind."

Mind! Laura wondered if he was being sarcastic. It must be as obvious to him as it was to her that her mother had been delighted when he asked to take Laura out to see the sunset. He must, in spite of his age, be a bachelor, or perhaps a widower, and he was obviously intended to be Laura's husband. He must, therefore, be very rich, as he was not titled. Laura's long day in the saddle was catching up with her. Her thoughts were disconnected, but one thought was quite clear. Her mother and father were united in wanting this match.

He stood beside her in a listening silence; he had said something and she had not answered.

"I beg your pardon," she said in confusion, "I did not hear what you said."

"It was not of importance. I asked if you had any objection to my smoking a cigar."

"Oh no, do. I am so sorry —"

"You are very tired."

"Yes, we rode up from Dhilpur today."

"That is quite a long pull. You enjoy riding?"

"Yes, very much." The flare of his match lit up a hard, firm profile, a mouth that looked as if it had been closed in determination many times. He had a scar on one cheek and his nose had been broken. Nonetheless he was very handsome, in a battered way.

He held the match to the tip of his cigar and then said, "Have you seen all you wish? May I put it out? It is burning my fingers."

Laura jumped. "Oh!" She felt as though the match had set fire to her whole body, she was burning with embarrassment.

"Please do not be distressed, Miss Laura. It is natural that you should want to have a good look at me. I was able to look at you as much as I wished in there. If what you saw just now pleased you even a tenth part as much as what I saw pleased me, well, I do not mind burning my fingers." He paused, and added in a lower voice, "Which I could very easily do. Very easily."

Laura could think of nothing to say. She was engulfed in the sudden paralysing shyness of the young. He was quite composed, and stood beside her, smoking his cigar and waiting. The silence between them grew, and was filled with the noises of the early night, rustles and movement in the trees, and a bird, which whistled a few notes sweetly and then, as if abashed by the audience below, was quiet.

"If you have had enough of the garden, and want to go up to your room, there is a stair at the back of the house – come with me and I will show you. You can get up to your room quite easily without having to go through the lower part of the house. I will tell your mother that you went in because you were tired and cold and that I stayed out here for a smoke. She will not be annoyed, I can assure you."

Laura followed him through the darkness, and when she stumbled, he took her arm in a firm grip and guided her to the foot of a little curving stairway.

"Not perhaps a suitable stair to Juliet's balcony, but never mind. I shall see you at dinner. I enjoyed our few moments alone very much, Miss Laura." There was a laugh in the deep voice. Without finding a word with which to reply, Laura went up the spiral staircase. There was a door at the top, which when she opened it led straight into her bathroom. Of course! the sweeper's staircase. She stumbled into her dark room, and found the bed and threw herself down on it, and was still lying there when Moti came in with the lamps and it was time to change her dress and go down to dinner.

The company was assembled in the drawing room; had they not all changed their dress it would have seemed that they had not moved since Laura was last in the room. The men were still standing before the fire, Honor and Lady Addison were seated on the sofa.

Laura had to summon every inch of her courage to go into the room, and felt her face flushing scarlet as the conversation broke off and her mother said in a voice that dripped sweetness, "Ah, *there* you are my dear! Come and sit near the fire, these evenings are very chilly. Did you enjoy your view of the hills?"

Laura murmured something in answer, caught a flash of a smiling blue eye from across the room, and sat down before her legs gave way.

He took her into dinner, and sitting beside him was easier than sitting opposite would have been. He did not speak to her very much, but was assiduous in small attentions. She dropped her handkerchief and he had bent from his chair and put it back in her hand before she knew that she had dropped it. Her mother's smile grew blander, her father was expansive, and as the meal went on, more talkative than she had ever known him to be.

Laura listened to what the men were saying because her mother and Honor were discussing a lady of their acquaintance, unknown to Laura, and she found this dull. She noticed that Sir Richard looked worried and Colonel Windrush said very little. Her father appeared to think that he knew what he was talking about; his voice was louder even than usual, and very emphatic.

"This time we will show them something. A quick campaign, all over in a couple of weeks, and after that, no more nonsense. They've been playing a silly game with our friends from the north, and they must be stopped. You agree, Charles?"

So his name was Charles. His deep, rather harsh voice had authority which her father's voice lacked.

"I do not think that a mountain campaign is ever very quick. In any case, I think this discussion should be left for a more suitable time."

Her father laughed.

"My dear Charles, if you are worried about the servants, you have no need. For one thing, none of them understands English, I will not have an English-speaking servant in my house. Furthermore, they are all men found for me by the Nawab himself."

"When you say 'The Nawab', do you mean Ismail Mohammed? Because he is not the Nawab. There is only one

157

Nawab of Pakodi, Ali Mohammed, and he has no heir, as yet. The Ruler of Lambagh is the Regent. Ismail Mohammed holds no position here at all, he is merely Ali Mohammed's nephew. I still say that this conversation should be left until a more suitable time." His tone brought the conversation to a standstill.

Laura's mother came competently into the silence with a question about plans for the following day, and in the talk that followed there was nothing of any importance except for one sentence. Charles Windrush spoke to Laura under cover of the general conversation.

"Feel fit to ride tomorrow morning?"

His blue eyes met hers squarely, and before she could answer he said, "Splendid. I'll see you outside just before dawn. It will be light then, though the sun will not be up. We will ride to Soonia Point, and see the sunrise from there."

Her mother was catching her eye, the ladies were leaving the room. Laura stood up and had her chair pulled out by Charles Windrush. As she passed him, he murmured, "You do not need candlelight, you are so beautiful," and she blushed hotly, and saw his mouth twitch into a smile as she left him.

Later, long after she was in bed, Laura reviewed the evening. There had been no more embarrassing encounters with the Colonel. The men had stayed late over their wine, and when she had asked her mother's leave to go to bed she had been allowed to go without argument. Laura had kissed Honor, and had said, "Good night, Mamma," and been awarded a peck and a smile of approval.

She was too tired to sleep, and she had too much to think about. Charles Windrush was certainly no fool. He must know what her parents intended. They were practically pushing her into his arms. Laura had been told all her life what her destiny was. She was to marry, and marry well, as she had had the bad taste to be born a girl. This man, Charles Windrush, was obviously her parents' choice for her, this man who looked so hard, and spoke with a snap in his voice, and who must be as old as her father.

But, thought Laura staring at the darkness, she liked him. There was something about him that she felt she could trust, a sort of tough honesty. If only her father could have been such a man! She tried to visualise her mother married to Charles Windrush, and failed. Perhaps people automatically married suitably. Her mother and father appeared to agree perfectly. Half asleep she tried to think of the kind of woman who would be a suitable wife for Colonel Windrush, and wondered why he was not already married. He must be a widower. Perhaps he even had children of his own, probably her age! She decided that she would take the earliest opportunity of telling him of her involvement with Robert Reid. It was the only honest thing to do, so that if he were looking for a wife, he would not look towards her and be disappointed.

This decided, she fell asleep at last, and dreamed that she was riding beside Robert in the woods round Moxton Park, and that the woods were all on fire.

She woke with a start to find Moti, lamp in hand, waking her. The night had gone. Outside it was barely light, the sky was silver and a bird was filling the early silence with a flood of bubbling song. It was time to get up and dress and ride out to see the sunrise.

Chapter 14

Laura hurried down the sweeper's staircase. For some reason she did not desire to pass beneath her mother's windows at the front of the house. Her mother never rose before ten, but nonetheless Laura had a strange feeling that this morning she would be looking through the curtains to see her daughter ride off with the approved suitor.

Charles Windrush was waiting for her just outside the stables. She walked across the small lawn that separated the garden from the paved stable yard and left footprints on the frosted grass. He did not speak, but smiled a welcome and helped her to mount. They rode off together in the strange silver light, Charles taking the lead. Laura looked up at the mountains. All she could see were the lower slopes, black against the silver sky; the towering peaks were still hidden.

The path they followed wound steeply up the mountain, slippery with pine needles from the trees that towered on each side. But the horses did not miss a step or slip. Silent on the thick carpet, they moved up the path at a walk, in single file. There was no sound anywhere, not a breath of wind, not a bird call. It was as if they moved inside a silver bubble, shut away from the ordinary world.

The climb ended as they came up a curve in the path. Rounding it, Laura found that they were to stop there, on a flat outcrop of rock large enough for two horses to stand side by side comfortably. Still Charles Windrush did not speak. He dropped his horse's reins on its neck and gestured at the mountains, and Laura obediently turned to face them and saw the beginning of the day.

The mist was shredding away, and the sky was no longer silver. One by one the peaks came into view, scarlet and gold, on fire with sunlight for a few minutes. Laura almost expected to hear a shout as the sun seemed suddenly to leap into sight, and the mountains flamed and then the peaks were sheer dazzling white, marked here and there with blue shadows as the sun rose higher.

The day had begun.

There was a wind, sharp and noisy in the pine trees, setting them in motion so that there was a voice for the wind, a sighing and whispering. Birds called, and smoke came from the village that she now saw for the first time, miles below her.

"Well?"

"Oh, there is *nothing* to say. It is like the world beginning again, absolutely new."

"And God said, 'Let there be light –' Yes. That is what I feel when I come up here to watch the sunrise."

"Do you come every day?"

"Yes. When I am here. I shall bring you up every day to watch the sun rise, and every evening we shall watch the sun set from a place I know. We will see it better there than we saw it from the garden last night."

Lost in the turmoil of her own thoughts, Laura paid no attention to the inference that she was going to be at his disposal every day. She was nerving herself to tell him about Robert. The night before it had seemed so easy, the most natural and sensible thing in the world. Now, still shaken by the magnificent moment of sunrise, it was not easy for her at all. The man beside her seemed remote, a stranger, which of course he was. Was she not presuming too much? After all, would a man of his age be interested in a very young girl, even if her parents were throwing her at him? Of course he would not. With a sigh of relief Laura turned to smile at him, and saw his eyes, and the way he looked at her, and spoke with no further hesitation.

"There is something that I wish to say, Colonel Windrush."

Her nervousness made her voice stilted, it sounded stupid in her own ears.

He looked at her and she could not read his expression,

except that there was that disturbing look of laughter in his eyes now. But she had seen his look a moment before, and ploughed bravely on.

"You see – well, I feel that I should tell you, Colonel Windrush, that I am in love." There. It was out. Her horse moved restlessly, and she put a calming hand on its neck, and sat staring straight between its ears, seeing nothing. Was he never going to speak? When he did speak, his voice was very grave.

"You are in love, Miss Laura?"

"Yes. Deeply."

"I see. It is something that happens to us all. I too, Miss Laura –" He turned in his saddle to look at her, and raised his right hand to lay it in the region of his heart.

"I myself, old though I am, have felt the wound of cupid's darts!" His tone was languishing, his eyes sparkled. Laura looked at him once and then looked away, her face colouring.

"It is neither fair nor kind to laugh at me when I am trying to be honest."

He changed in an instant, leaning over to put his hand on hers.

"No, you are right. It is insupportable of me. Forgive me, Laura. It was just that you looked so serious."

"I am serious."

"I am honoured by your confidence. May I ask *why* you are telling me this?"

Of course he would ask that. Why on earth was she telling him, Laura thought wildly, what a fool she was making of herself! Then she recalled the expression she had surprised on his face, and regained control of her thoughts. She looked him full in the face, saying, "You know quite well why I am telling you this, Colonel Windrush. My parents are doing everything, short of tying me up in paper and handing me to you as a present, to make you propose to me."

"Could you call me Charles, while we are indulging in these confidences. It would seem more – well, more friendly, would it not?"

"You are laughing at me again."

"Not unkindly, my dear Laura, I promise you that. I am only trying to lighten your self-imposed task a little. Believe me, I understand how difficult this is for you, and admire your honesty very much. Now, tell me more. Who is this fortunate man to whom you have given your heart?"

"His name is Robert Reid."

Her companion was looking at her steadily, his expression quite unreadable.

"Tell me, Laura, how old is this gentleman who possesses your love?"

"He is eighteen."

"Eighteen! Great God! I *beg* your pardon, Laura. But eighteen! Oh Laura, Laura, do not look so angry! You must understand how young you both seem to one of my great age. Is this why your parents do not approve of him? And yet he must be handsome, I have no doubt, tall and slim and unscarred by life or anything else. I can see him clearly, I can imagine exactly what he is like."

Laura had become very angry as he spoke, but his last words made her look away from his scarred face quickly, and her anger faded. He looked at her, his smile twisted.

"Laura, do not pity me. I want no pity. This scar on my face is one of many scars that I bear and does not distress me. I am sorry that I laughed, but you are so young to be so sweetly serious."

"Well, age has nothing to do with why my parents do not wish me to marry Robert. I am sure that you know all about it already, I am certain that my parents have already told you all about Robert."

"I assure you Laura, that *they* told me nothing."

"They must have done. They have told everyone else."

"Everyone? The whole continent?"

"Well, they told the Lees that I was unsuitably attracted, and must not be encouraged. Surely they spoke of him to you?"

Charles Windrush shook his head at her.

"Come, Laura, it would have been most unwise of your parents to suggest to me that your heart was already engaged, would it not? You yourself said that they were very anxious for me to become interested in you!" He looked at her downcast, shamed face and added quickly, "I can tell you, Laura, that it would have been very easy for me to become interested."

"There is no need for you to flatter me. I am ashamed enough of my parents' tactics; at least do not make me feel worse by pretending an interest that you cannot possibly feel. You know nothing about me."

"I know a great deal about you. Laura, did your Aunt Caroline never mention my name to you?"

"Aunt Caroline?" Laura's face was suddenly sparkling with pleasure. "My darling Aunt Caro! Do you know her?"

"Darling Caro. Yes, I know her very well. She wrote so many letters about you. I do not understand why she never spoke of me."

His voice was bleak, and Laura hastened to say consolingly, "I expect it was because she did not know that I was coming to India. I left from Jersey, you see. I doubt if she has heard from me yet." He did not reply, and a silence grew between them while Laura thought about a number of things. His thoughts were not evident, but Laura came to certain conclusions, and broke the silence, speaking accusingly.

"You knew all about everything, and yet you led me on to talk of my affairs in a stupid fashion. It was not kind of you to make me look foolish!"

"Laura, you could never look a fool. You were so sweetly earnest, you reminded me so much –"

"Of my aunt?"

"Indeed. You could be her daughter, you are so like her. You could be my daughter, my dear child."

But Laura was still offended.

"It must have amused you greatly, listening to me trying to prevent you falling in love with me, when all the time –" She broke off, too embarrassed to continue.

"My secret is out. I love your aunt, have loved her for years. But make no mistake, Laura, had I not been already enmeshed, do you suppose I would not have lost my heart to

164

you? It would have been all too easy. Two things saved me. A love that has lasted from the first moment that I met your aunt, and a strong sense of the ridiculous. A man of my age laying siege to the affections of someone as young as you are – ah no, Laura. However, as your parents do not seem to worry about the disparity in our ages, I have attempted to make life a little easier for you. Listen to me now, while I tell you what I have done." He leaned over and took her hand, holding it firmly while he spoke to her.

"Your parents have, from the moment I first met them, made their wishes and hopes so obvious that I realised that you would be put under great pressure to engage my attentions and would be made very unhappy. Therefore, last night I spoke to your father. I told him with truth that I found you most attractive, but that I thought you were too young as yet for me to attempt to pay court to you. I told him that under no circumstances was he to say anything to you, nor was he to exert any pressure on you. I made myself very clear, and I am hopeful that I have ensured that you will be left in peace, because both your father and mother will imagine that I am hooked. Forgive me for speaking of your parents like this, Laura."

Laura looked at him in astonished gratitude and could think of nothing to say. He smiled at her, and raised her hand to his lips.

"Dear Laura! Your young man is very fortunate. I know that you will be discreet, and will help to foster the illusion that you and I have an understanding between us. Only, when your young man appears, do not let him call me out – it would be very hard to be killed for no reason! Now we will ride back together, and I will cast languishing looks at you, but do not return them too warmly, or I might find myself becoming embroiled." It was easy then for Laura to laugh and forget to be embarrassed. She felt a lively curiosity about her companion's relationship with her aunt, but he began to talk about other things and she could not ask him questions, although she was beginning to feel that she knew him very well.

They rode back together and arrived to find several strange *syces* holding horses outside the stables, and the whole house ringing with alarm and rumour.

The Nawab of Pakodi State had been murdered in Bombay on the eve of his departure for Pakodi. It was said that his wife had fled from the Palace in Bombay and had reached safety, with her mother, in their own small state of Jangdah, where her father was the Khan. Richard Lees greeted Charles's return with relief. He said a hurried good morning to Laura and took Charles off at once.

"For God's sake Charles, Edward is impossible! He is speaking as if the nephew Ismail Mohammed was the heir, and talks of presenting his credentials to him as if he were a diplomat at the court of a king. This would not matter, but Charles – Said Tabib is here. Can I leave him to you so that I can deal with Edward before he upsets the old man?"

"Of course. But I must tell you that we are probably too late if Edward has had any time alone with Said Tabib."

"No, I saw to that. Honor is there, keeping the balance until I get back."

Honor had not succeeded. When Charles went into Edward's study, he saw Said Tabib's eyes above a tightly clamped mouth. Edward was in full spate, and Honor shook her head at her husband and raised resigned eyebrows.

"Well," said Edward, "there you are at last, Charles. Enjoyed your ride? Good, good. You'll have heard the sad news. Very sad, no doubt, but of course the fellow hasn't been here for years so one can't really expect anyone to be very upset. We've got the man who has done all the ruling anyway. First-class fellow, Ismail Mohammed. One good thing. It will mean the end of this stupid Regent business. No need for that fellow Kassim Khan to keep interfering now! No need for a Regent, in fact. Ismail Mohammed and I can manage the place very well between us, what? In fact," repeated Edward, quite oblivious of the various cross-currents in the room, "in fact you could say that whoever killed the Nawab has done the State a good turn."

He spoke into total silence. No-one moved or said anything

for a moment and then Honor, released by a glance from her husband, rose and made her farewells to the furious old man sitting beside Charles, and left the room.

Said Tabib, Lambagh's Minister to the State of Pakodi, who was there to represent his master the Ruler of Lambagh, Regent of Pakodi, sat as if he were turned to stone. He had a choice of insults to take offence at. When he spoke it was in the Lambaghi dialect, and his words were directed to Charles.

"Wah! This is the one your Government sent up to advise Kassim Khan Bahadur how to administer Pakodi State! I speak to you, Colonel Sahib, because you are as my son, and also you are the trusted friend of Kassim Khan. Does this fat fool know nothing of the manner of man Ismail Mohammed is? Deep in debt, dissolute and cowardly, and known to be in the pay of at least one enemy of the Raj, not to mention all the money that comes to him from the south. He is a paid agitator. He is not even of the blood. His mother was a low-caste woman who served Ali's grandmother. His father, he claims, was Ali's brother but it is known that by the time Ismail was born Ali's brother had long lost interest in women. This is the man the Agent would see ruling Pakodi State? Have you read the despatches he sends to Delhi?"

"Have you, Sahib?" Charles's voice held anger.

The old man laughed.

"Do not be angered with *me*, Colonel Sahib. Does one handle a snake with bare hands? If your Government sends us such a man, then you cannot blame us if we behave as he does. Yes, I have read all his despatches. He refers to Ismail Mohammed as 'The Nawab' and in one letter he wrote of Kassim Khan Bahadur as 'That Eurasian Raja'. *That* letter we destroyed. Today he sent a letter of congratulation to Ismail Mohammed, telling him that he would soon be coming to 'touch his hands' as a token of fealty. Colonel Sahib, rid us of this fool, before he does any more stupidities." As Charles was beginning to reply, Edward surged to his feet, ignoring Said Tabib as he walked to the door.

"Well. The man's been dead now for some weeks. Really can't waste any more time on this discussion. Have to be getting on now." Something about the silence of the others in the room got through to him and as he opened the door he nodded to Said Tabib, "I'll say goodbye to you – I presume you will be leaving for Lambagh now? Are you coming Richard? Charles? I have a horse I wish to see in the stables. Might be a very good buy. The Nawab sent the animal up, and he has a good eye for horse flesh." Richard shook his head in apology at Said Tabib and followed Edward Addison out, leaving a furious silence behind him.

"Tabib Sahib."

The eyes turned to Charles were quite expressionless, and the old man did not answer.

"Tabib Sahib, I am ashamed before you. In all races there are those who bring shame on their country. Such a one is this man Edward Addison."

"Yet he was chosen to advise us."

"This was an appointment my Government regrets. I give you a promise that he will be removed as quickly as it is possible."

"And who will be sent to advise us? Once the Government has put a man in, it never leaves a native State again. The cream of your service appears to stay in Delhi."

"That is not so, Sahib. How would you regard Sir Richard Lees as Agent in Pakodi State? Do you think the Ruler would object to him?"

"He is a friend to Kassim Khan Bahadur, and to Sher Khan also. He is respected and trusted, as you are. But it is known that he has other duties –"

"It is well said, Said Tabib, that a man scratches himself in Delhi and all the villages of the north begin to look for fleas. Is there anything you do not know?"

"Very little. We understand each other, Colonel Sahib. Sir Richard's presence here would be very pleasing."

Charles saw the old man ride away and then joined Richard who was attempting to impress on Edward Addison that he must have no further contact with Ismail Mohammed. Charles did not mince his words, and there was a torrent of protest from Sir Edward.

168

"Damn it all, Windrush, the fellow is a friend of mine. Dines here frequently. We have a hand of cards as a rule. Very civilised chap, one forgets he's an Indian. Clarissa likes him too. I find this attitude of yours most distressing. Very high-handed in fact, if I may say so."

"Sir Edward, I speak for the Government. For your own sake I urge you to listen to me. Leave Ismail Mohammed alone and do not offend the Ruler of Lambagh any more, because if you do, my feeling is that Delhi will not approve."

Sir Edward made an angry rejoinder and stamped off, but he was looking thoughtful. Displeasing the high-ups in Delhi was not something he wished to do.

Charles and Richard, left alone, sat down to make plans and do a number of things that were urgently necessary. Condolences were sent to the widow of the Nawab in Jangdah, and it was decided that Charles would leave for Delhi almost immediately. Richard went off to find Honor and tell her that their return to Delhi was doubtful. He knew that she would be delighted. The social side of life in India had never appealed to his dear Honor, and life in these remote hills would please her very much.

Chapter 15

It was dusk when Robert and Ayub entered Lambagh. Dusk and fire-lighting time, the time of the men coming home from distant upland fields and pastures, the time when lamps were lit, and food prepared. Blue smoke curled up to join the blue mists of evening, and the air was sharp with the cold of the high hills, and sweet with woodsmoke.

There was no ceremony when they reached the old Palace, which sprawled its magnificence over one entire side of a big grass-grown square. Robert had some idea that there would be guards drawn up and uniformed men guarding the Ruler. He saw that this was foolish. Here, in his own place, the Ruler needed no guards.

Men ran out to take their horses. Rabindra went away with them, and Robert followed Ayub through an arch, across a big inner court, and through a door which spilled light on to the paving stones of the court.

The room was large, and full of light and warmth and surprised voices.

Robert never had a very clear picture of the next few hours, but there were some things that he could not forget.

Kassim Khan, the Ruler, was so exactly as he had thought he would be that he realised all over again how much his mother had loved this man, because she had described him so accurately that Robert felt he had known him all his life.

Kassim looked what he was, a man of an old Princely family, who had, by his own efforts, superimposed on this romantic image the strength and skills of a soldier, the self-discipline of a dedicated Ruler. Robert felt the impact of a personality that was admirable, a man to admire, trust and love. This was the man that his mother had given her heart to long ago and had never been able to forget. Robert himself, another man's son, was, in his startling resemblance to Kassim, the strange proof of Muna's undying love.

He also remembered that first sight of the Begum Sara, his mother's adopted sister, small and beautiful, with a gentle manner and a flower-shaped scar on her cheek. She had reached up to hold his face in her hands and pull his head down to kiss him, and he had felt her tears on his face.

The young man with the copper-coloured hair and the bright blue eyes he remembered very easily, for he became a lifelong friend. Jiwan Khan, Kassim's only son, welcomed Robert as a brother, and as brothers they remained.

The woman who had stood silent beside Ayub Khan, her eyes seeing nothing but her husband for a few moments, had waited until the Lambagh family had finished speaking to Robert and had then been led forward by Ayub Khan.

Robert looked at her, astonished. Was this Bella, the Scottish woman who had been his mother's maid and later her friend and companion? The movement of her walking stirred her pale green silks. Her red, silver-streaked hair was strung with jade and pearls. She was fantastic, beautiful in an extraordinary way. Her eyes, enormous and ringed with black lashes, were the green of the water that runs when the first snow melts, the pale green of snow water.

"Bella?"

"Aye, it's me. You wouldn't remember me anyway, you were so young when I went away."

"I remember you very well. But in my memories you were different."

"Eh, well, I am older."

"No. On the contrary. You are younger."

"For goodness sakes! No need to use your honey tongue on me! If I am different it is because you never saw me in all these pearls and silks. This man of mine likes to give me these things and I wear them to please him – sometimes."

"He is right. A beautiful woman should wear jewels and silks. Bella, I did not remember you beautiful!" Robert was so

171

tired that he was talking nonsense, he felt sure, but Bella did not seem to mind. She took his hand and led him over to an arched niche in the wall. Set in the niche was a portrait. The face of the pictured woman looked gravely down at him. This was his mother. It was a replica of the picture that hung above the drawing room fire in his grandfather's house in England, except that in this painting Muna wore Lambagh dress. Seeing her there brought home to Robert that this place, too, was his home as it had been hers.

Jiwan Khan put a goblet in his hand, and after the first deep drink of fiery spirit it seemed that the evening blurred, until he found himself lying in bed with no notion of how he had come there, and Bella was with him, and Ayub Khan, and his wound was hurting abominably.

A week later Robert was up again and riding about Lambagh and the outlying villages, learning the hills and valleys by sight, as he had learned of them from his mother in memory. Jiwan Khan had taken a week's leave.. They spent the days together and became a familiar sight, so that all Lambagh called them 'The Brothers', and whatever story was told of Robert's parentage, no-one believed anything other than that he was the son of their beloved Ruler and the famous and loved Muna, the Dancer of Madore.

On the last night of Jiwan Khan's leave they spent the evening in the old Palace, and the evening stretched into the very small hours. Robert and Jiwan Khan were sharing the small white Palace on the shores of the lake, and when he rode back, the lake and the sky seemed to be constantly changing places. Jiwan Khan was not in very much better shape. Their bearers were waiting for them, and Robert felt his boots being pulled off, fell on to his bed, and was asleep.

No dreams broke his sleep. He woke just before dawn, still so confused by deep sleep that he could not remember where he was. Then memory returned and he jumped out of bed. This was the day he was joining the Forces, fulfilling the dream he had had for so long.

He went over to the window and as usual lost himself in

the view. He never tired of that view. He had heard about this place for so long that it was wonderful to him to be part of it.

The village of Lambagh lay below him, the morning fires were being lit and the smoke was rising in columns like blue transparent pillars in the clear air. The sun rose, and he saw it rise, and heard the birds begin their morning song. He stood in the window of a room in the Motimahal, the house his mother had spoken about, and looked and looked again, as he did every morning, filling his eyes as if he were satisfying an appetite long starved. All thought was brushed clean from his mind. His mother's voice, speaking of this loved place, sounded clearly in his ears, and he could not move from the window.

Ayub Khan found him there, still undressed and un- shaven, with his breakfast cooling, untouched on the table behind him.

"You have exactly ten minutes before you have to appear before Zulfikar Mohammed. You will be bathed and shaved and dressed, with all your senses about you – I trust."

Robert leapt for the bathroom and was ready in the stated time, but he went unfed.

He was presented to his Commander, a splendid-looking man, taller and broader than Ayub Khan, fiercely moustached and immaculately dressed. Under the piercing stare of his grey eyes Robert was glad that his uniform of dark green high-necked tunic and breeches was as well fitting as Zulfikar's own, that his boots were of the correct pattern and polished to a high shine, and that he had arrived on time. He could not imagine what would have happened to him had he been late.

They rode out to morning parade and Robert, riding behind Ayub Khan, found Jiwan Khan beside him. That young man did not speak, he merely smiled in greeting and rolled slightly bloodshot eyes.

The parade was long and arduous. Robert was glad that he was not expected this morning to take any part in it. He was merely there to observe, he would be allotted to a troop later.

173

He was relieved to hear that the words of command were those he knew; Sandhurst was with him again as the horses wheeled and turned, orders were barked and obeyed. Robert concentrated hard, watching everything. So far he had not found anything that he did not understand.

Parade over he was taken round the Fort, which was part of the wall that had once surrounded Lambagh village. Most of the wall had now gone as the village had expanded, but the Fort still stood, and the big gate that was still called the Sowar Gate.

The Fort was a thick-walled white building, two storeys high, with a tower that rose higher than the rest of it and was surmounted by a crenellated parapet. Stables lined three of the walls of the Fort, and the other wall contained a forage store, outside which two black cats waited with concentrated interest. There was a farrier's shop, an open barn filled with freshly cut green stuff that made Robert shudder as he looked at it, and a large cook house. The tower contained the orderly room, the armoury and the guard room.

The Fort was old and not very large. Robert wondered where the rest of the men were housed, and asked. It was thus that he learned that the standing Army in the State was not large – but that every man in Lambagh of a certain age, provided he was healthy, was a fully trained soldier and could be called to join the Force at any time.

Robert watched everything. He saw the chaff-cutters at work, watched the horses being watered, and suddenly, sharp in the morning air, heard a familiar trumpet call. As the notes floated out Robert stopped, and turning, smiled at Ayub Khan and Jiwan Khan. His face expressed the most complete contentment. Robert had found his place, the home of his heart. Here waiting for him was work he knew he could do, and the place where he wanted to live. He had come home to the Valley at last.

There was silence after the trumpet call, and he could hear the horses stamping in the stables and a pigeon cooing on the tower parapet, and on the breeze, blowing strongly from the lake, he smelt the familiar smell of incense. There must be a

174

temple nearby, with worshippers burning incense before their gods. It must be very close, the smell was as strong as if he were standing in his mother's room while she made her morning prayers.

Jiwan Khan's plaintive voice broke into his thoughts.

"Would you care to continue to walk round and round this Fort for the rest of the morning, upsetting the men, turning out the quarter guard, and filling the duty Dafadar with suspicions – or can we, in the name of Allah, go and get some coffee and something to eat?"

There was no smell of incense. The breeze smelled of stables and cooking fires and nothing else. Robert turned away and took Jiwan Khan's arm.

"Why not? What are we waiting for? I am starving."

Robert fitted into his new life as if he had never lived anywhere else.

Very shortly he had made his personality felt in the Forces. He knew every man in his half troop as if he had been brought up with them. He was beloved by the men and popular with the officers. He was a born soldier and was willing to do anything, go anywhere, and ride any horse – and he rode as well as all of them and better than some. His spare time was spent in the lines, or with Ayub and Bella, or with the family and the Ruler. His place in the Ruler's family was taken for granted. Here was Muna's son, come home at last – where else should he be? Jiwan Khan went everywhere with him; if one was wanted and could not be found, people looked for the other.

Robert volunteered for every possible duty, so in fact he had very little spare time. Jiwan Khan, steadfastly following, finally asked if Robert had ideas about taking over the State Forces from Zulfikar Mohammed, and Robert considered his question seriously before replying.

"I would like to have command one day, of course, but at present I am perfectly happy as I am. It is just that I want to know everything about soldiering. Everything possible. Otherwise how can I lead men, if I do not know what I am doing?"

"Dil Bahadur, it appears to me that we already know everything possible about soldiering, and quite a lot that I thought was impossible. For what are we volunteering tomorrow? Wah! What a wonderful life I led before you came!"

Ayub Khan, riding away from the Fort, heard them laughing before he saw them. They did not see him. They were riding back from an evening parade, riding like lunatics, but lunatics who loved their horses. He wondered if he should call them to order but could see that they would not hear him even if he did. They were riding their own horses and he decided that they were not his responsibility after duty hours. His own horse danced under the involuntary tightening of his muscles as they went breakneck past him, shouting to each other. They vanished through the gates of the Fort without slackening speed, just as the trumpeter sounded 'Guard and Picquet Assembly'. Ayub Khan wondered who the unfortunate duty Dafadar was who would have to sort out the disorder caused among the guards and picquets falling in during Robert's and Jiwan Khan's headlong arrival.

He saw them both ride out later at a more subdued pace, and take the path that led through the village to the Palace. He turned to go back to his own home and Bella.

Bella was sitting on the steps of their house waiting for him. This time of night was their longed-for hour together, the hour when the dusk was not yet come and the lake was streaked with colour caught from the sky, and all the birds of the heavens seemed to be winging home to roost either in the dark trees, where the dusk had already deepened, or among the gold-tipped reeds and sedges of the lake.

There was no-one else there. Bella always sent their servants off at this time, and in spite of all the comfortable divans and cushions that were strewn about the *chibutra* it was always on the steps that she waited. She had dragged a cushion down for him too, and he sank down beside her with a grunt of pleasure, took the goblet she held out to him, and put his arm round her to pull her close to his side. He told her of the day's doings, sitting like this, and finished with the story of his sight of Robert and Jiwan Khan riding into the Fort.

"I sometimes ask myself if they will either of them live long enough to inherit anything, or if they will both break their necks together."

Bella sighed and shook her head.

"Their lives stretch ahead of them, Ayub Khan, fear no evil for them. But it will be Jiwan Khan who will take the Guddee. A shadow follows the other."

"What? What shadow?" Ayub Khan was alarmed, and not without reason. Bella had glimpses of the future, which were always right. Ayub was afraid of her when her eyes looked past him, seeing something he could not see. He took a firmer grip of her, and repeated, "Bella, tell me – what shadow?"

"Ayub, I cannot see clearly but there is a shadow behind him."

"But you said that his life lies ahead of him – a long life?"

"I do not know. Yes, a long life. But his path is shadowed by something. No, Ayub, there is nothing you can do." Ayub had started to get up, muttering about putting a guard on the two.

"Sit," said Bella, "sit, and take your drink. There is no guard that will keep a shadow from a man's path, if it is written. You know that. Also, I do not see clearly any more. The sight is leaving me. When I lived alone for all those years, and my blood was cold like a snake in winter, my mind was free. But now –" she paused, and something in her voice arrested Ayub's attention which had been dwelling on which man should be put to guard Robert, in spite of what fate might have written for him. Ayub Khan was a man of action, and had no patience with sitting and waiting for fate to strike. But he loved his wife very dearly, and her voice had sounded strange.

"Green eyes, what is it with you this evening?"

"Nothing. Only I had the sight, which was like being a bird, free to fly anywhere in the world or beyond it. Now my wings are clipped."

"How – clipped?"

"I see very little ahead now, only dimly, as if smoke were blown aside for a moment. My heart obscures my sight. I live in the flesh now, Ayub, as well as the spirit, and the spirit and the flesh are both yours. Only for you could I have given up my mind's wings."

Ayub had no idea what she was talking about, but he held her warmly and they shared his drink together, and presently she was laughing and it was time to go indoors, for the darkness and the cold had come down together, and all the birds were quiet.

Miles away across the valleys a man got up, stretching, and trod out the small fire that he had built carefully, well hidden so that it could not catch any eye. As he stamped on the embers they flared, and for a second his shadow was thrown dark against a rock. Then the flame died under his foot, and the darkness came back and he was hidden, and it was safe for him to travel.

The weeks passed, and all the Ruler's family were scattered. Robert and Jiwan Khan were off with most of the State Force, going to the northern passes on the borders of Pakodi State on their yearly exercises, which were also useful as recruiting drives. Kassim Khan, his Begum, Ayub Khan and Bella had gone on an inspection tour of the posts on the Jindbagh–Lambagh border with India. Afterwards the Begum and Bella had the promise of their husbands that they would camp and rest and do nothing for at least a week.

Both parties went off in holiday mood, the men of the Forces looking forward to a splendid month of mock fighting, with possibly an opportunity to settle a few scores across the border when their officers were not looking.

Dil Bahadur, who was looking less like anyone who could have ever been called Robert every day, and Jiwan Khan rode in front of their men and sang loudly, and behind them, also singing, rode Usbeg, who had been called up from his watching below the Lungri Pass. Instead he had been given the duty of following Dil Bahadur and guarding him against any possible danger. The task was greatly to his liking. He

178

sang as lustily as his charge, and thought with pity of Rabindra who had taken his place below the wind-torn pass.

While Robert and Jiwan Khan spent their days among the rocks and ravines and high plateau of the northern borders, a month passed pleasantly for the rest of the family.

On the borders of Jindbagh and Lambagh, where the Kanti river widened into a deep pool before plunging down the hillside in an enormous waterfall which carried the river on through the ravines and lower valleys to India, a small village of tents waited for the Ruler and his companions.

The Begum Sara and Bella stayed in the camp. When the sun was high they swam in the ice-cold waters of the pool, afterwards sunning themselves on the boulders, grey and traced with lichens, that rose from the still waters of the pool, so calm there, so noisy a hundred yards further on where the falls began.

The friendship between the Begum and Ayub Khan's leopardess had been a difficult thing to establish. Every time Bella looked at Sara she remembered that other woman, adopted into a Princely family, with everything that was good and easy in life apparently ahead of her. Muna, who had loved Sara her adopted sister so dearly that she had thrown that easy life away, in order that Sara should live in peace.

Bella had loved Muna. There had been a bond between them from the first moment they met, and their understanding and love for each other had lasted, unbroken by any moments of doubt, until Muna had returned to England and her death, and Bella had come up to Lambagh, the wife of Kassim Khan's most trusted friend.

Bella had closed her mind to Sara completely at first, seeing her as a woman who had always had life as she wished it. But as the days went by in the valley the two women were thrown together more and more, and slowly Bella began to feel as if she had not seen the Begum very clearly when she had first met her. This was no spoiled, selfish beauty. Sara's gentleness, her love for everything alive, and her adoration of her husband, touched a chord in Bella. It was as if at the back of her mind a voice was whispering, urging her to move closer to the Begum.

Now, three years later, the women were friends, enjoying each other's company, full of understanding for each other's foibles. Sara knew how much Bella had loved Muna, and what a terrible grief her death had been to the older woman. Bella saw that same grief mirrored in Sara's beautiful eyes, and so, once again, Muna healed a breach that might have grown beyond healing. Even after her death, it seemed, Muna was a living force in the memories of all those who had been close to her.

Sitting in the sun, watching the light shift and change on the mountain slopes, they would often speak of Muna. It was as if she were not very far away, just beyond their sight, or waiting somewhere round a corner for them to come.

Bella spent a great deal of time walking the hillsides, collecting plants and herbs that she dried and used in the simples and powders that she made. Bella was still a healer, a woman of wide powers, and the people of the valley had come to value her skills.

Sara spent quieter days. She would sit looking at the waterfall pounding its way down the rocky hillside, watching the birds that flew through the spray to their nests among the bushes that grew thickly near the water. Her entire day was centred on one thing. Sunset, which meant Kassim's return. An hour before sunset she would bathe and dress, and be ready, fresh and smiling to greet him. However tired he was, he would relax as soon as he saw her, as if this were the crown of his day also. So it had always been for these two; they renewed each other each time they met after an absence, however short. Sara had a habit of sitting with one hand covering the scar on her face, but if Kassim saw her doing this he would take her hand and hold it, telling her in the same words each time, "On your face it becomes a flower", and Sara would come back from memories that contained fear, and close her eyes, too much in love still to let him see her thoughts when he said this. Robert Reid's father had saved her from extreme danger, and had risked his life bravely in doing it, but in her memories of that terrifying flight from Madore to the hills, when she had so nearly been captured by Hardyal, the then Raja of Sagpur, it was Kassim's voice she heard, saying those words the first time he had seen her scarred cheek. There had been no-one in her heart but Kassim, from the moment that she had been old enough to know what love was. Because of him, her thoughts were free of fear; she rested through the days thinking of nothing but his return each night.

Kassim Khan and Ayub were busy. They went off every day, riding out of the camp before dawn. They were inspecting each of the small white forts that were strung like beads along the border between Jindbagh and Lambagh. The forts had not been in use since the first Ruler, Kassim's great-uncle, had joined Jindbagh, Diwarbagh, and Lambagh into one State, Thinpahari. There was no need for forts on this border. But nonetheless they were still there, though not guarded, and Kassim and Ayub rode out every day to look at them.

There were six old forts. For five days Kassim and Ayub went to one after another, finding nothing but quick-moving lizards, or a vixen and her cubs, or bundles of old rags and broken pots left from the days when the forts had been used in the winter as a shelter for the high-climbing goat-herds and their agile charges.

On the sixth day, as they rode up to the last fort, Kassim Khan's hand dropped to his sword hilt and Ayub Khan pulled out a pistol and rode up to pass him, but the Ruler prevented him.

"Wait, you. If this is an enemy, we take him together. But I think there is nothing here but what we wished, so wait, Ayub, before you go in fighting, to be sure that you do not break something we value."

"I value your life," said Ayub Khan, but fell back, and they rode into the fort side by side. The man who was waiting for them stood up and salaamed.

He was old, but erect and strong, wearing duffle robes and a pointed hat that came from a region very far north from this

181

border fort where he now stood. His face was not the slit-eyed flat-nosed face that belonged with his clothes. His eyes tilted at the corners indeed, above high cheekbones, but his nose was thin and straight, and his eyes were as grey as Kassim's own. When he spoke, his tongue was pure Lambaghi, and the words he used fell easily into the silence as their shadows slanted through the doorway of the room where he had waited for them.

"My life for yours, Lord, now and always," he said, and fumbled at his rope-girdled waist to tilt his dagger hilt towards Kassim's hand.

The three men sat long in that room with its dusty floor and crumbling window embrasure. The old man talked, and Kassim and Ayub listened. When he had finished speaking, Kassim thanked him; there was no question of payment for services such as his. This man had risked his life for many years in the service of Lambagh, and was going back to Tibet many days' march away to continue his work; his name was written on a list of men working for the Government of India, survey work among the hills and valleys. He was paid very highly for this work, which was full of interest to the men in Delhi, but before they had any news from him it had been told to the Ruler of Lambagh. Lambagh was his country, he was, before anything, the Ruler's man. He knew the value of his services to Lambagh, but expected no reward. His home was in Lambagh village. He had a family there. He knew that so long as the present line of Rulers reigned in Lambagh State, his family and their descendants had security. This was his reward, and it contented him.

Presently Ayub Khan and the Ruler took leave of the old man, leaving him resting in the late afternoon sun. He would be gone by nightfall, walking with the long slow stride of the mountaineer, the pace that never alters and eats distance.

The Ruler and Ayub Khan were late returning to the camp that evening because they stopped to talk. They tethered their horses in a copse of silver birch, and climbed a small promontory and sat, just below the skyline, out of sight of all but a questing eagle.

The news the old man had brought had not surprised them. There had been rumours and whispers of the growing friendship between Russia and the Dalai Lama. Great Britain was taking the rumours seriously, but that was nothing new either, as both men knew. Great Britain was given to excitement over anything that Russia did on the borders of India. But this time it sounded as if they had some reason for excitement.

The reason was a man called Dorjieff. His name had been first a whisper, then a rumble, and finally a shout of anger. He had been seen, it was said, on Indian soil, on his way from Lhasa to St. Petersburg. No-one could yet be certain of this, but even the suspicion was enough to fan curiosity into anger. Tibet had been steadily refusing to have any contact with any foreign power, and this included Great Britain, despite the Viceroy of India's efforts to open a correspondence with the Dalai Lama. The information that the Dalai Lama was writing letters to Russia, a power with whom Tibet had no treaty nor any common border, was something that could make events take a very serious turn. Russia and Great Britain had been scoring off each other in various ways for some years, playing a game that both enjoyed on the northern borders. However, if Russia was now going to try and move in on Tibet, Great Britain would move first, and in strength.

"Oh this great game that these two powers play! It will start in good earnest soon, if what we heard today is true. Tibet is a much more interesting board on which to play this game than Afghanistan has proved to be. Well, it appears that we are fortunate. All that we will be asked to do is to keep the borders of my State secure, *but* if we do not, then it will give the British a splendid excuse to put troops and an Agent in the valley, and then Russia has an excuse in turn. I will not allow my State to become part of this game. I will not have my country used as a trade route or as an easy route to India. Russia is no friend of ours, but I have no intention of allowing my State to become a pensioner of the British. We do very well as we are, and we are fortunate that we have the

183

strength to remain so." He paused and watched the eagle soar upwards on a sudden current of air, his face very grave. He remembered what had happened in the past to some of the States to the north of Lambagh. One after another, Mhira, Sukhara, Jhokundi – where now were the Rulers of those States, where the customs of the country and the quiet lives of the people? Those valleys were now part of the Tsar's wealth, the Rulers and their descendants dead and forgotten, the very names of the valleys changed. Watching the eagle so high above his own mountains, he vowed to himself that as long as he lived he would fight to keep his country for his own people, so that their lives could go on, secure and peaceful, unchanged by any other nation, for any reason.

He turned to Ayub, sitting deep in thought beside him.

"Ayub, what think you of this fellow who captured Dil Bahadur and is now living disguised in the Temple of Amarana in Faridkote? The boy thought that he is German. Could he be the man that is setting Delhi by the ears, Dorjieff?"

"Him that they called Tovarish? No. This man is a young man. Dorjieff was seen back in Tibert according to your informant today, while Tovarish we know is still here – hiding in Faridkote. Why does he wait here? Russia is not interested in the doings of a monastery!"

"As you say. But Russia is interested in keeping an Agent near the State that could be used as a throughway down into India. As long as I am in power, and as long as men of my family rule Thinpahari, then there is a wall across their path. But if something happens to take me from the Guddee and damage the succession, break our hold on our State and the northern passes – then, Ayub, how quickly would the wolves come down. That is what Tovarish waits for. News of disaster."

"But what disaster?"

"Allah knows. There could be so many. Also, another waits, who would pay anything to bring us down. You know the man who has a bottomless purse and uses his gold to cause trouble."

"Yes, I know! What a partnership. The Raja from the south, Sagpurna, and Tovarish." As Ayub spoke the names, the eagle swooped down out of sight with a cry that echoed back from the rocks, the echo following so swiftly on the cry that the two together became the sound of mocking laughter.

Kassim looked into the empty sky and stood up.

"Ayub, perhaps that bird is right to laugh. Perhaps we are two men who chase shadows, men who remember too much."

"I wish I could be sure of that. Or that I could be sure of what I fear."

"What do you mean?"

Ayub shook his head. "That is the trouble. I do not know what I mean. But *I think* that Tovarish is paid by the Raja of Sagpur, our ancient enemy State, to cause trouble, and more than trouble, to us of Lambagh. Sagpurna holds the purse, but Tovarish is the brain, and I do not like to think of that. The shadow that Sagpur drew over our family years ago still has not lifted, and now it seems to grow darker."

A wind rose and the clouds raced, and the setting sun, clear for a moment, sent a long ray of golden light over the rolling country at their feet. The eagle sailed back into view, his prey held in his talons, his neck arched as he pecked downwards.

Ayub sighed. "Eh, Kassim Khan! Let that be an omen. That bird was not chasing shadows. Let it be so for us if we have to chase our enemies. Let it be a good, quick capture, with death at the end of it for them!"

"As Allah wills. Come, if we do not get back, they will have searchers out for us."

They went down the slope and mounted their horses, and rode back to the camp where the lanterns had already been lit in the blue evening and the fires were burning, and their wives were waiting for them.

Thereafter, as they had promised, they spoke no more of games of power and State. They spent a peaceful week, each in the way they most preferred.

Kassim and Sara stayed together, close to the camp, happy

185

to be alone, with none of the interruptions that beset people in authority.

Bella and Ayub ranged the hills and valleys, returning long after the others had retired for the night.

Ayub enjoyed watching his wife on these day-long treks. She took the steep slopes as easily as he did, she was as tireless and agile as a girl.

Sitting at ease beneath a tree that grew twisted and gnarled by the wind on a high slope, Ayub looked at his wife and marvelled to himself. There she lay, propped on her elbows, looking out over the slopes and valleys beneath them, and she looked as cool and relaxed as if she had just been strolling in her own garden.

"Green eyes, when will you grow old?"

"When you do, Ayub." Her clear eyes turned to him, green eyes that could look as cold as snow water, but which were now warm with love. He leaned over and pulled her up into his arms, and she said, "We have discovered the secret of eternal youth, for I, held in your arms, am a girl. We will be for ever young, and for ever together."

The evening wind rose, and the tree shook all its leaves into whispers, but the two lying beneath its sheltering branches heard nothing but their own voices and the sound of their own hearts.

The week, which had stretched ahead when they thought about it for happy centuries, was after all only eight days long. It went away from them into the past, became a pleasant memory. They went slowly back to their daily life in Lambagh, and were content that a little of the peace of the week stayed in their minds.

Chapter 16

That morning, after watching the sunrise with Charles Windrush, Laura bathed and changed from her riding clothes and breakfasted alone on her balcony, wondering what was happening downstairs. She let her coffee grow cold, looking at the line of peaks, blazing white in the sunlight, impossibly high, with blue shadows showing where the deep gullies ran down to the tree line.

Two women walked past on the path that curved up the hill below her balcony. Their graceful carriage and free stride reminded her of Muna. Thinking of Muna was only a short moment away from the thought of Robert. She dreamed in the sunlight, lost to everything.

An eagle dipped and floated in the blue, cloud-dappled sky. Beyond those sparkling peaks, that high wall of mountains, lay Lambagh, and Robert, she was sure, would be there soon. She looked at the swooping eagle with envy, longing for wings.

Her peace was broken by the arrival of her mother, billowing in a brocade dressing-gown, full of questions about the morning ride, prying questions with sly thoughts behind them that made Laura blush. Charles had imagined that his request to Edward Addison that Laura should be left in peace would be honoured. He had not counted on Clarissa Addison. She poked and pryed among Laura's feelings, sullying the beautiful morning. Laura had been away from her mother and among loving people for so long that she had forgotten her mother's determined curiosity, and her temper flared. She forgot discretion and asked a question of her own, and the battle was on.

"Why shouldn't you marry Robert Reid? The son of that

Indian fly-by-night?" Clarissa's eyes protruded with anger. Laura's voice trembled but she spoke bravely.

"No. Why should I not marry Robert, the son of Colonel and Mrs. Reid. Mrs. Reid was the adopted daughter of Sher Khan, the old Ruler of Lambagh, Mamma."

"Adopted daughter! Mistress more likely! That woman! She was no more than a common whore, a dancing girl! How she caught Alan Reid was obvious. Mary Boothby, a friend of mine, was engaged to marry Colonel Reid. She broke her heart when he came back quite changed, and married to that – that *creature*. Lady Reid was quite distraught."

"That is not true, Mamma. Lady Reid loved Muna very dearly." Laura's words were unheard. Clarissa was in full spate.

"Mary Boothby – poor girl, she never married – she told me that the woman used to wander about stark naked. What went on with every manservant on the place was terrible. She was insatiable. An insatiable animal appetite. You *force* me to mention an aspect of life not normally brought to young girl's attention because of course you yourself came under that depraved creature's influence. Heaven knows what you learned from her! I shall never forgive your Aunt Caroline. Never."

"Aunt Caroline! I love Aunt Caroline with all my heart, and she loved me as if I were her own child." Laura was backed against the rail of the balcony, looking with astonished distaste at her mother's flushed face.

"Caroline Addison made a friend of that woman because they were two of a kind. Man mad. Disgusting." The fact that her own Edward had shown plainly that he would certainly have proposed marriage to Lady Caroline Sutters if his elder brother had not already done so was part of the reason why Clarissa hated Caroline. Added to that, Caroline had been Lady Caroline Addison for years, while Clarissa, married to a younger son, with no title of her own, had been Mrs. Addison. When at last William Addison had died childless and Edward had inherited the title, there was still the Lady Caroline Addison, charming and amusing and a constant

188

thorn in the flesh of her sister-in-law. The very thought of her infuriated Clarissa. Now Laura made matters worse by rushing to the defence of her loved aunt.

"Aunt Caroline could never be disgusting. She is the most wonderful, wise person I have ever met, and I love her."

Clarissa looked at her daughter with real hatred.

"It is obvious that we got you away from her influence in the nick of time. You are a very fortunate girl. Colonel Windrush has spoken to your father. Thank God you will be off our hands soon and making a good marriage, which I fear is more than you deserve."

"I will make a very good marriage. I will marry Robert." The words hung in a silence that became terrifying. For a minute or two Laura thought her mother was going to strike her. Clarissa looked her daughter up and down, patches of scarlet flaring on her cheeks.

"I wonder just how much liberty Caroline saw fit to allow you. Mary Boothby wrote me of one or two things, but knowing the pain it would cause a mother's heart, she may not have told me everything. Are you pregnant?"

Under the brutality of her mother's tone Laura flinched, and the flush of anger died out of her face, leaving it very white.

"No, Mamma. I am not. A loving mother would not ask me such a question."

"How dare you speak to me like that? Well, if you are to be believed, you are not pregnant. Just as well for, if you were, the child would be born black. Which is why you are not going to marry Robert Reid with his very strange background. I will not hear another word from you, Laura," said Lady Addison and swept from the balcony, her trailing brocade skirts hissing along the floor behind her like a snake.

Moti, who had been watching the scene between mother and daughter, tried to comfort Laura. She then went to Honor and asked her to come.

Laura told Honor everything, holding nothing back. At the end she lifted her tear-swollen face and said, "A black child! I would love my child with all my heart because it would be

189

Robert's child. The colour of the child would not matter to me. But Robert told me what he suffered when he was a little boy at school. I could not bear a child of mine to suffer like that."

"Your child, if you marry Robert, will be no darker than his father. In any case, married to Robert here in his mother's country your life would not be affected by the attitudes of the English in England. Laura, dry your eyes. There are many battles ahead of you before you can marry your Robert."

"I do not care what my parents do or say. I shall marry Robert. I shall run away if necessary."

"There are also Robert's Lambagh connections to consider."

"Do you mean that his family might be against our marriage?" Laura's tone was outraged. Honor took her hand and removed from her fingers the soaked ball of her handkerchief, replacing it with a clean one.

"Laura, there is every reason why they might. Your father has gone out of his way to offend the Ruler. Also, you must know that in this country Robert could have his pick of the beautiful daughters of various wealthy Indian families. The Ruler has declared him the heir to the Lambagh States should anything happen to the Nawabzada Sahib, Jiwan Khan, the Ruler's heir."

The thought that the opposition would not all be from her family was a daunting one for Laura. Supposing Robert had changed, had already fallen in love with one of these beautiful Indian girls! But even as the thought came to her she dismissed it. She had no doubts of her own love for Robert, and none of his love for her.

"Robert loves me," she said quietly, "as I love him. We will marry, and be together always." As she said the words she seemed to hear another voice repeating them; like an echo the words hung in the silence that fell after she had spoken. Then Honor bent and kissed her.

"I am beginning to believe that you will indeed marry him. Dearest Laura, I wish nothing but happiness for you! Now let

Moti put you to rights and come downstairs with me."

While Moti bathed Laura's swollen eyes with cold water and brushed her hair into shining silk, Honor told her about the murder of the Nawab of Pakodi and his wife's flight. Laura, never having heard of the Nawab or his young wife, was unable to be very distressed, but she was sorry to hear that as a result of this tragedy Charles Windrush was leaving Mehli.

"Oh what a pity! I like him so much. Did you know that he was a friend of Aunt Caro's?"

"A friend? My dear child, he has been devoted to her ever since he first saw her."

"Why did he not marry her?"

"I presume because she was already married to your Uncle William."

"Well, Uncle William has been dead for some years – surely he could marry her now?"

Honor laughed. "He could indeed, if she would have him. Come, Laura, we must go down. It is almost time for luncheon."

If Charles Windrush noticed that Laura had been weeping and that her mother was in a vile temper, he said nothing. But he was very attentive to Laura, and the thundercloud that brooded over Lady Addison's face began to lift. Obviously her words to Laura had done a great deal of good. When Charles took Laura out into the rose garden her good temper was quite restored.

She would have been furious had she heard their conversation.

"Laura, I have to tell you that your father, having gravely offended the Ruler of Lambagh, is about to be transferred from Mehli. He will return to Delhi and be posted elsewhere."

"Oh no!" This was disaster.

"Yes. However, I hope that you will remain here with the Lees. I have made it my business to let your father know that I shall be spending a great deal of time in this part of the world."

"So he will let me stay because he imagines you will be courting me?"

"Yes."

"Thank you very much. I hope that you will not have to play-act for very long."

"It is no hardship for me, Laura. Meanwhile, may I suggest that you learn Urdu? A friend of mine is coming to see me shortly. I feel sure that he would be willing to teach you. You will like him. He is a most intelligent and charming old gentleman."

"I would love to learn to speak Urdu! Moti has already taught me a little. You see, you do think it will all come right and I shall marry Robert and live here!"

"If it is going to make you happy, Laura, then I hope sincerely that your love story ends happily. But do you understand all that it means? You will be living in Lambagh State for most of the year with very little contact with British families. Are you sure you will not be lonely?"

"How could I be lonely? I shall be with Robert!" Laura had clean forgotten her first impression of India, the sights and smells, the heat and the discomfort. She thought of Sher Khan's beautiful house, and looked at her present surroundings. Everything was beautiful. Charles looked at her serene face and could say no more. How could he possibly destroy that beautiful confidence? He did not try.

Later he introduced her to a tall old man who spoke beautiful English, and it was arranged that he would come every day and give Laura Urdu lessons. After the old man had gone Charles had a talk with Honor.

"It has been arranged that Laura stays here with you. I hope you do not mind?"

"Mind! Charles, I am delighted. But how will you get Clarissa to go down to the plains with Edward in the middle of the hot weather?"

"Very easily. I have already planted the seed. I told Edward that a new posting was on its way and that he would have a great deal of entertaining to do as soon as he took up his new appointment. Clarissa will certainly go!"

"Where on earth will he be sent?"

"Where he can do no harm. Calcutta."

"The Capital! But surely that is promotion!"

"Exactly. Kicked upstairs. He will merely get the credit for work done by brilliant subordinates. Two years at the most, a suitable decoration and out." Honor was still looking her astonishment when her husband came in and flung himself down.

"Charles, I have a great deal of news. The pigeon post has brought news. The Ruler is sending Ayub Khan up here, or rather, into these part. Jiwan Khan the heir and Dil Bahadur are north on a recruiting drive somewhere in the mountains on the borders of Pakodi and Zhara. They know nothing about the death of Ali because they are out of touch. As soon as Ayub finds them, Jiwan Khan will come here to replace Said Tabib."

"And Dil Bahadur is –"

"Dil Bahadur is Robert Reid."

All three sat in silence. Then Charles asked how long it would take to find the young men.

"Two or three weeks, I imagine. They are really in the wilds. If we are very lucky the Addisons will be gone."

"But not Laura."

"No. I wonder if perhaps, after all, it might be better to let Laura go too."

"No!" Honor's face was flushed with anger. "You cannot be so cruel, after telling her that she could stay here. Her horrible mother will make her life a misery. I am determined that she shall stay here with us."

"Well, Honor, there are difficulties. Kassim Khan Bahadur feels that it would be good if the Addison family fell off the edge of the world. Allowing Dil Bahadur to ally himself with the Addison daughter – he might dislike this very much, and suspect me of plotting."

"He has only to meet Laura, Richard. Look at Sher Khan and Bianca. They adored Laura."

There was no more argument. Laura was to stay.

The following day, Charles took Laura to see the sun rise,

brought her back and breakfasted with her, and then left for the plains. Her mother's efforts to leave them alone together to say their farewells infuriated Laura. If it had been Robert, how differently would Lady Addison have behaved. Laura felt that she hated her mother, and once having admitted it to herself, knew that she always had hated her. Charles, however, was sure that Laura would be left in peace with the Lees in Mehli. His last words were for Lady Addison to hear. "I shall see you again very soon, Laura – I hope you enjoy your stay in Mehli."

The following morning Laura rode alone to Soonia Point. The miracle of sunrise held her there, dreaming beside her horse until all the scarlet had gone from the sky and the birds were in full song. She rode slowly back to the house, and met Richard Lees walking near the stables. A *syce* came up to take her horse, and Richard and Laura walked through the gardens together. The air was full of the noise of pigeons, their sleepy wooing voices and the clap and flutter of their wings. "*Listen* to those birds," said Laura. "There must be millions of them."

"Not millions, but certainly a great many. Have you not seen the Kibutarghar? Come along, there is time before breakfast. It really is worth seeing."

On the far side of the house behind a screen of bushes there was a small circular building with a high domed roof. This was the Kibutarghar, the House of the Pigeons. The air drummed with their sound, as if a hand were plucking the strings of a bass viol. All round the dome were small arched entrances, in three tiers. Each entrance opened on to a wide ledge, and here the birds preened and strutted, sat fluffed and contemplative or took off into the air with sharply clapping wings. The highest tier of all had a stair, narrow and twisting, leading up to it. The little cells opening on to that high ledge had doors, most of which were shut.

"That top tier is for the Dak pigeons, the birds that bring messages or are sent out. Some of them fly in from Lambagh and other nearby States, others from as far away as Madore. Don't you remember seeing the Kibutarghar in the stables of Sher Khan's house?" Laura, watching the birds, enchanted, shook her head. She was looking at the top tier. Above each of the little cells there was a bell. As she watched, a grey pigeon landed on the high ledge and went straight into one of the cells. His pressing, plump body made the bell ring, and a boy sitting near the foot of the stair ran up, and putting in his hand, took out the little, panting traveller and at Richard's order, brought it to them. The bird was perfectly tame, and lay without struggling between the boy's hands as Richard took from its pink leg, above the delicate clawed foot, a small silver cylinder. The boy then opened his hands and the bird, after cocking a bright eye about him, flew up and returned to his nest, and the bell rang sweetly again.

"There you are! Now you have seen a message arrive. I imagine it will be something from Lambagh. We'll take it in. You see – it is written small, on oiled paper, and rolled into this, which is no bigger than the amulets that the people hereabouts wear round their necks on a chain. The amulets contain charms. These little cylinders contain news, or messages."

"I would love to see a message sent out."

"You shall. I will let you know when I send one off, and you can come and watch."

Laura went in to the house, and even her mother's lecture on the impropriety of girls riding alone could not spoil her pleasure in what she had seen.

Her days went by very happily. She rode every morning, usually to Soonia Point, sometimes with a *syce* in attendance, or if he was free, with Richard Lees.

She enjoyed her Urdu lessons. The old man who taught her was charming, and he taught her beautiful Urdu, insisting that she learn to write the flowing Arabic script as well. She enjoyed her talks with him after the lesson was over and they relaxed with little glasses of lemon tea. He told her a great deal about the valleys and their people and customs, and she listened eagerly and asked questions and learned much more than just the language he was teaching her.

In the afternoons she walked and climbed with Honor, searching for wild flowers for Honor to paint, or views where she would sit and sketch. They often took a tea basket with them, and had their tea sitting in some upland meadow, watching the shadows of clouds chase each other on the slopes of the mountains, and listening to the birds.

One afternoon as they lay lazily in the sun they saw a bear, lumbering through the trees, a green shoot hanging incongruously from his mouth.

"He's looking for honey," said Honor, watching him shamble slowly out of sight.

"There isn't anywhere as interesting or as beautiful as these valleys." Laura stretched out her arms as if she would embrace the whole country. "I *love* India, Aunt Honor."

"I do too. But India isn't all like this, my dearest girl. Some of it can be horrid." Honor thought of dusty cantonments, and flies, and heat, and cemeteries where children's graves lay in long lines. She thought of the long boredom of the hot weather in the plains, when the heat grew every day until it seemed the body would burn away in the closely shuttered room where a rattling, flapping punkah only moved hot air. There were many things that she felt sure Laura would hate in India.

But Laura was laughing at her. "I cannot believe there is anything horrid about India. The more I see it, the more I love it." She lay back on the thick softness of a sheepskin rug and closed her eyes against the bright sky. Laura was happy, her face showed no strain, no shadows, but it had a waiting expectant look. Honor recognised it for what it was. Laura was waiting, happy in the calm certainty that she would see Robert Reid again, and that they would marry.

They sat in silence together until Honor looked at her watch and rose with an exclamation. They gathered up the remains of their picnic lunch, and began to walk back. Laura was very quiet, and Honor did not interrupt her thoughts. As they came up the drive they saw that there were three men on the verandah, talking to the Addisons. Richard was with them. The three strangers did not see them, for which Honor was grateful.

"Heavens, Laura! Your mother appears to be entertaining, and look at us – let us go round to the back, and up that stair. I really cannot appear like this, and nor can you."

Safely in her room, Laura stood stock still, looking at nothing, her heartbeats shaking her. There had been three men in splendid uniforms and emerald green turbans talking with her parents and with Richard Lees. There was no doubt in Laura's mind who one of them was. The squared shoulders, the arrogant tilt of the green turban – Robert had worn his hat tilted like that, and no-one else stood as he did. Robert was downstairs, on her mother's verandah, within reach at last. It was enough. Laura had no thought of changing her dress, or of tidying her hair. By the time that Honor had realised what the emerald green turbans might signify, and had hurried, half-dressed, to Laura's room to warn her, Laura was gone, had run lightly down the stairs and was in the drawing room, looking through the glass doors.

Chapter 17

The night before Laura's picnic with Honor, Robert had been only two hours' journey from Mehli.

He lay beside a crackling fire and threw dice with Jiwan Khan while they waited for their evening meal.

They were stiff after a day's gruelling work. For over a month every day had been a hard one. They had climbed along mountain ridges, where the long-haired goats had started away at their coming, astonished to find their high territory invaded. They had inspected forts that stood in ruins on the very edge of the snow line, and they had found others where they had been fired on before they could make themselves known to the guardians. The ground had been so rough, rock-strewn and mountainous that most of the travelling had been done on foot. They had walked, or ridden when they could, all along the difficult mountain frontier that lay between Panchghar and Pakodi. This day had been like all the others. Now as evening came down they rested, feeling each muscle in their bodies relax in the warmth of the fire. Behind them tents were going up, and new recruits, raw both in body and spirit, moved about clumsily, fighting with guy ropes, tent poles and pegs, under the vigilant eyes and lashing tongues of Jiwan's troop.

Ayub Khan, who had arrived that morning while they were on one of their forays, came to sit with them. He looked tired and depressed which was so unusual that the young men put away their dice and began to talk to him. Robert thought to cheer him with news of a peaceful area.

"There is certainly no sign of trouble. As usual, a ruined, neglected fort, but no-one but goats or wild cats had been there. This border area is quiet."

"It is early in the year for border trouble. But those forts must all be manned. They must be repaired, made habitable and left in good hands. How is the recruiting going?"

Jiwan Khan shrugged.

"They come to join us as usual. Father brings son or brother brings brother, and we have, as you see, the usual collection of web-footed buffaloes to train. One thing – Ayub Khan, has anyone else been asking for men about these parts?"

"Why?"

"One of the grandfathers bringing in a posse of grandsons to join us spoke of a man who came and offered money, much money, if the young men would join his army. The old man said that the young ones did not go with this man because he offered so much money that they were sure he was lying. Had you heard of this?"

"Yes. It happened about six months ago at the time of the first thaw, when the logs are brought down from the higher forests. Two men came with an interpreter, and they went about the valleys, but had no success."

"They would never had come as far as this if Ali of Pakodi had been here looking after his State," insisted Jiwan. "My father said as much when that Englishman was put into Mehli as Agent."

"Well, it was the Englishman who dealt with these men who interfered with your recruiting. He himself, the Agent, is a fool, but has a good man with him, who gave firm orders, and the men who were trying to bribe the youths were sent out at once. They made the excuse that they had mistaken their way and had crossed the border in error."

"Russians?"

"Who else?"

"Wah! The English must have been enraged! Ayub Khan, Ali of Pakodi deserves to be deposed. He has a good State, with loyal people who hold him in respect although they never see him. He is a fool."

Robert, drowsy by the fire, remembered the day he had spent in the Pakodighar, and how he had thought then that the Nawab was a good man spoiled by self-indulgence. He moved restlessly, not caring to hear the man decried.

Ayub looked gravely at Jiwan Khan.

"Say no more against Ali, Jiwan Khan. He was a good man."

"*Was?*"

"He was murdered in his garden a week after I left with Dil Bahadur. His Begum escaped with her mother, and is now safely in her father's house."

All Robert could remember now was the Nawab's laughter, and his generosity. His hand fell to the hilt of his sword, the Nawab's gift.

"He asked for a week to settle his affairs! That man Stepan! Ayub Khan, I should have known that Ali of Pakodi was dead when I saw that great brute among the men who took me."

"Yes. I think now that Stepan was the man who was told to capture you in Ali's house in Bombay. I think he terrorised Salih into bringing poisoned wine to Ali, and then when the plan failed, he killed Salih in case he talked. I did not tell you – Stepan tore Salih's tongue out. Now we know why."

"Oh *God*," Robert turned away, sickened.

"I did not know Ali of Pakodi" said Jiwan Khan, "and I know few details of what happened in Bombay. I regret that I spoke ill of him. What will happen to Pakodi State now? My father is Regent. I presume there is no heir?"

"There may be an heir in due time. It is said that the Begum believes herself with child." Ayub Khan did not look at Robert, but in any case Robert had quite forgotten the girl who had pretended to be a dancer and had lain in his arms in the garden of the Pakodighar. Jiwan Khan raised his eyebrows at Ayub's words.

"That will upset the nephew! He will most certainly attempt to gain the Guddee."

"But he has no right at all – besides being in debt, your father told me. Deeply in debt."

"Yes. But Dil Bahadur, do you know who owns him, body and soul? The Raja of Sagpur. The contender for the Guddee of Lambagh. It would suit him very well to have his creature in power here. He will help the nephew if the Guddee of Pakodi can be bought."

Sagpur again! Ayub Khan wondered at the threads that bound the north and the south together, twisting and spinning webs of intrigue and danger over so many years. He looked at Jiwan Khan and Dil Bahadur, contrasting them with the man who ruled in Sagpur, also a young man, but already so depraved by drugs and dissolute living that the State of Sagpur had fallen into the despair and poverty of those who have a rich despot as a Ruler. He recalled the face of the handsome young Raja who had so loved Muna the Dancer, Robert's mother, that for a short spell he had found strength and manhood and courage. If Muna had lived and stayed in India, would that have held the Raja, Sagpurna, steady? Ayub Khan sighed and turned away from his thoughts of the past.

"The Ruler will deal with the nephew. I have orders for you both. They came up with the same message that brought news of Ali's death. Tomorrow you both put on full dress, and with me as your attendant, we go to call on the Agent in Mehli. We go to condole with him on the death of the Nawab, and to make it clear that Lambagh holds Pakodi State for the heir of the late Nawab, and to indicate quietly but firmly that while the nephew Ismail Mohammed has been promising that he will provide men and horses for the British, and a safe passage through the States of Lambagh and Pakodi should the British decide to mount an expedition into Tibet, no-one, no-one can promise anything in this State except the Ruler now that Ali is dead. Kassim Khan does not wish anyone to have passage through these States. This is to be made very clear to the Agent. We leave four hours before sunset tomorrow. Understood?"

It meant nothing to Robert that he would meet and speak with English people for the first time since he had stepped onto Indian soil. England had moved far away and was fading from his mind as if it had been a dream. He stared into the red heart of the fire and there, unfolding like a flower, he

201

saw Laura's face. He remembered her sharply, suddenly, as if she had called him. He forgot everything else, and thought of her with love and longing, the only part of his English life that he really missed.

The following afternoon, the collar of his brocade coat tight round his neck and his turban cocked at a precise angle over his eyebrows, he walked with Jiwan Khan up the steps of the Addisons' house and was presented to Lady Addison and two men, one of whom was the unpopular Agent, the other Sir Richard Lees.

He had never met Laura's parents, and had no idea that they were anywhere near Pakodi State, nor had he known that the Agent was Laura's father. The name Addison was a shock to him. Frowning, he turned from bowing over Lady Addison's hand to find himself confronting the tall man who had been standing behind Sir Edward. He bowed to him, heard him introduced as Sir Richard Lees, and began to frame a question as a babble of conversation, social and led by Lady Addison, broke out behind him.

Richard had watched the two young men come up the steps and had been conscious of being in the presence of fighting men, suave, well-mannered, but trained to a hair in both brain and body and as potentially dangerous as a pair of young lions. As they had bowed and exchanged courtesies with Sir Edward and his Lady, he thought that if these were an example of what the Ruler's Forces could produce, the Ruler was fortunate indeed. The Nawabzada Sahib, Jiwan Khan, the Ruler's son, was a good-looking young man, with a charming smile that did not touch his eyes when he turned them on Sir Edward. But the other – he had been introduced as Dil Bahadur, with no other title. This was Robert Reid, who was heir to the Guddee of Lambagh should any disaster befall Jiwan Khan. This was Muna's son. As he straightened from his bow, Richard studied the handsome face. Here he could see nothing of Muna's delicate beauty. This was a young face with the shape of strength and leadership already showing on it. Here, looking at him, was the young Kassim Khan as he had known him years ago. If he had thought,

202

deep in his heart, to renew for a moment by looking at this boy his memories of Muna, he put the thought away. This was a man to reckon with.

Robert discarded various permutations of words as he met Richard's gaze.

"These people –" he said baldly, "the Addisons – do they have a daughter called Laura?" He saw his answer on the other's face, and continued quickly. "Where is she?"

"She is here – no, *not* in the house yet," said Richard, putting out a detaining hand. "She has gone out with my wife and will be back shortly. For God's sake, boy!"

Robert swallowed, and put a hand to his head.

"Sorry," he said, almost beneath his breath, "Sorry. But someone might have told me. I presume her parents have not realised that Dil Bahadur and Robert Reid are one and the same. But you know?"

"Yes. The Ruler sent up word."

"What will *they* do when they find out? Have me whipped from the garden?" The question had a note of steel in it.

"They will not find out, unless you go on shouting it aloud." Again the young man was abashed. For so much leashed power he also appeared to have a charming respect for his elders. Richard found himself liking Robert a great deal. Now there was another question in the clear grey eyes. Richard answered it before it was spoken.

"Yes, you will see her alone. I shall arrange it. But a little patience and discretion, please. As you no doubt know, the Ruler does not care for Sir Edward Addison. I do not wish to be sent away in disgrace for encouraging a liaison between an heir of Lambagh and the daughter of a man who is not in the Ruler's favour."

"A liaison? I would like to assure you that Laura is my affianced bride –"

Richard kept his face expressionless as he saw the flutter of skirts vanish round the back of the house. He mentally allowed another half-hour for dress-changing and the doing of hair. Robert was fidgeting with his sword hilt in an unnerving manner, and glaring about him.

203

"Please, young man! Your expression is scarcely social. I am sorry if I used the wrong word. But it is a fact that we cannot be sure that the Ruler will be any more pleased about your attachment to Laura than her parents are."

Richard spoke to empty air. Robert had turned towards a glass door that led into the drawing room, and was standing rigid, his hand reaching for the door knob.

Laura, her eyes enormous, her lower lip caught between her teeth, was staring at Robert through the glass door of her mother's drawing room. Everything else vanished like blown smoke from Robert's mind. He opened the door and went in and Richard, after a moment's hesitation, closed the door and stood with his back to it, blocking with his broad person all view of the room. He looked at the others. Lady Addison was now holding a difficult conversation with Ayub Khan who was an old friend of Richard's. Sir Edward was being pompous to Jiwan Khan, who was obviously bored, and was raking the verandah with his eyes, looking for someone to rescue him. Richard sighed deeply, and leaned his shoulders against the glass door. He reckoned on allowing the two young people a quarter of an hour together before Lady Addison stopped ennunciating in slow English to Ayub Khan, who in fact spoke English fluently, and began looking for the second Nawab.

In the drawing room Laura and Robert looked at each other and could find nothing to say. Laura saw a stranger. Robert had grown a moustache. His face appeared to have been remoulded in some indefinable way, it was the same, but harder, his expression was different, he looked fierce and older.

Robert saw Laura as he had never seen her before. He had last seen a girl, barely out of childhood. This beautiful creature was a woman, and she took his breath away. He could not even say her name. Under his stare she blushed and looked away. Once before – how long ago! – once before, the first time he had kissed her, he had frightened her, and she had called his name as if she were not sure that it was he. Now she did the same thing, saying his name softly, questioningly.

"Robert?"

The spell that held him was broken. This was flesh and blood. He saw with clear eyes her ruffled untidy hair, the old blouse and short walking skirt above stout little boots. He moved to take her hand and instead found she was in his arms and his mouth was learning her face as he had so often dreamed that it would.

"Laura!" Oh God, a woman's voice. How often had the name been called before they heard. Was it that terrible mother?

No. This woman was pretty, with a gentle face and a mouth more used to smiling than looking stern.

Laura stepped back from him without haste, saying, "Aunt Honor, look, how wonderful! Robert is here!"

"So I presume. Laura, had your mother come in then you would have been unlikely to see Robert again."

Robert took Laura's hand and held it firmly, and she looked up at him, her face filled with happiness and a perfect trust. Honor might not have spoken. Even as she prepared to be firm, Honor thought what a wonderful moment it was, when life became perfect and secure because one particular person was near you. She smiled, but began to insist. Laura must go and change, and come out and be introduced properly. Robert must come out and take his place with the others. A family row would help no-one.

They behaved sensibly to her relief. Robert kissed Laura's hands and she went quickly as if even so short a parting were so much pain that if she looked back she would be unable to leave. Robert stared after her with a look that made Honor fear he would follow.

"Robert!"

He turned then, and smiled.

"Lady Lees. You must not call me that."

"I beg your pardon. I felt I knew you – however, if you prefer, Mr. Reid –"

"No, no! You do not understand. I am now called, by the Ruler's wish, Dil Bahadur."

"I see. Very well, Dil Bahadur, we must go on to the

verandah. I trust you have not been missed."

"Your husband has kept *cave*. I think all is well."

It was. Richard moved from before the door. Honor saw him looking at her as a shipwrecked man would look at a sail in the horizon. She gave him a reassuring smile, and then with grim determination made her way over to Clarissa Addison, leaving Richard to talk to Robert.

Jiwan Khan was still trapped with Sir Edward. He watched the drawing room door and wondered what was going on. Dil Bahadur had gone into that room like a dog after a rat, and had come out again with his turban knocked awry, and the expression of one who has had an unexpected glimpse of the glories of paradise. There was a girl mixed up in this, Jiwan Khan was sure. Why did no-one rescue him from this fat fool? He caught Ayub Khan's eyes, and with an almost imperceptible movement of his head, beckoned him over.

Ayub Khan took pity on him, and came over just in time to hear the Agent say, "Furthermore, the Nawab was telling me yesterday –"

Jiwan Khan had lost all interest in the drawing room door. He turned fierce blue eyes to the man who was speaking.

"The Nawab?" His voice was silky, and Ayub Khan began to watch him with interest. This was Kassim Khan's voice when he was becoming annoyed.

"I did not think that the Nawab was here?" the silky voice continued.

"Eh? Oh, I mean the Nawab Ismail Mohammed, of course. He told me –"

"What he told you can be of little interest. For one thing, he is not a Nawab. In fact he has no title at all. For another thing, he is a fool, and has no right to say anything in this State at all."

Edward turned bright scarlet. This young sprig! Obviously the boy they had brought out from England to join the State Forces. He had heard that there was an Englishman coming out, and this was not the heir. The heir was that boy on the other side of the verandah, the very image of his father, the Ruler. Looked better-tempered, though, at the moment. The only time Edward Addison had met the Ruler he had been far from pleasant. He set his mouth and turned to annihilate the young man beside him.

"Well, young man. You seem to know a great deal about everything! I do not think that I heard your name –"

"My name is Jiwan Khan Bahadur, and I am the son of the Ruler of Lambagh."

"So!" said Ayub Khan to himself. "So! We have a good man to follow the Ruler. Here is a Ruler indeed." There was an aura of authority and power about young Jiwan Khan that augured well for the valley in the future.

Edward Addison looked up into angry blue eyes, and bully that he had always been, could find no strength or truth of purpose within himself to meet the strength of the young man confronting him. He was saved from making a greater fool of himself by Richard, who had been watching, and brought Robert up to join the others. He started Edward off on the safe subject of horseflesh, and drawing Ayub Khan on one side had a low-voiced conversation with him. This was interrupted by Laura's arrival on the verandah.

Laura had done exactly what she had been told. She had gone upstairs and changed and allowed Moti to do her hair. Now, dressed in pale silks, hair coiled and gleaming, her great eyes glowing, she stood before them all. She looked radiant, a girl who was in love, and was sure that she was loved in return. Robert, like the tide pulled by the moon was at her side, and although they were not looking at each other, the joy on both their faces was open.

Jiwan Khan had stopped listening to what Sir Edward was saying, and was about to make an excuse and leave him. Richard watched him do it and admired his civil dignity and complete determination.

Both the young men were beside Laura, and Jiwan Khan was a splendid cover. Their laughing conversation together included him, but their eyes spoke promises and vows and longings that they could not say in words.

Ayub Khan, watching, said to Richard, "Is that the girl? The daughter of this – this Agent?"

"Yes."

"Sweet like a rose, beautiful as the morning."

"As you say. But the Ruler?"

"The Ruler will not expect Dil Bahadur to marry the father. No, provided the parents keep away, I think there will be no trouble. Does the girl have great affection for them?"

"None, I suspect. They have treated her without love all her life."

"Such a gentle child. Look at those eyes. Well, it is good to see youth and beauty. But we also had days when the wine was never sour, did we not?"

"We did. We still have. How is your leopardess?"

"Well, thanks be to Allah." They were interrupted by a bray of laughter from Sir Edward, where Honor was nobly holding both the Addisons in play.

"That man must go," continued Ayub, turning back to Sir Richard. "I understand you come instead? That is very good news. There will be a great deal to do."

"The expectation of trouble, or the prevention?"

"Both. The Raja of Sagpur is travelling. It is not yet known in what direction, but we know that he has been free with his money in any quarter where it will cause most trouble for the Ruler. Sahib, for the sake of peace and security, have this Agent sent away soon." On Ayub's tongue the word became a gross insult. Richard laughed, and promised to do everything he could.

The lawn was barred with long shadows, there was the sound of jingling harness. The horses were being brought round.

Chapter 18

The visit was over. It was time for the two young Nawabs and their companion to start back to their camp across the valley, and they were making their farewells. Robert was standing beside Laura.

"Goodbye, Miss Laura." Jiwan Khan had called her that, and in view of what Robert was going to attempt later on, it seemed wise to cling to his Indian self. His lips said goodbye but his eyes asked a question, and Laura, with the heightened perception of love, understood, and nodded. Her voice was very low, her eyes were looking down, so that her mother, standing a little behind Robert, saw nothing on her face but disinterest.

"Goodbye," said Laura, "goodbye, Nawab Sahib. The staircase at the back is perfect."

It was beautifully done, a girl adding a few civil words to her farewell, and no-one heard her actual words except Robert.

After the visitors had ridden away, impatience began to torment Laura. Every hour that had to be passed before Robert would come seemed to stretch ahead of her like years. The period spent in the drawing room before dinner was endless. Dinner itself went on for ever, with her father discussing every moment of the afternoon's events, and enlarging on how unsuitable he thought the young Nawab-zada Sahib would be as the representative of Lambagh State in Pakodi State. "In any case, as I have said before, I do not understand why Lambagh State is still interfering. Nothing to do with the Thinpahari States. Typical of this Lambagh fellow, he has always thought a great deal of himself." Expressionless, efficient, the servants moved about the table, removing plates, pouring wine. Richard watched their still faces and wondered which of them would carry the story to Lambagh. What a fool Edward was! While he was engaged in trying to change the subject, Lady Addison was fluting about the charming young men whom she constantly referred to as 'Their Highnesses, the Princes'. Laura hid a smile as her mother said complimentary things about their looks and their manners. "Not at all like natives, so civilised." It was obvious that she had no idea of Dil Bahadur's true identity.

Honor watched Laura. Laura ate and sipped her wine, and answered when she was spoken to, but it was only a beautiful simulacrum of Laura who was sitting at table with them. Her eyes were full of dreams, all she could see was a young man with broad shoulders and dark hair under an arrogantly tilted green turban. Honor saw the burning impatience on her face. It was not difficult to imagine that she might be expecting a visitor. The young pair would be bound to try and meet. That snatched embrace, those few moments together in the afternoon, were not going to content that wild young man Honor had met that day. Nor would they be enough for Laura. The girl's eyes were like lamps, every movement she made was alive with impatience. Romeo and Juliet, thought Honor, and then prayed that this pair of lovers would be more fortunate. She saw her husband's eyes resting thoughtfully on Laura, and then watched him cut Sir Edward short in the middle of a rambling conversation, and blessed him for the kindness and understanding that had always been one of his attributes.

There was an hour to get through in the drawing room after dinner. Lady Addison was convinced that 'Their Highnesses' might call again that evening, and therefore was in no hurry to retire. To relieve the wild irritation she saw growing on Laura's face, Honor went to the piano.

"Perhaps you will turn the pages for me, Laura?" As Laura came obediently to stand beside her, Honor said quietly, "Be patient, Laura –" and was rewarded with a glance of such love and gratitude that she was afraid.

What a power of loving this girl had! The room seemed full

of her passionate longings. Honor played, and the pages were turned, and at last Lady Addison declared that she was going up to bed and the long evening was over. Laura kissed Honor good night with burning lips, and escaped to her own room.

But only to wait. She undressed because it gave her something to do. Laura was no practised coquette. Robed in creamy muslin, her peignoir ruffled about her, she did not look in the mirror to see the seductive picture she presented. She sat, first by the window, and then, growing chilled, she lay on her bed. She heard the little owl that haunted the garden calling mournfully and his cry struck an answering grief in her heart. It was late. Too late. Robert was not coming.

Laura found tears on her cheeks without knowing that she had wept. She was emotionally exhausted.

The owl, seeking his food, cried again, and Laura wept herself to sleep.

Robert, riding back with the others, also found time was standing still. There were firm rules about men leaving the camp at night. Robert, about to break these rules, had to wait until the camp was quiet.

The wait seemed endless. At last Ayub Khan went off to his tent, having arranged for an early trip into the mountains in the morning. Then Jiwan Khan went off to the tent he shared with Robert, and Robert, pleading that he was wide awake and wanted to think, stayed by the fire. The fire died down to glowing ash, and one by one lights went out, until only the lanterns at the guard post remained. The last voices sounded sleepily, and then were silent.

Robert got up, shrugged into a *poshteen*, and went down quietly to the enclosure where the horses were tethered. The men on duty challenged him, then seeing who he was ran to bring him his horse. If the young Nawab, the favoured second heir of the Ruler, beloved of all of them, wished to go riding in the right, who were they to stop him? Robert mounted and rode away, his thoughts outpacing his horse.

As always, Usbeg Khan had been awake and watching Robert. He was close behind Robert when he rode out of the camp, but dropped back a little as it seemed to him that this was a journey that the young lord might prefer to make alone. However, he had had his orders from Ayub Khan. He was not about to disobey that honoured and quick-tempered man.

Even lost in the pleasure of his thoughts Robert's trained ears caught the sound of hoofbeats behind him. He reined up and heard the horse behind drop to a walk. He was being followed. He waited to be sure, then while his horse was still moving, flung himself off and slapped the animal on its rump so that it cantered off down the path, bridle jingling. Robert began to run back the way he had come, his feet silent on the thick carpet of fallen leaves that covered the path.

The horseman who had followed him was sitting his horse in the middle of the path, peering through the darkness. Robert stopped running and went behind the trees at the side of the path, working round so that he came on the man a little from the rear, loosening his dagger in its scabbard as he moved. He was tensing his muscles for a leap when something in the pose of the rider became familiar. He relaxed and walked out on to the path.

"Usbeg. What do you here?"

The convulsive leap that Usbeg gave as he heard Robert's voice behind him almost unseated him and upset his horse considerably. The next few minutes were crowded with action for Usbeg as he regained his seat and quietened his dancing animal.

"Well, Usbeg?" asked the implacable voice beside him.

Usbeg heard in his head Ayub Khan saying, "And remember. Dil Bahadur is not to know that you guard him." Well, there was no chance of him not knowing now.

"I follow you, lord," said Usbeg.

"Yes. I see that. Why?"

"I always follow you when you go abroad at night, lord, if you go alone. Ayub Khan's orders."

"Tonight, Usbeg, I do not need another man. Go away."

"You did not need another man when you visited the House of Many Pleasures in Lambagh, lord. But I was there."

Robert obviously did not believe him. Usbeg proceeded to enumerate the number of times he had accompanied Robert to the famous House in a certain lane in Lambagh and Robert flung up his hands.

"All right!" You were there, it is seen. But tonight I do not go to a house of pleasure. Where I am going tonight, I go alone."

"Indeed, lord. But I follow, and I wait outside. What do you think Ayub Khan would do to me if I disobeyed his orders tonight, with the news of the killing of Ali of Pakodi fresh in his mind?"

"I too regret the killing of the Nawab of Pakodi, but I do not understand why his death makes it necessary for you to run about after me."

"No? Dil Bahadur, why do you think Ayub sets me to guard you? To spy on you, to see which girls you favour? Lord, it is to guard against the knife that flies through the air, the shot fired from behind a rock, the cord about the neck. I am responsible for your life, lord. The hand that took Pakodi's life could take yours as easily, and for the same reason."

"Because I know who it is, and why another man was tortured to death," said Robert slowly, and master and man looked at each other in silence.

"Then who guards Ayub Khan?" asked Robert finally, standing in the dark shadowed road with the trees rustling in the wind. "Who guards him? For he also knows the man, as do Yar Khan and Dost Khan. Are they all guarded?"

Usbeg shrugged. "Who knows? I know nothing about them. *I guard you.*" His tone was final. It would be a waste of time to go on arguing, and Robert had no time to waste. He shrugged, and Usbeg shook his reins and cantered ahead to catch Robert's horse and bring it back to him. Robert mounted and continued his ride, and two horses' lengths behind rode Usbeg, a young man of single mind, determined to carry out his orders.

213

Just before they entered Mehli, Robert reined in his horse and waited for Usbeg.

"I go to the house of the Agent. The place is guarded like an arsenal. There is no need for you to stay awake all night. I shall tether my horse in a grove of trees at the top of the slope behind the house. I shall go in by the gate that leads to the stables."

"It is well. I have friends in the stables. I will tether your horse in the wood, lord, leave that to me. May your night be as long as your pleasure."

"I shall come back to the grove after an hour. I tell you –"

"There is no need, lord. Do not tell me anything. You have just said that I do not need to stay awake all night –"

Robert began to say something, thought better of it and rode on, Usbeg still two lengths behind. In the grove of trees Robert dismounted, threw his reins to Usbeg and walked out of the grove, going quickly through the back gate of the Addisons' house.

He stood in the shadows and waited, looking up at the house. There was only one light, and that was in the window of a room at the top of a curving outside staircase. That must be her room. Romeo and Juliet and their tragic story did not come into Robert's mind. He needed no thoughts of other love stories, his own love was enough.

He had waited long enough. There were no other lights, the house was quiet. He moved forward and set his feet on the stairs. The third step creaked abominably. He waited, holding his breath, but nothing happened. No lights glowed behind the dark windows. He went on up the stairs, saw a line of light under a door, put out his hand and opened it, and entered Laura's bedroom through her bathroom.

The door that led to the balcony was open and a fresh breeze blew in, moving the muslin curtains and bringing the smell of trees and grasses into the room.

Robert stood just inside the door and looked about him. He did not yet look at Laura, asleep on her bed; it seemed to him that he must not look at her while she was asleep, it would be an intrusion.

The quiet room reminded him, in its atmosphere of calm orderliness, of his mother's room. He looked through the door of the dressing room, where mirrors gave him back his own reflection, staring wide-eyed like a man exploring a strange place. He recalled his mother's table, scattered with little silver pots of rouge and antimony and blistered glass bottles of precious oils and scented unguents. There was none of that feminine clutter on Laura's table; it spoke poignantly of her youth. Only ivory-backed brushes, a comb, and an oval hand mirror lay there. Robert thought of the things that he would give her, and for the first time in his life thought with pleasure of his wealth. There was nothing that Laura could not have. Her brushes should be backed with silver, everything that she used would be beautiful and costly. A kaleidoscope of jewels, fine horses, gold and shimmering silks ran in splendid confusion through his mind. He turned from the door of the little room, and his attention was caught by the bowl of white roses on a table near Laura's bed. The flowers in their gentle delicacy seemed to be made for Laura. As he looked, without a sound petals fell from one of the roses. A voice spoke deep in his heart. "What do you do, dreaming there? Time passes, days vanish into the past before you have lived them, as the petals fall from a rose. Look at your girl, look now while she is young and lovely. Time goes so quickly, and cannot be called back. Look now."

Robert took a step forward and at last looked down at Laura and saw the sum of all his life, everything he had ever done, all his dreams and desires gathered and centred round that sleeping face, the gentle curves of that relaxed figure. Laura, his first and only love. For a single moment he knew the future with complete certainty. This was his future, this the only woman, in youth and in age, here lay the dear companion of all his years.

The certainty lasted for a breath. Then everything was swept away in the passion of feeling that overwhelmed Robert when he saw the tear stains on Laura's cheeks. He bent and gathered her into his arms.

215

Laura's awakening was sweet. She woke to his kisses with a little murmur of pleasure, put her arms tightly about his neck, and was presently returning his kisses with an innocent abandon that put a great strain on Robert's self-control. He freed himself from her clinging arms, and walked away from the bed to the balcony, reaching for a strength that he was not sure he could find.

"Rob – don't go so far away!" The voice from the bed was imploring.

"I am not far away, my rose. Just here. It is," said Robert mopping his forehead, his breathing chaotic, "it is a little *warm*."

"But wait – how stupid I am! I have some wine here. Moti smuggled it up for me. It is cold, look, the bottle is still frosty."

Unwillingly, he looked. Who Moti was he neither knew nor cared. The wine in a generous silver goblet was being held out to him by his little love, standing with every line of her body gently drawn through her light night robe by the lamps behind her. His hand shook taking the goblet, and when he touched her hand it was as if he touched red coal. The goblet fell ringing to the ground as Robert, driven past discretion, caught Laura up into his arms and carried her back to the bed. He put her down among her pillows, and looked at her with a question in his eyes. Even Laura's innocence understood and she opened her arms to him with nothing in her face but pleasure. She was a beautiful young woman to any eyes. To Robert she was his girl, warm-hearted, innocent, loving, holding all his future in the palms of her hands. He vowed under his thundering thoughts as he looked at her with love that if it were humanly possible she would never have a moment's pain through him. Then he bent and set his lips to hers in a kiss as gentle as a moth's wing, compelling in its schooled passion. Under his touch, Laura caught fire, and there was neither fear nor shyness in her from then on.

At some time during the night they reached, among their mountain peaks, a plateau of peace, and were able to talk together and look at each other with the wonderful intimacy that love-making brings to lovers. He noticed the deepening husky notes in her voice, the new glowing beauty of lambent eyes and skin as she lay looking at him, her hair all about her in a sweet disarray of love. She was too happy to say very much. At this time it seemed to her that nothing could ever go wrong in her life again. She put out a hand and traced the hard line of his jaw, and smiled into the steady adoring eyes. He caught the hand to his lips, and she said slowly, "Robert. You have changed. Your face used to be so gentle."

"Gentle? How horrible! But I am gentle anyway, if I am with you."

"No. You do not look like a poet any more, or like a prince out of an old fairy tale . . ."

"Laura, don't tell me that you loved me even though I looked like a poetical fairy prince! Great gods! What on earth do I look like now?"

"Like a man. And I," said Laura simply, "I like your looks very much."

"Thank you, my love. Have I ever told you how much I like your looks, my rose of desire?"

"No. Not in so many words. Tell me?"

So he told her, and showed her, and the splendid night of their delighted loving stretched out like a beautiful strange country made for them alone.

A bird called from the garden, and then sang as if it were the last song it would ever sing. From the village below cocks began to converse with the sun. A long finger of silver light inched through the curtains and lay on Laura's white breast. Robert woke and watched her sleeping; he had no feeling that he was intruding now.

While he bathed, they made plans. They were so sure of their happiness that it seemed there was no need to plan. He would come back that night, and then in a week or two he would speak with the Ruler, and with Laura's father. From the heights of bliss where they rested, it all seemed gloriously simple.

Saying goodbye was protracted. The silver pre-dawn light

was gentle on dew-soaked lawns when Robert finally climbed the slope to the trees where he had left his horse. Usbeg was not there. With one eye on the growing light, Robert waited impatiently.

The night before, Stepan had followed Robert and Usbeg, running and dodging behind rocks and through gullies, as soon as he had seen them enter Mehli. He had been confused by the darkness. He had seen both men ride into the small grove of trees behind the Addisons' house, and as he had seen horsemen enter, he had not expected to see a bare-headed man leave the wood on foot, and therefore had not seen Robert hurry through the shadows and into the garden by the back gate. When Usbeg rode out of the trees, intent on reaching his friends in the stables, the watcher was alert. He saw the rider go into the stables, and although he could not see the front gate from where he hid at the side of the road, this did not worry him, as he reasoned that this narrow gate was the quickest and easiest way out of the stables and he would hear the horse if the rider decided to leave any other way. Stepan settled down to watch the back gate.

Usbeg drank a little with his friends, and then settled down in the straw of the stable where they had put his horse. He woke well before dawn, and shared a glass of tea with the relieving guard before splashing his face with stinging cold water and twitching his clothing into place. He retied his turban, and set it back on his head at the identical angle preferred by Dil Bahadur. He said goodbye to his friends, and prepared to ride out and wait in the trees until Robert came.

It was still dark, the long dark hour before the sky would lighten as the sun rose behind the mountains. The lantern on the stable gates threw Usbeg's shadow before him on to the road, the shadow of a tall horseman with squared shoulders and a precisely tilted turban.

The knife thrown in a deadly parabola caught no light, made no sound as it curved through the air, unseen but successful. Usbeg fell without sound, was dragged on the silent cushion of pine-needles, and finally fell free on the side of the road, to see for a moment the shadows of trees against the paling sky before the shadows blurred together into a final darkness and he saw no more.

The frightened horse stood, true to his training, and presently was no longer afraid, for Stepan, the brute, in spite of his brutality had one overwhelming love. He loved horses and understood them, and there was no horse that he could not manage.

The animal comforted and quiet, Stepan went back to retrieve his knife. His foot kicked against the dead man's turban and he picked it up, shaking it free of the hard pointed Kulla round which it had been wrapped, and thrust it into his belt. He bent and turned the quiet body at his feet on to its back, and looked down into the dead face. The face of the wrong man.

The wrong man! Stepan stood glaring down at his victim as if it had been Usbeg's fault that life had ended so suddenly for him at the beginning of a new day. As the light brightened Stepan went swiftly away, leading the horse silently on the thickly fallen pine-needles, hurrying to find shelter before the light discovered him.

Robert waited until he could wait no longer, wondering where Usbeg had gone. Then he turned his horse and rode fast for the camp, knowing that he would already have been missed.

He went straight to Jiwan Khan, who was wrestling with check lists of camping equipment and harness stores, cursing to himself. He looked at Robert with a sardonic eye.

"Where were you all this long sweet night, Dil Bahadur? What fields and woodlands did you hunt?"

"The fields and woodlands of my heart."

"Indeed. I trust you had good hunting. You have a busy day in front of you. You follow Ayub Khan to the Barradurri."
The Barradurri was a high plateau in the mountains that formed the natural barrier between Panchghar and Pakodi. It was a very high plateau, over thirteen thousand feet and a three-day climb over difficult country. Robert looked his

dismay, but it did not enter his head to refuse. This was his life. The longed-for – already *desperately* longed-for – return to Laura would have to be postponed.

"And you, Jiwan Khan, what do you do?"

"I check these thrice-accursed lists. Then I go back to Mehli with a message to the man Lees from Ayub. Then –"

"Never mind any more 'thens'. Listen, Jiwan Khan, if I write a letter, will you deliver it?"

"*Write* a letter? You are mad. Ayub Khan will take your head if you delay any longer. You are supposed to meet him at the Gaddar Pass. He was not pleased to find you absent this morning. You have no time to talk, certainly not to write letters. Start changing your clothes, or do you fancy climbing in that coat and those boots?"

Cursing, Robert ran for his tent, followed by Jiwan Khan who helped him change, hauling off his tight dress boots and finding warm clothing for him while Robert gave him a variety of messages for Laura which had to be delivered to her in privacy.

As he helped Robert into his *poshteen*, Jiwan Khan said, "Dil Bahadur, I will not be allowed to see that girl alone. I shall say you are not returning for six or seven days, and will he please tell the lady of your heart. Do you wish me to give her also through Lees your undying love, or shameless one?"

"Yes I do," said Robert outside the tent, and mounted his horse, which was held for him by Dost Khan. This was unusual. "Where is Usbeg?"

"Lord, I know not. He has not returned." Robert frowned, remembering Usbeg's determination of the night before. He told Jiwan Khan where he had last seen Usbeg.

"Probably drank with his friends in the stables and has not yet woken. Take Dost Mohammed, he is ready. But go, Dil Bahadur, in the name of God, or Ayub Khan will have my head too."

Robert went off, his horse going from a canter into a gallop, Dost Mohammed rattling over the stony path behind him. They would be able to make good time as far as the pass; after that it would be walking not riding. Jiwan Khan watched them out of sight, and consigning his lists to the devil decided to ride into Mehli first. Usbeg's absence worried him. The young man frequently got into a great deal of trouble, but since he had been given the special duty of guarding Dil Bahadur, he had taken his work very seriously.

Jiwan Khan arrived at the Addisons' just before twelve, taking two men with him, and avoiding meeting Sir Edward Addison by sending one of his men ahead to say that he would like to speak with Sir Richard Lees, and that he was at the guard post by the main gate. Richard came to him there and he gave him Ayub Khan's message. Richard read it and smiled. "This will please Laura – Miss Addison."

Jiwan Khan, who knew what was in the message, looked surprised. Richard explained, and sent a servant to call Laura to the Kibutarghar so that she could watch the bird be fitted with the cylinder containing the message and sent off. He and Jiwan Khan walked up to wait at the Kibutarghar with its busy inhabitants.

As they stood talking in the autumn sunlight they saw Honor coming quickly down the steps from the house, Richard, watching his wife, thought with pleasure of the grace with which she moved. She checked her step when she saw he was not alone and his marriage-trained awareness of her told him that she was worried and distressed, although she smiled easily as she came up to them, greeting Jiwan Khan and turning to her husband to say, "Such a pity, Richard, Laura is not feeling very well and is keeping to her bed today. So she will have to watch a pigeon being sent off on another occasion."

"This is truly a great pity. There will not be very many more occasions once the winter sets in."

Honor agreed with him. Her manner was absent and abstracted. She watched the message, written on a thin strip of oiled paper, rolled into the tiny silver cylinder and sealed at both ends. The cylinder was fitted into a clip on the bird's leg, and the pigeon boy climbed up the ladder, past the top tier, to a flat platform. There he held the little sleek body above his head and tossed it as a boy tosses a ball into the air.

221

The wings spread, the bird circled, took direction and was suddenly a small speck in the blue sky.

Richard turned to Jiwan Khan, holding out his hand.

"I would like to say, Nawabzada Sahib, that I am delighted to hear that you will be in Mehli as the representative of your father. Most excellent news, do you not agree, my dear?" Honor bowed and smiled and added her congratulations, but she was plainly very preoccupied. Presently she excused herself and returned to the house, leaving the two men to stroll in the garden, deep in discussions of policy.

Honor was indeed distressed and worried. That morning she had intercepted Richard's message about the pigeon post and had taken it to Laura's room herself. Laura was not there, and Moti was worried. The Miss Sahib had ridden out just on sunrise and had not returned. Moti had sent a *syce* to Soonia Point, but he had seen no sign of Laura, or her horse, nor any sign of trouble. Did the Lady Sahib know where the Miss Sahib was?

Honor had shaken her head, but she felt unhappily certain that Laura had eloped. She had rushed out to tell Richard, and finding him with Jiwan Khan she had hurriedly told a lie. Then, as soon as she could, she went back to Laura's room to look for a note. She questioned Moti. Had the Miss Sahib given her a letter? No. She had only said that she was going to see the sunrise. Moti was more schooled in keeping her face expressionless than Honor was.

Moti was certain she knew where the Miss Sahib was. She had seen the young Nawab Dil Bahadur climb the stairs to Laura's room the night before. As soon as Laura had ridden out Moti had examined Laura's sheets, and had at once changed all the bed linen, keeping the sheets folded carefully. They would be used to prove that her mistress had come virgin to her husband's bed when she married Dil Bahadur. Proof of virginity was always needed after marriage. Moti would keep the proof safely. She liked Honor, and was distressed that she was worried about Laura's safety, but she would tell the Lady Sahib nothing. She was not going to have her mistress followed and taken away from the man she loved. So Moti, her face closed, continued to tidy the room while Honor searched for a note from Laura and found nothing. Finally, she decided that she would have to take Moti into her confidence.

Moti was delighted to conspire with her. Between them they concocted a story that Laura had been stricken by a bad cold. This would ensure that Lady Addison would keep out of her daughter's room. She had a pathological horror of the common cold.

Moti almost spoke when she saw that Honor was on Laura's side, but she decided she would keep silent a little longer. If the two were escaping together, the more time they had the better.

"Let us hope that the Miss Sahib returns before nightfall," said Honor, tacitly admitting that she knew that Laura had gone away with Robert.

Moti nodded, bright-eyed.

"Indeed, Lady Sahib," said Moti, convinced that Laura was now with Dil Bahadur for life, but agreeing with Honor because she did not like to see the shadow of unnecessary worry on Honor's face. By nightfall, the truth would probably be out in any case, thought Moti, and after Honor had gone she packed a case full of things she thought Laura might need.

The discovery of Usbeg's body came about an hour later. The *syces* ran to Jiwan Khan as Usbeg was one of his men. He went to the empty stable where Usbeg's body had been laid and looked at the quiet face, thinking of how Usbeg had always done everything to excess, riding too fast, running and leaping into danger until he had been given the duty of guarding Dil Bahadur. Then he had become a responsible and a faithful guard. The *syces* told of Usbeg's night in the stables, of his early start in the morning, and of how they had found his body lying behind the trees that lined the upper road, his rifle still slung across his shoulder, his sword still in its scabbard, but his horse gone. He had been killed by a throwing knife, but there was no sign of a weapon. The *syces* whispered together and made big eyes of fear, speaking of

223

djinns, and demon killings. Jiwan Khan ignored them, knowing that Usbeg must have been killed in mistake. His death had been meant for Dil Bahadur. Usbeg had been wearing the emerald green turban that all the men of the State Force wore. Now he was bare-headed, the turban had gone too. Usbeg lay on an old string bed as if he slept, and Jiwan Khan covered him with a quilt and made arrangements for his body to be taken down to his family in Lambagh.

He was sad and angry when he went to see Sir Edward Addison to ask, as a matter of form, that the police and the small State Force that Pakodi had maintained and which was stationed in Mehli should be turned out to search for Usbeg's killer. He could have given the order himself, but felt that courtesy directed that he should ask Sir Edward to order the search.

Sir Edward was not willing to do anything at the request of this young man to whom he had taken a strong dislike the day before.

"No need for a search at all. Fellow was probably squabbling over a girl. Notoriously quarrelsome, these hill-men. Young louts, without enough to do."

"Usbeg is a Naik of my father's State Forces," said Jiwan Khan, his voice very quiet.

"Well, there you are then. What was he doing down here? No, no, I will not waste my men's time. Obviously an undisciplined young man, up to no good. Too many of these young hooligans rampaging about the hills for my liking. Ismail Mohammed, who is a very good soldier, has often told me of the trouble they cause. Of course Ismail Mohammed knows how to handle men. He went to Harrow, you know. In England, you understand. Very good school." He made a dismissive gesture and turned away.

Jiwan Khan, schooled in England at the premier public school and only eight months out of Sandhurst, went out seething to look for Richard.

Richard, faced with the flat demand that Edward Addison and everything belonging to him should be out of Pakodi State within the week, tried to placate the young man who

224

now looked remarkably dangerous. He did not succeed.

"In the name of the authority entrusted to me by my father the Ruler, who is Regent of Pakodi State, I require you to send this man away before he does anything more dangerous than he has already. He is still dealing with Ismail Mohammed. Sir, I know who you are. Do not imagine that your fame and your abilities and your power in your own Government are not known to me. My father gives me his confidence. I am asking you, sir, as a favour to do this thing. Get him out! Do not, I beg of you, put me in a position where I have to use my father's authority to have this man taken out of the State. I would do it gladly. Only for your sake am I attempting to save his face."

Richard argued no more. In fact, inwardly he agreed with Jiwan Khan, because with Edward gone, Ismail Mohammed would no longer have access to the British Residency. Richard was most unhappy about the situation he had seen developing. Edward's transfer was probably already on its way. He would jump the gun.

The news of his immediate departure was broken to Edward by Richard with a spurious despatch in his hand. There was the maximum amount of face-saving. It would have been unnecessary. Edward Addison was thick-skinned to the point of being iron-clad. He took his sudden transfer as an honour. He expounded to his wife on the necessity for them to leave at once.

"Calcutta my dear, no less. We go to Delhi first, of course. I knew I would get Calcutta one day," said Edward, speaking as if he were about to be Governor-General at least, "but I had not hoped for them to send for me in such a hurry. Richard speaks of it as an immediate posting. No time to waste. Just pack what you need, the other stuff will follow."

Clarissa, delighted at the thought of the bright lights and social festivities of a big city at last, made no demur.

Meanwhile, Jiwan Kahn had ordered out the villagers to search for Usbeg's killers.

The day had gone, and Laura had not returned. Honor was

sure that she was with Robert. She was hurt that the girl had not spoken to her, and at the same time wondered what she would have said if she had known that Laura was going to elope.

Moti saw the night come down and smiled. She thought of the two lovers, together and happy, and because of their happiness, thought of Dost Mohammed, her lover, and longed for his return.

Jiwan Khan, to his astonishment, was offered the hospitality of the Residency by Clarissa. He was asked to dine, and was offered the guest quarters for the night. He accepted both offers. The house in any case belong to the State, and he was anxious to be within call of Richard in case news came in of the capture of Usbeg's killer. He was not hopeful, for nearly a whole day had been lost before the search started, and it would not continue through the hours of darkness, the terrain was too rough. He wondered if Laura would appear for dinner. However, Honor made her apologies, her cold was very heavy.

"Poor child," said Clarissa, moving a little way away from Honor who had presumably been in the sickroom. "I dare not venture within a yard of her with my chest."

Jiwan Khan's slightly raised eyebrows upset Richard's sense of humour and encouraged Clarissa to continue her description of the agonies she suffered if she caught a cold. Honor was looking absolutely miserable; she caught her husband's eye and then looked away again. He could not imagine what was wrong with her, she seemed on edge and very worried. Laura must be really ill. He had no opportunity of speaking to her before dinner, and during dinner Edward held the conversation firmly in his grip, aided by Clarissa who described the glories of Calcutta to a very bored Jiwan Khan.

In the servants' quarters Moti was listening, horrorstruck, to what a *syce* was telling her. When he had finished his story, she told him to wait, and hurried back to the house. She decided to speak with Jiwan Khan, and had to wait for a long time before he said good night to his hosts and came out of the drawing room, crossing the verandah to reach the guest quarters.

Moti was waiting for him, her *chaddar* pulled discreetly over her face, and asked for leave to speak to him. Jiwan Khan was impatient. This did not look like a bazaar woman hoping that he would pay her to share his bed. Therefore it was a woman come to ask favours. He had a brusque refusal on his lips when Moti said quietly, "Lord, hear me. I am the woman servant of the Miss Sahiba, who is the beloved of Dil Bahadur Khan."

Arrested, Jiwan Khan followed her to the stables. The *syce* was there, and repeated his story just as he had told Moti. His brother's son was a shepherd and spent long nights out in the uplands with his sheep. He was bringing them down to the village sheepfolds at the onset of winter, moving slowly to keep them in condition, and sleeping in make-shift sheepfolds each night, with great fires to keep off marauding wolves. He had twice seen a man on the goat paths, lying up behind rocks. The shepherd had been occupied with his sheep and had not told his story until the sheep were safely driven in and he could rest. No-one in any case was very interested in men hiding among the rocks. The winter was not far away and he could be a man with a private feud, or a man seeking refuge from an enemy. But this time, because of Usbeg, the *syce* had listened, and had come straight to tell his story, telling Moti because he knew her well; he was her mistress's *syce*.

"What manner of man was this one who hid?"

"My brother's son spoke of him because of his looks, lord. He was a giant, with the duffle coat and the fur-lined hat of those from Tibet or beyond. Lord, he frightened my brother's son. Just to see him was enough to make the boy afraid." The *syce* had no more to say. Jiwan Khan gave him some silver and then turned to Moti.

"You have more to say, woman?"

"I have, heaven-born. The young Nawab Dil Bahadur was with my mistress last night. He took her in love, and therefore, when she did not return, I was glad for I thought that she must have followed him. But with this evil man abroad – lord, I fear – " She stopped speaking, Jiwan Khan's hand gripping her arm to make the wrist bones grate together.

"Are you telling me that your mistress is not in her room?"

"Nay, lord. She went out after Dil Bahadur, just on sunrise. I thought to give them time to get away together – I did wrong?"

"You did wrong. Allah knows where your mistress is now. She is not with Dil Bahadur. He returned to camp alone and has gone into the mountains for eight days." Jiwan Khan turned away, leaving Moti standing in the stable with the *syces* whispering behind her.

Richard had followed Honor upstairs, had found her weeping, and had then heard her story.

"I could not tell you sooner. I have not seen you alone all day, Richard." This was true. Richard comforted his wife as well as he could, but she was very distressed. "I did not think Laura would do this. I thought she would confide in me at least."

"Yes, but my dearest, she may have wished to save you from having to dissemble."

"Well, I've dissembled all day, and I did not care for it."

"You did very well, my love. This may be the best way out of a difficult situation. They cannot stop her marrying him now!"

It was then that there was a quiet tap at the door. A servant was outside, asking that Richard should go downstairs again, the Nawabzada Sahib wished to speak to him. Wondering if there were news of Usbeg's killer, Richard hurried down.

Out of all the horrified conjecture and discussion that followed one fact stood clear. The Addisons must not be told. They must be got out of the hill States before the news broke. Richard was now the one who was adamant about this. He had a picture of Sir Edward calling on Ismail Mohammed to take over the State of Pakodi, from the hands of a Ruler whose guarding of the State was so incompetent that Sir Edward's daughter had been kidnapped. He saw Clarissa ringing the last ounce of drama out of the situation, and he went upstairs and told Honor, who sat down slowly, saying something that he had not thought about.

"Richard, we have lost hours when we could have been searching for Laura, and it is my fault."

"Honor, Honor! We are not even sure that she is with this man —"

"Then where is she?"

Unanswerable. Richard took his wife's arm. "My dearest. Your task in this is to ensure that the Addisons leave this place without knowing anything about Laura's absence. Can I trust you?" He had done his best for Honor. Now, with something difficult to do, at least she would not panic and alarm the household. He went slowly downstairs to where Jiwan Khan waited for him by a dying fire. They had nothing to do but talk, and the talk proved depressing. They were both convinced that Stepan had killed Usbeg, thinking he was Robert. He had found out his mistake and then, seeing Laura, had taken her instead.

"But we can't be sure of this," said Richard desperately.

"Then where is she? I know that she is not with Dil Bahadur. Would you rather she was lying with a broken leg, crying in some ravine?" Richard, remembering tales he had heard of Stepan, was silent. Jiwan Khan, too, thought of what Robert had told him of the man, and said quietly, "Forgive me. I did not think of what I said." Further talk was fruitless. Richard went to bed, and Jiwan Khan went down to the village and sent a courier to Lambagh.

The Addisons left in great state, Clarissa in a palanquin, Sir Edward in a white canvas carrying chair, holding a green-lined white umbrella. He had made no effort to see his daughter, but Clarissa had opened the door, seen the huddle of pillows and blankets heaped over a hunched, coughing figure, and had backed off, calling her farewells. The door safely shut, Moti scrambled out of the disordered bed, but continued to cough. Outside Clarissa was making tentative arrangements for Laura to be brought down to Calcutta as soon as she was well enough. It was so insincere that Honor felt no sense of dishonesty as she assured Lady Addison that of course she would be delighted to chaperone Laura down.

"It depends of course on Colonel Windrush's wishes. The engagement is to be announced shortly, as you know," said Clarissa.

"Yes," said Honor, and waved the Addisons away with nothing in her heart but acute relief that they were gone.

Now every available man was out searching. Jiwan Khan put most of his faith in the villagers and the shepherds who knew the country so well. Both men and women searched, and they could be heard calling to each other from one height to another, their voices high and shrill and clear, vying with the cry of the hunting eagle.

But another day passed, and there was no news of Laura, and no word from Lambagh. There were no pigeons to send, as none had returned. Despair settled over the house, and Honor wept in Moti's arms, their tears mingling, guilt and sorrow.

The following morning there was news. An old woman and her grandson were brought to Jiwan Khan and Richard. They had not been part of the search for Laura because they had been out searching for a lost sheep. The search had taken them several days and they were over ten miles from the village when they had found the sheep and the old woman, the animal safe, had decreed that they must rest. Sitting in the shelter of some great rocks, they had slept in the sun, and had woken to the sound of horses on the path below their shelter. They had looked down and had seen a big man in a *poshteen* with two horses. He had a girl lying across the saddle in front of him. She had looked like a bundle of rags, covered with a blanket, but the wind had blown the blanket aside and the boy had seen the girl's face. Then the man had pulled the blanket tight and ridden on, out of sight.

"Was the girl alive?" Jiwan Khan's voice was quite calm as he asked, but Richard could see his eyes, and knew what he feared.

"I do not know, lord. But she had a green rag in her mouth and her hands were bound."

They could tell nothing more. They went off, rewarded,

and Jiwan sent out to cancel the search and send men posting off in the direction the old woman had indicated. But it was a hopeless quest, and they knew it. It was already three days since the old woman had seen Laura. She could be anywhere now.

Richard and Jiwan Khan shared the same fears. Laura could be on her way to Sagpur.

"The Raja has been pouring money into Ismail Mohammed's pockets. Supposing – just supposing that Stepan's leader *is* Sagpurna, then of course that is where they were taking Dil Bahadur. Now Laura. But this time I think Stepan has made a terrible mistake." Something in his voice made Richard feel very cold and afraid.

"What do you mean?"

"Sagpurna is currying favour with certain elements in the British Administration. The last thing, the very last thing he would want, would be a young English girl delivered to him as a bargaining counter. He'd go mad with rage. He'd refuse all connections with such a thing. He wants Lambagh, and he is trying to get it by proving that he is an excellent fellow, so that his claim can be considered, as the claim of a Raja who is very friendly towards the British." Jiwan Khan stopped talking and walked over to the window. The long day was ending, the garden was full of shadows. Richard followed him over.

"What are you trying to say, Jiwan Khan?"

"I am wondering what they will do with an unwanted hostage."

They stood and looked into the grey-green shadows that were gathering the daylight out of the garden. As if their thoughts speeded the darkness, the shadows thickened, the dusk filtered down through the trees, and it was suddenly night.

Chapter 19

After Robert had left her Laura lay re-living the night, unable to believe that any of it had happened. But her body told her otherwise, in sweet and satisfied languor, in pains that did not matter because of the memories that they brought. Now she knew everything, everything that lovers knew. She stretched, and winced, and laughed, and pushed her heavy tangled hair away from her face. She jumped out of bed and ran to her mirror to see if she looked different. Surely she must! She saw wide shining eyes with deep shadow printed round them, and a mouth burned red with kisses, and blushed at her own thoughts and sudden longing.

It was still early but she could not go back to bed. On this day of days she wanted to see the sun on the high peaks, the peaks that could not match in beauty the ecstasy of the heights that she had scaled with Robert during their long night. When Moti brought her early tea Laura was already bathed and dressed and Moti was sent scurrying to order her horse brought round. Laura was glad that Richard was not about, and she did not want the company of her *syce* but sent him back to the stables and rode off alone through the bright morning. When she reached the Point, she dismounted and stood leaning against the warm shoulder of her horse, watching the colour glow and flame into the sky, reminded of how Robert's love-making had brought her body to burning pleasure.

Stepan, lying hidden among the rocks, watched her. He had seen her riding often, either with an Englishman or with a *syce*. Now his slow brain saw her as a prize, one that would win him praise, and make up for his failure to kill the young Nawab. She came from the big house with the guards on the gates, she rode on splendid horses, she must be very important. Perhaps she was the bride of the young Nawab. Then he would come after her. Planning furiously, his future looking bright, Stepan began to move from rock to rock, getting closer to Laura and her horse with every silent step.

Laura soothed her horse, which was restless. She was standing at its head when Stepan's great hand closed over her mouth and she was pulled into his rib-cracking hold. She could do very little but she fought, using every bit of strength that she had. Her body was young and she was more difficult to hold than Stepan had expected, and she managed to bite the palm of his hand. He dropped his grip to her throat and squeezed until she lost consciousness in a red, choking haze of pain. He carried her up to the place where he had hidden Usbeg's horse, dragging her horse with him, and by the time she had regained her senses she was tied and gagged and could only lie, dazed and terrified, while he sat beside her planning the best way to get back to Faridkote with his prize. Finally he took Laura's saddle and threw it down the *khud*. He rolled Laura into her own saddle cloth, pulling the folds over her face, and put her across his saddle before him, and leading her horse he set off, thinking of nothing but the praise he would get when the leader heard of his cleverness.

Autumn was almost over. On the high passes snow was falling, and the people of the valleys to the north of Pakodi were already bringing their sheep down from the hill pastures and shutting them safely into the stone-walled folds within the villages.

The Sharpan Pass was still clear of snow. With Laura lying bundled across his saddle in front of him, Stepan rode Usbeg's horse and led the other, moving as fast as it was possible towards that pass.

Rabindra, hiding some miles from the pass, saw, in the midst of boredom, the two horses being hurried up the rough path, and inched closer to see who was in such a hurry. He had never seen Stepan, but had been given a description. Even without this, the horses in the hands of a hill man in filthy duffle robes would have been enough to alert him. That horse, ridden by the man, was Usbeg's horse. He let them pass before climbing back up the hill and then, out of sight, began to run for his own horse and a fast trip to Faridkote by goat paths and short cuts known only to the devoted band named by the Ruler 'The Sons of the Rose'.

Stepan crossed the Sharpan Pass in the teeth of a biting wind, and the mist closed behind him as he took the first of the slippery slopes that led to Faridkote.

It was night when he and his prisoner reached the outskirts of Faridkote. The wind had dropped when they left the heights. Now it was a still night, very dark, with a river mist rising to lie like smoke, waist-high above the water. The river ran fast and noisy, creaming away from the banks which in a bend had flattened to a sandy shore. Here Stepan halted. It was impossible to cross the river in that mist-haunted darkness. He struck flint and steel and lit a small lantern. By its flickering yellow light he examined his capture properly for the first time. He saw that the day's riding, muffled and gagged and flung like a bundle of rags across his horse, had worn the girl almost beyond recovery. It would be necessary to remove the gag that he had thrust so hard into her mouth that the corners of the soft lips were torn and scabbed with dried blood. When he took the gag away her dry retching worried him only because a hostage to be of value had to be alive. He untied her legs and indicated by coarse gestures and words that she was free to relieve herself. He made no effort to leave her in private while she did so, standing over her, staring, but Laura's needs were urgent and she ignored him. When she had finished he half dragged, half carried her back to where he had tethered the horses. He saw that it was perfectly safe to leave her free. She was crippled with muscular stiffness, and if she cried out there was no-one to hear, and in any case the voice of the river drowned all sound.

He lit a small fire and boiled water and made tea, and Laura drank as much as he would give her, though she refused the coarse dry chapattis which were all he had as food. Finally he threw a horse blanket to her, and taking one himself rolled it round his body and went to sleep, lying close to the fire. Laura too fell into an uneasy sleep, too tired to stay awake. Her sleep was almost a coma, she knew nothing, felt nothing, until towards dawn the cold woke her.

It was a terrible awakening. The fire was dying. Close to her was the strip of cloth that had, all the long day before, been muffled round her head and stuffed into her mouth. In the fitful firelight it appeared to be green. She could not control her thoughts, her brain was full of terrors, and slowly she became convinced that the monster who had captured her had first killed Robert. This green cloth was his turban.

The dark sky where the morning star burned above the ridge of mountains seemed to belong to some strange planet. She had fallen off her known world and lay, comfortless, in hell.

By the dying fire, Stepan was also wakened by the cold. He got up and threw more wood on to the fire, and kicked it into life. Then, as if a thought had come to him, he looked over at Laura and saw she was awake. He walked over and squatted down beside her, and her whole body clenched within itself at his expression clearly illuminated by the bright flames. The look she had seen in Robert's eyes and had answered so gladly with her own awakening passion was here in this man's animal face, the rictus of lust in its crudest form.

The words 'a fate worse than death' were often heard, said in undertones in women's gossip, or read in novels. They had meant nothing very much to Laura. Now, looking into Stepan's pig eyes, Laura's body warned her by its instinctive recoil that there was indeed a physical torment that a woman's body could suffer that would be far worse than the private act of dying. If this creature invaded her body there would be no way of ever erasing that invasion from her mind. As long as her life lasted she would be a ruined woman, unable to accept or take pleasure in the act of love because of the memory of rape. She lay helpless and looked with this new knowledge at Stepan, shuffling closer on his knees as his hands fumbled at his waist, untying the loose trousers he wore beneath his duffle robe. In the growing silver light he loomed above her, a creature of eternal night. With one hand he imprisoned both her hands, futile with weakness. As his heavy weight covered her body and his hand began to force her legs apart, Laura, her mind a chaos of fear, called on the one person she still saw clearly. Her cry she knew was silent, for her mouth was closed, but the cry was there all the same.

"Robert!"

Chapter 20

In Mehli the skies were grey and heavy and the snow line crept lower down the mountainsides. There was very little time left before the high passes that led from Pakodi down to the plains would be blocked with snow. Robert must be told, and soon, so that he had the chance of getting over the mountains before the passes closed. They could wait no longer for news from Lambagh.

Honor was left in the empty house with a strong guard of Jiwan Khan's men. This latter precaution was by Jiwan Khan's own wish. His face was twisted with rage as he issued the orders.

"In these valleys," he remarked to Richard, "in these *our* valleys, it has been our pride, since the first Ruler, that our women could live in safety. Now we have danger with us, danger for women, and this danger has come here from outside, assisted, I am convinced, by money from Sagpur. Anything to make it seem that the Lambagh family cannot rule its people."

There was nothing Richard could say to comfort him.

They set off at dawn for Barradurri, where Robert could be found. Jiwan Khan set a furious pace. Their horses took them as far as the Gaddar Pass, then it was walking. They stopped for short periods of rest, but as the day declined and the lights appeared ahead of them, so high that it was impossible to tell if they were stars or the lights of a village, Richard stopped.

"I am sorry. I am beaten. You go on, Jiwan, and I will follow as soon as I have rested."

It was a hard admission to make. Richard was proud of his strong, well-disciplined body. Against the agile muscular youth of Jiwan Khan, he saw himself suddenly as an ageing man.

Jiwan Khan stopped and came back to lean against the mountainside where Richard stood, back to the rocks, gasping for breath.

"We are there. Those are the lights of Nansing Monastery. We will find their camp very shortly. But we must go, for this part of the journey cannot be made in darkness. Can you?"

Richard dragged himself into movement again. Jiwan Khan led the way. He turned off on to a path that ran twisting like a thread on the side of the mountain. In the grey milky light, Richard saw the river, tiny at the bottom of the ravine, and heard the distant roar. The path twisted round a shoulder of rock and there, magically, was a wide, flat plateau, and firelight on thick walls, and voices, questioning and welcoming. Clearly he heard Robert's delighted shout and Ayub Khan's deep-throated greeting. He felt himself gripped and half lifted across a doorstep and into a warm room, shining with lamplight, and a big fire that flamed and sputtered. The warmth in the room was almost painful after the biting chill of the evening air.

Richard saw Jiwan Khan looking at him with a question in his eyes. Behind him he saw Robert, smiling with pleasure, no doubt thinking to get a message from Laura. Ayub Khan was beside him. That wise face showed nothing, though Ayub Khan must have been very curious to know why they had come. Richard, before Robert's smile and his welcoming words, closed his eyes and admitted cowardice. It was Jiwan Khan who told their news, and Jiwan Khan who walked out of the room with Robert, his arm tight about Robert's shoulders. Suddenly they heard Robert's voice, in a single desperate cry.

"Laura!" The sound echoed and was flung back to them. "Laura!" repeated the rocks and then "Laura" again, until the echo whispered itself into silence. It was dark outside, the twilight had gone. Richard shuddered. So might a man call to his beloved if he saw her carried away on the boat that Charon rowed. He turned to Ayub Khan, feeling the need of firm sanity and common sense to help him out of the desperate despair that seemed to fill the room as the cry had filled the valley.

Ayub Khan was waiting to hear everything that Richard could tell him. Richard was hoarse when he had finished and Ayub Khan called, and a man brought hot wine, spiced and heady. They were both drinking quietly when the two young men came in. Saying nothing, Ayub got up and poured a full goblet for each of them. Robert was very pale and his eyes were desperate but he was in command of himself, and his voice was steady when he spoke.

Ayub Khan stood beside him, one hand on his shoulder, and forced him to sit. Jiwan Khan sat on his other side, and it seemed to Richard that Robert took strength from the wall of love and friendship the two men had set about him. As Robert drank, and spoke, and drank again, Richard watched him, astonished at his calm and control. Apart from the expression in his eyes and that one wild cry, Robert behaved as if nothing had happened. Richard admired his self-discipline.

Ayub Khan watched Robert, and came to another conclusion. This was the calm of the eye of a hurricane. He remembered Sher Khan's controlled strength, and Kassim's cold, murderous rage in battle. How had this boy, who had none of their blood in him, got their characters blended in him? For a moment his thoughts blurred, the sounds in the room faded, he thought he heard a woman's voice speaking. "Love," whispered the voice, "love is strong." Ayub Khan blinked and looked round the bright room. Love is strong? Perhaps the wine was too strong, for there were no women to speak here. He wished with all his heart that his wife were there. He knew, with dismay, that Robert was going to take action, that he was planning as he sat there so quietly. When he had decided what he would do there would be no argument, nothing that would change his mind. He waited, in apprehension, for Robert to make his plans known.

Robert, drinking his hot spiced wine, might as well have been drinking water. The room, the walls, worst of all, the fire, were all screens on which his mind painted pictures. Pictures of Laura frightened and alone and in the power of a man Robert knew was a monster. He remembered the horror he had felt when he had looked into Stepan's eyes. A man who took pleasure in the agonies of others. Robert had no way of blocking the pictures from his mind. All he could do was endure, and in that way try to share a little of what Laura was enduring, and plan for her rescue. He turned away from any thought that she could not be rescued, might not even be alive. Those thoughts he put away completely. He sat and drank, and made his plans, and the other three watched him while the fire leapt and crackled and leapt higher, as if it were dancing in partnership with its own shadows on the walls of the room.

Tension had built up in the room to such an extent that when Robert finally began to tell his plans, at the first sound of his words the others jumped as if reaching for weapons to repel invading enemies.

"Ayub Khan," said Robert, noticing nothing, "Ayub Khan. You remember where they were taking me, when I was their hostage? Safed. The House of the Pundits. Was that it?"

"Yes. But —"

"Ayub Khan, listen. Tomorrow, I go down to Gaddar Pass and take my horse, and go to Safed by the same route that they took me. For that is where Stepan will take Laura. She is his redemption. He killed Usbeg thinking it was I. Then he must have seen Laura on that horse of hers, branded with Sher Khan's brand, and seen her as a member of the family, and taken her to make up for his mistake. I tell you, I *know*. If we go by the same route, we will either catch him on the way, or find him in Safed. A man like Stepan cannot be hidden, and we have the name of the house. I say 'we' for I think you will come with me, Ayub?"

Richard looked at the other two. Which of them was going to say that the chances of Laura being anywhere alive were very remote now? There had been no further news from Faridkote, and it was obvious that an English girl was not a hostage that Tovarish would wish Stepan to take to Sagpurna, who would certainly be furious. Who would bring this sharply to this boy's attention?

None of them, it seemed. Ayub merely nodded. He would then set off on a wild goose chase to Safed, where they would both be killed, if Sagpurna were there with his courtiers. Richard knew enough about the men of the south to know that the higher castes were wonderful fighting men. He had heard that the Sagpur Forces were well armed and well trained in Hardyal's day. That was the present Raja's father. No doubt they had not changed. Robert and Ayub would be entering the town alone. As his thoughts ran from one alarming possibility to another, Jiwan Khan moved, and getting up to pour himself another goblet of wine took Robert's empty goblet to the table too, and filled it.

"Why do you suppose that I shall not be coming? Dil Bahadur, do you imagine I will not help to rescue the girl who is as my sister, being your beloved?" As Robert turned with the first emotion he had shown to take Jiwan's hand, Richard rose.

"You, Jiwan Khan, are going nowhere except back to Mehli with me. For two reasons. The first and most important is that you are not only the Ruler's representative in Pakodi State, but also the heir to the Emerald Peacock. Had you forgotten that?"

By using the name of the famous necklace that was only worn by the Ruler of Lambagh, Richard stressed the importance of what he said. The Emerald Peacock was seldom mentioned by name, and only seen on State occasions. It was said that the man who held the Emerald Peacock held the three States, once known as Thinpahari, now always called by the name of the principal valley, the Lambagh valley. Jiwan Khan straightened his shoulders and turned to face Richard, his glance very cold.

"And the second reason?"

"The second reason is that I cannot get back to Mehli alone, and we – Jiwan Khan, I stress the word *we* – must return to Mehli. The Ruler accepted me as Agent there, and gave you authority. I cannot break my trust and duty, and nor can you.

Jiwan Khan, I must tell you this. As Agent, I cannot allow you to leave Pakodi State without your father's permission. You once asked me not to place you in a position where you would give me an order. I now make the same request to you."

Jiwan Khan's voice cracked with rage as he said, "No! I will not allow you to give me an order. Nor will I allow Dil Bahadur to run into danger without me. I speak to you as the Nawabzada, the next Ruler of Lambagh, Sahib!"

"Gently, gently!" cried Ayub. "I too have a little word to say here. Jiwan Khan, sit down and listen to me. You behave like an untamed tiger. Listen you to me, both of you!" His voice louder than the others in the room, Ayub stood in front of the fire and stared Jiwan Khan's angry eyes down. Robert, who had risen to stand beside him, sat down, and Richard, feeling remarkably foolish, with both young men glowering at him, resumed his seat and looked at Ayub Khan.

"Now. You, Jiwan Khan, will do as the Agent – chosen, remember, by your father to advise on the running of Pakodi State – says. You will return to Mehli with him, and then if you wish you can go straight away to Lambagh State and ask your father's permission to follow us. I go with Dil Bahadur. This business is now finished. If there is to be any argument," said Ayub, standing large and bulky in front of the fire, "if any wish to disagree, we will not do it with our tongues. I would remind you that I am, in a manner of speaking, your great-uncle, Jiwan Khan, and therefore you will respect me. Dil Bahadur, you will also do as I say, if I am to accompany you."

The silence in the room after he had finished speaking was broken by a servant coming in with wood, followed by others bearing trays of food. Richard noticed that they were all men of Nandakhu, a State outside the borders of both Pakodi and Panchghar. If there were no men of Lambagh here, it meant that Robert and Ayub would go to Safed completely alone. He sat doing rapid calculations in his mind, to do with the distance between himself, in both time and miles, and his precious pigeon post. He must get word to the Ruler. His thoughts were broken by a touch on his arm. Jiwan Khan was standing beside him.

"Sir. If I spoke in my own language I would assure you that my head was covered with the ashes of remorse. In my other natural language, I would like to make my apologies for being very rude. Of course I shall return with you. Please forgive my bad manners."

"My dear boy – I beg your pardon, Nawab Sahib, but you could easily be my son – there is nothing to forgive. This is a disastrous situation." He looked behind Jiwan Khan, and seeing Ayub Khan occupying Robert's attention he said quickly, "I must get word to your father. They cannot be allowed to go alone."

"It is a more distressing situation than I think you realise, sir. Have you thought? Safed is a town in British India."

Richard sat down as if his legs had been broken. Of course. No State Forces could go in strength into Safed without causing a major incident. He looked up at Jiwan Khan and saw the same dismay on the young face that was filling his own mind.

Ayub Khan had refilled Robert's goblet. The boy must have a head made of teak. The wine was running in Richard's brain, and he was glad to eat the hot savoury vegetable stew that was given him. Robert ate very well, to Richard's surprise. He was not to know that Robert was eating because he would need all his strength for the next few days. He tasted nothing, neither the food nor the wine. It was necessary for him to eat and drink, and so he did, his eyes still seeing terrible pictures, his hand steady, his mind full of horror, forced down by iron control. There was something in the back of his mind that he knew would help him, but it eluded him. It was so on another occasion; he recalled the evening in Ali of Pakodi's garden when he had tried to remember something. Now, eating and drinking, answering when he was spoken to, moving like a puppet, controlled by a hand unknown to him, he searched his mind for the thing that was trying to come to him and could not lay hold on it. At last the merciful wine took hold of him. His head nodded, his plate slid, deftly caught by Jiwan, and

Robert fell into sleep as a tree falls to an axe.

Richard looked from his unconscious body being carried into another room by two men to Ayub Khan.

"Drugged?"

"What else? He has a capacity for drink that would drain the ocean. He will sleep well and wake the better for it. My leopardess gave me the powder, lest I should be wounded and need sleep for healing."

It was late when Ayub Khan and Richard slept, rolled in blankets in front of the fire. Jiwan Khan slept in the same room as Robert.

It snowed in the night. Richard woke once, and knew the silence, breathless and total, that snow brings. He slept again, and finally woke to a piercing light that came in through an unshuttered window, brilliant even through the thick, clouded hide that filled the frame. Jiwan Khan was fully dressed and shaved. In answer to Richard's enquiry he said, "He is still asleep. Ayub Khan is outside and would like you to go with him to the Abbot."

There was no dressing to do. Richard had slept in his clothes and felt crumpled and unsuitable for morning calls. He went out, rubbing the white stubble on his chin, and found Ayub Khan seated at ease in a sheltered corner, being shaved by a smiling Nandakhi. Richard waited his turn, and when the razor was stroking his face, Ayub told him that they were going to the monastery to ask a favour. "I must send a message to the Colonel Sahib."

"The Colonel Sahib? Windrush? Good *God*!" said Richard and got a cut on his chin for his pains. Of course. Charles Windrush could send men to Safed – any excuse would do! And I, thought Richard humbly, as the Nandakhi scolded and tried to staunch the trickle of blood on Richard's chin, I am supposed to be advising these people!

They were dancing, the monks of Nansing Monastery, whirling, the skirts of their robes many-coloured, flying free to the beat of a drum and the wild lonely howl of a horn. The dance was solemn, in spite of the whirling colour. It matched the steady rotation of the prayer wheels in the hands of older monks who sat watching. The courtyard was full of snow, and the air above was full of pigeons, flying and returning, circling and landing to strut, courting, high above the courtyard where the monks danced.

The Abbot was very old. He received them in a small room where they crouched before him, two big men shoulder to shoulder. Ayub Khan had brought ceremonial gifts, but as well as the silk, fringed scarves, there were blocks of green tea, and cloth bags of salt and of sugar. The Abbot gave them tea, rancid with yak butter. He nodded when Ayub had spoken with him. Then after a little more talk, Ayub Khan and Richard backed out over the paved floor and followed a young monk up steps, and up again to a place where one wall was entirely given over to nesting places for the pigeons. Down one side was a block of closed netted doors, and above each door was the bell that announced an arrival, and symbols inscribed in thick, smudged black ink. The young monk went to a small door, and opened it, and putting in his hand brought out the messenger. Ayub had his message ready and in its cylinder. Watching the bird tossed into the cold blue air, Richard asked, "If it snows?"

"The bird is hardy. He will get home. He has been impatient for some days." It was the monk who answered, smiling. Only then did Richard think to ask where Charles was.

"In Madore, thanks be to Allah. I had word the day I came up here. He went to consult with Sher Khan. Now, Sahib, we go back, for otherwise Dil Bahadur will leave without me. If any worse harm has befallen that girl, then may Allah aid us all."

The young monk who was the pigeon keeper bowed them out, his hands hidden in his sleeves.

In the courtyard the monks still circled, the drum thundering like a throbbing heart and the horn calling to its own echo among the high, windowed walls.

Ayub Khan and Robert travelled with Richard and Jiwan Khan as far as the Gaddar Pass where the horses had been left. If Richard had thought that the pace of the journey he had made with Jiwan Khan was fast, this day's speed was killing. Flying through the morning on impossible rock-strewn paths hanging between high mountain ridges and deep narrow ravines, Richard followed as well as he could. Watching the two young men he thought again, as he had when he first saw them, of two beings who had been trained and polished and honed like swords sharpened for war. He found time, watching, to pray that the strength of his disciplined body would help Robert Reid's tormented mind.

The four parted at Gaddar Pass, Ayub Khan and Robert vanishing down a steep track, gone out of sight in the valley mists even as their farewells were sounding in the still air.

Richard and Jiwan Khan turned for Mehli, and rode in silence the whole way there.

Chapter 21

"Robert!"

The sky was a silver wheel, turning through space. Laura thought the voice was caught in the wheel, that Robert's name would go out into space and echo there for ever, screamed down the steeps of time. She could hear the echoes, and yet her lips were pinched tight by hard painful fingers, so she could not have made a sound.

Suddenly his weight lifted from her, she was free. She opened her eyes and saw him standing a few feet away, ordering his dress with hasty, fumbling hands. There was sound, loud clear voices shouting from somewhere – from the other side of the rocks.

Saved, not by her unuttered cry, a cry that had only been within her mind, but by the voices of men, shouting to each other to be heard above the noise of the river. Safety was close. Laura filled her lungs and screamed.

Alas, not even Stepan, only a few feet away, heard her. She had no voice. Shock and exhaustion had taken it away, she could only whisper. Laura lay looking up at the brightening sky, blurred by her tears.

Stepan came back, but this time he did not molest her. He held a glass to her torn mouth, and raising her head, forced her to drink. The liquid had a bitter, smokey taste, and she tried to turn her head away but his grip was too brutal. If she was not to choke, she had to swallow. She was sure that he was drugging her. When the glass was empty he released his grip on her head, letting it fall back as if she had no feeling. She was already very cold. Now from the pit of her stomach a deathly chill seemed to be invading all her limbs, and her body felt heavy and helpless. The morning light was fading; it seemed that the wheel of the sky was reversed and night,

247

black and without stars, was returning. Laura's last coherent thought was that this was death, she would never see Robert again. She tried to hold his image in her mind, but darkness swooped over her like a bird with beating smothering wings, and she saw nothing, and thought no more at all.

Stepan had moved quietly down to the river's edge and looked in the clear morning light to see what the men on the other side of the rock were doing. What he saw interested him, and the plans that came into his slow brain pleased him. He watched both sides of the river for a few minutes and then, smiling, returned to the unconscious Laura. He bound her hands and feet, and from his saddle bag he took a cotton sheet and wrapped her from head to foot, covering her face as well. There he left her lying on the ground and walked boldly round the rocks, and choosing a spot not far from where a group of men were sitting round a great pile of wood, he began a task that was so usual on that strip of sand that no-one paid any attention to him. He built a funeral pyre. He finished his work, went back behind the rocks, and picking up the shrouded body of Laura, carried her round and laid her on the pyre he had prepared for her. The other men were walking away, and did not turn as he put Laura down. He went back and made sure that the horses were within reach of both food and water, and that they were tethered securely, and as an afterthought hobbled them as well. He dragged his saddle bags behind rockstrewn sand banks, and satisfied that everything was as it should be, began to walk down to the ford. He crossed the river easily, and entered Faridkote with no trouble by the Gate of the North.

A girl with turquoise earrings seated close to the gate, her basket of flowers before her, offered him tight bunches of roses and garlands of marigolds, skimped and small, the last flowers of autumn. He ignored her and went slouching on, the spurs on his skin boots rattling on the cobbles. After a few minutes the girl lifted her basket of flowers on to a padded circle on her head and swayed off towards the inner part of the city.

The man selling hot *samoosas*, three-cornered flaps of

pastry filled with vegetable curry, fared better than the flower seller. Ravenous, Stepan stopped to eat, and tossing down a coin asked the shortest way to the temple. He walked off in the direction indicated and a small boy who had been sitting nearby, throwing knuckle bones, playing left hand against right hand, stopped his game as the food seller called him over. A few minutes late the boy ran off, singing to himself as he went.

Stepan entered the temple by the big main gate, shouldering his way through the groups of beggars who hung round the gate like starving crows, raising their hands as they croaked their requests for alms. Stepan threw no coins and gained no blessings. He wandered about in the temple precincts, his dirty duffle robes conspicuous among the holiday attire of the few pilgrims – the season was long past – and the daily worshippers and the many priests. Presently he saw what he was looking for and stopped beside a small altar where a solitary man sat telling his carved wooden beads, a prayer wheel beside him. Stepan approached and squatted down a few paces behind, and pulling out a string of wooden beads began to mutter, the beads rattling through his dirty fingers. The man in front of him finished the prayer he was making, rose and walked away, and Stepan stayed where he was, watching, the beads forgotten, his eyes on the man's back.

Tovarish went back to his cell and sat in fury, wondering if Stepan had been followed. The fool, to come up to him in broad daylight! Ach, he should have killed Stepan directly he had lost his head and murdered the Nawab of Pakodi, putting them all in jeopardy. He was a bad servant, a dangerous companion in any conspiracy. Now he must have come in triumph to tell of the successful killing of that inconvenient young man Robert Reid. At least with that task completed he himself would be able to go south and report. His sojourn in the temple was beginning to try him. He thought of drink, and women, and shivered with longing. The ascetic life of a priest had never appealed to him.

The *chela* that the priests had allotted to him and who had

249

become his devoted servant appeared at the door.

"Twice born, there is one who asks for you. A hill man. Will you see him? He says he has a message for you." Tovarish nodded, and Shanker opened the door wider and admitted Stepan.

Stepan's interview with Tovarish did not go as well as he had expected. His mistake over the killing was very ill received. The outburst of rage that came from Tovarish was not less virulent because it was perforce delivered in a low monotone lest it should be overheard. Stepan's attempts to tell him of his successful capture of a girl of importance were useless until Tovarish had talked himself out. Then into a seething silence Stepan told his story, and waited for praise. Tovarish said nothing for a few minutes. All his rage had left him and he spoke quietly when he finally asked his questions.

"A girl. An English girl? You know that she is the daughter of an Englishman in Pakodi State?"

"Yes," said Stepan triumphantly. "She is indeed English. Her father is a lât Sahib, he is there in Mehli to teach the Ministers and Princes how to rule. The girl will be a useful tool for the leader, he will be pleased, will he not?"

Something in the quality of Tovarish's silence began to worry Stepan. Where was the excitement, where the praise?

"So you have kidnapped an English girl, the daughter of a member of the British Government," said Tovarish, still speaking in that strange quiet voice. Then he said, "Where is she?" and suddenly fierce, "Is she alive, you great fool?"

"Of course! Listen while I tell you how I have been clever. I have her safe where no-one will think to look. There is a holy place here, on the banks of the river where they burn the dead. I have her there." Stepan was smiling at his own cleverness. "It was so good a place. They wrap the dead from head to foot in white cotton and lay them on a pyre of wood. I had already drugged her lest she should call out. Then I built a pyre of wood and laid her on it, and she lies there as many others do, waiting for flame to be put to the pyre. No-one knows that she is not dead and waiting for her family to come and break her skull and set fire to her pyre." He sat back, leaning against the wall of the cell, sure now that he would be praised – and every word he had said had been another nail in his coffin. Tovarish had only one idea in his mind at that moment. To kill Stepan as quickly as possible. God in heaven! To kidnap an English woman! He would bring every authority down round their ears – the English would never rest until they had found her and caught her kidnappers. He imagined himself trying to explain to the southern Raja who paid him so well and his heart failed him at the very thought.

Outside the cell Shanker, his ear to the door, had heard everything. He knew nothing of Laura but it was enough that an English girl had been kidnapped in Mehli. Also, and even more important, here under his hand were both the men that Ayub Khan wanted – the men who had been implicated in the kidnapping of the young Nawab they called Dil Bahadur. Shanker's thoughts leapt from one possibility to another. How best to handle this sudden complication? Janki! She would know what to do and how to send news to the Ruler. He moved away from the cell and out of sight, and began to run, going down twisting dark passages and through long-forgotten and unused parts of the temple. Presently he came out into a neglected walled garden, and found a man, a naked ash-smeared fakir with wild matted hair streaming over his thin shoulders. He sat in contemplation, sitting so still that he was one with the tree beneath which he sat, and a bird fluffed its feathers at ease an inch from his head. Only the fakir's eyes lived, looking at eternity and the circle of earthly lives. As Shanker came up and knelt in front of him the bird flew off with a cry. Shanker leant close and put a handful of copper coins in the calabash in front of the crossed ash-smeared legs. The fakir raised a hand and muttered a prayer and Shanker, speaking low, replied, and ran back the way he had come. After a few minutes the fakir rose, and picking up his begging bowl and his stick with its padded top that fitted under his armpit, he walked to a door in the wall while the bird chirped in the tree where the fakir had sheltered.

Stepan was still sitting in the cell when Shanker returned. Shanker scratched at the door, and then went in.

"Master, it is the hour for your tea and your hookah. May your servant bring them?"

"Yes." Shanker's eyes flicked to Stepan and Tovarish shook his head, and Shanker bowed and went out, closing the door, and then leaned close to listen. He could hear in Tovarish's voice that the man was holding his temper with difficulty.

"Stepan," said the cold voice, when Stepan had thought to have praised heaped on him, "Stepan. Are you sure no-one knows you have the girl?"

"I am sure. How could anyone know that I was near Mehli?"

"Fool. Because of the dead man you left on the road. The *wrong* man. Remember?"

"Ach, he could have been killed in a brawl. I did not leave my knife there."

"And his horse? And the girl's horse?"

Stepan heard the rage in the quiet voice, and hesitated.

"Well?"

"I stripped the saddle from her horse and threw it away. There was no-one to see us! I did not meet one person on the road. The horses are hidden by the river."

"I knew you would have the horses. Well, listen and do as I tell you. Go swiftly and put flame to the pyre. Yes! Burn the girl. She is probably dead now in any case after your treatment. Burn her body. When it is utterly consumed take the horses, and go. Do not re-enter the city. Go by the circular way round the walls and make for the Great Road, and so, as fast as you can, go to Sagpur."

"And my reward?"

Reward! Tovarish felt his throat constrict with rage. This fool had put them all in jeopardy and now expected a reward. If he would only go! Tovarish was waiting for a message from Sagpurna and did not want Stepan there when the messengers came, nor did he want the whole city in an uproar while the English searched for the stolen girl. He bit the inside of his cheek as Stepan again asked for his reward.

"You will be rewarded in Sagpur. That is a promise." He spoke as calmly as he could, helped by the knowledge that Stepan would be rewarded by death in Sagpur. The

Raja would be glad to dispose of him after all his bungling.

"Promises buy no bread."

"Very well. Take this and go. Go, Stepan, and make no mistake about burning that girl." The purse he threw to Stepan was heavy, but it was the threat in his voice that made the big man hurry out.

Shanker was there to smile at Stepan with sympathy and fawning admiration in his voice.

"I have food and drink in my room. It was discourteous of my master to forget to offer you anything after your journey, but he is a man of prayer, not a man who has seen action as you are. Such a body needs feeding. If you will honour my poor place?"

His tone was balm after Tovarish's acid tongue. It could make no difference if he spent a short while refreshing himself. He nodded his assent, and Shanker took him down a long covered passage with small rooms on each side and showed him into his room with ceremony, bringing water for him to wash his hands, and then giving him a dish of steaming vegetable curry and some chapattis.

"Is my lord thirsty? May I bring wine? I will first take the tea and the hookah to my master, and when I return I will have wine. Eat and enjoy."

The silver hookah with the amber mouth-piece, and the glass of tea with mint floating in it were put beside Tovarish, who settled down on his string bed to await the arrival of news, which could not be long delayed. Shanker left him, knowing that in a very few minutes he would be asleep. The drug smouldering under the charcoal would ensure that he slept for some hours.

Stepan had almost finished the stew and was lying in an untidy heap on the floor, the remains of his curry spilt across his body. Shanker, with a grimace, cleaned the floor and took up the smashed bowl. The man was breathing heavily, snorting and choking, and while Shanker bound his hands and legs securely he wondered if he had put too much of the drug into the curry. Well – he had other worries. He put a gag into the open, drooling mouth, and threw a blanket over him. He went out, securing his door with a padlock and chain, and went in search of certain young priests. Two of them came shortly to his cell with sacks of charcoal on a hand cart. When they had loaded Stepan's blanket-covered body onto the cart among the sacks they left the temple gardens by a small side door and came, after a quick run through the back streets, to the House on the Wall, emerging again from that place with an empty cart. Almost all the charcoal that was used in the House on the Wall came from the temple to Janki, so their arrival and departure was unremarked.

At the same time as the two priests delivered the unconscious Stepan and the charcoal they gave Janki word that Shanker needed a messenger. He had more news and no-one to send. They could not leave the temple for very long. She watched Yar Khan drag Stepan's unconscious body into an empty stable and leave him there, locking the door after him.

"Shanker needs a messenger. Yar Khan –" She broke off and made a dismayed grimace.

"Yes, Lady of Sense. If I am seen wandering about in the largest Hindu temple between here and Benarsi, the priests will cry on the gods and start a riot. I do not think you can disguise me as a Brahmin, can you?"

"I can, but not in time. Rabindra is now halfway to Lambagh with the news of Stepan's arrival. There is only one person to send. Meeta, my child, come, let me tell you what to do."

Yar Khan said immediately that Meeta could not go. "She cannot walk about the streets alone." His tone was final, and Meeta and Janki both looked at him astonished. Meeta spoke first.

"I cannot go through the streets alone? Why? I go out alone every day and no-one says anything or thinks anything except that I am a girl from the House on the Wall, going to the market for my mistress. What else? I am not a *purdanashin* of family, Yar Khan. I am Meeta. I know every lane and byway in Faridkote. I have taken trouble to learn them. Janki has taught me very much."

"Then take my horse."

"Aiee! You think that would not cause me to be watched?

254

Nay, Yar Khan, I thank you, but I go on foot. Tell me, Janki, what you wish me to do."

Half an hour later a hill girl with great lumps of jade in her ears and long shining plaits swinging below her waist, a little embroidered cap tilted on her head and her face innocent of paint, arrived at the temple. She carried offerings, a mound of rice placed on a fresh green leaf and decorated with silver beaten as thin as chicken skin, and several garlands. These and the leaf dish of rice were arranged on a brass tray. She went in, throwing a coin to the swarming beggars. She walked to the shrine of a goddess whom she had feared and reverenced ever since a certain night, when a voice had spoken to her in a dark grove, giving her comfort and hope. She made obeisance before the many-armed statue of the dancing goddess whose necklace was of human skulls carved in stone, and who stared at Meeta out of painted eyes above an open mouth daubed with scarlet, from which her pointed tongue protruded. Meeta placed her garlands and her leaf dish of rice on the low altar in front of this figure. She put a pinch of incense on the fire burning before the goddess, and the smoke curled up, scented and blue, and hid the terrifying mouth; only the eyes were left to look at Meeta above the scented smoke. Meeta joined her hands palm to palm and bowed over them. She turned away then and mingled with the crowds outside in the temple gardens, walking slowly, pausing before one altar after another, until she stopped before the figure of a god seated in contemplation. There a low voice spoke her name. It was an old shrine and empty. She stood, half in shadow, half in sunlight, her gaze on the many-coloured throng, and listened while Shanker told her his news. Her face, schooled to show nothing but the curiosity of a hill girl seeing the great temple for the first time, hid the thoughts that filled her brain as the crowds filled the temple gardens.

Shanker spoke of a white girl, the daughter of an English *burra sahib* in Mehli. Shanker did not know who she was but Meeta did. Her brain sharpened by love and jealousy knew at once. This was Dil Bahadur's girl, the girl he had called to in his delirium. Laura, he had called her, a soft word, like a dove in the trees in spring. Laura. Let her die then! Then Dil Bahadur would

255

turn to her. She remembered, behind her still, listening face, the tenderness of his touch on her hair, the close warm clasp of his hand. He was a man who liked women. If there were no girl with this name that was like the sound of a dove calling, if this *Laura* died, perhaps he would turn to her, Meeta, and take her from the House on the Wall and keep her as his mistress in the *bibikhana* of his house. It would be very easy to catch his interest if this English girl was dead. She might be dead already, lying cold and alone on the shore of the dead, with the pyres of others burning round her. Let it be so. Delay a little, do not do anything, she would die. The thought lasted for only a moment. Then a voice spoke to her under her thought, under the voice of Shanker. "My daughter," said the voice that was no voice and yet sounded as clearly as a plucked guitar string in a silent room. "My daughter. This is not for you. Turn your heart and do not think of the young man. I tell you this, I who see down the years."

Meeta bowed her head. She could have been praying. Tears fell on her clasped hands but her low voice was steady.

"Where is the pyre? There must be many on the shore of the dead."

"I do not know. I could not question that animal and he did not tell Tovarish. But I know there are two horses nearby. I drugged Stepan because he was on his way to set flame to the pyre by Tovarish's orders. He was then to go to Sagpur. Tell Janki. Tell her also he killed someone in error. He had orders to kill the young Nawab, but killed another man in error."

"That we know. He killed a man called Usbeg. Shanker, I must return. What other message have you?"

"I need help. I cannot take Tovarish alone. I fear him. Send me armed men. Let them come to the old side gate – Janki knows it. Also –"

He stopped speaking, and Meeta heard him move. Then she heard his name called, heard his reply, and then a murmur of voices. Then his voice, clear and raised.

"I come now. My master has been expecting visitors, I will take them to him. Then I must came back here. I have not finished cleaning this shrine. The god must wait for me without anger, for I will come back." She heard his feet on the bricked path, and then she sank down before the seated god whose eyes were not painted and who gave her no message save that of patience.

Shanker ran to Tovarish's cell. There was no possibility that he would be awake yet. Shanker grew very afraid when he saw at the door of the cell three men whose shaven heads and duffle robes did nothing to make them look priestly. These men were dangerous, trained and, at the moment, angry. They had been knocking and could get no answer, they said, and the door was locked. Where was the Abbot? Shanker, who had locked the door on the drugged Tovarish, said that he did not know. Possibly the Abbot was eating the air in the temple gardens? Two of the men turned to follow him, but the third said brusquely, "No. He is within. I heard him snoring."

"Then he sleeps. If you would give yourself the trouble to come to my room until he wakes –"

"We wake him now. We have no time. Knock." Knowing it to be pointless, Shanker knocked and called, and finally the man who was spokesman for the others told him to move aside. The door was strong, but the man merely put the hilt of his dagger into the hasp of the lock and pulled it from the wood. The door swung open and Tovarish was there, the silver hookah by his side, the tea cold in its glass. The man whom the others called Narain bent over the bed, and then looked at the hookah. He put his fingers into the top of the hookah and crumbled some of the cold stuff that had long burned out. He smelled his fingers, and looked at his two companions.

"He is drugged. What does he smoke? Opium it appears."

"No, that is impossible. He would never take anything."

"Then he has been given something. Hold the boy, and keep him quiet." One of them gripped Shanker, who made no resistance or outcry. There was no-one to help him and he would bring trouble on his friends if he caused an uproar.

Narain and the other man did some unpleasant things to Tovarish who finally woke groaning. After they had helped to douse his head in cold water, and he had finished drying his face and put on fresh clothing, he was in command of himself, heavy-eyed and pale, but a leader once again. He looked round his soiled disordered room.

"Let us get to the boy's room. We cannot talk here."

They walked out, pulling the door shut, Shanker in their midst, all of them talking to him like men who are delighted to be back with a friend. And so they made the short journey to his room and no-one saw them.

In Shanker's room, with the door shut and one of the men standing in front of it, a knife in his hand, they began to question Shanker. He told them that he had taken tea and the silver hookah to his master, and had left him there as he did every day while he himself went to buy food for the evening meal. "Why should I drug you, lord? You have been a good master to me. Has your disciple not pleased you? Must I be accused?" His argument was persuasive. Tovarish remembered the priests bringing him Shanker when he had first come to stay in the temple. There *was* no reason for Shanker to drug him. He had found the boy attentive and obedient, and totally without curiosity. There were many other more likely suspects: Stepan himself could have come back, perhaps. While he was thinking Tovarish had stepped back a little from Shanker and his foot struck against something. He bent, and found his own purse at his foot, the purse he had given to Stepan that morning. Holding it in his hand he turned to look at Shanker, and the others all looked at what he held in his hand – even the man in front of the door moved a little to see. The way was clear, and Shanker was young and loved life, and made a mistake. He barged the man at the door aside, wrenched it open and was racing to safety down the passage. They would not dare touch him in the open.

The thrown knife flew straight to its target like a stooping hawk, catching him in the back, hilt deep, and he fell. To them he had declared not his fear, but his guilt.

Narain dragged him to one side and then, seeing an empty cell, threw him in. With no hesitation then the four men walked quietly out of the temple and turned, under Narain's low-voiced instructions, for the Arabsarai.

Meeta waited and waited. The thought of the girl lying on the river bank grew large in her mind. At last she got up and looked for a suitable person to question. She saw a novice monk, and stopped him. "I am the sister of Shanker who is the *chela* of an abbot. Is it possible that I speak with Shanker? I have news from our mother." It was not allowed but Meeta was a pretty girl and the novice was very young. He directed her to Shanker's cell, and got a smile in return that sent him off with his mind full of unsuitable thoughts. Meeta forgot him as she turned away. She hurried to Shanker's cell and found it empty. It was already afternoon. She could not wait any longer. She was turning to go when she heard a long, shuddering sigh, and stopped, her breath held. The sigh came again, and ended in a sob. Meeta turned and ran swiftly towards the sound, and in the darkness of a small windowless cell she found Shanker, and saw his blood and heard the bubble of his breathing, and bent down and took his head to her breast. He was very young, and in great pain and fear, and he was weeping as a lost child weeps. Darkness had come over his eyes. He was a child again, waking afraid in the dark and reaching for his mother to comfort him. Meeta's arms and her soft breast were a refuge for him. He turned his face against that tender breast, and sighed, and the blood bubbled out with his sigh.

"Hai my mother – I had such a dream! Stay with me for it is very dark, and something hurts me – mother, I hurt –"

"Hush, my son. Sleep now. I am here, nothing will hurt you. Sleep, son of my heart." Meeta's soft voice was the last sound that Shanker heard. His head fell back, he sighed again, and on a great gush of blood his young life left him.

Meeta laid him down and then bent and put his limbs in decent order and left him, going back down the passage to his own cell where the charcoal stove that would never warm him again glowed red in the corner. She locked the door, and looking round found his leather box in which he kept his clothes. She took off her blood-soaked clothes and dressed herself in the duffle coat and loose trousers she found in the box. She and Shanker had been almost the same build. When she had wound the rope girdle round her waist the clothes fitted well enough. She pulled on an ear-flapped felt cap, tucked her hair up into the high pointed crown, rolled her own clothes into a bundle and put them in the leather chest. She took off her jade earrings and put them into the embroidered pouch at her waist which also contained flint and steel and a floss of dry tinder, and a few coins. She pulled the door close behind her and locked it, and walked out into the afternoon sunshine, a boy from the far north, totally unremarkable. She walked quickly through the precincts and out through the main gate of the temple.

Outside the gate she stopped twice, once at a stall which sold flasks of oil and powdered incense in cones of thin silver-birch bark as fine and pliable as paper. With these purchases tucked safely away she went on until she found the flower seller with the turquoise earrings, back at her post just inside the North Gate. She stopped there to buy a garland of marigolds, choosing carefully and arguing about the price. The flower seller threw in a white rose only half open, and when her customer had left her, she put the round padded circlet on her head, lifted her basket and walked away, her face very solemn beneath the flower-laden basket.

Meeta did not take the lanes that led back to the House on the Wall. She walked away from the North Gate, and finally left Faridkote by the Gate of Mourning, and turned towards the river where it curved away from the flat sandy shore. The path was well trodden. She crossed the river by the shining black stones that stood out of the foaming river where it ran shallow as the banks widened. Then she was at the place of burnings, and her nostrils were filled with the smell of scorched cloth and wood smoke and the sickly smell of charred and roasted bones and flesh. There were several pyres, some burning with a few men waiting beside each pyre until the body should be consumed enough for the ashes to be cast into the river and carried away. The river ran eventually, many miles away, into the Ganges, the sacred river that every good Hindu wanted to die beside. The river ran fast here, the ashes and the bones that were not always entirely burned were soon lost in the tumbling water and carried out of sight. At one pyre men were praying, and pouring oil on the heaped wood. The corpse was uncovered and a young man was about to crack the skull of the old man who had died, before setting light to the timber. Meeta hurried past, looking at nothing, holding her breath against the stench. She reached the end of the sandy strip of shore. There was only one pyre left, built a little distance from the rest, a small sheeted body lying on it. This must be the one she wanted. She went up to it and stood, for a minute or two completely at a loss. She knew nothing of the rites of a funeral. Then she realised that a burning *ghat* was not a place where anyone asked questions. No-one would watch her; all who were there had duties to perform as quickly as possible so that they could leave again.

Meeta put down her garland and took out the incense and the oil. She must make sure that this was the girl before she did anything else. She walked round the great heap of wood and gently lifted the swathed cloth away from the face of the form on the pyre. She looked down at closed eyes that seemed to be sunk in blue hollows, at a dead white face, and a gentle curved mouth that had the marks of dried blood at the indented corners. She put her hand gently on the white forehead and withdrew it, her heart sinking. Surely the girl was dead, her flesh was icy. Meeta covered the still face and looked around her. There was a straggle of trees and rocks close by. If this was the girl, and she was sure it was, the horses would be hidden somewhere among those rocks. Meeta walked slowly over to the rocks, her eyes on the ground as if she was searching for something. Once behind the rocks she began to run towards the trees. There she found the horses, two of them, tethered and hobbled. She took a small sharp knife from her waist pouch. There was no time to loosen the hobbles. She slashed through them and led the horses back to the rocks, tethering them there to a leafless tree that grew on the bank. She snatched off the saddle cloths that covered the horses, and went back to the sheeted body on the pyre.

Fortune had turned her way. There was a thick pall of sickening smoke blowing in her direction from a newly lit pyre below the bend of the river. One of the worst of her problems was solved – how to remove Laura's body from the pyre. While the evil smell of burning flesh surrounded her, and the thick smoke made a curtain between her and the rest of the people on the shore, she rolled Laura's body from the pyre onto one spread saddle cloth, and dragged it behind the rocks. Far from safe yet, but it was a beginning. She rolled the saddle cloth into a bundle, adding the second cloth from the other horse. She saw the Peacock insignia embroidered on one of the cloths. So she had been right. This girl was Dil Bahadur's girl. Working at speed she formed the two saddle cloths into the rough semblance of a body, and ran back to the pyre. She put the roll of cloth where Laura's body had lain, choking in the smoke that mercifully was still hanging about in thick greasy coils. She poured her scented oil over the roll of cloth, threw on the resinous incense, and taking flint and steel and the lump of dry tinder she struck sparks that caught at the tinder and smouldered in the oily cloth. The wood was dry and there was plenty of bark. Soon flames began to lick round the roll of cloth. Meeta stayed long enough to see the whole thing flare into flames and rolling swathes of smoke and then ran back to the girl behind the rocks.

Laura, unwrapped from the shrouding cotton, blue-white and deathly cold, appeared to be dead. Meeta put her head down on to her chest, and felt, faint as the touch of a feather against her ear, the flutter of Laura's heart. She began to rub the stiff limbs and call softly, her desperate fear, the fear she had kept in check till now, beginning to grow. The killer, or killers, of Shanker – did they know about the girl? Yes. She remembered Shanker saying that Stepan had been told to set light to the pyre by the man he was watching in the temple. She also remembered Shanker saying that he was afraid of the man and asking for help. Well, there was no help for Shanker now. But supposing Shanker's killer came to make sure that his orders had been obeyed? The thought made her frantic. She looked at Laura and went over to put her ear to Laura's heart. Again, faint as the ruffle of a bird's feathers in a wind she heard the heartbeat. Soon it would not matter if the killer came or not. The Nawab's girl would be dead in any case. Untempted now by any desire to let her die, Meeta began to plan, and as she planned she acted. First she collected all the dirty, matted blankets and rolled Laura into a shapeless bundle, securing each end of the roll with strips of cloth torn from a filthy bit of green muslin. In spite of her activities she was shuddering with cold, and finding Stepan's *poshteen* she put it on. Then she led the big horse closer to where Laura lay and began to tie a blanket on to his back, using the rope that had tethered him. She could not use the saddle if she were to take Laura in front of her, for the saddle was of the type that was used by the horsemen of the northern plains, with a high pommel and crupper. The horse stood patiently and finally she put the bit between his teeth, and fastening the check straps, let the reins drop on his neck. Everything was now ready. They could leave as soon as help came.

It was very cold and the river was louder it seemed. She peered round the edge of the rocks that stood between her and the rest of the shore. The curtain of smoke was thinning, soon it would have drifted away altogether. Where was Yar Khan? If Phuli had delivered her message he should be here. She saw from the lowering sun that several hours had gone. She could wait no longer. Something must have happened to Phuli, the flower seller, and Meeta did not care to think what that might be.

Chapter 22

Phuli the flower seller had hurried across the city toward the House on the Wall. She had almost reached the final turning when she saw four men coming fast, on foot, from the direction of the temple. By their dress they were monks from the north, an abbot and three of his followers from one of the lamissaries. But in such haste? Phuli was intrigued and suspicious. All the men and women who were members of the band known as the Sons of the Rose had been given full descriptions of Tovarish and Stepan. Stepan she had reported on that morning. This band of men hurrying away from the vicinity of the temple looked furtive and strange to her. The Ruler's orders had been clear. Every move the man Tovarish made was to be reported. Nothing and no-one was more important. She put down her basket about twenty yards from Janki's gate and began to run, silent in her felt boots. She caught up with the four men at the Gate of the Arabserai, and dropping to a walk went in behind them, entering the chaos of the crowded, noise-filled courtyard, and joining some women who were preparing to leave, rolling up their bedding, busy and in haste lest they should be late and the caravan would leave them behind. "At what time does the caravan go?" she asked one of the younger women who was sitting cross-legged on the ground, feeding her child, while the others ran about carrying bags and bundles to a central point. She shook her head, smiling down at the child at her breast.

"Eh! There is time, and time again! We do not leave till moonrise, and already these others run about like hens for no reason. Do you come with us?"

"Yea, if my man returns in time." Phuli invented a totally fictitious husband and sank down beside the woman and her baby, with an excuse for watching the crowds while she herself was inconspicuous. She had seen the men go into the stables. When they came out she almost missed them, for they were no longer dressed as monks led by their abbot. First, on a splendidly accoutered horse, came a man in a fur hat and richly trimmed woollen robes. He was attended by a servant almost as richly dressed, and two men in duffle robes and ear-covering bonnets, leading a laden mule. Rich Mongol traders on their way north, after a successful trading venture. They had come abreast of where Phuli was sitting and were about to go by when she saw, under the fur hat, the steel-blue eyes of the master. Without a word she left her companion and ran after the Mongol traders.

Outside the gate there was no sign of them, but she heard the ring of shod hooves on the cobbles of a street that turned down towards the North Gate. The street was empty; there were no dwelling houses here, *godowns* lined the street on both sides. She ran as a lapwing flies above the fields, head down, concentrating on nothing but speed. The street curved, she ran round a corner and straight into the arms of a man who was waiting for her. The three others waited a little further on.

With her own silk scarf they gagged her. They dragged her down a dark side lane, and there stopped.

The blue-eyed man, Tovarish, spoke. "Is this the girl?"

The man who held her nodded.

"She was standing at a door near where we came out of the temple. Then just as we went into the Arabserai she was behind us. When we came out, she followed us."

"Why?" Tovarish looked directly at her, and the man holding her loosened her gag. She answered in her own language, shaking her head, saying she knew nothing, her eyes wide and puzzled. She was startled when Tovarish answered her in her own Tibetan tongue.

"You were not following us. Then why do we see you everywhere?"

"I have never seen you before, lord," said Phuli and the fear on her face was not feigned. "I went to the Arabserai to be with my sister, she goes north tomorrow. As for the rest of what your man said, I do not understand Urdu so well. I sell flowers in this place, and do no harm. It grows dark, lord. Let me go."

Tovarish nodded slowly. "Yes. As you say, you should go. It does indeed grow dark. Narain, whether what you think is correct or not, we have all been seen now. She must go."

He spoke quickly. Phuli did not hear all he said, nor understand him. He turned his horse and rode away and she still thought that she was going to be released when Narain broke her neck as a man would snap the stem of a flower, and tossed her body into the open drain that ran down one side of the lane.

Outside Janki's house the basket of flowers stood, the blooms beginning to droop a little.

By the river, behind the rocks, Meeta was struggling to raise Laura's inert body up on to the horse. She could not help the rough handling she gave Laura. She had not the strength to lift her, and had to drag her, and push and pull her body into position. Finally Laura lay across the animal's withers, her head and arms drooping limply on one side, her legs and feet on the other. She lay face down, entirely rolled in the dirty blankets. It was the best that Meeta could do. Laura showed no more sign of life than the roll of cloth that she was disguised as. Meeta hoped that she still lived, but had no time to find out. She untied the second horse and knotted its rope halter on its neck, leaving it free to follow if it would. She dragged herself up behind Laura so that the reins came over Laura's body, and she could help to steady Laura if she showed signs of slipping.

She guided the horse out of the sheltered cove and on to the path beside the shore of the dead where the pyres winked red eyes in the rising wind. As she rode, several crows flew up in front of her like brown-black shadows, startling her with their raucous cries and making the horse toss his head and sidle nervously. She turned and saw the crows land again, and shuddered. The fires did not always burn everything.

The horse was cold and was pulling, anxious, after being hobbled and tethered so long, for swift movement, but she dared not let him out of a walk, fearing that both she and her burden would fall off.

At last they came to the ford. It was now grey evening, the sun had gone. The light tempered by the rising river mist was milky. She had to dismount and lead the horse over, stepping herself from one slippery black stone to another, steadying Laura with one hand while the animal slipped and floundered in the swift-flowing water.

Meeta knew that she was only just in time. If it had been any darker she would not have been able to cross. She heard the other horse splashing behind them, and then stepped from the last stone and felt sad beneath her feet. The horse was blowing and stamping beside her, the other horse still slipping about in mid-river. The water was shallow, only touching the horse's chest, but very swift. Running through a wider channel with fewer rocks it was quieter. She mounted again, crawling up onto the horse like a man scaling a difficult slope. As she gathered the reins, she heard a sound. It was distant, but coming closer, and unmistakable. It was the sound of a horse being ridden hard. She had no hope that it would be Yar Khan. Yar Khan's horse was unshod. This one was striking iron on the rocks of the rough path.

At first it seemed there was no hope. She was trapped, and the Nawab's girl, if she still lived, had lost all chance of continuing to do so. Then, as she despaired, all the efforts of the day, the fears and the griefs, seemed to come at her at once, and with them came rage, and a great and glorious courage.

Now it was almost dark. The river ran pale foam beside the black rocks, giving false reflections of trees and shadows that were not there as the evening came closer. Meeta caught the second horse as it splashed ashore and pulled it with her, riding on the sand until she was inland, and on grass. There she tethered both horses. She did nothing to the bundle that was Laura, there was so little time. She ran back to the river bank and began to cross the stones again, hurrying, unable to see black stones against black water except for the white foam that laced round them. The sound of the oncoming horse was loud in her ears, first on road, then splashing into the water.

267

By that time she was across and running like a blown shadow over the sands of the shore of the dead until she reached the pyre where Laura had lain. She did not know what she would do, but somehow this man must be prevented from finding Laura.

The fire still smouldered. The saddle cloths had burned to white ash, which showed as a little red fire leaped into life as the wind blew on the smouldering coals.

The man and the horse had come up. He dismounted and left his horse to stand, coming over to bend above the pyre. Meeta knew what he was doing. He was sniffing, trying to be sure that a body had burned down to that ash. But there was no smell of burning flesh on that pyre. The wind moaned in the thin trees behind her and the river rushed and roared around the rocks, and the flames of the pyre leapt up to illuminate the intent face of the man bending over the pyre, his dilated nostrils, his frown. He picked up a smouldering stick and blew on it. The wind helped him and in moments he had a flaring torch, and Meeta drew back into the deep shadows behind the rocks. He went round to where she had spent the afternoon and looked at Stepan's scattered belongings and the sand churned up by two horses' trampling feet. Then he went back to his horse and mounted, and began to ride slowly along the path, bending over to look at the ground, the torch throwing a clear light for him. Meeta knew he was following her tracks.

If he continued to the ford and crossed it, as he obviously would, he would follow her tracks to where Laura lay helpless on the horse. This must somehow be prevented. Meeta's prayer had no words. It was as if her whole being reached out, crying for help, and, as if she were being answered, a plan presented itself to her, whole and perfect, so perfect and so easy that it was as if she were being told what to do.

Scudding down the shore, close to the river's edge, she ran to reach the ford before the man riding slowly on the longer way of the path. She entered the river beside the stones of the ford. The river came to her chest and the current was strong. Grasping with wet hands from stone to stone she felt her way until she reckoned that she was in the centre of the river where the water ran fastest. She heard the horse and rider arrive and splash into the water behind her, heard the man urging his horse on, and then heard him curse as he dismounted and began for the second time to cross the stones. Then she knelt, the water rising to her chin. She snatched off her felt cap, and her round black head, the wet hair plastered to the skull, was a stone among the other stones. She thrust the cap into her belt and pulled out the long sharp knife she had taken from Shanker's box.

The man was hurrying, pulling at his horse, holding his torch high. The horse was not only disliking the river, he was frightened of the flaming torch. As the man stepped from stone to stone, his attention and his eyes were divided between his slipping feet and his plunging animal. He might well have put his foot on Meeta's black head, but as he came to the stone beside which she knelt, the wild-eyed horse reared, and the man missed his footing. Meeta did not have to seize his leg above the cuffed felt boot as she had planned. He fell, his feet flying up in front of him. He was a big man, and he fell hard, in a sitting position. Meeta, her dagger gripped in both fists, saw the torch falling, shining on a darker flood in the dark water. He had fallen on the dagger which entered his body between his legs, going deeply into his groin where an artery pulsed. He lay face down in the water, kicking, while his terrified horse reared and kicked behind him, and then, freed, it turned and went back the way it had come, splashng back to the shore of the dead and galloping into darkness.

Meeta retrieved her knife and pushed the body free of the fording stone against which it now lay. The current took it and it vanished down river, going as the logs went in the spring when the snow melted.

Sick and shivering, her hands gummy with blood, Meeta went back to the place where she had tied her horses. She mounted from a tree stump and this time she led the second horse. Laura lay still and cold across her horse. Meeta's hands were cold, but she shrank away when she touched Laura's flesh to see how she was. Laura was like ice. "Dead then," thought Meeta, "dead and finished, and all I have done is to be sure that the crows do not pick among her bones."

Now she rode fast. She seemed to have lost all fear. She rode up to the Gate of Mourning and clattered through it so fast that the guards had no time to stop her; all they saw was a wild-haired boy and two horses coming back late from the shore of the dead. Meeta did not risk the dark back lanes. She rode to the Main Gate, and called to the man on duty to bring out Zaman Beg.

"Who calls?" The guard eyed the ragamuffin boy with all his goods bundled in front of him on a superb horse, and leading another.

"I, Gulab Beg, his brother." The guard raised incredulous eyebrows, but Zaman Beg was a man from the northern valleys. This could be his brother, the horses were good. In any case, Zaman Beg was not a man to trifle with. If this boy were not his brother then Zaman Beg would soon deal with him. He called, and Zaman Beg came out, going straight to the boy on the horse. He had no brother, but the combination of Gulab, meaning Rose, and brother could mean a message, and an important one. It was always a signal to the Ruler's élite band of watchers.

Zaman Beg had been often to the House on the Wall. He had seen Meeta and had been among those who admired her polished delicate attraction after Janki had trained her. He did not now recognise her. He looked up into the dirty exhausted face of a young boy, and heard him say his name.

"Zaman Beg –"

"Well?"

"I have goods for Janki, and news. These are precious goods. My name is Gulab Beg, I am your brother, a son of the Rose. Help me."

Zaman Beg lifted up his voice, the other guard was close.

"Wah, youngling! You have grown, and how dirty! I did not know you. How is our mother? Well, we will talk later. Come with me. I have lodgings nearby." He took the rope halter of the other horse and mounted, leading the way down the twisting lane that led to the House on the Wall. Meeta, her hand free to steady Laura's body, sighed deeply. Dead or alive, she had brought the girl in.

The day in the House on the Wall had been very long after Meeta left. Janki sat idle, her hands opening and closing on nothing, her eyes watching the sun move on the balcony and the pigeons flying in and out of their circular house. Yar Khan groomed his horse, polished the harness, cleaned his rifle, and then stamped up to Janki's balcony.

"How much longer do we wait? She has been gone too long. I have looked to that creature's binding and he is still asleep, the gag tight in his mouth. The chain and the bolt are both on his door. He can do you no harm, so do not be afraid."

"I am not afraid of him! I am afraid of what foolishness you may do. Yar Khan, if you go close to that temple you could cause great suspicion. What would a Moslem soldier do riding around a Hindu temple? Come, Yar Khan. Do you think it is easy for me to wait? Stay and bear it with me."

"Janki, I cannot stay here, where the walls are high and there is no news. I cannot. I will ride as far as the House of Paradise only. I must do something."

Janki nodded, knowing exactly why he could not stay. She sighed. It seemed a long time ago since she had planned so carefully that he would notice Meeta, desire her, and be the first man to take her – and now here he was, half mad with worry over Meeta, and the gods alone knew where Meeta was or what she was doing. Janki closed the gate after Yar Khan had ridden out, and heard the sound of his horse grow faint, and then there was nothing to listen to but the sound of the pigeons strutting on the balcony railing. The pigeons! She had four special birds living lives of secluded luxury, Dak pigeons, to be kept in case Faridkote was attacked so that help could be called from Lambagh. Where had her mind been? This was big trouble, news that the Ruler must hear.

Janki sat down and took a block of black ink and a fine-pointed brush, moistened the brush and the ink and began to write beautiful curving characters on a tiny strip of rice paper. She could write so little; after she had said that Stepan was taken, what more could she say? A feeling of disaster was on her, she was afraid. She put a cry for help into her writing. "The news is small but bad. We know very little, and the messenger has not returned from the temple. Our lives are yours, Lord of the Hills, but send us help."

Janki had never asked for help in her life. She looked questioningly down at the paper and almost tore it up. Then she made her mind firm, and rolled the paper small and fitted it into the cylinder. She sealed each end of the cylinder with black wax, soft and malleable, and then went out onto her balcony and climbed up the thin ladder, her strong, henna-painted feet firm on each rung, and reached up to open the closed door of one cell. The other birds were so tame that they buffeted about her hands with their soft bodies. She took out the messenger, feeling its heart fast against her fingers. She fitted the cylinder into its holder on the bird's leg, threw the feathery handful into the air and watched until it was beyond her sight. There. For good or ill, she had sent for help. She felt a little ease in her mind, and went down to the lower room.

The girls came, her two best girls who had been trained from childhood. They went to their rooms chattering to paint their faces and dress each other's hair, and prepare for the night. Janki too took time to wash her face and paint her eyes, and comb and twist her hair into its high coil, but every minute she was listening, waiting. Meeta had been gone all day. It began to seem certain to Janki that Meeta would not come back. She fanned the charcoal stove into glowing life, set out the tea kettle and the glasses in little silver filigree holders. This was for the first part of the evening, for the men who came to sit and talk. The wine in silver flasks and the hammered silver goblets were arranged, and the room, glowing warmly, welcoming and peaceful, was ready.

It was after sunset. The men would be coming soon in ones or twos, the talkers, the lonely who needed an ear, and then later the strong men, laughing, asking for wine and music and the girls and soft beds. The evening would be so ordinary, so normal!

But there was nothing normal in the way that Janki sat and

listened, her eyes looking at nothing, so deep in thought that Dina, coming in with a willow basket, had to speak to her twice.

"Eh, Janki! See, these garlands are withered! Why were they left outside the gate in the sun all day?"

Janki came back to the warm, scented room, and to Dina, who was holding a limp garland in one hand, the flat willow basket balanced between her hip and the other hand.

The basket.

"Where did you get that basket?" Janki was staring at it as if it were a basket of snakes.

"It was a little, small way from the gate. I could see no fresh garlands so went out to look for Phuli, thinking she might be late. But she must have put the basket down and gone. Perhaps she knocked, unheard –" Dina stopped speaking. Janki's eyes were wide with horror.

"Janki! Akam, what is it? Speak to me, tell me. What has happened here today?"

Dina and Shanti too were both skilled watchers and news-gatherers. Dina called to Shanti, and they knelt beside Janki and listened to her story of the day's events. Phuli's worth as a message-carrier was great. The deserted basket, left outside a place of safety, was frightening. Fear came into the warm room and took away colour and comfort. Dina slowly put down her withered garland, the orange petals scattering round her feet.

"Should we not close the small door and bar the gate tonight?"

Janki set firm lips. "No. The House closed would be something to make people ask questions. If there are horses brought in tonight, the stable at the end is locked and must not be opened."

The knocking on the outside gate sent them all running. But it was Yar Khan and his horse and anxious questions. He had no news. When he heard about Phuli's basket he was on his feet again at once.

"Enough. I go into that temple and take it to pieces, stone by stone and priest by priest until I find Meeta."

"Be still, Yar Khan. You cannot do that. Tomorrow we should have word from Lambagh."

"Tomorrow? Have you run mad, Janki? Rabindra will only arrive in Lambagh tomorrow with the news of Stepan's arrival. Will he fly back with the Ruler in his mouth? Let me go."

"Yar Khan, I sent a pigeon three hours before sunset. I asked for help, and said that the lack of news was strange and bad."

The knocking on the gate was peremptory. There was a trampling of horses in the lane outside the gate. With smiling, painted, desperate eyes, Janki went out to let her customers in.

The door in the wall opened to Zaman's knock, and both horses went in. Yar Khan and Janki, without news since that morning, were waiting. Zaman Beg dismounted as Janki came up to him.

"The boy says he has important news and precious goods for you — so I brought him. He has the words."

Boy? Janki looked at the dirty little tattered figure perched on the big horse that Yar Khan was recognising as Usbeg's horse. Then Meeta slid down and told her story, and as they listened they were carrying Laura's body into light and warmth and unwrapping it. Janki looked once at the stiffening body, bent in the position in which it had been carried for so long, then took a clean sheet and wrapped Laura in it, and took her up the winding stair. Meeta watched her go, her heart very sore. She looked at Yar Khan, ready to leave, and her lost, weary eyes raised to his had so much sorrow in them that he went over and put his arms round her.

"All for nothing," said Meeta, the bright room whirling round her. "All for nothing. I would have saved his girl for him. But at least the crows did not get those blue jewels that were her eyes. I saved her from the crows."

The room tilted, the whole world shifted, and only the strong arms holding her were real. Meeta lost hold of even that reality. Her head fell back and she had no more sorrow to endure. Yar Kahn held her, and looked at her dirty little face with the dark circles of exhaustion printed under the closed eyes, and the short upper lip caught up so that Meeta's mouth seemed to be about to speak, even though she was unconscious. He lifted her and put her down near the charcoal stove, but no-one had any time for her. One of the other girls, her face painted, her hair plaited with flowers ready for her evening duties, came running to put bricks to heat beside the stove. Janki was upstairs. Zaman Beg was outside dealing with the horses, and he, Yar Khan, should go, for one thing had come clearly through Meeta's message. The man Tovarish was loose, and had probably left the city. But Meeta, lying like the dead beside the stove – if she were left like that she *would* die; her robes were heavy with water, her hands frozen to the touch.

Yar Khan unbuckled his sword and picked Meeta up. He carried her across the room, and kicking the curtain aside with his foot, went into one of the small rooms. He put Meeta down on the string bed against the wall, turned up the oil lamp and undressed her, taking the filthy felted robes from her body without thinking of anything but the need to get her warm. He saw the blood on the upper robe and examined her for wounds but there were none, though her hands were caked, the fingers stuck together with dried blood. Yar Khan brought water and a cloth and sponged the little body and the hands and the dirty bony face, pushing the damp hair back from the childishly rounded forehead.

The skin of her body was as smooth as silk under his hands, her little breasts, still only half grown, were high and tight and reminded him of the golden-skinned apples he had picked from his father's trees when he was a boy in Lambagh Valley. He sat back suddenly, the towel in his hands forgotten as he looked down at her, and saw her as he had not before. Her eyebrows, fine and silky, were a little drawn together as if she puzzled over a problem. Her eyelids were dark with the shadows of fatigue and her lashes were long and black against the half moons of utter exhaustion. He found that he was leaning closer, longing to put his mouth over hers and waken her. Desire was heavy in him, and as if, wherever her mind had gone, she felt something, she moved and murmured. Yar Khan was a young man who had taken many women. Now for the first time in his life he stood back from something he wanted, and picking up a *rezai*, he covered Meeta.

The heavy lids lifted and she looked up at him, her frown deepening. Then she smiled and said in a drowsy, broken little voice, "Janki *said* there would be a man, a tall young man who would make me forget everything. Will it be you, Yar Khan?"

"And if it is I?"

"If it is you, it will not be as hard as I feared. Not so strange – a friend to learn from."

It was plain that she had forgotten the day's events. She was almost asleep still. Even as he bent over her again, her eyes closed. She slept, and Yar Khan put a gentle finger on the lifted upper lip, and closed it.

"It will be I, Meeta. Sweeter than wine will our kisses be. A friend, a teacher? I shall be your lover." Yar Khan made it a promise, this longing of his, as he looked down at the sleeping girl. The voice calling him from the courtyard was insistent. He looked a moment longer, and then hurried out.

Zaman Beg was calling, consternation in his voice.

"Yar Khan! He has gone!"

"What?" Yar Khan needed no name. He knew who had gone, and cursed himself for not checking. No need to look at the open door of the last stable. The room was empty.

"How? What happened?" He asked the question automatically, but there were the shards of a broken *chatty*, the ragged ends of slashed rope, bloody and fraying, and high up, the small window torn from its frame. He had underestimated Stepan's giant strength.

Zaman Beg was almost weeping.

"I opened the door because there was no sound and I imagined him dead. Dead! He has gone, alive and well."

"And we do not know how long he has been gone. Now he ranges the city a man-eater. Where? We can guard this house tonight, but in the morning they go, the women, all of them, to the House of Paradise. At least there they can be guarded. For now, bar the gate, and put out the lanterns outside the

276

door and the gate. The House is closed, no strangers enter here tonight."

A hand fumbled at the catch of the small door used by customers who knew their way. Yar Khan drew his sword, and Zaman Beg had a silver-chased pistol in his hand as Yar Khan opened the door.

At first it seemed there was no-one there, and then a man moved forward from the shadows of the lane.

It seemed to Yar Khan and Zaman Beg, both brave young men not given to imagination, that the man was darkness itself in human form. He was almost naked, and the ash smeared on his dark skin was like the bloom on a peach.

"Who are you?"

"My name is Nothing. I am a beggar of the gods." He held a begging bowl in one hand and his crutched stick was under his arm. He was a travelling fakir, a holy man. Yar Khan remembered seeing him about the city. But surely this was no time to come begging! He had barely formed the thought when the man, his eyes almost phosphorescent in his dark face, said calmly, "I do not come for alms. I bring news. Phuli is dead. Do not look for her coming. She lies with her neck broken in a drain behind the Arabserai. The men who killed her have left the city, three of them going out by the Main Gate. The fourth left by the Gate of Mourning."

It seemed that apart from Meeta's safe return there was no good news on this dark night, with the coming winter sending harbingers of fog to wreathe about the lanterns over the door and blot out the stars.

The fakir's eyes turned to the half-open door of the last stable.

"I bring you news of him too." His voice was deep and seemed to echo, as if it came from some place enclosed. Zaman Beg put up his hand and held the tiny silver amulet that hung on a black cord round his neck. There was a half-smile on the Fakir's face.

"What news of the big man?" Yar Khan was afraid too; he did not care for holy men who read his thoughts.

"Bad news. He is free. He chose to hide in the temple. He

is evil, but we do not take life. However –" The fakir paused, and began to walk towards the house.

Yar Khan had had enough. He leapt across the courtyard, his hand out, but the fakir shook his head.

"Touch me not, brother of war. I do what you cannot do. I promise you that not one limb of that monster shall rest in its socket."

"You say you cannot kill. Tell us where he is. Ay – you say we are brothers of war. Then tell us!"

"He is where you cannot touch him. Leave him to the gods – and to Phuli's friends. I go to give news of her death – stand back from me, brother. Remember me, when you next see a beggar, and give alms."

He was climbing as he spoke, a shadow among shadows, up the ladder to the pigeon loft, where the sleepy inhabitants stirred and complained and rose in terror into the dark sky, wings clapping, a minor thunderstorm of feathered fear. Then the shadow that was the fakir vanished, and Yar Khan heard the smack of his bare feet on roofs, and a tapping on shutters, and the first few whispered words, "Phuli is dead – killed by a monster!" After that there was only the sound of running feet, growing fainter, and then gone.

"But the big one did not kill Phuli?" said Zaman Beg. Yar Khan shook his head. "No. But his friends killed Shanker, and Phuli, and he would have killed if he could. Let be. Tomorrow the women go to the House of Paradise. Now we guard this place until morning."

Stepan had got into the temple easily enough. He found his way to the cell where he had spoken with Tovarish, but no-one answered his knocking. He had hidden then, slipping from shadow to shadow as it grew dark and lamps were lit about the temple precincts. His head ached, and he needed Tovarish to direct him. He had always obeyed Tovarish slavishly, with the obedience of the serf who recognised a master. At Tovarish's bidding he had taken service with the Nawab of Pakodi but he had made mistakes, killing when he did not have to, and then killing again and running away. He had wanted to kill the young man they had kidnapped, but had been prevented. Then he had been sent, after all, to take his life. He had gone gladly, following, watching and waiting for the chance to do the one thing he did well – murder. He had lived miserably among the rocks and valleys, the cold night winds and the high peaks. It had been terrible for him, that mountain country. He had been born on the flat plains of Tartary, where the grasses blew like the manes and tails of the horses he loved. He bore all the trials of the high valleys because he had been ordered there. He had killed the wrong man, and for the first time in his life had performed an action without an order, thinking to win praise. Now, with a sore head and a confused brain, he looked for his master, knowing there was something he must do, but unable to remember what it was. He went back to Tovarish's cell and sat there in darkness, waiting.

Outside through various houses in the city went the news. Phuli was dead, the little flower seller; her people gathered, passing the word from one to another, and the fakir returned to the temple.

An hour before dawn, two priests found Stepan slumped in uneasy sleep beside the empty cell. They told him Tovarish had gone, and that he must leave the temple. Like a bull tormented by flies he looked from one to the other, and started for the main gate. No, they said, not that way. That was shut at night. They would show him the way; he might find his friends if he went the way they would show him.

They led him down a flight of steps into a dark passage. All along the passages were alcoves, in which stood innumerable gods. No god or goddess seemed to have been forgotten in this multitude of altars, on which the flames bent sideways in the wind of Stepan's hurry as he followed his guides. They disturbed a host of little bats which swooped and squeaked about Stepan's head, little shadows given voice and substance. There was the creaking reluctant sound of a door that had not been opened for a long time, a breath of sweet cool air, free of the heavy scent of incense, and Stepan found

279

himself standing in a narrow lane, with the big door through which he had come closing firmly behind him.

It was just before dawn, and the sky was silver. The crowd that blocked both ends of the lane were silent. They did not speak, but like an incoming tide they began to move, feet quiet on the cobbles, quiet, quiet, determined, overwhelming.

Chapter 23

For three days Robert and Ayub travelled down to the plains, slowly searching and questioning, listening to the talk round camp fires at night, taking side roads to speak with villagers known to Ayub Khan, and finding nothing, hearing nothing.

Robert travelled like a man driven by the wind. If he could have done he would have gone straight to Safed. It was Ayub Khan who persuaded him to travel more slowly. "If we find her on the road, we save her sooner." It was enough. Robert slowed his pace, redoubled his watching and questioning.

Turning away from the fire in a camping site, he said to Ayub Khan through tight lips,

"Gold speaks loudly in these parts. Someone is bribing these people. That last man was lying. I swear he has seen something or heard something. Let us wait and take him when he comes away from the fire, and try another form of persuasion."

"Torture? Eh, Boy, have you forgotten Bombay?"

"No, I have remembered. To find my girl I could see a thousand men tortured, and smile. Would you not do the same for your leopardess?"

"Indeed, no man knows what he will do if a certain string is pulled. Yes, I could torture for my woman."

"Yes. I thought torture would sicken me. But to save Laura a moment's pain or fear I could take a man apart slowly, with my own hands, and hear him scream."

Ayub Khan tightened his lips. Then he said very quietly, "I too. Alas for those who love."

Three days' journey from where Robert and Ayub Khan were camped, a camel caravan was on the move. Travelling slowly, avoided by horsemen and feared by almost everyone, the camel train was making its way north with empty bags, deliveries of various kinds completed in the southern towns and in the big sea ports. Now they carried small packets of various drugs, some smuggled gold, and one camel was laden with rice. No one interfered with them, these camel drivers; they were people who moved swiftly and quietly up and down the roads of India, carrying with them an atmosphere of timeless secret trade, of things known and understood only by them. They were left in peace.

The tall woman, muffled to the eyes, stalked beside the camels, her eyes all that showed of her face. Strange, light eyes that moved restlessly, seeking. Other travellers moved aside, and some put a hand up to touch the amulets that hung at their necks. The woman saw everything, and smiled behind the cloth that covered her mouth. She had three tall men with her, leading the camels. They moved through the hot day and as the crows began to fly back to their roosts in the short twilight of the cooling evening they came to a small *parao*, and choosing a place well away from the other travellers, made a fire and began to cook their evening meal. The three men went about the camp, their eyes and ears busy. The woman guarded the fire, moving about the outskirts of the parao to gather sticks to augment the handful of dried dung that was glowing under her cooking pot. Her face was unveiled but she was wrapped in such cold aloof dignity that no-one stared at her. Her eyes were quick to see the smallest, driest twigs, and she stooped and gathered them and stood, moving closer and closer round the fires. She gathered an armful of suitable dry tinder under a wide spreading neem, where the darkness of the night seemed to have already gathered round the fire that burned in the shelter of the tree. The men at this fire had no woman with them; they were dealing with their own food, and had lit a large fire, which reflected brightly on their faces and their rich clothing. Embroidered waistcoats, large turbans, full white trousers – Punjabi's from the big cities of the north, Lahore, Jullunder, Meerut, not horse traders, but men of substance. One, sitting close to the fire, was twisting a ring on his finger, staring into the flames as if he saw something there that he did not like. The woman pressed closer, and trod on a dry branch, which snapped loudly, louder than the crackling of the fire beside which the man sat alone. He looked up with a start, straight into her eyes. She was a brave woman, but her heart beat faster as she met that straight, cold look. Strange eyes, like holes in his face, through which she imagined that she could see ice, the ice that forms over the rivers of the high far mountains. She saw something else in his eyes, and the woman repressed a shudder, continuing on her twig-gathering way, only pausing long enough to give him the conventional greeting of the people of her country.

"May you never be tired."

He did not reply, merely continued to look at her until she moved away, and the suspicion that had made her go so close became a certainty. This was not a man of the country to which he appeared to belong. He was therefore disguised. She took her twigs back to her fire, and looked into her pot of savoury stew, and settled down to wait until her three companions returned. When they came back she served their food, a good portion of the stew put on to thick chapattis, cold and tough, but an excellent substitute for plates. They carried very little water for washing, what they had was for drinking, and precious. While the men ate, she retired a little distance from them and sat, with her back turned to them, as was correct, watching the other camp fires with disinterested eyes. As soon as the men had eaten she brought a little water to pour over their hands, and then sat down to eat her own food. While she ate, her shoulder turned to the men and the rest of the camp, she listened to the three men, her brothers, as they told her of the news they had gleaned from the various camp fires they had visited. Any of this news might be worth selling further north. They spent their time gathering news, the people of the camel trains.

The woman had seen her prey. When her brothers had eaten they rolled themselves in thick, quilted *rezais* and slept. But she built up her fire and sat close to it, so that the light played on her fine features and on her long tilted eyes. Her loose tunic was open at the neck, and the rosy light spilled over her face, and down her strong throat into the deep cleft of her breasts. Her headcloth had fallen back a little and now she took it off altogether, and loosened her hair from its long light plait, beginning to comb it out with slow stroking movements of the long fingered hands that were remarkably beautiful in spite of the hard work they did. Her comb was silver, studded with turquoise, and she wore heavy silver ear-rings, also ornamented with the greeny blue stones. She sat in the firelight and combed her hair, and sang softly to herself about a far country of green valleys and deep lakes, and a man who would give her his heart to wear round her throat. Beneath her long lashes she looked at the shadows under the neem tree and thought she saw movement there, and stretched herself a little, the firelight bathing her in warm colour, from her shining black head to the toes of her arched foot that thrust out from under her loose black trousers. All her clothes were black, and they served to underline the brilliant colour of her skin, and her slanting grey eyes, and her scarlet mouth. She sang, and stretched, and combed her hair, moving like a sleepy black cat in the light of her fire. She had seen a look in the strange eyes of the man who had sat beside the fire under the neem tree, and like the cat she so much resembled, she waited, watching her prey, in no hurry, but supremely sure of herself.

A step sounded behind her. She turned and looked up into the pale eyes. She saw the urgent question in those eyes, the question she had known she would see, and rising slowly, her black hair loose on her shoulders, she walked away from the firelight and into deeper shadows beneath the trees beyond the *parao*.

Towards dawn it grew cold. The woman sat up and drew her tunic over her, and the man beside her stirred and woke. Without a word he pulled the cloth from her, and threw it aside, and began to make love to her again. She had never had a European before, and found his love-making and the effect it had on him very strange. He kissed her a great deal, which was unusual to her, but he took very little trouble to satisfy her, being more interested in his own pleasure. She did not care. Her mind was on more important things. He said things in a language she could not understand, and she had to put her hand over his mouth at the last for he was noisy. When he had finished, she rolled him aside, with a determined hand. It would be light soon. She dressed herself without haste while he watched her, and then stood, magnificent in the growing light, plaiting her hair into a long thick rope before bending over him with her hand held out. For the first time he showed discomfort, opening an empty hand to her, but she smiled as if it was of no moment, and then, with a swift movement, took his hand and pulled off the ring he wore. For a moment he resisted, and then suddenly smiled and shrugged, and she took the ring and put it on her second finger, admiring the green stone that was already beginning to burn in the growing light. She made him a sweeping salutation that was mocking in its respect, and then turned to leave him, walking away without a backward look. Throughout the night he had not heard her speak.

The men were waiting for her beside the ashes of the dead fire. They had charcoal burning in a small clay stove, and had the *chaikhalta*, the embroidered tea bag, open, and a kettle of water steaming on the stove. While they drank their scalding hot tea she showed them the ring.

"This ring must be known, it is a ring from a King's treasure, not a ring for a Punjabi trader. We strike camp and go. There is no need to follow him. They go to Safed, to a house there. In the heat of love he talks, that one. His appetite is great, and he told me how to get into the house in Safed tonight, so that he can satisfy himself again. But I do not like his smile. He gave me the ring too easily. I think that if I were fool enough to join him tonight, as he thinks I will, he would take the ring back and leave me dead. I am sure we will find some one looking for this ring."

As she talked, her voice low, she had been preparing to leave. The few things that they had removed from one of the laden camels were replaced, the camels unfolded themselves reluctantly and silently on the thick dust at the edge of the road and the caravan moved off, the woman, her headcloth pulled close across her face leaving only her eyes free of the thick folds, walking at the head of the leading camel, its headrope in her hand. As she walked she sang softly, plaintively, the song she had been singing the night before. The hand that held the rope was the hand on which the great emerald in the ring she had taken from her companion of the night gleamed and burned in the early sunshine.

Just before lamplighting on the third day, Robert and Ayub rode round a corner and met a string of camels. The horses were tired, but not tired enough to receive the impact of these long-legged, head-bobbing shadows who bubbled at them from sneering lips. When the pandemonium had died down, and the camels were pasing on one side of the tree-lined road while Ayub Khan and Robert Reid held their dancing beasts steady on the other, Robert, who was watching the woman who swayed on the neck of the leading camel, suddenly exclaimed,

"Ayub! Look there! That woman – the woman riding the first camel. She has my ring on her finger!"

"*What* – it is not possible! Come."

They raced down the road after the camels, applying stick and spur to keep their horses from bolting altogether.

The camel train stopped reluctantly, and Robert leapt off his horse and standing beside the camel looked up into the face of the grey-eyed woman sitting easily on the beast's back. She held a thick, short bamboo pole in one hand, and the rope that led to the camel's nose halter in the other. On the index finger of the hand that grasped the rope glowed the green fire of the Peacock ring.

"May you never be tired," she said composedly.

"May you live long! Tell me, woman, the ring you wear – I have seen it before."

"You have?" The woman held her hand out, turning it so that the ring flashed wickedly, and the three men with her came back and stood close, their eyes on her. Robert knew that they were waiting for a signal from her, and that when she gave it he would either be attacked immediately or they would return to their posts at the heads of the other camels. Ayub Khan sat his restive horse and could do nothing but watch; if Robert was attacked he could try to shoot, but a sudden move from him now would start the ruckus.

Robert's eyes were steady. He looked again at the ring, and said to the listening woman, who watched him as closely as he watched her, "That ring was given to my mother by the Ruler of Lambagh. She gave it to me shortly before she died. It was to be a betrothal gift for my bride. But it was taken from me by a band of men who kidnapped me. I have been looking for those men."

"Are they not my brothers – or my husband and his brothers? You do not fear to tell a stranger on the road the story of your ring?"

"No. I do not fear to tell you my story."

"You see and recognise the ring. You see my face. The police *thana* in Sanjur is only four hours' swift riding from here. They would be glad to hear the story of your ring."

"I do no swift riding tonight. The horses are tired from my search."

"All for a ring, you search for these men? Your mother's ring has such value for you?"

Ayub Khan shifted in his saddle, and spoke for the first time.

"We search for the woman of his house, and the men who took her."

The woman put her hand to her head and peered under it to see where Ayub sat on his horse in the shadows. Her brothers stepped back, and Ayub Khan relaxed his grip on the butt of his pistol.

"May you never be tired," said the woman, and dropping the rope she held, tapped the camel sharply about the head until, grumbling and grunting, it folded its legs beneath it, swaying first forwards and then back, until it was seated on the ground. The woman slid easily from her perch on its back and stepped up to Ayub.

"The ring is worth much?"

"But not as much as news of the woman I spoke of."

287

"I have no news. There was no woman with them."

Robert groaned, like a man who has been dealt a severe wound. "But the man who had the ring – he was a big man?"

"Nay. He was of medium height. There was only one *feringhi*. The others were from the south, from Sagpur. One I have seen before, he comes and goes often. The man who had the ring was very angry. Some plan had miscarried, and at least two of their party are missing. One was sent to look for the girl. He did not return, and the others blamed the stupidity of the big man. They left from Faridkote, the three men and a servant."

Ayub Khan leaned forward. "Had they the girl with them when they left Faridkote?" He held up his purse, and she smiled.

"No. For they were complaining of time lost, waiting for news of the girl." Ayub tossed her the purse and she tucked it away in her waist belt without looking. Her eyes were on Robert.

"Ho, young lion! Do you know the Mahal on the lake and the man who lives there?"

"How not? He is my grandfather."

"How this one pours his life-blood into the hands of strangers! How do you know that I and my menfolk here will not take you and sell you to that band about whom you ask questions? I think they would give us much gold!"

Ayub Khan answered her.

"We know that you would not sell us, Woman of the Hills. How did you come to join a camel train, and who are these men you call brothers?"

"You ask many questions. I joined the camel train years ago when my man was killed in a border skirmish and I was taken, so had no choice. I like the life now, I could not return to the quiet valleys and the high hills. I see the life of Hind, from the south to the north and back. I hear everything before it happens." She turned back to Robert.

"I saw your girl when she first came to Hind. I saw her riding the Great Road towards the hills. If you wish for news ask us of the camel trains – if you have gold."

"We have gold. Tell us where the girl is!"

"I will tell you what I think. She is in Faridkote. Go to the House in the Wall, to Janki." She saw surprise on Ayub's face and laughed.

"Oh, I know Janki, and she knows me. I keep my tongue quiet, and I watch. I have a good life. But sometimes – sometimes I remember the hills and the cold breath of the snows beyond the black hills, and I hear the eagle scream, hunting the skies for food. I remember these things and for a little time I am sick for the old days. These last few days I have remembered many things. I saw that ring. I had seen it before on Kassim Khan's hand when I played outside my mother's house in Lambagh. So when I saw it on another hand I was interested." She paused, and Ayub Khan, watching her face, leaned forward.

"Woman of the Hills, you were right to be interested."

"Yes. If I had an allegiance to any place, it would be to Lambagh, and if I had an allegiance to any person, it would be to the Ruler."

"Yes. And?"

"I would know my enemy then, and I would not look north. The enemy in the north is still playing a game. The enemy for me to fear – *if* I had an allegiance – is in the south, as always." She turned her strong clear gaze on Ayub Khan. After a minute she said, "I tell you what you already know?"

"You give certainty where there was suspicion. Woman of the Hills, be our eyes and our ears as you travel and you will be rich."

"And hang gold in my ears and sit on a silk cushion? Nay, that life is not for me. I am my own mistress, freedom is my companion. For the sake of my childhood and my memories I have told you some things. Look in Faridkote for news of the girl. If she is there, Janki will know. *I* know that your girl is not on the roads between here and the south. As for the man from whom I took this ring, he goes to Safed to the House of the Pundit to meet the one who pays him to trouble your borders and discredit Kassim Khan. Tell your English friends that."

"You know a great deal. Some of your knowledge is dangerous."

"You think I will wake with a slit throat one day? Perhaps. But until then, I travel the roads and I see and hear everything and sell goods to the ones who pay me. Not always do I sell for gold." She turned then to Robert, standing in the dust beside his restless horse.

"I wish you well in your search, son of Muna."

"How do you know me?"

"As I know many things. Here, take your ring."

"I had thought to leave it on your hand as payment."

"Your *mother*'s ring?"

"I said before – the ring is not worth as much as the news of my girl."

"I strike no bargains with your mother's son! The Peacock ring belongs on your hand until you give it to the woman of your choice. Take it." It had become very dark. The ring in the darkness had no glitter or gleam, it was only a green stone, cold to the touch. Robert took it, and slid it on to his finger, and turned to the woman beside him who stood as tall as he. She held his horse's bridle as he mounted.

"You who know my mother's name have not told me yours."

"I? I have forgotten my name. I am the woman of the camel train, the woman from the hills, the Pahareen. I have neither mother nor father to remember my name, nor husband to find a new one for me in the night. I go free. But if one should need me, the camel trains will carry a message, and the name Pahareen will bring me. Go laughing, son of Muna, go in hope."

Robert dismounted and handed the reins of his horse to Ayub.

"Make no farewell speeches to me. I go nowhere with joy until I have travelled a little distance with you, Pahareen. Will you lead me to the man from whom you took my ring?"

The woman looked at the grim young face, the bunched muscles at the angle of his jaw, the hard eyes under the straight black line of his frown.

290

"Eh, lord. You think to kill him? Cover your eyes when you look at him or you will never come within sword's length. Even a friend would run from that face!"

Ayub, listening, leaned from his saddle to put his hand on Robert's arm. "Boy, leave it! Did you not hear what she said? We can find your girl first and then, knowing her safe, we will go to the Colonel Sahib and with troops go seek out Tovarish."

Robert turned his head, and Ayub took his hand away quickly. The cold eyes that looked at him were the eyes of a killer. Ayub remembered the way men of the Lambagh family fought and was again amazed at the likeness Robert showed to Kassim Khan in all his moods. "Lord, I ask your pardon, but if we are to go after this man without aid –"

As Ayub spoke the hard glare left Robert's eyes.

"Ayub, my friend. Forgive me. I was uncivil. There is no need for much explanation. I go to kill my enemy. The man has haunted my every step since I arrived in India. Now he has caused fear – at the very least, fear – to the woman of my heart. Would you have me turn my back? Enough. We waste time." He turned to the watching woman.

"You will help me, Pahareen?"

She made him a sweeping obeisance. "Lord, my life for yours! I will take you with us, for you will travel in safety thus. Your quarry will be close to Safed now, but I can take you by short ways and a forced march. You must dress as we do." She walked over to a kneeling camel and, measuring Robert with her eyes, took out a bundle of clothing. She chose a pair of black trousers and a black *kurta*, a long loose shirt. She gave Robert the clothes, adding a black quilted waistcoat and a length of black cloth for his turban. Robert went to the side of the road and when he came back he looked exactly like the other *surwans*, the camel drivers, dressed in dusty black, tall, silent and dangerous.

He put his discarded clothing into his saddlebag. "Ayub, you go to Faridkote and see Janki. Find Laura for me and tell her I am coming."

Ayub did not argue. He watched them go, vanishing

silently into the deepening shadows of the evening, and then he mounted and rode back the way he had come, leading Robert's horse. He did not ride for Faridkote and the hills. He rode as fast as he could, encumbered by the led horse, for Madore. On the road he hoped to meet Charles Windrush and troops if his message had got through. If not, then he had no doubts that, whatever laws had to be broken, Sher Khan would break them to help Muna's son.

Chapter 24

Tovarish and his party spent little time resting at camp sites. They rode hard, and reached Safed as the sleepy night guard was unbarring the gates of the town.

Minutes late the camel train swayed through the gates, tired and dusty. They went by back streets to the *serai*, where they became part of the general turmoil of arrivals and departures. The brothers unloaded the camels, and the Pahareen paid for a room that was built into the back wall of the *serai*, away from the main gate. Unloaded, the beasts were led to the stables, separated from the main courtyard by a wall pierced by many wide arches. The stables, too, were in confusion. A band of men in the pay of the Raja of Sagpur had arrived with horses, baggage mules and a State elephant on which the Raja had travelled. Now the elephant stood, twitching his grey skin and shifting uneasily from foot to foot, the focus of chaos for the horses and mules, and the cause of great anxiety to his Mahout. The beast was irritable and would not settle. Please the gods it was not the beginning of an attack of *musth*. An hysterical bull elephant in a small crowded place – it did not bear thinking of. If only there was somewhere quiet to take him! The Mahout looked bitterly at the press around him, spoke soothingly to his charge and threw some peeled sticks of sugar cane down in front of him.

"Come, Janpat, King among elephants. Eat and enjoy and be calm. Eat, beautiful wise one –" The beautiful wise one picked among the sugar cane with a sensitive, fastidious trunk and rumbled in his stomach, his little eyes red and wicked. The Mahout sighed and sorted out some opium pills to mix with sugared water and give to the great beast in the hope that it would quieten him.

In a house not far away, Tovarish was having a difficult time calming the elephant's infuriated owner. Neither the cooled wine nor the peeled sugared fruit spread before him on silver plates could calm the Raja of Sagpur when he was told of the bungled attempt to kill the heir to the Lambagh throne. He glared at his companion, his face swollen with rage.

"But to take an English girl! If this is traced back to me, I will lose my State. *Where* is my man, Narain?"

"He is the reason why nothing will be traced back to you, Raja Sahib. The girl is dead and her body burned. Narain stayed in Faridkote to be sure this was done and also to find and silence Stepan."

"Stepan! That ape! Why you wasted my money on such a useless fool I do not know."

"By this time he must be dead, Raja Sahib. I suggest that you calm yourself. After all, the boy we tried to kill was not the true heir, but the second heir."

"He was another life between me and the Lambagh Guddee. And he still lives. I tell you, Tovarish, I would have filled your saddlebags with gold if you had brought him to me."

The Raja's raised voice, harsh with rage, sounded clearly in the garden outside where, at the foot of the steps that led up to the verandah, a tall young man in dusty black clothing stood bargaining with a guard over the price of a tooled and ornamental cartridge belt. The voices of anger from the room above faded, the bargaining was completed and the cartridge belt changed hands. The young man walked away tossing a few silver coins in his hand.

In the room she had rented the Pahareen was preparing a meal. Robert, leaning against a wall, watched her and tried to keep awake. The doorway, a bright oblong of sunlight, was darkened as two of the camel drivers came in. Hamid and Afzar had admired Robert's tireless stride on the night march. They sank down to sit beside him, offering him a *bidi*, a native cigarette such as they were smoking. Presently, as the room filled with the rank smell of the strong tobacco and

294

the smell of the cooking food, the Pahareen turned from her stove to ask a question.

Hamid nodded. "Tovarish is here, in the House of the Pundits. Nurulla is seeking news of the others who are there. We think it is Sagpurna himself; there is a riding elephant in the stables sending all the horses mad."

The food was ready, and they ate and had almost finished when the third brother, Nurulla, came in. He was younger by some years than the other two, tall and still gangling with adolescence. The Pahareen gave him a bowl of stew and a chapatti and watched until he had eaten it all and was rubbing round the inside of the bowl with a bit of chapatti to sop up the last drops of gravy, then asked him for his news. He answered her slowly, frowning to himself.

"The Raja of Sagpur is there. They were quarrelling."

"Quarrelling?"

"Yes, the Raja was displeased. The Russian was not made afraid, but answered the Raja quietly. Do we have business with the Raja? He is a man of great wealth."

"We have business with the Russian."

"The business that you started the other night?" He laughed and looked meaningly at her hand where the emerald no longer glittered. "You give your rewards away and have to earn more, perhaps?"

"Perhaps."

"It is a pity that we have no business with Sagpurna. He is a very rich man and pays well. The Russian? Who is he? He travels the roads as we do, and speaks softly to the rich Raja, but I do not think that he pays for services." He looked again at the Pahareen's ringless fingers and said suddenly, "What share of payment comes to me for the news I brought? I had to go into the garden to talk to the *chaukidhar*, the house guard, who is a man of this town. It was no use speaking to any of the guards at the gate, they were men of Sagpur. Those dark men! They wear silk and scent and make eyes like women. What do I get for risking my neck in the garden?"

"I do not see how you risked your neck. As I recall, the *chaukidhar* is well known to you. When we were here in the hot season you spent much time with him in the garden of that house." Hamid spoke in anger, looking at his young brother in no very friendly fashion. But the Pahareen smiled and said quietly,

"Nurulla did well. You have my thanks, little brother."

"Thanks? Thanks has no sound of gold or silver about it."

"You ask payment from your own blood?"

"Why not? Will you not be paid? I ask for a share, that is all."

"There should be no talk of payment here. What do you need with gold and silver, little brother?"

"I need – oh, I need many things. In any case, while we speak of blood, you are not of my blood – and nor is he." Robert looked up to meet Nurulla's bold stare. Hamid spat, his face furious. "Think shame, Nurulla. The woman in our house has tended you since you were an infant, has cared for you like a mother. You show disrespect to her, and to our guest."

"I feel no shame! This man here, we do him a service. He has wealth, being a Prince. Do Princes not pay for service?" The Pahareen's voice was very soft when she answered.

"Why should you think that our guest is a Prince, Nurulla? Why?" Her quiet voice was without expression, but the boy shifted uneasily as he answered her.

"Oh, I do not know. I heard talk as I went to get news for you, here in the *serai*, maybe. I do not recall where I heard this talk."

"Empty talk, like your own. Go you and feed and water the camels before I become angry listening to you."

Nurulla looked sideways at Robert and seemed about to say more. He was given no chance. Hamid got up, his expression ugly, and the boy went out quickly.

There was silence for a few minutes after he had gone, and the Pahareen finished washing the used dishes and put them away. As she pulled the lid of a basket over the cooking dishes, she spoke over her shoulder to Robert.

"Lord, this news of Sagpurna the Raja is not good. I think he is very dangerous for you. It is common talk up and down the roads that he is a bitter enemy of the house of Lambagh. Are you still of a mind to take Tovarish? Now it will be very dangerous and difficult, for many reasons."

Robert turned, and she saw his face, his expression set and cold with purpose. She said no more about a change of plan. She sat down in the doorway, and looked out at the bustle of the courtyard. "We will wait for darkness," she said.

There was a lizard on the white wall, moving with caution towards a moth. To Robert the hours to darkness seemed to move as slowly as the lizard. He dozed, and dreamed of Laura, seeing her dimly through a mist. She seemed to call him, and he could not hear what she said; her lips moved without sound. He woke full of distress, and longing for action. The slow lizard crawled on the wall and the shadows changed and shifted with the sun. Robert finally fell deeply asleep and the woman got up and, with the two brothers' help, pulled him into a more comfortable position and covered him with a quilt. Robert did not waken. He had passed beyond dreams and was sleeping soundly.

When he woke the setting sun was painting the walls of the room with gold, and the billowing clouds of blue smoke from many cooking fires made the courtyard a place of mystery where people moved, now in full sight, now hidden. The Pahareen still sat in the doorway but there was no sign of the brothers, and there were no bags or bundles in the room. While he slept, the men had loaded the camels and gone.

"They wait outside the town, about two kos from here, where the road forks for Madore. It is better thus. When we go, we will have to leave quickly, by ways where camels could not go. Are you ready, lord?" She looked at Robert and smiled at her own question. The man beside her was young and strong, trained in the arts of fighting and killing, and filled with a burning purpose.

The sun vanished below the edge of the plain and darkness came down, the sudden darkness of the east where the twilight lasts only minutes. The courtyard was still misted with smoke, but now lanterns glowed everywhere, and with the light from the fires the place was blazing with rosy light.

"Come," said the Pahareen and walked out. They crossed the courtyard, threading their way through the confusion of shouting men, restless animals and unyoked bullocks being taken to the stables. There were palanquins and long shafted carts and bucking, jerking, half broken ponies, and everywhere it seemed, little crying children. One sprawled in front of a shying horse, inches from the flailing hooves, and a woman's shrill scream cut through the noise. Robert made a long arm and scooped the child up and handed it to the clamouring woman, then followed behind the Pahareen. They went past the stables and saw the elephant being led towards the main gate, his riding saddle of padded cotton already strapped to his back. Robert saw the beady glitter of his eyes like black jewels in the glow of the rosy light. Then they were past the dusty restless bulk and away from the crowds. The Pahareen stopped outside an arched doorway, took a key from her waist and opened the door. Robert followed her into the room.

With the door closed, the room was dusky with shadows, the splinters of rosy light that came in through the shuttered windows lying like flames on the walls and floor, confusing the sight, dazzling instead of making the room lighter.

"Why here?" Robert spoke below his breath. "Why have you brought me here? I thought we would go to the House of the Pundit."

'Not so. He likes to have a place apart from the others. So he told me when I spoke with him on the road."

"How did you get the key?"

"The *serai* Master buys my silence. I saw him kill and steal. He fears my tongue." Her voice was a breath of sound against his ear and he smelt the heart-catching scent of sandalwood oil rising warm from her flesh. Many memories assailed him as he smelled it. The girl in the garden at Bombay; women he had taken in passion in the pleasure houses of the valleys, but above all those other memories that the scent called to his mind was the memory of his mother, and he closed his eyes to see her, small and clear, like an ivory carving on his eyelids. He had loved two women deeply in his life, his mother and Laura. Now in this scented darkness there was only his mother. The smell of sandalwood did not remind him of Laura.

The Pahareen's whisper broke into his thoughts.

"See, lord, here is the privy door. Go out and turn to your left and you will find yourself close to that window. You will hear everything that is said in this room. He will be here soon. We have been watching him. He comes to dress himself for a *nautch* in the House of the Pundit, with the Raja of Sagpur as his host. Wait until you hear me begin to sing the love song of Anarkali, and then come in. Do not wait to fight cleanly, lord, for he will not. Kill as a hunting leopard kills, and then we will go swiftly for there is danger here."

Indeed, Robert thought, there is. Like a snake, peril seemed to be hiding close by.

"Now that you have brought me here, why do you not go, Pahareen? There is no need for you to stay."

Like a moth, her lips brushed his ear.

"You waste time, lord. Go out. Remember. Wait for the song. Go laughing, lord —"

The love song of Anarkali was well known, sung by soldiers up and down the roads of India. Anarkali had been the beloved of a Mogul Emperor. She had loved the Emperor's son, had been discovered and had been walled up in the wall of the city of Lahore. Robert remembered the haunting beat, the first few words. 'I am alone, my love, and my bed is warm . . .'

It was not warm outside. It was dark and a little chill wind was blowing. In the courtyard beyond someone was making music. There was the liquid sound of a sitar, gentle as a spring dripping into a pool, and the tap of a hand drum. The beat of the drum became the beat of Robert's heart as he waited.

"What do you do here, Woman of the Roads?"

Tovarish spoke so close to his ear that Robert started and turned. The man was just on the other side of the shuttered windows. Robert held his breath and his hand felt for his dagger.

"I wait for you, Master."

"For me? Why?"

"For the same reason that you told me where you would lie in this town. We both drank wine the other night from a flask that we left unfinished. I have come to help you finish that rich, sweet wine."

Robert heard a sudden movement and an indrawn breath. Tovarish's voice was muffled when he spoke again.

"Rich wine, indeed. Heady and sweet. But alas I have no time –"

"There is always time. I will wait. What do you do that is of such importance?"

"I sup with the Raja of Sagpurna, a disappointed man, and therefore not to be kept waiting."

"Then do not waste time. Let me help you."

His ear against the shutter, Robert heard the rustle of silk and the chink of metal. She had taken his sword and his dagger. He knew he could be going in soon, and turned towards the door, putting everything from his mind but the thought of killing the man who had been his enemy from the moment he set foot in India.

In the room, Tovarish sighed. "Time! You are right, I must hurry, so that later I can have my cup full and overflowing with the rich wine of your loving. I will have the long sweet night later –"

"I promise you, Master, a long night. Listen, Master –" Her voice rose true and full in the old song,

"I am alone, my love, and my bed is warm,
I have a song to sing that you should hear,
And wine to drink that I would share,
With someone dear to me, with someone near . . ."

Robert heard no more than the first notes of her voice. He opened the door of the room and walked in.

Tovarish was fastening his long embroidered coat. He was

smiling to himself as if the sound of the woman's voice pleased him. The smile was still on his lips when he looked up at the sound of the opening and saw Robert and the long dagger in his hand. He felt for the pistol that should have been at his waist. But the belt and the pistol were in the hands of the Pahareen, who was standing near the door watching the two men, the echoes of her song still sounding in the room.

Tovarish looked at the face of death but his voice was steady.

"So, Nawab Sahib, you come to fight an unarmed man?"

"I do not come to fight. I come to kill. I shall kill you as I would kill any other poisonous creature." Robert took a slow step forward, his dagger hand as steady as if the weapon and his arm were one.

The scream that rang through the room was a terrible sound, tortured, demented. It was followed by a moment's silence and then the whole world seemed to explode into noise as people began to shout and run about outside. Robert turned his head, and that moment's inattention was all that Tovarish needed. As Robert lunged at him he leapt to the side of the room where the Pahreen stood and had her in his hands, holding her body between himself and Robert's furious attack. Robert saw this too late to check his leap. He almost fell as he tried to alter the upward thrust of his dagger. He succeeded, but it was such a close thing that the Pahareen's leg ran with blood. Tovarish strengthened his grip on the woman's body, now holding her throat so that she was still. The belt and the pistol fell to the ground, but Tovarish did not stoop for them. Holding the woman as a shield between himself and Robert's weaving dagger, he moved to the door, opened it with one hand, and throwing the Pahareen into Robert's arms, he ran out.

The Pahareen was fighting for breath, but Robert saw that her leg wound was only a slight one. He left her and followed Tovarish into the noisy night.

The courtyard was like an ant-heap with the top removed. Men ran, lanterns tilting crazy bars of light ahead of them.

301

Riderless horses charged through the press of people and women screamed to their children. The noise of the crowd was tremendous, but it became nothing as another terrible cry echoed into the night sky, drowning all other sound. As if driven by that dreadful scream, people ran without knowing where to go. Fear was everywhere, and worse, the contagion of panic.

Robert heard and saw nothing now. As the needle of a compass steadies on the north, so he turned, and in spite of the chaos of running figures, he saw the one man he wanted, conspicuous in his richly embroidered coat that caught the flickering lamplight.

Tovarish ran for the stables, where he knew he could get a horse, and Robert lengthened his stride and shortened the distance between them.

There was a scattering of blankets around the dying cooking fires. Robert caught his foot, stumbled and fell hard, the dagger flying out of his hand. Tovarish looked back to see how close he was, then turned and ran back. He snatched up the dagger and stood laughing, his face the face of a fiend. Robert struggled to his feet, dodging the quick thrust of his own weapon, and so narrowly escaped that the coarse black shirt he wore was slit from hem to neck and a long thin cut oozed blood down the length of his side.

Tovarish feinted again and Robert dodged, watching the man as he would have watched a striking snake.

Something moved, huge and silent, behind Tovarish. Robert saw the movement and stared, not believing what he saw. Tovarish laughed.

"Do not think to make me turn my head by making faces of fear at something behind my back. That is a trick as old as time. No, Nawab Sahib. I kill you, and I take your body to Sagpurna, who will be very glad to see me then."

Robert still watched the movements behind Tovarish, and the man saw that now other people stood behind Robert all looking afraid. Suddenly fear seized him. Something soft and fleshy touched the back of his neck, lingered a second and moved lower. Like most Europeans, Tovarish had a horror of

302

snakes. He jumped round, cutting at the air with the dagger. The dagger point slashed the elephant on his sensitive trunk. Already maddened and desperate in the throes of an attack of *musth*, Janpat flung up his trunk and screamed his terrible trumpeting cry. As Tovarish turned to run, Janpat seized him in his trunk, raised him high and flung him with force to the ground, where he then put a great foot on him. Tovarish's shriek was silenced. As the elephant turned to trample again men ran with spears, the Mahout heading them, and drove him back.

Remarkably, Tovarish still lived. Robert found his dagger and went back to the mewling thing that had been his enemy. Tovarish could not see him, but he whispered desperately, "Kill –"

"You deserve no mercy but I will grant you ease in the name of humanity." Robert leaned down and despatched him cleanly and stood back, wiping his dagger.

Tovarish dead was nothing but a blood-stained heap of rags on the ground. The long chase was over. Now he must find Laura. Pray God the Pahareen was right, and she was safe with Janki, now surely in Faridkote.

He began to walk away from the stables and heard running feet behind him.

"Lord! Lord, wait! The woman in our house sent me to find you. I have news –" The voice was breathless. Robert turned to find Nurulla beside him, his eyes bright with excitement.

"What is it?"

"Lord, our stars are good. Your man from Lambagh, the big man who rode with you, is here. He brings news of the girl you looked for. Come, I will take you to him." Robert was already hurrying the way Nurulla pointed and the boy took him out through the main gate. They turned then to the left and went quickly down a short narrow lane to a gate that opened on a big garden and white-washed single storey house. Robert took the steps at a run, outstripping Nurulla. "Which way?"

"Here, lord, through this door."

Robert opened the door and ran in calling "Ayub! Ayub

303

Khan?" It was a large room with a dais at the end. The man
on the dais smiled and leaned forward among his cushions.

"Ah, indeed. Ayub Khan, the friend and the relative, I
believe, of the Lambagh family. But he is not here." Robert
heard a step behind him, and dagger in hand turned to fight.

Once she could breathe and move again, the Pahareen
hurried to the stables, arriving in time to see Robert going
with Nurulla. She went after them, strangely uneasy,
keeping in the shadows, and saw Nurulla take Robert into
the House of the Pundit. There was no guard on the gate
and the anteroom was empty. She heard the buzz of men's
voices and followed the sound until she came to a closed
door. She tried the door, it opened easily and she stood in
the shadows.

Robert stood shirtless, with blood on his face, his hands
bound behind his back. On a dais at the back of the room,
lounging at ease, indolent, handsome, was the Raja of
Sagpur. The Pahareen had seen him often when the camel
train had visited his State. He lay among the cushions and
looked at his captive with lively pleasure.

Robert, furiously angry, was demanding to be released.

"Oh come, Nawabzaida Sahib! Do not be ridiculous. How
splendid a son Kassim Khan has got himself! Such eyes! How
do they call you, Dil Bahadur? Lord of Hearts. *Such* a suitable
name. You give pleasure to the eye of a connoisseur. As to
your release – well, it lies in the hands of your father. If
Kassim Khan does what I ask you will, of course, go free."

Robert's angry shout cut across his words.

"Kassim Khan is not my father."

"Come, Nawabzaida Sahib, with that face you try to deny
your paternity?"

"You know my father, I think Raja Sahib." Robert spoke
coolly now, as if he had decided something. "My father is
Colonel Alan Reid."

There was silence from the Raja and everyone looked in
that direction. The Pahareen began to move quietly up
through the shadows of the room towards the pool of light

that was the dais. She had her dagger in her hand, hidden in the folds of her robe. She walked with the cool, devouring purpose of a hunting lioness.

Sagpurna's voice cracked. "You lie, Dil Bahadur!"

"I do not. I am the son of Colonel Reid and of his wife, Muna."

Sagpurna's leap from the dais belied his earlier affectation of indolent boredom. He stared Robert up and down, studying him as a man looks at a horse that he would buy.

"You have proof?"

"I have. But untie my hands." Sagpurna lifted his hand, and a man stepped forward and freed Robert. He brought his hands forward and began to rub them into life. Sagpurna saw the flash of the emerald ring, looked closer and drew in his breath.

"I last saw that ring on Muna's hand. Where did *you* get it?"

"She put it on my hand. I told you, I am her son."

Sagpurna looked at him and smiled suddenly as if he were smiling at a friend. In the silence that had fallen in the room Nurulla's voice sounded loud.

"What of me, Protector of the Poor. What of my reward? Give it to me and let me go – the gates will be closed soon." He choked suddenly and Sagpurna stepped back quickly as a little blood trickled down to the floor from Nurulla's mouth. The Pahareen at his shoulder withdrew her dagger with a skilled twist, and the boy fell and lay looking up at her, his young face full of astonished pain.

"You have your reward, little brother, and the gates are open for you. Go to whatever place it pleases Allah to send you. Go swiftly, child of sorrow."

Nurulla took a few minutes to die, fighting for breath, and the Pahareen watched him until he lay still. Then she pulled her headcloth over her face and walked to the door, and no one stopped her.

The door opened before she touched it, and suddenly the room was full of uproar and fighting men.

Sagpurna sighed and turned to Robert and put his arm

about him and Robert felt the cold steel of a dagger touching his back.

"Now we wait for Ayub Khan," said Sagpurna calmly. "Keep still, son of Muna. Very still." Gradually the fighting ceased and out of the wrack and bluster of the room came Ayub Khan, wading through his angry troops as a man wades in rough surf, his bloodied sword in his hand.

"Stop, Ayub Khan! What you value is at the point of dagger." Ayub halted, his mouth tight with anger and fear.

Then Robert laughed and turned in Sagpurna's arm. He leaned a little against the sharp prick of the dagger and felt it pulled back but not removed. He pressed back again and felt warm blood on his back and the dagger clattered to the floor. Ayub Khan looked down at it and back at Sagpurna, but Sagpurna was looking at Robert. He pulled a kerchief from his sleeve and gave it to Robert. "You bleed," he said quickly.

"A fool's trick," said Ayub, and bent to pick up the dagger. "What if it had been poisoned?" He turned to Sagpurna. "Raja Sahib, tell your men to go. There be men of Lambagh with me and it is better that this is known as a drunken brawl. There is a detachment of British soldiers on the road, but I think you will not wish to wait for them."

The Raja looked down the disordered room. There was a great deal of blood on the ground, but the only corpse was Nurulla.

"So. As you say, a drunken brawl. The Ruler of Lambagh must be very sure of himself to risk this in British India!"

'Oh, he is. Very sure. It was a mistake to take a British woman, Raja Sahib."

"Yes," said Sagpurna heavily, "it was. But not my mistake. My only mistake was to use bad tools." He looked Robert up and down, smiling. "Son of Muna, be careful. Perhaps another day the dagger will pierce your heart." He walked away, spoke to one of his men, and the room emptied. Robert's urgent question was forestalled by Ayub's understanding.

"Boy, she is alive and with Janki in Faridkote. That news we heard in Madore. Is that balm for your heart?"

"My thanks, Ayub. My heart is full."

"I heard the tale of the death of Tovarish in the *serai* where I went to find you. What do you wish now, Boy?"

"Now, Ayub?" said Robert, turning to the door, "Now we go to Faridkote. *Now*."

Standing in the shadows outside the house, the Pahareen looked at Robert and smiled. "You have good news, lord?"

"I have. Pahareen, there are words I would say to you – I do not know how to give you thanks."

"Say nothing, lord. There are to be no words between us. I said all the words that are needful when I said, 'My life for yours. Go laughing, lord'."

She heard the sound of their horses grow faint along the road, and went back into the house to take out her dead.

Ayub Khan's men were waiting just inside the gates of Safed. They were a hand-picked company and most of them were known to Robert and were delighted to have rescued him. Slightly above themselves with success, very little damaged, they greeted him with full-throated enthusiasm, to be smartly ordered into silence by Ayub.

"You wish to be taken by the Town Guard? Who knows what power that serpent Sagpurna has in this town? In the name of Allah, let us get safely on the road before we make celebrations." Robert was sharply reminded that these men had no right to be here at all. They were far into British-controlled India, and they were State Forces. He looked a question at Ayub Khan, who grimaced and shook his head.

"Nay, Boy. The authorities may try but in truth they can take us for nothing, for we have done nothing. Merely an escorting party for you, who attended a *nautch* and, getting drunk, fought a little with no harm done. None killed, and not a shot fired. But it would be foolish to become conspicuous." Subdued, the party gathered themselves together and rode through the gates in a compact bunch.

They rode fast through the day, and camped that night, well off the road, and away from other travellers. For two days they made good speed, arriving at the fork where one road led off to Madore, and a smaller road wandered up

307

towards the foothills and the high valleys. Here all but six of the men left them, and it was again brought home to Robert that Sher Khan had sent his own personal guard to rescue him. Mixed with his gratitude was fear. This fear had been growing in him as each day of the journey passed. Ayub Khan had said that Laura was safe in Faridkote – but was she? If Sher Khan had taken his safety so seriously that he had sent his own men into a part of India where they had no right to be, would it not be possible that he had instructed Ayub Khan to tell him a lie in order to get him safely back to the Ruler's territory? Robert fell without warning into deep depression, and was not helped by the fact that Ayub Khan was noticeably quiet. If Laura was safe, then why was Ayub Khan so withdrawn? The men riding to Madore had grown small in the distance. With a heavy heart, Robert followed his own party as they turned towards the foothills and the winding narrow road that climbed them.

Trees closed in, and then were gone as the road climbed, and the far mountains came in sight, black against the darkening sky. A wind blew, chill with rain on its breath, and the road grew steep and turned and twisted and the horses slowed their pace. It was time to stop for the night.

After they had eaten, they lay, wrapped in *poshteens* and blankets in front of the camp fire. In the rosy light Robert saw Laura's face. He did not feel the cold wind that flattened the flames so that the light died a little and the night leaned closer, dark and silent. Ayub, looking at his face, shivered suddenly, and pulled the collar of his *poshteen* closer round his neck. What devils were driving this boy now? He touched Robert's arm, telling him it was time to sleep, but Robert did not hear him, he was hearing Laura's voice, calling to him in the night wind, and trying to understand what she was saying. Finally Ayub let him be and rolled himself into his blankets and slept, and Robert watched the night pass, alone with the echoes of Laura's voice saying things that he could not hear.

He was heavy-eyed when the morning came, a morning veiled in a cold mist. The great mountains were hidden. One of the men brought him a bowl of hot tea. As he drank it, Ayub loomed up through the mist and sat down beside him.

"We will have to wait until this lifts. One slip on the path further up, and we will lose a horse. Maybe this is the hand of Allah, granting us more time before we have to face the anger of Kassim Khan." Robert stared at him. "Why is Kassim Khan going to be angered, Ayub? With news of the death of Tovarish? He will be pleased, surely? I do not understand what you are saying, Ayub."

"We had Sagpurna in our hands, and we let him go. You could have killed him, with his own knife. Tell me what words we use when we give that news to Kassim Khan. Why did you let him go?"

"Why? You were present I believe, Ayub Khan, when Sagpurna saved my mother's life, or have you forgotten? Perhaps I should refresh your memory. Listen you to me."

Speaking in a low, hard voice, he reminded Ayub Khan of a day when Muna had been in deadly danger. He described accurately the Pool of the Women that had been for centuries below the white Palace of Sagpur, the Pool of the Women, a great cavern where an underground lake lapped on sparkling white sand, a cavern haunted by the ghosts of many Queens who had been led to their deaths in the dark green water. He spoke as if he had been there himself, and seen the place, where a blind white crocodile waited for its prey, and where Sagpurna's mother had lain writhing in the coils of a serpent, while Muna had been carried to safety by her son. He painted a vivid picture, and Ayub, remembering, put his hands over his ears and cried out.

"Enough! As you say, I was there, I remember, and I still wake sweating in the night from dreams of that time. That place was a stronghold of devils – you speak as if you were there yourself. How?"

"How not? My mother lived with horror afterwards. She told of that time and of Sagpurna's bravery."

"It is true. Half out of his mind with drugs, he led us there and got her out."

"Well then. Do you think Kassim Khan will ask me why I

did not kill Sagpurna? No, Ayub Khan. He knows that I owed Sagpurna a life." He paused for a moment watching the mist lift swirling from the moisture-pearled grass. His expression was bleak. "Yes. I owed him a life. The debt is paid now. There will be another meeting, but then there will be no debt to stand between him and death. The mist has lifted, Ayub Khan. Let us go."

A day later they were within sight of Faridkote; they rode down to the gate, were stopped and recognised with joy and relief, and were at last free to ride to the House in the Wall.

It was closed.

There was no answer to their knocking. The only sound was the flap and flutter of pigeons settling for the night. It was an hour before sunset, and already the sky was dyed crimson and gold.

Chapter 25

Janki was given the news of Stepan's escape as soon as it was light. She was so distressed about Laura's condition that she hardly listened to what Yar Khan was saying. However, when she heard that they were all to move to the House of Paradise, she protested vigorously.

"Yar Khan, she will die, this English girl. Her life hangs like a drop of water on a leaf."

"Better for her to die in a palanquin than to be taken again by Stepan. Come, Janki, you know that I cannot keep this house guarded. It is in the wall. Who knows where that man is? You know that what I say is wise." Janki had to agree. She hurried with her arrangements. Dina and Shanti loaded *kiltas* with things that were needed, and the conical baskets were put on the back of Janki's pack mule. The palanquin was brought out, and then Laura wrapped in quilts was carried down by Yar Khan. Her face was grey-white, she lay limp in his arms. He felt that he carried a newly dead corpse. Janki watched him lay her down on cushions in the palanquin, then drew a thick *rezai* over her and covered her face with a light veil. Everyone was ready. The gate opened, they went out and the House on the Wall was left shuttered and empty except for the pigeons rising and falling like blown feathers in the empty courtyard.

The cavalcade went quietly through the early morning streets. Although the streets were empty they were hedged about with guardians. From balconies and flat roofs, from behind shuttered windows, men and women watched their progress, passing messages ahead. Yar Khan rode in the van, Meeta's arms round his waist quickening his breath as she perched behind him. Zaman Beg rode at the back of the

311

cavalcade, and both men were alert and wary. They saw what appeared to be a large crowd blocking a lane near the temple, but it was not on their road and they went on their way, meeting no danger. They reached the high walls of the House of Paradise and went in, and the palanquin was set down in the courtyard. Yar Khan dismounted and turned to catch Meeta in his arms as she slid from the horse. Her smile was friendly but preoccupied, and Yar Khan let her go, promising himself that one day she would think of nothing but him.

He spoke with the Dafodar who commanded the detachment of men on duty at the House of Paradise, and the guard was doubled. Armed men took up position in the outer courtyard and in the garden beyond. There had always been a guard on the main gate since the place became the property of the Lambagh family, and on the small secret gate at the back. To an unknowing eye the House of Paradise was as it always had been, the guarded luxurious residence that the Rose of Madore had once owned, and then, leaving the north for a far country, had given to the Lambagh family forever.

Within, the house buzzed. The girls were not unaware of innumerable splendid-looking young men set about the house and garden. Dina's curving lips smiled, Shanti's painted eyes slid in sideways glances. They had, each of them, a feeling of excitement and pleasure. There would be no fat fumbling old men tonight, no young incapable drunks grunting through acts that the girls knew well how to bring to a perfect climax and seldom had the pleasure of a matching perfection. In the green shade of the garden, where the fountain sparkled and the parrots flew like blown leaves between the trees, the young men looked at the bright sky and measured the time of their duty with warm impatient eyes.

But in the beautiful room where, years before, Muna had set the scene for Bianca and Sher Khan to meet after their long separation, there was no feeling of excitement. Laura lay on the big cushioned bed, still and white, a plaster copy of a beautiful girl. Janki, heavy-eyed from a sleepless night, sat beside the bed on a cane stool and tried to drip brandy and

312

water between Laura's lips from a spoon. But the white lips were tightly closed, and Janki saw with fear the pinch marks of blue, like death's prints, beginning to show on either side of the pretty nose. Laura was certainly very close to death. Janki had sent earlier for Reiss, the European doctor who had once saved Bianca's life and reason, and had come to the House on the Wall when Robert had been at the point of death. But he was down in Madore. She had only herself to rely on, and she could think of nothing else to do.

It was Meeta who forced her to go away and rest.

"I will sit by her. You will be ill, Janki, if you do not sleep, and then who will help us? Go, Jenab, rest, trust her to me." Janki went, only because she could not watch death come and take this young one, this girl with the whole of life in front of her, to die so untimely. Janki went out of the room and closed the door behind her, and wept.

After she had gone, the room was very quiet. Laura's breathing was noiseless, indeed, Meeta bent to put her head to Laura's heart to be sure that it was beating. The long struggle she had made to bring this alien girl to safety had made Laura a part of her life, someone who was close, and if Laura's heartbeat stopped, Meeta felt she could not bear it.

"My sister," she said softly, "my sister. Waken to me. See, you are safe. Wake and let us look at each other. Wake!"

But the heavy dark eyelids did not lift, the black lashes, thick and long, were quiet on Laura's cheeks. Her eyes had sunk into deep hollows, her breathing was not discernible. The warmly lighted room, soft with brocades and silks and rich carpets, seemed bitterly cold. Meeta felt a terrible pain of loss, as if everything she had ever wanted, food, warmth, love, were all being taken from her as this girl lay dying. She became possessed with a desperation that made her pant with open mouth as she would have done if she had been over-exerting herself physically. She set her mind against death, and took Laura into her arms, holding her tightly, calling into her ear, shaking her, tears pouring down her own face as she did so. Her fingers dug into Laura's cold flesh, her voice broke as she called, knowing no name to call, crying on

Laura to wake in a tongue that Laura would not understand. Meeta put her frail humanity against the force that was towering so close. With dilated eyes she stared at Laura, seeing the shadow that had fallen over the girl's face, and within the shadow saw a movement, a small muscular contraction round the eyes as if someone sleeping were trying to wake.

Then Meeta cried aloud without words, and sent a desperate prayer for aid against this death. Laura's eyelids fluttered, and lifted, so that Meeta saw a slit of blue. The heavy lids fell again, but holding the cold body close against her heart, Meeta was sure that she had won her battle. Laura would live.

Afterwards, no drama, only hard toil. Janki, running in at the sound of Meeta's cry, took hold of Laura too. They tore the coverings off her body, and rubbed and slapped and kneaded until the white flesh was scarlet under their fingers. Brandy was dripped into Laura's mouth, not from a spoon now, but from the corner of a muslin cloth. Her throat muscles at last contracted and she swallowed. She choked, but some of the precious stuff had gone down. They wrapped her in sheepskins, and packed heated stones round her. Janki looked at Meeta, all tiredness gone from her face.

"Her heart beats. She is back, she is safe. Meeta, what did you do?"

"I called to her." Meeta's face was as exhausted as it had been the night before; it was all bones and had no beauty except for the wide glowing eyes filled with light and happiness. "I but called to her, Janki!"

"You called her back from the very threshold of Yama's kingdom, my little one. Indeed and indeed you have now served Lambagh State well for the second time, using your strength to its limits." As she spoke, Laura's head turned on the pillows; she sighed deeply and lay, sleeping naturally, the blue shadows gone from her face.

Somewhere a woman's voice said softly, "Love is stronger than death." Who spoke? Not Janki, bending over Laura. Not Meeta, who heard the voice and looked up. The words

314

sounded clearly, their echo chiming in the room long after the words had been spoken.

There was warmth after cold, light pressing against her eyelids, the aching exhaustion of return from a journey that had been very long.

There was a voice that said clearly, "Love is stronger than death." The words chimed sweetly like the sound of the glass wind harp that had hung in Aunt Caroline's bedroom window.

"Love is stronger than death."

Her eyelids were weighted with lead, stuck to her cheeks, the lashes gummed so that she could not open them. The chiming voice had gone, though the words still rang gently, ghost bells under the other voices that spoke a language she did not understand. Laura listened. Women's voices, anxious and kind, and full of love. A rounded, rich voice, and a young voice.

They faded too and were gone.

The light against her eyelids had changed when she next woke. It was a warmer light, and she tried again to open her eyes, and succeeded. She could see nothing, nothing but a blur of colours. Then, slowly, a face took shape, close to hers. Laura blinked, and the face became clear, young and tender and smiling, a girl's face.

"My sister wakes," said Meeta softly; Laura did not understand the words, but the tone spoke to her heart. Her hand weighed like a mountain but she moved it, and Meeta's hand closed on it, held it between both of hers, a white bird, resting, safe.

They bathed Laura's white emaciated body, the bones so close to the skin that it seemed they might pierce the delicate envelope encasing them. They washed her hair, exclaiming at its silky length, and combed it and let it fall heavy over her brocaded shoulders. Her robe was emerald, high collared, hiding the bony ridges that spanned her chest, giving green glints to the blue eyes. She was propped up in the big bed so that she could look out into the garden and see the topmost

315

jet of the fountain's spray fall glittering in the morning sun, and the green parrots flying through it. She could not speak very much, and in any case they would not have understood her, but she did everything they wanted her to do, eating and drinking as much as she could, and attentively following Janki's gestures, like a dancer learning a new dance.

"The Begum herself is coming from Lambagh – she will be able to speak with you, and we have sent word to the Begum Bianca, who will surely come at once. She is of your race, Precious Flower. Oh Rose of Snow, *why* can you not understand a word I say," said Janki, exasperated.

"Because you do not speak her language!" Meeta's laugh was loud, and free, and Laura laughed with her. Then she said slowly, "Begum Bianca?" Janki nodded furiously. Her white brow pleating, Laura dredged her memory and out of a past that seemed centuries old, dragged words she had learned.

"The Begum Bianca comes?" she asked in understandable Urdu, and Janki clapped her hands and laughed, and almost wept with pleasure. "She speaks! You speak Urdu! Why did you not tell us?"

But Laura, exhausted by effort, had dropped into sleep, and Meeta pulled the quilts higher round her and sat on the floor at the foot of the bed, while Janki went away to concoct yet more forms of nourishment for the girl who was so newly back from the dark place of everyone's future.

Chapter 26

At the gate of the House on the Wall, Ayub Khan raised his whip and knocked again. Now even the pigeons were quiet. There was no sound anywhere.

The closed and barred gate, the lack of response to their knocking were terrible. To Robert the dark, silent house meant one thing only.

"She is dead," he said, turning away.

"Not so. She lives." The voice that spoke was not Ayub's voice. A naked mendicant fakir sat near the gate. He looked up at Robert sitting his restive horse, and repeated, "She lives. She is in the House of Paradise." He had barely said the words when Robert was gone. It was Ayub Khan who stayed to throw a silver coin into the begging bowl and to hear that Stepan was dead.

"Nothing of him remains. There was not one bone upon the other when Phuli's friends had taken vengeance." The fakir lowered his eyes and intoned a prayer in gratitude. For what? The silver coin? Ayub turned his horse and rode thoughtfully after Robert. Robert was at the gate of the House of Paradise when Ayub caught up with him. Men ran out to welcome them and take their horses. Robert asked a single question, and answered by several voices, ran through the gates. The outer courtyard was already busy with tired men, and dusty horses stamped and blew on their way to the stables. There had been a previous arrival. Still veiled and in travelling clothes, a woman was standing, talking to Janki. In spite of the veil, Ayub knew the slender pliant figure at once. The Begum Bianca must have ridden hard to get there so soon. Robert did not even see her, he passed her without a word or a look. Ayub stopped beside her, and she turned to

317

say softly, knowing why his eyes were searching the court-yard beyond. "Be patient, Ayub Khan. Your green-eyed one comes within the hour. Janki had word this morning. All is well. All is well here too. Laura is sleeping in the upper room." Bianca's lips curved in a smile behind her veil as she thought of the beautiful room where Laura lay. "Her awakening will be sweet," she said. "It is good to think that we can have a wedding for two lovers after so much pain."

"What of her parents, Khanum?"

"They will have nothing to say but honeyed words. It has been made very plain to them, I am told by our friend Colonel Windrush, that to displease the House of Lambagh would be remarkably foolish in many ways. Also our wealth appeals to them. Can you not hear that terrible woman talking in the Calcutta houses of her friends of 'My daughter the Begum'? Oh have no fears, Ayub Khan. This is one marriage that will take place with no unpleasantness. As soon as Laura has her health back we will take her up to Lambagh, and your Bella will nurse her, and then – in the spring, the time of the blossom, they will have their marriage at last."

Laura had wakened. The room was full of sunset, so that the tapestries ran with splendid colour, dazzling before her eyes. The window, with the sparkling spray of the fountain caught in it, was like a living wall-hanging. Laura lay, her eyes on the water, and thought of nothing, and heard nothing but the cry of the birds settling before the night, and the whispering, falling water.

But Meeta at the foot of the bed heard the sounds of arrival, the questioning voice, the feet on the stairs. She got up quickly and went out.

Robert, at the top of the stairs, did not see her pressed against the wall to let him pass. She continued on down the stairs and went out into the garden where the fountain splashed, dropping diamonds and pearls like tears on to the lily pads.

Yar Khan, lounging against a tree, saw her standing looking down into the pool. She was looking at her own reflection when a brown and sinewy hand was placed across her eyes, and she was turned, still blinded, away from the water.

"What can you see, Meeta?"

"Nothing, Yar Khan." He took his hand away, and she was looking up at his face.

"And now what can you see?"

"You – what else?"

"So. Look well, little one. Look well. I make you a promise. One night or another night, soon, I shall come to you and thereafter you will see me wherever you look – and find me for ever in your heart." Meeta smiled at him and left him beside the fountain and he stood there looking down at his hand, wet with her tears – or was it the fountain's spray?

In the upper room Laura turned her head as the door opened. Robert was there, standing beside the door. Laura leaned up on her elbow, staring. Was this another of her dreams? She closed her eyes and opened them again and he was still there, hesitating as if he might go away.

"Robert!"

It was not a cry, it was a whisper. It pulled him to her side, and for a moment he stood by her bed and they could do nothing but look at each other. Laura saw a tired, grim-faced young man whose eyes were beginning to fill with a wild joy. Robert saw an exhausted girl, so frail that he was afraid to touch her – his beloved Laura. He put his hands one on each side of the cushion on which her head rested and looked down at her and saw youth and beauty flood back into her face as he looked.

"Laura –" Her name on his lips was an endearment. Laura said nothing, but he heard her indrawn breath, a soft sigh, the sound of a tired child safely home at last. He bent his head and put his mouth gently on hers. She felt the tenderness in his kiss, and the longing, and her whole body answered to that kiss. She lifted her arms and put them about his neck, and answered his kiss with her own.

"Together – always together –" said a voice somewhere, faint and far away. Robert lifted his head to listen, but there

319

was no one there. Only Laura, smiling at him, warm and alive and lifting her mouth for his kisses. Joy began to beat in his blood, rising like Laura's quickened heart beat under his hand.

The golden light of sunset grew and strengthened and then faded. The room grew shadowed and the whisper of the fountain was loud. But no one was listening to the fountain, nor watching the coming of night.